LA MAISON

EMMA BECKER

LA MAISON

Bedford Square
Publishers

First published in 2019 by Flammarion, Paris, France

This paperback edition first published in 2026
by Bedford Square Publishers Ltd
London, UK

bedfordsquarepublishers.co.uk

A Maxim Jakubowski book

ISBN
978-1-83501-418-9 (Paperback)
978-1-83501-419-6 (eBook)

2 4 6 8 10 9 7 5 3 1

Typeset in 10.8 on 13.5pt Garamond MT Pro
by Avocet Typeset, Bideford, Devon, EX39 2BP
Printed and bound in Great Britain by
CPI Group (UK) Ltd, Croydon CR0 4YY

The manufacturer's authorised representative in the EU for
product safety is Easy Access System Europe, Mustamäe tee 50,
10621 Tallinn, Estonia
gpsr.requests@easproject.com

For Louis Joseph Thornton, an admirable man and father
For Desirée
And for the girls, for all of us.

'This slit, this tapered scar that only ever opens onto a monstrous smile without end. Black. Gaping. A toothless smile. Strangely lascivious. Perhaps there is nothing else at the end of our worry, and as the only response, the uncontrollable mute hilarity of this sticky orifice.'

Louis Calaferte, *Septentrion*

YESTERDAY. I'M WITH MY SON, WHO'S METHODICALLY emptying the wardrobe while I make his bed. I'm looking for a quilt big enough to cover his mattress – and in the cupboard in the hallway, the first thing I notice is the three-by-three-metre bedcover I bought when the brothel closed. It's been lying there for five months, folded haphazardly, unwashed.

'Aren't you going to help me put the bedcover back on?' says Inge in the Red room. It's just come out of the dryer, it's still warm in our hands and almost a living thing. It's I who put it in the washing machine because a client spilt some oil on it, and Inge and I are trying, from either side of the vast bed, to smooth out the creases with our palms. We're chatting – but what about? There's no way of remembering. But I'm in a good mood, I've finished a bit early, and it's nearly time to go home anyway. Inge swooshes up the organdie curtains to air the room. The light outside is a miracle of late summer, not yet orange and of an almost supernatural brilliance. 'I'm going down-stairs. See you in a minute,' I say to Inge as I slip on my black coat. Inge sings a reply, like she usually does, and the door closes onto the landing where the smell of laundry and naked flesh lingers and fades.

It's this exact smell that has remained trapped in the bedcover, this wonderful thing that I bought for five euros, nothing, when the brothel had to close and the owner chose to sell us everything for a song rather than have the owners of other brothels come rummaging through our possessions.

I brought it home like a dog that had been abandoned on the motorway and for a long time I said I couldn't wash it because my machine was too small. But my refusal was really all about my fear of losing this smell forever. Without it, the cover would be only a piece of material of dubious taste, too big for everything, a pile of fabric taking up space that I would never make up my mind to get rid of. And there it is with its big fold in the middle, which, unless it's perfectly lined up, makes my mattress look askew. Next to the little one, who's still busy emptying his wardrobe, I bury myself in its still-pungent folds, turning my head from side to side like a spinning top in the midst of colourful memories. There's the smell of laundry liquid of course, and I could find the same brand if I had the time, the energy and the lack of scruples I'd need in order to impose on my family the familiar aroma of the brothel where I worked for two years. But how could I add to it the acid tang of the rest of the human juices that have dried in its fibres, and the noxious, sometimes unbearable notes of the blue soap that the guys used in the bathroom? Even if I didn't wash it, the bedcover once exposed to the air of the bedroom would end up taking on the little one's odour, and the ghosts of the brothel (of which I am one) would end up evaporating, and, day by day, I'd capture an ever-thinner trickle of it, until this three square metres of embroidered fabric would become a blank canvas, smelling of nappies and the clean skin of the baby.

I should preserve this bedsheet like a medieval book, only unfolding it very rarely and in the right conditions, without too much light or movement. By bringing it home, I was in some way convinced that the brothel would never close, that something or someone would save us at the last minute, that there would be other trinkets to hate or to adore — and that even if the brothel disappeared, it would surely blossom again, somewhere else. With everything I'd crammed into my apartment, the bed from the White room, the mirrors, the bedside table, the coffee table, the towels, it had to. But objects have such a gracious and discreet way of acclimatising…

*

When she visited us, my grandmother asked me, enraptured, where I had found such a superb, solid bed: caught off guard, I talked about a flea market in Reinickendorf, despite the fact that everything about the bed gave the game away about the brothel. Who would want a bedhead inlaid with a mirror and riddled with romantic trims, doves and sheaves of flowering laurels? But placed there, in the bedroom, it had lost all of its ridiculous eroticism. It had the humble look of an unexpected bargain, and when I announced that it had cost us less than thirty euros, my grandmother repeated that it truly was an adorable bed. How had we managed to get it home with us?

'Oh, it was a huge hassle,' I heard myself reply. It was raining that day and we'd got up at 7 o'clock in the morning to go and hire a van at the other end of Berlin because my eyes had been bigger than my stomach and because we had to fetch, as well as the bed, four mirrors, two tables and a considerable amount of crap that I would never have even looked at if I hadn't known them in this house. We parked up on the dropped kerb right in front of the door that several of my colleagues and a troop of Russian lackeys armed with tape measures and screwdrivers were going in and out of. This was the first time I saw this door so depressingly open between the two boxwood balls. It all reeked of a demand for back taxes, bailiffs, a rout. On the first floor, everything had already been emptied. As she passed, Jutta took in the room with a long sad look and sighed, 'What a waste, eh?' She left saying she had a meeting, but I think the bed disappearing from the room was a blow to her. It took us a good hour to dismantle it, because it was in three incredibly heavy pieces that were absolutely not made to be carried. Somebody had designed this bed to remain there, to never have to leave. The bed base was just a collection of massive planks of wood. You could jump on them with all your weight and not hear a crack. It was built for that, for agitation, for fierce thrusting, for honeymoon nights, wild and furtive embraces – not really for sleeping. But that's why you sleep so well in it. You sink into it, flattened by the exhaustion of all the people who exerted themselves in it for forty years. Anyway, nobody knows about this but me. And it takes me a few moments, closing my eyes because I'm always distracted from my tiredness by the need to look at myself in its mirror. When I turn my head, I always have the impression I'm going to see, behind the globes of my flatteringly up-tilted thighs, the white chest of drawers in which Inge stored the sheets, the star-shaped lamp, the sentimental painting of a blonde standing at her window, and I almost hear the musical soup emanating from the loudspeakers, which I fought with my playlist on the hi-fi system. That day, I really thought the bed would never make it out of the bedroom. That we were going to have to take it to pieces like they used to do with babies in the breech position who couldn't be birthed. Even after we'd taken out about fifty screws, the bed-frame split when we tried to lift it. It was impossible. We had to call the five Russians, who were dismantling another bed in another room, for help. They were like funeral-home workers. I looked at the wooden floor, paler where the bed had stood, thinking that at the moment when these wooden tiles had last seen light, the brothel owner was a very young woman and three quarters of the girls who would pass through this room weren't even born. The dust was the same age. We loaded the van and left tired out, covered in dirt, and that was the last time I looked at this house, these rooms, these boxwood balls, this Wilmersdorf street, and the last time I breathed in this smell.

Instead of which I stitch together my story of a felicitous flea market where a pair of mirrors that originally cost four hundred euros (as noted on the sticker on the back) were given to us for a fifth of the price. And this lamp, and these towels, and this trinkets dish… The only thing that really smells of the brothel is the bedcover that I hide like the wedding dress from a marriage annulled for tragic reasons. I couldn't justify buying it, it's a million miles from my usual tastes. Its value is purely sentimental. Feelings that seem impossible to justify – hence my writing this book.

And I don't really have the choice, because the little one has just thrown himself into my arms, buck naked after his bath, and has copiously watered the bedcover – which I will now have to wash. You can always count on children to forcefully turn over pages that you want to keep open. Separation starts here.

And so does my book.

'One couldn't go to the place where the lady with the great and beautiful dresses lived. Nobody spoke to her, nobody even said hello to her. She kidnapped little boys. Her house was full of them. Lots of little boys who were never seen again, who would never be seen again because she ate them one after the other. The lady with the grand and beautiful dress was a loose woman.'

a loose woman.'

Louis Calaferte, *The Way It Works with Women*

Doch die Leuten im besetzen Haus riefen: 'Ihr kriegt uns hier nicht raus! Das is unser Haus. Schmeisst doch endlich Schmidt unter Press und Mosch aus Kreuzberg raus!'

Ton Steine Scherben, 'Rauch-Haus-Song'

Season of the Witch, Donovan

WHEN DID I START SERIOUSLY THINKING ABOUT it? I've had quite a few stupid ideas in my life, but I think this one was always there, in my mind, to some degree.

Perhaps very simply twenty-five years ago, in Nogent, one fourteenth of December. Perhaps a decade later, when I started to distinguish between little girls and women in my head. Perhaps when I started to read. Perhaps when I understood that I couldn't keep Joseph and walked alone, sad, through the frost-covered main streets of Berlin. It may be that this novel begins on this precise night: Stéphane, who came to visit me and is no doubt kicking himself about it, is deeply asleep next to me and, not content with taking the whole cover, lets out a dull snore, heavy with meaning. If I'm unable to get to sleep beside a man who snores, and one who also snores because he's not twenty years old any more, that means I've lost my way again; it means that against all expectations, and despite my love for Stéphane, what I need is a boy with wide sinuses, brand-new – by extension, a boy my own age. Could that really be so?

Joseph, indeed. Joseph – thinking of this name in the dark, articulating it wordlessly so that my lips caress each other – is a kind of pain I can't find a name for. And perhaps it's for the best. Perhaps Joseph shouldn't be anything to do with this novel. When someone leaves, it's like a death – one that you can't get over, because the thought that this person is very much alive and not so far away, having decided not to exist any more, pours salt on the wounds for all eternity. It is a death. And I helped kill Joseph, as I've helped kill all the people I love, little by little.

I understand his hatred for me, his hatred that, compared with my own self-hatred, more resembles a vague dislike. I left for Berlin because I'm a coward and because I didn't see another way of making him understand that I no longer had any hope. That there was no hope for us. I was convinced I would find, in this city, people like me. I still don't know if there is anyone in the world like me, but the streets continue to call me, with loud cries, on the slightest pretext. Since Joseph left, I feel like I've been holding my breath whenever I'm not outside, when I'm not walking. And now Stéphane's asleep, as deeply as is humanly possible, I can't see what would prevent me from breathing again. So I get dressed in order to escape. When Stéphane wasn't yet here, I was dying of loneliness – and it only took his arrival for me to start missing myself as is always the case when someone, anyone, hopes for my company. Hence these spontaneous escapes; and everything, from the friction of my shoelaces that I tie holding my breath to the cracking of my knees when I bend over to pick up my bag, seems to play against me and in favour of the person who is asleep. But thank god, you could fire a cannon in the room and Stéphane wouldn't wake up. Closing the door behind me, I have that same feeling of stolen freedom as a guy who was wondering how to go home after chatting up and then fucking a girl he has met in a bar.

I've found myself stuck like that between women and men for several years. Oh, for forever, in fact. It's never struck me as much as in Berlin, during my solitary nocturnal walks on the big thoroughfare where the prostitutes bloom. They seem to materialise in front of me, by magic, wherever I go. Around 4 o'clock the street is empty, but as soon as the sun disappears (quickly, as it does in Berlin in February), there's hardly time to blink before the pavement is assailed by these legions of girls wearing thigh-length boots and with waists cinched by bumbags. Since I've been living here, I feel like I always bump into the same ones and, if I wasn't so shy as soon as women are involved, I could see myself greeting them as I do every shopkeeper in the neighbourhood. Perhaps in the end they take me for a plain-clothes police officer or for a possible colleague here to assess the quality of the working conditions. Not far from there, my haven of peace consists of a bench perfectly placed beneath a streetlamp; I position myself there and pretend to read, or I really do read, while also sneaking glances as their shadows spread out next to mine.

Each time I think, these are real women, women who are *only that*. Here are highly sexual beings who you can define without difficulty. If there was anything at all ambiguous about them, this duplicity would be drowned out by the profusion of adornments and pheromones in which they soak this little piece of pavement. From Joseph I have retained this absurd belief that a woman who fucks as much as a man – that is, in as casual a way – can only be a whore, however she dresses or however she looks at men as she offers herself to them. That indicates how difficult it must have been for Joseph to clearly define me throughout the three years we shared, constantly swinging between mad love and inexpressible hatred. If there was some misunderstanding between us at the beginning, Joseph did finally understand (but not accept) that the abandon and skill I demonstrated in bed were not reserved for him – far from it. And even better – that they hadn't blossomed into life with him. I imagine that he also understood that my desire wasn't directed towards any particular man but towards the entirety of the male species, and spiked with incomprehensible drives that had no relationship whatsoever with the raptures of the flesh. I spent so many years intellectualising desire, the body in general, that in me the satisfaction of it could happen almost without removing any clothes at all. How? I have absolutely no idea. That's no doubt why I continued, and still continue, to fuck, imagining that the solution will, against all expectation, be found there.

The truth is that since Joseph's departure, any idea of physical relief has evaporated. I don't even think about it any more, it's the least likely thing – coming with anyone other than him. My pleasure comes from that of the other, who I look at stretched out beneath me as I hold the mystery between my thighs, not understanding any of it, convinced of only getting close to it via these cavalcades in which only my brain is involved. My body gives itself willingly to this masquerade, but however much I try, however I submit myself to the most devious of contortions, there's still a calm, cold voice in me, one of a predator in wait: 'He might come soon. If you caress him like that, that's what will happen. If you slow down a bit you'll slow it down, but look at his hair standing up on his chest, look at the goosebumps on his stomach – he's getting near the end. He's looking at your bouncing breasts and this is the vision he's going to take with him into the abyss.'

And behind this voice rises the indecently childish voice of that part of me that got stuck at age fifteen and can't get over it. So, it's the movement of your breasts that's going to make him come, your own breasts, these tiny breasts that you would never have believed were anything other than decorative. It's your body, your smell, the way you move, the noises you emit – you're nothing but an envelope and this envelope is sucking all capacity out of him, and isn't that a sort of miracle in itself? You, a body? A body that makes someone come? Good god!

Over the several years that I've been engaging in this activity, you'd have thought that the initial astonishment would have been blunted – but no. Every man who talks to me and conveys with greater or lesser subtlety his desire to share his bed with me gives me the feeling of an opportunity to be grabbed pronto before it disappears. As if I risked waking up again in the skin of that kid who despaired of being to the boys anything other than a bespectacled mate. And I wonder, in fact, what must happen in the mind of a whore, how her ego is built, her appreciation of herself. The one I always watch from my frozen bench is a very young blonde who pretends to smoke a Vogue as she paces around a sliver of pavement. She's wearing what her colleagues all over Berlin wear: thigh-length leatherette boots that reflect the streetlights and catch the eye and won't let it go. Pristine white, with platform heels that scream 'For hire' louder than their lascivious glances. Sunken into her boots, pale jeans moulding her touchingly adolescent thighs, a fluorescent bumbag swelling, in a curiously intentional way, her short fake-fur jacket. In the freezing-cold wind, she shows a pink, slightly damp nose and long strands of almost-white blonde hair, which flutter in her wake, sparkling in the grey smoke of her cigarette.

The face she pulls as she spits out the smoke tells me she's at least five years younger than me. Five years. She's hardly twenty, and yet what artfulness in her way of moving, what self-awareness. For starters, there are the heels: nobody could walk in those, certainly not me, yet they seem like an extension of her legs as natural as bare feet. And this noise, this languorous clicking, over the ten steps there and back that mark her territory… Listening to it, you know that this expert rhythm can only be produced by a wobbly girl in danger of twisting her ankles – behind this rhythm there has to be a woman, aggressively seductive, in full possession of herself. And then these clothes, this hair, this make-up: my god, such an eye-catching caricature! How can she, at her age, bring together all these ruses, all these cock snares, without looking like a kid who's just ransacked her mother's wardrobe? And does she know this herself? How must it be to be aware that in every man she passes she evokes a sexual thought, involuntary or otherwise. What does it do to you to be like that, in the street, right in the middle of the cars and passers-by, a thunderous, implacable reminder of the prevalence of desire over everything?

And what would he say, Stéphane, with whom I no longer dare wear such outfits – ever since, in Paris, wearing exorbitantly priced high-heeled boots, I fell and splayed myself over a pedestrian crossing? Several seemingly interminable seconds followed during which Stéphane and a few onlookers, barely suppressing their hilarity, came to my aid – and I had no knickers on to spare decent-minded folk the sight of my gaping bush. Even as time went by, Stéphane and I never laughed about it. It's a non-event that lived on between us, grave and heavy like a subject that, if even touched upon, would lead to an argument. From my side, I never tried, for obvious reasons of vanity and pride, but I never managed to work out what was holding Stéphane back, except perhaps simply the fear of annoying me by reminding me of that evening (because what followed, far from making up for my fall, was nothing but a series of rejections from swingers' clubs – in short, a slow and painful fall from high heels for our egos). Either that or he didn't think it was funny. It's a possibility that leaves me very thoughtful: perhaps Stéphane and I don't have the same sense of humour, which would explain the code of silence applied to this scene and to others, harmless, that all include me clad in frivolities that womanhood can manage as easily as we do breathing but that proved unmanageable for me. Thinking about it now, the idea of joking about it would occur to him as little as the idea of laughing about an obese person bellyflopping in a swimming pool – because one shouldn't make fun of any kind of handicaps. And perhaps that's how I seem to him, perched up on my heels, hiding my suffering poorly. If he could see how I see, now, the grace of this late teen stamping around a few metres of pavement without showing the least discomfort, he would have to admit the degree to which my lack of talent for these things is innate.

Could that be the answer to the questions I ask myself when Stéphane is in my vicinity? This constant feeling of wanting to reconcile two parallel worlds, separated not by space but by time, in such a way that to feel close to Stéphane I would need some science-fiction machine that won't be invented for a century or two. Wearing heels doesn't affect our closeness in any way – it's only a symptom of it: for him, I'm not a woman. Or not yet. Or if I am one, and when I'm naked the evidence for that is striking, I'm lacking decades of sophistication acquired under the yoke of masculine desire. What

I'm lacking in order to fascinate Stéphane is this goodwill and this indifference when I try to walk in platform boots on the nasty little paving stones of Paris or in staircases without handrails leading to overrated clubs where we are turned away, and that also probably because my pain, my immaturity, are written on my face. What I'm missing is the haughtiness of these women when they're dressed to kill, these eight, ten centimetres of provocativeness, this illusion of dominating men. What I'm missing, in fact, is treating him with disdain as I do any other man, one I don't give a fuck about.

I feel it, when we walk or have dinner together: I sense that beyond certain shared views and an identical sensitivity, we are one of the worst-matched couples you could imagine. He can't bear that one might think he's a father dining with his daughter living in Berlin. And how could it be otherwise, since I prefer to dress like his daughter and not risk, by showing a little elegance, looking like an escort taking her client out? I'm sure he'd prefer that. Stéphane would never let himself kiss me in public, he keeps his gruff tone and brusque manners of a guy lost in the space between friend and lover, and when he laughs and part of me melts hearing such a grown-up laugh, such a sexy laugh, I tighten my hand on my thigh under the table out of fear of grabbing his. It's also occurred to me that he neither kisses me in public nor hugs me not out of regard for other people but because he doesn't want to, because our walks in Berlin, which he thinks are too long, exhaust him as much as my incessant questions, my thirst to know him better and better; that my uninterrupted flow of words, due to my timidity, to my fear that he's bored, far from entertaining him actually stifle him, and that with me Stéphane ends up missing his solitude just as I miss mine. The time we spend out makes us both visibly uptight; it's only in bed, far from the eyes of the world, that Stéphane and I – or at least our skin – achieve a kind of serenity. That is, before he starts to snore – a new factor that, in my romantic fantasies, I hadn't taken into account – and that's where I realise that if I'm too young for him, Stéphane is perhaps also too old for me. That would explain why, by wanting to get close to him, I also feel as if I'm trying to fit together the pieces of two different jigsaw puzzles. And why, when he leaves and the relief sets in of not having to pretend anything any more, I have the eternal regret of not having been able to be more tender, more understanding, to not have made him be in love with me.

I imagine him already on his plane home, this rugged bear of a man who fills my bedroom with moans and takes the whole of the cover, this guy who refuses to carry on walking the second I admit to having no precise aim to our wanderings, who gets impatient when I get street numbers mixed up, this man older than my father, who the idea of being, if only vaguely, a kind of a teacher or a mentor terrifies me, who is irritated by my curiosity, and who does however have such a way of saying my name when he comes…! There's a holy moment when I'm on top of Stéphane, higher than I will ever be, and he takes on the look of a man about to drown and the whites of his rolled-back eyes send me back an imperial, almost mythological image of myself – and he says, 'Emma, darling, darling, oh, Emma,' like a man lost inside a woman, of whatever age, whatever background, not like a man who is coming – or not only that – but like a man really in love. And afterwards, this fire that flickers and extinguishes itself little by little makes his skin boiling hot; with his head between my breasts he sighs in comfort, blind and deaf. When he opens his eyes again, I close mine, because the power that my niche talents seem to have given me don't lessen at all the fact that this man impresses me. That's the curse of what I call, in spite of everything, our love. The only moments of closeness are when he is inside me. That's the magic of our story, these moments after making love when I look at him looking at me, propped on his elbow, caressing my hair with the gentleness that men show to women they've just possessed, and you could see in that a normal scene between two lovers were it not for the perplexity in his eyes at the idea that this pleasure could have come from me, from this kid who he will never love. We are fully together and more alone than ever. Then suddenly, it seems it would be possible to love each other. In this silence and this contemplation, I realise that even a single word would break this very fragile state of grace, our fleeting understanding of each other; and yet I have so many things to say, that's maybe my main problem, my avidity to speak when silence is enough. I'd like to say that there is very much a moment and a place where Stéphane and I love each other, even if it's a tiny spot – and the fact is that this cubbyhole is enough to contain both of us until the edge of sleep, before evaporating during the night. In the morning, we've returned to our respective places, Stéphane with his faults, me with mine, but I can't listen to him complain about the cold or about distances without remembering the day before, when we were so in love. I'm waiting patiently for the evening to repeat the experiment on this melancholic writer, to extract from him this abandon and this strange lucidity that make him write, when he's on the other side of the world, 'Perhaps ultimately, you are the only one.' That's a lot of uncertainty in one sentence, or in one context. To receive this kind of declaration, a certain number of factors have to be present at the same time: Stéphane has to be sad, or at least freed of his cynicism by orgasm, and one of his wives or mistresses has to have packed up and left. But what separates me from *You are the only one* is this first *perhaps* and the *ultimately,* which should be translated by *against all logic and after carefully examining my situation* – yes, but: Raymond Radiguet wrote that when a man says I love you to a woman, you can suppose he did it for a whole pile of reasons external to love, you can think he was lying; however, something, at that moment, pushed us to say *I love you*, and therefore it's true. There are moments when Stéphane and I love each other. Most of the time it's an absurdity. Sometimes the truth of this lie moves me, and then the world seems to me like highly hostile terrain where he and I are fighting side by side – which is better than hostile terrain where I'm alone against everyone, isn't it?

As a police car glides past the pavement where the girl is marking time, for one terrified moment I imagine that if the cops came to ask for her papers, they could also demand those of this strange chick who's reading, at 4 o'clock in the morning, on a bench in the cold. And because I came out without anything and because that's all I need, to spend a night at the police station because of a misunderstanding (although I'd probably sleep better there than next to Stéphane), I slip into the shadow of a chestnut tree until the car has gone. the girl has flown away too, and without her there remains only this piece of tarmac soaked with drizzle, which beneath her feet seemed to be in bloom.

In the doorway, I look at Stéphane's body stretched diagonally across the whole mattress. He's not snoring any more; either the sound of the key disturbed him for a minute, or earlier my presence or my warmth produced the ideal conditions for snoring. I undress slowly, and I sit down on the edge of the bed in the space created by his raised knees and his face. I don't often have the chance to see the details like this; in fact, it's a unique occasion – Stéphane has never slept with me. And naturally, seeing him like that, in a state of complete abandon, I'm struck by the realisation that we are *nothing to do* with each other. It's blindingly obvious. Fifty-five years old. Think about it. He may look younger, but nobody would think he was twenty either. Everything about him screams maturity, right down to his sleep, because even then he looks serious and preoccupied. If I take off my glasses, in the artistic haze of my nearsightedness his contours are less pronounced, less sharp, and I manage to see him as he was around thirty – not at my age, no, Stéphane at twenty-five, that's a sort of eldorado that's undoubtedly documented in archives – like in that photo taken when his third book came out. One could easily superimpose this sleeping face on the round and joyful face of the young writer who couldn't take a single step in Paris without falling in love ten times. I'm not making it up, I read it, and when I have trouble believing it, I read it again. So I don't forget that thirty years ago he was gruff, slow to unravel, and that this was an armour to conceal from the world the hysteria that women invoked in him – Stéphane is a very controlled fire, and one whose heat flares up. I wonder if he would have fallen in love with me: Stéphane's thirties, in the thrilling 1980s when I was still floating along my father's epididymis, feel like a promised land when nothing was impossible. I see myself towering up, fascinating this young animal full of sap, parading him through Paris, solving the mystery of this woman, the only one he loved enough to give her a child. And perhaps I too would have given him the idea to reproduce, in order to keep me with him – and he would have loved and then tired of me, and would have ended up hating me for sacrifices that no one had asked of him. I would have become this routine, lying in the next room with the kid, exhausted and full of milk, weary of knowing him so well, weary of his weaknesses, of his acts of cowardice, of his promises, disdained and dishonoured during rants between men lasting whole nights – I would have known Stéphane's anger, his reproaches, his incoherent moments, his acts of deceit, and perhaps even his tears. And I could have said, after years of living together, that, my god, there was nothing to worry about, that he was just a man like any other. We would have torn each other apart for valid reasons, shouting, breaking things, and at night, feeling guilty; I would have come and sat on the edge of the bed, like now, and like now I would have placed my hand on his hair, and Stéphane would have opened one eye, would have looked at me in silence, hesitating as to what emotion to feel, and he would have sighed, and he would have said *Oh, darling…!*

'Oh, is that you?' Stéphane shakes himself, turns over, and mutters in the tone of someone who's already fallen back to sleep:

'What the fuck have you been doing? You're freezing cold.'

'Nothing. I went out for a little walk.'

'You're mad. Come back to bed.'

Which, note, is perhaps exactly what he would have said to me at the time. I make myself a place in his warmth, keeping my extremities far from his. All my naive tenderness has receded to the back of my mind. I return to the familiar sensation of sleeping beside a family friend who was too late to try to book a room and who accepts with some good grace to share mine.

STÉPHANE AND I ARE WALKING ALONG DANZIGER Strasse, beneath a timid sun. It's a tricky walk because of the snow, and one without any aim (in any case, in five hundred metres I won't know where I am any more) – but Stéphane doesn't really seem to mind, he hasn't seen snow in a long time and it's making him a bit giddy. A little earlier, as we were going back up Kastanienallee, I saw him smile without any particular reason; he'd loved the cake at breakfast, and the shops too. And he gave me huge pleasure by declaring, in the middle of a silence that actually wasn't that embarrassing, and when I hadn't asked him anything, 'I could really live here.'

What would maybe prevent him, except his work, is the weather in Berlin. Too cold for him.

'Yes, but look how pretty it is too, an all-white city.'

'It's true,' he concedes calmly, all dreamy, looking at the buildings that look like jewels beneath the sun and the snow. 'But in London…'

A pretty girl surreptitiously separates us, almost sliding between us, enveloped in a fur coat that supplements the smell of her perfume with a note of damp sheep's wool – and she flicks this decent family man out with his daughter a lightning-fast glance that causes Stéphane to turn around. I'd be a bit annoyed were she not wearing these shiny thigh-high boots whiter than snow, as if designed for touting for business in winter.

'Ah, there's something you don't have in London.'

'Pretty girls?'

'No, idiot. Whores.'

'Was that a whore?'

Stéphane turns around again, unable to believe that this girl, who looks like a student, can be a whore, even with those boots on, and what's more, that she can walk around like that with an attitude of complete indifference to the police.

'But is it legal here?'

'Everything is legal. Prostitution, brothels, escorts.'

'Well, it's heaven then!'

Stéphane's eyes, suddenly alive with fascination and longing, follow her to the corner of Schönhauser Allee – and that's the gaze I fell in love with. The gaze he bathed me in the first day, after we had shaken hands. While I was moving away from him, I'd turned around to study the effect of my skirt on this man who was far too grown-up for me – *this* gaze. And as I like to believe that this is not a form of attention destined solely for sex workers, I conclude that he looks this way at all women who, through a mix of flippancy and provocation, are living symbols of desire, self-assured in their omnipotence and disdainful of worshippers. So that's what I was to him, before my lyricism gave me speech and initiative and I lost in sparkle what I gained in intimacy.

I'd been too affected by this almost indecent gaze, unreadable by anyone but me, to ascribe it any meaning; all that remains of it are a very vivid memory of warmth and a feeling of urgency to run away quickly, quickly, before my appearance lost some of its glory. Now that I see these same eyes riveted to the fur and the insolent thigh-high boots, I wonder, with my forensic coldness: *What's he thinking right now?* If I asked him, he'd reply *Nothing*, but I would see his face suddenly change expression. There must be images parading in front of his eyes, images of her naked, in impossible positions, and in his head everything he could ask her if he allowed himself this fleeting control over her. Is he thinking, even furtively, of taking her back to ours?

'Do you think she's shaven?' I let slip, out of a cunning motive that he grasps immediately, the animal, trumpeting:

'Are you jealous?'

'Jealous? I'm mesmerised, actually.'

We're now in the heart of the lawless zone, the badly lit part of Prenzlauer Berg: a little further back, the whores have begun their watch.

'It was like this too, on certain streets in Paris, twenty years ago,' notes Stéphane.

'Where do you think they go, with their clients?'

'No idea. In cars? Maybe they have sleazy apartments?'

There's a tall brunette, gaudy, too fat, who's squeezed herself into a corset – and the sight of this mass of flesh above and below her strangulated waist fills me with terror and elation. Brushing against Stéphane, she gives him a look of disdainful invitation, lasting barely a second, before going back to her line of sight, which I imagine must be the end of one street, the beginning of another and, among these thousands of men, one who will allow himself to be tempted by a cosy stop-off. I don't know if she even saw Stéphane: if after a while people like him who only glance in passing (however insistently) don't all blend into one hostile, laughing crowd, who would like to but can't, who'd love to but daren't, who wouldn't even like to but who get excited on their way home – a crowd who won't spend a penny to devour her with their eyes, this woman who achieves the miracle of being both more clothed than me and more naked than a statue, presented this way, moulded into a corset pulled down over her down jacket.

'Why have you never been to a brothel?'

'I've never needed to go to a brothel.'

'It's not about need, is it?'

'Let's say I've never felt the need to pay a woman. You know about my proverbial stinginess.'

'It's about money then? Don't tell me it's about money.'

'Why would I go paying for it when I can have a woman who wants me for nothing?'

'Oh Stéphane, I don't know, for the *poetry*?'

'It doesn't particularly excite me to fuck a girl who I know has only accepted because I'm paying her. If you were a man, you would understand what I'm saying.'

I burst out laughing and, in my momentary obsession, I have the impression that the little blonde whore who's looking at us is also smiling at me.

'If I was a man? Darling, if I was a man, I would be following them around all the time.'

'Yes, that's what you think.'

'Well, perhaps not the ones in the street. But I'd go to a brothel. Don't you think that's fantastic? I'm not even talking about going, I'm just saying it's possible. Imagine, you go to work and a desire to fuck comes over you, and on your way home there's a little brothel with fifteen or so pretty girls who...'

'Who don't give a fuck if it's me or someone else.'

'Let's say it's early, okay? The brothel has just opened. They're still human beings; perhaps among them is one who's also woken up horny, like you.'

'I don't know how long you can be horny for, doing a job like that.'

'Oh Stéphane, we're not talking about robots.'

'No, but you have no idea what it can be like to fuck ten times a day. After a while, I think the spirit and the body together get resigned to it, and horniness becomes something not only decorative but also extremely rare. Imagine... Oh sorry, Madam...!'

The whore who Stéphane nearly barged into is a blonde with lips so red that the rest of her white face almost disappears; one can see nothing beyond this bloody stain. 'Sorry,' Stéphane repeats, a bit flustered, and the smile she gives him in reply turns her mouth into a bouquet of red, white and pink. She steps back on her enormous heels to let us past and, because this man who never pays women is still staring at her, she produces for him a knowing look, her head bent towards the entrance of a grey building, lifting the mass of her full cleavage with her gloved hands in a movement so filled with promises that I'm a bit regretful that Stéphane shakes his head. 'She was cute,' he concedes.

'I don't understand how one can imitate desire so well, arouse it so easily in others, if one has totally forgotten what it is.'

'There is a desire, though – but it's a desire for money.'

'Yes, but to deliver such a successful imitation, without saying a word, to provoke desire in the fraction of a second, and within that second, making every man forget that it's a game…'

'It's acting.'

'Yes, but it's *good* acting. It's high art. Either that or male desire is completely crazy and all a man needs, to believe it's reciprocated, is for a woman to show her breasts.'

'You know how stupid men are.'

'Okay, let's say men are stupid. But not stupid enough to…'

'They are.'

'Oh, don't be annoying, I saw how you were looking at her.'

'Because she was pretty!'

'I'm delighted to hear you say that. And you've proven I'm right: perhaps their job, when it comes down to it, is just to be pretty and desirable, but the difference between the ones you look at and the ones you ignore is the extra soul they put into snaring you.'

'So they're actresses.'

'Possibly the greatest actresses of all. A whore who gives you the impression of truly possessing her, a whore who makes you forget what she has cost you, that's the quintessence of being an actress; they don't need anything else.'

Stéphane smiles at me:

'It's an easy take when you don't do that job. I'm sure your clients in Paris were totally satisfied. But it's because you were doing it for a laugh. It didn't require much effort from you to pretend – if indeed you did pretend – because this money didn't pay your rent or your shopping but the things you considered a luxury. Now, if you talk about these girls…'

'I'm just saying that pretending, and doing it in such a way that no one realises, may be inherent to being a woman.'

'Oh really? And what kind of woman?'

'All women.'

'All women or just you? Your problem is this tendency to generalise to reassure yourself.'

'I'd be surprised if I was the only one. What pains you about whores is knowing they are pretending, and that that makes you come anyway.'

'You know how easy it is to make a man come.'

'Yes, a machine could do it. But that doesn't stop you carrying on with it, right? It may all be false, from the start, even with your mistress or your wife – but that doesn't change the fact that when you get an erection, when you want to fuck, you're only thinking of the warmth of that body against yours, and of the noise the girl is going to make, and of the way she wriggles around beneath you – as long as she seems to want it, you don't imagine for a single second that it can be acting?'

'So, in your view, all women are faking it?'

'A whore is still a woman. It's an abnormal job, but that doesn't make them abnormal women; you have the same risk of disaster and the same chance of triumph as with any other.'

'A woman who doesn't spend her days fucking – you have more chances of getting through to her and making her feel something. Because she's not cloaked in her personal indifference.'

'You can also fuck guys who leave you a bit indifferent. There are many reasons to fuck without thinking about flesh.'

'And they are?'

'They are?' I look at Stéphane and suddenly feel further from him than ever. There's no doubt that if he was a girl we would be the best friends in the world – but what perhaps prevents him from understanding is this supernumerary member between his legs for which fucking means coming, implies coming. Fucking and coming are unfailingly linked, the cock and the brain don't lead parallel lives during the act – they travel hand in hand and fuse at the moment of orgasm. If I reduced him like this to his prick, Stéphane would scream bloody murder, shout about it being a gross oversimplification – with the bad faith necessary for that.

Two hours later at Hamburg Station, Stéphane, who doesn't mess around where art is concerned, leans towards me as if to share some thoughts on the work we're looking at (which happens to be a sinister installation by Joseph Beuys):

'I've got a hard-on.'

'Why?'

'Just like that. I don't know.'

We move crab-like towards the opposite wall, on which several sketches that seem to have been made using blood or strawberry juice have been pinned. No longer interested, Stéphane reads the labels in a rush, all feverish, looking for a dark corner. He finds it in the form of a darkened room where experimental short films are being projected, and as we melt into a small crowd who are standing listening, he whispers:

'Give me your hand.'

'It's you who dragged me to this exhibition.'

'I don't know what's got into me, I've had a surge of testosterone…'

'It'll pass.'

'You don't want to know what I would do to you if I could. Right in the middle of this room.'

What do you mean, I wouldn't want to know? Suddenly, just as I was getting interested in the exhibition, I hold out my hand to Stéphane, who slips it into his pocket, and I wrap it around his cock. And it's fascinating to realise that once he's grasped hold of this way, this man hasn't an ounce of reason left in him – we've walked two kilometres in the snow to get to this museum that he was insistent he wanted to see, and not without arguing three times because I'd had too much faith in my sense of direction. Stéphane began the visit as if no one merited the title of artist as much as

Beuys, but here we are with a hand, a warm little hand around his dick, taking away all his capacity to think.

And it doesn't occur to him that the excitement I feel, that I share with him, is totally detached from my flesh. It doesn't occur to him that my body doesn't care but that my brain is turned on – that it's his excitement, the images that go through his mind, that arouse in me this elation. Isn't this exactly the name of this lie he and I have going? He pretends I'm the source of this erection, and I pretend to be in tune with this desire that doesn't belong to me, which was probably brought about more by the brutal change in temperature between the street and the museum: women fuck for a whole host of excellent reasons that have nothing to do with physical pleasure. How could a man know? How could Stéphane suspect that my own very good reason, right now, is to make the two continents that we represent touch, continents that, without these passing meteorological conditions, this storm, would never get close to each other. I do it for this magic – to see him abandon himself, become as young, as malleable as me, to hear his serious voice take on the high-pitched desperation of a little boy when I ride him, and to watch Stéphane open his eyes wide, seemingly petrified by the power that I take on, when I'm astride him.

OCTOBER 2010, JOSEPH IS CELEBRATING HIS TWENTY-FIRST birthday; we are so in love that a gift could seem derisory. Our happiness would be perfectly content with a silly little thing like a pullover or a concert ticket, but with my craze for grand gestures, I've hatched a diabolical plan that gives me such joy that it's been impossible to keep it secret. I'm going to offer him a call girl so we can have a threesome. I've found the hotel, the time, I have a whole program in my head, I just need the girl.

I've found one, Nathalie, who would be perfect, as she specialises in couples. Her body, for all that that matters to me, looks pretty, and the description on the site gives me hope that she doesn't act in an overly professional way. The problem is as follows: her face is hopelessly blurred. Despite my polite request, she refuses to send me a photo, and her body may well be perfect, I can't see myself taking the risk of signing up a girl whose face might overturn everything.

After a few tergiversations, I fix upon a Larissa, unearthed thanks to an English escort site; a ravishing Russian about twenty years old, blonde with fine features and big almond-shaped glacier-blue eyes, a photo of whom I very proudly show to Joseph. It's an understatement to say that we spend the two weeks between then and the big night getting each other overheated, imagining exotic acts between Larissa and me while he gorges himself on unforgettable images, his swelling cock in his hand: the horrors that we watched separately on the internet seem, miraculously, two steps from becoming reality. Larissa, this languorous name, comes into everything we talk about during our long preparations.

I met her in Café de la Paix.

It was cold and sunny that day, I was shivering on the terrace as I waited for her, while she was waiting for me inside. I should have turned away at first sight, but I was impressed – how do you react when the head waiter leads you to the table of a towering Russian wrapped in fur, busy shelling the claws of a lobster while drinking champagne? Everything about her smelt of money, even the smile that took over her face without lighting up her eyes. The velvet of her painted face captured the light flooding the room, and men's gazes studied, warily, the duo that we formed. She smelt of something strong and sophisticated, Guerlain's violet, and her little teeth shone like pearls when she pretended to laugh.

Had he been with me, Joseph would undoubtedly have seen what I was too feverish to notice: that she had too much make-up on, that she didn't care about sleeping with a girl or a boy as long as she was being paid – you don't come to reside on Rue de la Paix if you have standards. Above all, that she didn't look like her photo – no trace of the nymph, only the very high cheekbones had resisted the photographer's retouches. I should have thanked her and looked for a new hetaera, but the timing was too tight for me to allow myself this fantasy; we'd already dreamed too much of Larissa.

Once relieved of most of my money, I forced myself to include the real Larissa in our fantasies, putting aside the fathomless indifference that she inspired in me. When Joseph asked me how it had gone, my heart raced and I lied: 'Oh, you'll really like her.'

Bang on 6 o'clock, we're in the room. I've taken out the champagne and the coke, which will turn out to be especially bad – but there's no question of me slagging off my own gift. Feverishly, to keep face, I roll a joint that kicks the legs – already weak – out from under the cocaine. The mixture of the two, watered down with warm champagne, doesn't help my anxiety.

It's 8 o'clock. Larissa hasn't arrived, and I'm at the point of confusedly hoping that she has vanished with my money – the idea of only two of us fucking is suddenly more exciting than the possibility of making a mess of it between the three of us. Joseph is as scared as me. When I take him in my arms, as I did every two minutes in those days, I feel behind his beautiful broad torso his heart palpitating, distraught.

Against all expectation, honest Larissa finally knocks genteelly at our door, plunging me to the depths of discomfort. Thank god, the room is too small for me to be able to discreetly ask Joseph what he thinks of her – and in any case we're too panicked to consult each other, too anxious. Larissa, with her shoes on, is almost five foot nine and a head and a half taller than us. It's clear she wasn't expecting such a small room, undoubtedly used to the insane proportions of Parisian palaces, and that's exactly what I should have booked, a suite at the Ritz that would have overpowered us with its flash luxury. If Larissa hadn't ruined me, that's what I would have done; the cute crampedness of the room becomes stifling, I'm embarrassed there's only one chair to sit on, and I offer it to her while we fall back on the edge of the bed like two naive girls. Larissa looks huge, adult; we stink to high heaven of innocence. All she sees is how young and fearful we are. The best thing would be to pretend not to have noticed anything, but psychology is evidently not her forte because, after a long look in Joseph's direction, she chuckles, in English: 'Are you sure you're eighteen?'

As we nod in confirmation, Joseph bright red and me scandalised, I feel my desires reduce to nothing. I thought that a young couple in love would feel more like a tip than real work, but what shines in her large eyes is unquestionably condescension and the impulse to laugh – and suddenly I feel a bit sorry for us; I should have booked a young one. A beginner who wouldn't know how to distinguish between work or pleasure or between work and experience, and who would have been transfixed with admiration for Joseph's beauty – this breathtaking beauty of an animal at the peak of its glory.

But I've paid, and I find myself in the uncomfortable position of a client who's going to try everything to drag out of a whore a few shreds of free interest. As the atmosphere isn't lending itself to a voluntary orgy, as neither Joseph nor I would think to jump on her, I initiate a clumsy conversation in English – a language that the three of us massacre with our heavy accents.

And I've never met a woman as glacial as her; despite the fact she's smiled, giggled at my pitiful quips; despite the fact she's worn just a very short dress, I've never felt so distant from anybody. The coke that I offer her out of obligation, and that she takes out of the same obligation, far from cheering her up probably only adds to her grievances against us, ignorant novices ready to buy any old white powder as long as it's finely ground. That can't play in our favour, this bottle of champagne stolen from my father and this gram of nothingness laid out in ridiculous lines: *Relax baby, sniff a bit of Canderel, sip a glass of fizz.* Ah, the wretches…!

Time passes, inexorably, without anyone turning the situation around. I don't know who deserves the most slaps, me for chattering and chattering, Joseph who has decided to play the DJ with his iPod, or Larissa (whose work it is after all, for fuck's sake), who is making herself comfortable, her long legs crossed over this jewel for which I painfully amassed more than a half of the annual minimum wage. No doubt telling herself that she's already racked up three quarters of an hour – and I would understand that if we were two old lechs, but could she even dream of clients easier to satisfy? Just a kiss, a tiny kiss on the mouth with the tip of a slightly wet tongue would transport us both to heights of ecstasy, she must know, she must have sussed out that neither of us will demand improbable contortions of her or some stupid role-playing. Because she is here, we are ready to pretend to be happy with nothing.

If there is within her not the slightest trace of spontaneity or any gift for acting (but spontaneity can be feigned as much as the rest), I have to recognise in her a form of meekness: I was making things so difficult for us that she must have felt it, and after an hour it's she who asks me to accompany her to the bathroom. An embarrassing moment during which, practically stuck to me between the shower and the toilet, Larissa demands I give her the remaining 350 euros before suggesting that Joseph and I take a shower. Which we've already done so much we've virtually ripped the skin off each other's groins.

Her money in her hand, Larissa can begin. It's impossible to think of what follows without wanting to laugh, and I'm sure that if I spoke to Joseph about it, if today it was possible for me to talk about anything with Joseph, we'd laugh together. Oh lord. Forgive me, Joseph. I would never had thrown us into that had I known – but I so wanted to give you pleasure, I so wanted to offer you a little slave to grope together.

As if everything had suddenly changed, as if we hadn't just spent sixty per cent of the allotted time making conversation, Larissa abruptly took off her dress before climbing onto Joseph. Kissing him on the mouth, would you believe, generously forgetting that whores don't do that – and perhaps that was her own attempt to relax us, perhaps she had already understood that nothing else would happen.

For me the sight of other lips than mine on Joseph's is, always was, fascinating. While nobody is paying attention to me, I undress and fit myself into the strange couple that they form. Silence would be quite enough, but Larissa is emitting teasing porn-movie mews, and I force myself to not catch Joseph's eye – because it's tacitly admitted that the situation has nothing much sexual about it; what's holding us back from giggling is shrinking at a rate of knots. Even our kisses sound fake to us.

I make sure to get into his trousers first because I know he won't have a hard-on. I hope with all my heart I'm wrong, but objectively there's no chance of that. I know we can only limit the damage, and

I'm counting on my powers of persuasion. But Joseph, the man I only know to be impeccably hard, just stays soft – no, his cock seems to have literally collapsed into his belly – and despite my gentleness or my persistence, it remains as it is, giving me the obstinate stare of a child refusing to walk. I can hardly blame either of them, Joseph is at least as sorry as me; this is not at all exciting. An erection would make this circus less painful, but wouldn't it be in bad taste, in fact, to get a hard-on for this pantomime?

Nothing is further from what I like in a woman than Larissa. She has that exasperating look of perfection, superb pert breasts, a small but completely round arse, skin with the whiteness and softness of milk, entirely hairless down to her tiny pussy – inside, the simulation of a vulva by Polly Pocket, so fine and so pure that one wonders if Larissa doesn't moult every morning. I search in vain between her legs for a slightly animal, slightly human smell, some detail, some imperfection that would bring her closer to me; but her arsehole could feature on a stained-glass window to which the masses kneel down, just a barely-there crevice, pink as a baby's cheek, neutralising by its absolute beauty any impure thoughts. And me with my messy hair and hairs, my skin neither moisturised nor made up, my smell of cigarettes, I sniff avidly the nooks and crannies of this indifferent show dog. As well as hugely depressing me, the soul-wrenching smallness of her clitoris, of her lips, as well as hugely depressing me evokes something almost illegal. It's only my saliva that gives some taste to her slit – as if Larissa was nothing but a sort of receptacle taking the form and the colour of the fantasies of each client, keeping her soul warm behind layers of apathy. Even a sixty-nine, with her on top, feels like you're wearing a pretty piece of minimalist headgear; and Joseph, normally panicked by this position, looks at us with semi hard-on, as if he's wondering if he's in a bad movie or a nightmare. Slipping a condom on his cock at top speed, I give him a look that says, *For the love of my 700 euros, for pity's sake, fuck her.*

Hardly has he penetrated her when he comes out soft, reduced to impotence by these icy entrails – but Larissa, galvanised, desperate to get it over and done with with these two vile kids, grabs hold of him and shakes him frenetically, standing over him, groaning at the top of her voice, 'Come now, come for me', despite the evidence that's blinding me: Joseph has never been further from coming. You don't need to be an expert, it's common sense: he doesn't have an erection, for god's sake, which pains us more than it does you – and if you want my opinion, being trapped between your sharp nails isn't helping him, no, knowing him as I do, he must be praying that you don't just pull it right off.

How, with all my good intentions, was I able to get us into all this? While I'm conscientiously licking her, I look for Larissa's eyes – in vain, because Joseph, who's sucking her nipples, is obstructing my field of vision. I can't convince myself to abandon the idea that we are not so different, and by caressing her along her mute thighs, I try to transmit to her my prayer – Larissa my sister, my soulmate, understand me, just try for a moment, forget this man between us who is absorbing both of us, albeit for perceptibly different reasons. I've been where you are now, of course it's annoying he doesn't have an erection, we don't really know how to make use of the time we have left. It irritates me as much as it does you. But I'd like to believe that we can still, the both of us, sort out the situation. Larissa, you were once my age, you had a lover, you also perhaps had 700 euros spare to give this lover an ambitious gift. I'd counted on giving him, with your help, an earth-shattering orgasm, but this possibility now being ruled out, all you'd have to do is emit some strident cries that insult all of our intelligence: that you feel what I'm doing to you down here. Because it can't be so disagreeable, to have your pussy licked when you counted on a gymnastics session. If you could gratify me with a sigh, just one – bloody hell, if you just placed your hand on my neck, if you opened your tiny little pussy and looked as if you were involved; if you just faked an orgasm that could really trick a 15-year-old kid…! Can you see in his young man's eyes the hope of seeing this spontaneity that no one can buy from you shine for a moment? Even a fart, Larissa, an uncontrollable gassy emission from your elegant rump, would suffice for him to think you're human and to get an erection.

Larissa now fakes an orgasm, cleverly timed at the moment Joseph adds his tongue to mine, right in the middle of this command deck she has in place of a vulva. I tend to think we're only overstimulating the infinite nerve endings of her clitoris, which would probably get by just as well with a sparrow's feather. But anyway, she's faking it, in a way that's not too insulting. And as Joseph has the wild air of a hunter who finally sees his moment arriving, five fucking minutes before the end of the allotted time, Larissa, whose face has hardly changed colour, sits up and, a cold smile on her lips, delivers the fatal blow to him: 'Listen, I think your *little friend* is tired.'

The little friend, I understand, stupefied, doesn't refer to Joseph but to his cock. He and I smile stupidly, paralysed by shame, and his dick goes back into its nest in mortification, weary of the snubs.

When Larissa finally leaves, it's difficult to describe the texture of the silence that follows the slamming of the door. I'm almost afraid to look Joseph in the eye, and afraid of us bursting out laughing – because that's the only thing to do. Seven hundred euros! How many pairs of April 77 jeans could I have bought him with 700 euros, jeans that would never have stopped him getting a hard-on? That's one purchase that would have made both of us happy, at least, instead of making us both feel like two inexperienced lice, and me naive.

Larissa unleashed a miracle that she will never know about. Suddenly, without this cold atmosphere that she took away with her, we both get hot again, and the idea of making love, just Joseph and I, of doing it as usual, so well that it gives us tears in our eyes, is as atrociously exciting as if we'd never kissed before.

'Come here, my fighter plane,' purrs Joseph, reaching for me with those beautiful arms modelled by love and by a year of working out, which if I was an escort would make me refuse any payment.

His cock is hard enough to explode.

'Did you see how soft her skin was?' I ask with my arse in the air, crushed between his large, intelligent, violinist's hands.

'Yes, she had soft skin,' he concedes. 'Almost too much so, don't you think?'

He bites into one of my thighs; the cry of protest that I let out isn't to be taken literally and I don't ask him to stop. Joseph has his pretty nose between my legs and is sniffing, avidly. I lift my dress to see his shining, smiling eyes.

'Did you see how tiny her pussy was?'

Joseph nods, drowning in a confusion of lips and unruly hairs.

'I'm still not sure she has a clitoris.'

'It makes me depressed, this kind of pussy. Even those of little girls are more formed.'

'And how do you know that, you nasty boy?'

His teeth shine, and I sigh:

'Her arse didn't smell of anything…!'

'Whereas yours…'

The end of his nose passing through my thighs, he takes an interminable breath in, his eyes closed, as if he was at the top of a mountain:

'Feel how hard I am.'

'So you are. Why now?'

'It's your arsehole.'

Hardly has his cock parted the entrance to my pussy than my mouth is full of saliva, full of obscene words. Reality itself overflows with birthday presents for a boy in love. 'Can I ravage you, for my twenty-first birthday?'

And what's 700 euros? Compared to this miserly sum, what are Joseph's smell and the halting of time worth, time losing all meaning as soon as we're pressed against each other, dazed by pleasure that has never so much resembled death – without that being frightening for a single second?

But I'm getting lost.

The presence of Larissa, this shadow cast by the grand light of our love, didn't prevent us from having the most charming weekend possible, giving an impetuously romantic shine to everything right down to the *magret de canard* savoured the following morning on the terrace of a bar on Rue de Rivoli. A bar that, by coincidence or otherwise, was for four years the refuge where we came to put sticky plasters over our arguments, all our dramas, where we learnt to love each other again in front of a bottle of too-sweet Coteaux du Layon that made us both dreamy and sentimental. Joseph would arrive angry, having had enough of me, and when he sipped this nectar, while I was praying our creator to grant me again, if only one more time, the grace of a kiss from that superb mouth, I would see his grumpy eyes light up with pleasure: he was ready to talk now, to hear me pitifully lay out my poor excuses for cheating again. And this caress in the form of wine whispered to him that he mustn't really hold it against me. That he mustn't believe what my lies seemed to imply. That I loved him.

One of these lies, for four years, was seeing Arthur. Joseph could never believe that Arthur and I were no longer fucking. I got caught up in umpteen fibs so I could down bottles of rosé with the latter – because who else could I have told these pathetic exploits to? A few days afterwards, when I'd furnished him with the tiniest details while sitting on his sofa, I thought he would never stop laughing. Arthur laughing washed away my annoyance.

'What an idea, also, to get a Russian girl!'

'I know. I wanted her to be beautiful.'

'A Russian who meets you at Café de la Paix.'

'I know, for fuck's sake. Don't make it worse.'

'Russian women are for businessmen who don't give a fuck. I dunno, don't you have a girlfriend who would have been excited by that…?'

'No, I don't have that kind of friend. Do you know how complicated it is, to suggest to a friend that she fucks you and your boyfriend? Even if she's interested, add the fact that it has to happen on a specific date, in a specific place, without meeting beforehand… No, it's a mission for a whore, I can't think of an occasion better suited.'

'Yes, but it's you who expects too much from the whore. Whether she's Russian or not, in fact. It's a job, for these girls. It's obviously less fun for them than you to have a threesome with Joseph. Can you imagine having to want it every time?'

'So you're saying that a young couple like us is on the same level as some horrible fat sixty-five-year-olds?'

'Not for us, because we're not whores. For her, it must have been less annoying with people like you, but deep down maybe yes, maybe it's even more complicated if she's not used to young people. And clearly, that was the case.'

I had a moment of intense reflection, as I often do with Arthur, the frequency of whose voice changes even the most inflexible opinions.

'All I'm saying is that the job of whores is, in the end, to provide an illusion.'

'That's what you had, an illusion.'

'An illusion you can believe in. Not a circus in which one can smell acting a mile away. That's what differentiates a good whore from a bad one.'

'It still remains an illusion, because that's the deal. You know that. But maybe a woman is less credulous than a man, or less easy to satisfy. Obviously, it's better when it's well done and you can get taken in, but I think guys are tacitly agreed on the fact that it's playacting. I can assure you that at Porte Maillot, where you can get sucked off in your car, the girls don't take too much trouble pretending.'

Arthur raised an eyebrow:

'Well, it is around thirty euros.'

'Ah!' I whelped.

'How much was yours?'

'Seven hundred for two hours.'

Arthur burst out laughing again and that ended up annoying me.

'Stop it.'

'Oh, bloody hell! *Seven hundred* euros!'

'For seven hundred euros, I think I have the right to demand world-class theatre.'

'Well quite, my prince!'

'Because in the end, it's work, fine, but when you earn a lot of money, there's still space for some simple goodwill, don't you think?'

'*Goodwill*? Now I'm listening to you. I think we're onto a brilliant concept.'

'Anyway, that's what I'd do. I'd pull out all the stops.'

'We all know you'd make a fantastic whore. The very best.'

'That's not what I'm saying.'

'It's what I'm saying.'

We did nothing wrong, Arthur and I, that night, I'll maintain that to the end.

Monolith, T. Rex

WHEN EYES OTHER THAN MINE READ THESE lines, a considerable chunk of Berlin will have disappeared, to widespread indifference. This type of thing happens every day, so all Berliners are grieving for one or two places they thought of as eternal and that one day evaporate. And the little street discovered by chance during an aimless walk, because you were looking for something else you won't ever find, will always have this air of fleetingness for you alone.

I don't know how people survive this type of loss. I'd never been faced by this situation – generally, it's I who abandon the places that are dear to me, only to see when I come back that I wasn't indispensable to them functioning properly. In this precise case, I have a cowardly technique that works quite well – I avoid thinking about it. I avoid looking at that side of the Métro map and, as nothing forces me to go into that neighbourhood, my nostalgia, while constant, is light.

Except that yesterday I got lost on my bike and, in an attempt to get back to familiar main roads, happened upon the junction where my bus used to stop less than a year ago. I recognised the bakery, the DIY store. Every now and then, the bells of the immense church a few steps away chimed in a way that sounded, from the bedrooms, like the reproving growl of a parent either too distant or too old to really inspire any good behaviour. The church, which seemed even vaster stuck up as it was against a brothel, laid a shadow across the café where the girls drank shandies after work. An icy feeling seeped out from its walls, air from a tomb that washed the damp heat from you, the intoxicating odour of twenty females breathing the same oxygen in and out.

The House was like that, straddled on either side by a holy place and a nursery school: it wasn't surprising they'd tried to close it down – and succeeded. The church bell told us the time and the children's nursery rhymes made the girls sleepy as they smoked in the garden.

There was a time, not so long ago, when as I parked my bike I looked up and could see, just from the curtains in the windows, who was already hard at work. Behind pink, mauve or yellow organdie slipped silhouettes I recognised right off. Behind the screens of the balconies, I saw spirals of smoke and the shadows of stretched-out legs. Now there's nothing left to see. Between the school and the church is a building mixing flats and offices. Offices…! It's enough to make you cry. You don't need to go into the courtyard to know that the garden has been transformed into a designer terrace carpeted by a toxic fake lawn – I can just imagine the space from where I am: a few little tables, plastic benches, a pastel-hued ashtray so one can have one's fag and drink one's latte during the break allowed by the owner-guru. *Oh I hate you, you bunch of hicks,* I think as I try to spot through the uncurtained windows at least one face on which to focus my disdain.

At that moment, a swarm of kids crossed the street, with about half-a-dozen nursery workers dotted around them. I recognised her, as she walked near me, by the gentle inflections of her voice. She was holding hands with two little girls and trying to bring back into the herd a boy fascinated by a kebab vendor slicing his meat. She was wearing her thick hair in a strict bun and a slightly faded skirt with espadrilles. It was when she caught up with the little boy that our eyes met – and it took a few seconds for polite indifference to turn into interrogation. And when she finally placed me, I saw a shudder go through her. I'm sure she rushed to speak to me out of fear that I call her by a name she no longer uses.

*

'Hey! How are you?' Her smile full of anguish. A glance over the group she's with – a silent prayer. What on Earth could I be to her: an old neighbour, a cousin, a niece?

'I was in the neighbourhood. What a surprise! Are you well?'

'Very well, yes!'

The two kids she's holding hands with are watching us. I nod in what I hope is a friendly way, but I've never been a natural with children and they carry on staring at me, mouths open, with their too-intelligent eyes. We are surrounded and she's squirming a bit.

'I have to go.'

'Me too. It was nice, while it lasted.'

Aided by her relief, she smiles, then laughs, and hearing her laugh, so many memories come back to me that I go hot and cold at the same time, and I want to cry. It doesn't help that she suggests, in a rhetorical fashion, so as not to just run off like that:

'We should have a coffee sometime.'

'With pleasure.'

'Let's call then.'

And as she goes off, flanked by the cloud of buzzing kids who once were our soundtrack, beneath what used to be our windows, two thoughts assail me: the first, which deep down is relatively unimportant, is that she doesn't have my number and I don't have hers. The second, which lingers in my head that day, or in any case for as long as it takes for me to have a look around Kreuzberg, is that that backside of hers bouncing beneath her flowery skirt hasn't changed at all. And despite the months that have passed since the last time she was naked in front of me, if her name has slipped from my memory, her arse is deeply engraved on it, the wobble of her white flesh and the constellation of beauty spots on her lower back, this beautiful plump arse of a courtesan now walking through Berlin disguised as a nursery worker.

Spicks and Specks, The Bee Gees

I HAVE TO REMEMBER EVERYTHING. THERE NEEDS to be, somewhere, a precise description of what The House was and that this description evokes powerful images – images as close as possible to the truth. Even though, when all's said and done, exactitude is unimportant. And if I will need a bit of talent to recreate the layout of the rooms and the colour of the curtains, I'm most concerned about how to explain the soul of this place, that pervading air of tenderness that made bad taste something splendid. I don't need many words; the right words would suffice. A decent writer would manage in ten pages. I've written two hundred about it and not once do I feel I've got close to what really interests me – the only interesting thing. I approach the subject from thousands of different angles and it escapes me every time, leaving my head even emptier from having been so full for a time.

Arriving by Métro, as many of the girls and the clients did, you have to walk up the big road starting at the church bell-tower. But before that is the park, lush in summer and in winter as lugubrious as can be were it not for the lake covered in ice, framed like a slightly sad painting by tall murky trees powdered by hoarfrost. After the park, the Biergarten, which the girls walked past with their heads lowered, not wanting to run into clients. The crèche, the nursery school. The bakery, the tanning studio. The kebab shop, and the florist opposite. A neighbourhood of former East Berlin without the slightest appeal to tourists, to which no one but locals would have come were it not for this door, at number thirty-six. Hardly visible between the two rows of boxwood balls. Amidst all the doorbells that look the same, one ancient copper doorbell stands out; the door opens as soon as you ring and you're right into a slightly dark entrance hall with a chequered-tile floor, a bourgeois ambiance. The worn little wooden door at the end, forgotten during the recent restoration, leads to a yard where the smell of The House already hangs in the air, where you can hear, muffled by the double glazing, the laughter of the girls and the chimes of the doors opening and closing on men.

Behind the rain-washed screens you can see ribbons of blue smoke rise: sometimes a woman's name is released aloud, breaking the silence with its suave, untruthful vowels. It could be nothing but a garden flat, that was how it was thought out. Unless you go into The House, which is what I'm planning on doing, there's no way of knowing where these murmurs, these chirrups, these smokers' coughs come from.

From the second entrance hall, which was judged morally unworthy of being renovated, ascends a staircase in worm-eaten wood, finely wrought beneath flaking paint. By closing my eyes, I can still feel, I always will feel, its curves, its opulent design, the reptilian slide of it beneath the fingers. In the time it takes to emit a single sigh it takes you to the first floor – a mezzanine, in fact, that's called the *Hochparterre* here. Incongruously for this old building, there's a heavy armoured door where someone has nailed in gold letters the name The House, accompanied by this whimsical description: Self-publishing. As if a self-publishing firm could afford such a door, or such lettering.

My finger lingers on the doorbell; inside, stifled, a desultory trill, the ruckus of little girls, which stops suddenly and starts again at half the volume. I already hear the steps of the *Hausdame* but, in the brief moment it takes her to slip through the girls, I fill my lungs with the air that is stagnating on the doorstep, this air that is already working as a filter. It feels like the women's perfumes are rising from under the door, mixed with those from the laundry room on the first floor – where this fifty-or-so self-published writers are washing napkins and knickers. The merging of these two constant breaths has something childish and obscene, it's like sniffing the laundry of a pack of schoolgirls hiding in the toilets to smoke – and in the rooms they fill with their cries, someone's squirted a somewhat vulgar scent, somewhere between bleach and cheap deodorant, burnt five different kinds of incense in a vain attempt to hide the smell of tobacco, damp armpits and on tacky fingers the smell of the men who are always just passing through: it's a hint of acridity, barely perceptible. In ten years, when the space will have had twenty different lodgers, been painted over and over again, there will always be on this doorstep this smell that no one will be able to explain – or only the Berliners who remember cocks taken out in the half-light of the rooms and pussies douched with plenty of water, with plenty of noise, in bidets long since destroyed.

The door opens; the body odour intensifies, both more present and better camouflaged by the army of candles burning away on a little side-table in the entrance. The dancing halo of the flames almost succeeds in bringing a bad reproduction of Klimt to life – turns it into a beautifully framed poster. In this octagonal room are two doors: the first opens onto a small salon resembling a boudoir. There's an armchair in white leather, a low table covered with old editions of *Der Spiegel* flicked through with the same distracted angst as people do at the doctor's surgery; a forest of fake plants snakes from the floor to the ceiling, disappearing here and there beneath the curtains and sticking out again further along, around a Jugendstil lamp that bathes the room in a half light. Yet you can see better in here than anywhere else; it's here that the men come in; they sit in the white armchair and a few minutes later the women join them, one after the other, their silhouettes replicated from every angle by the mirrors on the walls. They call this room the men's salon, even if it has only ever belonged to the girls; men are only ever a lurking presence, devoured by the armchair that has swallowed so many others. Infinitely interchangeable, whereas each woman brings, as she enters, a perfume and a universe that linger for a long time, a long time after she's gone.

The second door always stays half-open. It leads into a corridor with a burgundy carpet shredded by the steps of the girls and their clients. On the walls are Belle Epoque posters, many of them French. Klimt's *The Kiss*, again, hangs above another door; it's the one to the Yellow room with its dark-oak floor. On the left, as soon as you enter, is a chest of drawers in pale wood and a bouquet of plastic woodland flowers. On the right, a sofa covered with a yellow fabric, a night table and a trinket tray where nobody ever puts anything. But what irresistibly draws the eye is the bed in the middle, a bed that immediately makes you understand that the chest of drawers, night table and sofa are only distractions, ornaments aimed at the shy ones intimidated by this hefty bed. You only sit on the sofa to get used to the spectacle of the girl climbing onto the little platform, stark naked, to stretch out in the midst of the cushions of bronze and peacock-green satin, placed between two vast triptychs. One is sixty years old; one of the first live-in girls unearthed it at a flea market. I can't look at it without asking myself what it must have seen before moving here and before contemplating, twenty to thirty times a day, the more or less baroque couplings of men who ejaculate with their eyes closed and girls who straddle them while keeping an eye on the reflection of the clock. Just next to it is the Mauve room with its feel of a slightly grubby motel, dimly lit by dark neon. The floor is a white laminate that bubbles in the corners, the soles of high heels have left marks near the bed – it's a bit murky, the Mauve room, and we only go there when the other rooms are taken. It shares a wall with a second tiny salon where men wait and are sometimes forgotten about, on very busy days.

When you retrace your steps, after passing the men's salon, there's a vestibule from which another stretch of corridor snakes off. This is a primordial observation post, unsuspected by any creature who doesn't wear a skirt. The constantly fluttering purple theatre curtain marks the frontier between the world of outside and the unique closed vessel of a universe that the girls reinvent every day from 10 o'clock in the morning to 11 o'clock at night. If the front door stands open for a man, the cold air is automatically reheated by the humidity of the large living room that pulsates behind the curtain. If they were more attentive, if the blinding need to rut and the *Hausdame* didn't drag them straight to the white-leather armchairs, perhaps they'd see, through the slit in the curtain, long legs sheathed in black voile coming and going, half of a squinting face, false nails keeping the drapes closed.

Everything behind this curtain attracts me, but as it fades, the memory of the rooms becomes more necessary to me. I didn't love them enough.

The corridor makes an L-shape where a stucco Venus fountain pours, with the sound of a peeing child, ginger-scented water. Straight after that is the Silver room, like a box of sweets papered in prune from floor to ceiling. The dimensions are Lilliputian, the bed is right in your face, stretching from one wall to the other. At the end, beneath the canopy embroidered with stars, a small window lets in the warm air of the courtyard and the children's songs during break-time. Stashed behind the door, a sink, flanked by a pile of folded towels. In this part of The House, all the scents sprayed to mask bodily odours convene to such an intensity it makes you dizzy: it creates an irrepressible desire to let yourself fall back onto the bed and to crawl towards the window. The paintings on the walls, the sole witnesses of this poisoning, look like hallucinations – perhaps because in a normal world they would have nothing to do next to one another, this Kama Sutra etching, this poster from a ball in the Roaring Twenties, and this Lempinska reproduction in the midst of mauve voile curtains. It brings on a feeling resembling indigestion; in this room arise frenzied embraces followed by silences that are incredibly hard to break. When you get out of it, the foul air of the corridor gives you the feeling you're walking in a forest.

After the Silver room, a door leads to a cupboard blocked by a padlocked grill gate, originally designed to hold men during domination sessions. I remember it when it was still lit by a red bulb, before they realised it wasn't very practical to have anything at all right in the middle of a corridor with girls slipping through and naked men coming out of the bathroom. Now, when you open the door that squeaks like that of a real dungeon, you see two cardboard boxes that are getting filled up with girls' lost and found items: single shoes, cheap corsets, knickers and bras, in a not unpleasing odour of dust and feet.

Next to it, between the cage and the Studio, is the men's bathroom; the floor is a grey marble veined with black and gold, pretentious and adorably ugly, so slippery you had to cover it with a bathmat for the safety of old or clumsy clients. When the sun is in the right place, the scene doesn't lack charm; the floor looks like a still pond with giant lilies floating on it. A shower cubicle, toilets at the end, and a framed reproduction of an embrace between Pygmalion and Galatea. Almost invisible above the door is a small button you press when you've finished your ablutions; a little bell then sounds in the women's salon to let the relevant girl know that her client is ready to be brought back into the bedroom. This system of buttons in every room minimises the risk of the various men meeting – an employee and his boss, a husband and his brother-in-law, a mother and a son. Though of course not all the girls or all the clients are as careful; and often these pairs do meet, the girls chuckling, revelling in their justified indifference, the men lowering their eyes as if they've been caught out, unceremoniously pushed by their fleeting companion into a convenient recess.

At the end of the corridor there's the Studio. When The House closed, one of the originals anonymously bought all its contents for a derisory sum; I love picturing a whimsical old client who felt so at home in the midst of the wooden horse and the bamboo canes, but the most likely story was some brothel keeper who wanted to fit out their own establishment. Everything in it is red and black, with anti-spatter linoleum on the floor, black leatherette and paint the colour of fresh blood on the walls, from which a slanting workbench bristles with whips and hammers and other objects of different shapes and colours – everything the human brain has been able to dream up for the rear end. As soon as you go inside, there's an armchair in varnished leather that would make you feel pity in daylight, patched up as well as possible with black and silver scotch tape. From the armchair, you only have to reach out an arm to reach, on a glass table, an English magazine specialising in female domination – *Victoria*. The edition has never changed, it's always the same girl naked under a fur coat and in white thigh-length boots. The kind of literature ordered in a discreet wrapper and to which one would have undoubtedly masturbated twenty years ago. You can see its yellowed photos of bare-arsed men, straddled by women in an uncomfortable-looking way, making them lick their muddy heels. To ensure the reader doesn't miss anything, some starving writer has created a little story to accompany the images, with a variety of dialogue that must have made him die laughing and sweat with shame – but the dehydrated brains of the horny readers wouldn't know what to do with good dialogue. Facing the deep armchair is a strange rack with a hole in it, and I've never understood what's supposed to go through it. Two vast mirrors reflect to infinity the person tied up there, or on the bench under the window. In one corner, a round chest with drawers stuffed with ropes and instruments, each more fascinating than the one before; and such a range of handcuffs and ties that you never know which to take and end up always using the same ones or moving the bottom ones to the top, as if rotating a stack of plates. We mainly stuff clients in the Studio at busy times; most don't dare sit down for fear of tacitly approving the choice of rooms. Men are afraid of the Studio, girls make their phone calls there or spend ages checking that the seam of their tights lines up with their suspenders in the mirror. The red light falling from the ceiling flattens the guys' skin but flatters the girls', projecting a play of shadows onto their faces or their sparkling eyes with an excess of white.

I retrace my steps towards the theatre curtain from which the laughter and whispering are emanating. Here I very often longed to be a man, but then again, I could never have slid behind the curtain or even wandered around The House by myself – I would have missed ninety per cent of the essence of the place. Of course, I could have thrown a sneaky look into the girls' bathroom, glimpsed the sink where they spit out mouthwash with the gusto of tobacco chewers, and the sacred bidet – Hildie astride it, curls fluttering to the rhythm of her hand between her thighs, whining about how long the last client took, or Gita drying herself roughly while talking about hers, fishwives slipped into the bodies of young courtesans. I wouldn't have been able to follow them as they trotted, knickers still down around their ankles, toward the large women's salon, the purple curtain twisting around them as they go through it. Wouldn't have known the constantly steamed-up kitchen where the girls eat and talk in the din of a market hall, nor the work surface they clear with the sweep of a hand to perch up a buttock, nor the half-open window letting in the ruckus of the market on the square. Nor would I have seen the big mirror at the exit to the kitchen, Esmée in front of it in a suit, make-up bag wide open between her thighs, creating provocative eyebrows for which many clients travelled from the far depths of Brandenburg.

Most of all, I would have missed out on this overview from the doorstep of the salon; I always stopped there, at one remove from the agitation that started up when the bell sounded through the brothel. Time stood still, just for me, and I gorged myself on images. The L-shaped sofas backing onto a row of crates piled up to the ceiling; Agnetha sitting where a bookcase stands, filled with books you only ever have time to skim. Birgit turning the pages of a novel while trying to follow the lively debate between Fauna and Tinkie, one standing in the middle of the room, fiddling with her navel piercing, the other smoking on the balcony but with her torso bent inside. Birgit has her legs folded, her high-waisted panties bunched up between her lips – it's a spectacle we're all used to but that always seizes my attention for a moment, like Fauna's large breasts with their almost transparent whiteness. Standing motionless in front of all these naked women who weren't looking at me, I had, for two years, the feeling of being a man disguised as a woman, and so well that as I walked past them I was on the receiving end of the rough tenderness of hussies: slaps of varying degrees of loudness, a vaguely maternal caress on the top of my skull that actually improved the look of my purposefully messy hair. I don't think they were ever suspicious of this curiosity of mine, like that of a naughty child, nor the feeling of debauchery that occasionally took hold of me when I saw the vulva of a girl in the middle of painting her toenails: if they felt anything at all, it would have undoubtedly been the indifference of those whose job it is to be beautiful and looked at, but who don't care how graceful or otherwise their wiggling flesh looks.

In the midst of the sofas, a low table, still messy, loaded with books and plates, and headphones abandoned by girls when clients have taken them away from a podcast. Against the wall, jammed between other crates, is the desk where the Hausdame has her papers and the two landline phones, as well as her private mobile phone and the one the owner calls her on, as do the escort service and the handyman who can never find his tools in the cupboards stuffed with knick-knacks. On the table, the list of the rooms on which the girls write the arrival and departure time of the men, and their stage name noted on Post-it notes that are peeled off at the end of the day, leaving just the number of clients and the takings. Another list shows which girls offer which specialities, a Word document printed so long ago that you can hardly make out the names between the coffee stains or mentally separate those who still work there from those who vanished years ago. On a corkboard are pinned dozens of restaurant menus, numbers of taxis who are happy with a customer ID, the contact details of accountants one can *maybe* trust – and right at the bottom, notes specific to the girls:

'Carsten can't meet Christina!', 'If Thomas happens to call, he can't see Sarah!', 'For Birgit, only meetings of 45 minutes and longer', and this slightly contrite note, 'Lola forgot to put 210 euros in her envelope, please pass on the message.' But Lola left without notice two months after my arrival, owing roughly the same as other girls – it's said she now works in Munich; Genova says she saw her scoring coke in a champagne bar and it's obvious The House can shove those 210 euros where the sun doesn't shine. It's ironclad faith that keeps our note pinned there, faith in a kind loyalty that doesn't take into account, or very little, the versatility of the girls who do this job, the contrary forces that draw them to The House and at the same time keep them at a distance from it. This kindness bordering on sincerity extends to the doors of the lockers, some of which bear the names of workers who left a long time ago, their writing effaced by new girls' fingers – inside, probably, is dust that still holds their perfume.

Behind it is a lovely wide balcony, open in the middle onto a small staircase of white stone: four antique-looking steps bordered by wide railings descend languorously to the garden that gave its name to The House. Obviously, that has to be taken with a pinch of salt: it feels like there was a lawn here when the owners had use of it, but all that remains today is a square of earth vaguely fluffed up with green – like lichen or moss, with an occasional blade of grass or some puny little flowers poking out in the shadow of the church. As for the smell, it's almost that of a place where things actually grow and creatures move about. To protect the girls from neighbours' gazes, they've built a mesh sky and a decent amount of ivy mixed with white bindweed is growing over it. What nature refused to hide has been replaced by climbing plants made out of plastic: the rain and the snow have washed out the colour, but it has a kind of roguish charm, like a bargain-basement Versailles. There are some weathered lanterns hanging from the balustrade, placed there to give it the feel of a hermetic box. The result is that you can only see the garden by going into the building's courtyard, especially on a summer's evening. It's a green bubble that seems animated by a slow inhalation and exhalation; silhouettes move around in it, and smoke of varying degrees of dubiousness, a vulgar whiff of incense, emanate from it.

If the garden had been designed for the clients, more effort would undoubtedly have been made, more money invested in elegant furniture: but this is left to the girls, and some have added their own ramshackle contribution to the original cheap bric-à-brac. A squeaking swing chair embellished with a thick blue and white cover, folding garden chairs with peeling yellow paint, an almost presentable deckchair, and, in pride of place, the still-majestic carcass of an old Wannsee *Strandkorb*. At the beginning of summer, near the pot of rhododendrons, they inflate a small kids' pool in which the girls soak their heavy legs before, eventually, the clumsy ash of a cigarette falls into it and turns it all into a mosquito incubator. On July afternoons, I spent an eternity with my eyes glued to this threadbare yard. The stretched-out girls, the big straw hat over Elsa's loose hair. Birgit and Ingrid, ankles plunged into the water, still clean at the beginning of summer. Eddie hiding behind the raspberry bush, but only on principle, because everyone knows she's actually rolling a joint. And all the others, including me, coming and going, looking for signs we're getting a tan, bringing cool drinks out into this unmoving furnace. In winter the picture is no less charming – although it's less practical in the snow and ice in teetering heels. And it's exactly this vision that I especially cherish: Gita and Eddie in their furs, tottering around the garden, exhaling big clouds of smoke – silent in the pink light of an early morning in December, limping graciously like two young swans who have just learned to master their frail legs. It snowed the night before and fat flakes are still falling at a languid rate, powdering Gita's blonde curls, Eddie's black chignon. All that can be heard is their steps in the squeaky snow; they finally find a place to sit, and as they lower themselves they raise dust clouds of snow that sparkle for a moment in a thin ray of light, exclaim all at the same time *How lovely it is here.*

Gita's half-open jacket shows her burgundy corset, a bit of breast squished out by the bones of her bra; for a moment she takes the shoe off her foot sheathed in flesh-toned nylon, moves her toes – I only ever had eyes for Gita when she was at work. And as if she felt it, she turns her doll's face towards me. 'Are you coming, Justine? It's easier to breathe here than in the kitchen.'

I always wondered how I fitted into this picture – and if there was anyone on the balcony in whom it inspired the same tenderness.

Sitting there, in the old *Strandkorb*, I can see the second-floor balcony, the other bedrooms, between the plants on the wire fence. I don't have to go up to remember. The staircase that smells of food; the door to the first apartment; a long corridor with red carpeting; a low chest of drawers stuffed with towels. The kitchen where the girls come to look at the clock and sigh that *good god time's going slowly*, smoking an illegal fag right in the middle of an appointment. From this room you can hear the noises, stifled, in the Golden room, about twenty square metres of opulent purple upholstery illuminated by small orange lights – and intensifying that, a red sofa and a credence table on top of which sits a photo of two girls snogging. The bed is wide, robust, covered with a golden fabric. Once you're lying on it, all you have to do is hold out your hand towards the mahogany floor to find the little basket full of condoms and the indispensable roll of paper towel. It's a room much loved by the girls, but my favourite is opposite it, at the end of a dark little corridor. It's often changed name: from '1001' it became 'Jasmin', then simply 'Red', and ultimately it deserves all of these monikers. The grandiose bed, which is bespoke, occupies half of the volume of the room, from the ceiling fall kilometres of curtain, an ocean of organdie in the middle of which sparkles a small, vaguely Arabesque sconce. Daylight is channelled by red and gold embroidered curtains. Here the girls' skin seems completely purple, their loose hair is surrounded by flames. Opposite the bed an electric fire blasts out air – when it's lit during the big freezes of January – as hot as the fires of Tartarus. There's a big, exquisitely deep velvet armchair, dotted with white stains – the ageless calling cards of the woozy girls who have come there to smoke, bare-arsed, their post-coital cigarette – and the rug jammed beneath it is completely worn out, faded from their feet marking time as they wait for the men to get dressed again.

In the neighbouring apartment, Tropical is a little room that smells of jasmine the second you walk in. Fake plants respectfully frame a hideous crime of a fresco that some cursed artist committed opposite the door – a jungle landscape rammed with flowers and animals, such a muddle of them that after two years I was still discovering new and strange details. Opposite this aberration, a ravishing painting of moonlight over the Baltic, with in the foreground a woman the colour of sea foam taking off her dress. But when you're lying on the bed, the most fascinating painting is without contest the mirror hanging on the ceiling, as if levitating, even if the butterfly stickers that flutter around the nudity reflected in it give the pallor of the naked bodies the look of a bad Snapchat image. Right next to the Tropical and its bathroom, the Clinic, white-tiled from floor to ceiling, awaits men who want to sit a girl down on the gynaecologist's chair. It smells of alcohol and disinfectant even though nobody ever goes into it except to get a glass of water from the sink; yet the anatomical posters, the trolley overflowing with surgical instruments, the surgical gowns hanging on hooks bear witness to the original hope of bringing trainee doctors to this room that everyone detests.

At the end, a third apartment contains The House's two last rooms – the White and the Green. The White, which is completely pink except for the ivory laminate, is stupid enough to make you cry, with its Liberty curtains and its flurry of flowers. The bed and its pretentious carved wooden frame resemble the erotic fantasies of an old maid. But if the sun shines, even timidly, all of a sudden the curtains set the room alight with a pink glow, the flowers disappear, the trinkets fade away in this bath of vaginal light and, instead of being trapped in an old maid's fantasies, you suddenly find yourself enclosed in her, comfortably engulfed by her thighs with the only sign from the outside world being the suave music spread through the whole house via the ceiling speakers, and which is unbearable in the long term. Next to it, the Green room has a good-natured elegance, without any over-exuberance beyond a glass fountain that doesn't work most of the time. When it does work, either because any risk of electrocution has been removed for the day, or because the handyman has given it a good hard kick in the right place, a musky humidity fills the room and becomes dizzying. In this apartment, the over-large kitchen overflows with treasures left behind by the girls and their clients. Love letters, hairbands, mediocre cravats, soaps, lipsticks, CDs left behind in the hi-fi system that say so much about the girls they belonged to.

At the end of a day, you could work out the moods of some of them, how their dispositions have evolved. Esmée, who starts at 11 o'clock in the Golden room – with a grumpy guy who thought she was slimmer in her photos – and who finishes at 5 o'clock, is grumbling, after dragging her three subsequent clients into the more flattering half-light of the Red room. Gita, who has her period and will only work in the Studio today, getting her nerves shredded by a half-dozen men on their knees before her breasts wobbling to the rhythm of the rod. Ingrid and her new haircut, going from the White to the Red room to admire and elicit admiration for her blow-dried fringe in the excellent mirrors. Agnetha, who comes out earlier than expected because a somewhat over-enthusiastic client has scratched her. And that one. And those ones. And the frustrated sighs when someone opens the cupboard where the keys are kept and the desired room is already taken. And the excellent reasons not to go there despite the man's requests, *I have backache and it's hellish making the bed in the Mauve, I can't breathe in the Silver, there's a chestnut tree flowering opposite the room and I'm allergic to pollen, the lights in Tropical make me look like I have a huge arse, I feel lonely in the Golden room, Genova is right next door and her cries distract me…* And the entire worlds they invent, that they invented, in these rooms that are now let out as holiday apartments, in this garden where other slaves of a different kind now smoke – and of these places once lived in so intensely, where has the soul gone?

Little Bird, The White Stripes

DOROTHÉE, FULLY NAKED, IS RUBBING LEMON OIL on her long legs and its smell mixes with that of the soup that one of the girls has allowed to go cold on the edge of the coffee table. I'm pretending to read, but her nudity is robbing the words of all their meaning; there's only a black and white mush of letters, and the only spectacle worthy of my attention, just above them, is this girl who doesn't like me much and who no doubt thinks showing me her white bum is the ultimate gesture of disdain. As she pours the oil on her thighs, kneading them to make it soak in, I glimpse a darker pink stain, some tiny dimples of fat – and it's precisely this lack of modesty, this free and easy manner, that delights me. It's this not caring about her body being so devoid of artifice that moves me – I have the impression of seeing her more naked than when she comes out of the bedrooms, streaming with sweat.

I don't really know how or when Dorothée started to stop liking me; I suspect it's when I sent her the fat Frenchman, in spite of myself. But at that moment, I already knew enough about her to speculate about her inner life. I learnt, from somewhere, that she was a nurse. Nurses must make up fifteen of the fifty or sixty girls in our team – including Nadine, who I can imagine easily, with her kindness and her smile, saving from despair patients who would be stupefied to learn how she tops up her earnings. Dorothée may be one of those bad-tempered nurses, although she isn't always like that. There are days when, even with me, she's in a delightful mood;

she laughs at the other girls' stories, she tells some of her own, she defends The House against criticism from new girls who have come from places where they earn much more money. Which leads me to think that her bad mood isn't down to The House or to this work, but just to these dark states of mind that often come over whores, the fact of ageing, of seeing young women arrive, becoming less able to bear the empty hours between clients. I feel that Dorothée's rage isn't directed against us but against all of Earth, against the very machinations of the world. And if I spoke better German, if I was well placed to tell her this, I would want to tell her, as she twists around to rub oil between her thighs, that there are many young women here who are less pretty than she is; that some have never had, and never will have, this impeccable skin and this flat stomach in which two children grew without leaving any stretch marks.

Here's Esmée back, a towel wrapped around her head.

'You're back already?'

'What do you mean, already? I've been here since midday.'

'That smells good, your thingy!' exclaims Esmée, and without even asking permission, with this closeness between women who are shut in together, which always amazes me, she leans on Dorothée's shoulder to smell her, her eyes closed.

Almost two years in a brothel have done nothing to instil in me this boldness I envy in them. Two years immersed in a world where they sniff one another from every angle, and yet I still blush when a girl kisses me on the cheek. Nothing excites me in the way Esmée smells Dorothée; it's this confidence in her gender, the normality of this reflex, that I find moving. Perhaps because they don't spend most of their day fantasising about one another like I do, although that's not even in a sexual way, more as my way of pinning them down like butterflies to contemplate them in my own fashion.

'Are you coming back, tomorrow?' Esmée asks.

'No, I'm knackered. My plan for tomorrow is to go to the lake and drink one or two beers under a tree.'

'So I won't see you before Tuesday, pet?'

I'm making up 'pet'. Esmée undoubtedly used *Mäuschen*, little mouse, and that doesn't really matter – but sometimes I'd like to write the German to translate the affection conveyed by all these words ending in *-chen*, in *-lein*, making a caress of the most banal words.

'I'm not here on Tuesday. My husband comes back on Sunday.'

'How's it going between the two of you?'

'Really well, at the moment. I booked a hotel, the children will be at my mother's.'

It's astonishing, their indifference to the idea of fucking four, five, six men a day at The House, and the way they chuckle as soon as they're talking about a hotel and children at their grandparents'. Am I right in thinking that Dorothée's husband doesn't know she works here? He's a salesman or something of that ilk that requires a lot of moving around, undoubtedly he has no trouble imagining that his wife cheats on him – but the idea that she's cheating on him in this way is certainly miles above what he is thinking. If there's one thing that's not talked about when brothels are discussed, it's how to manage the quantity of sex. And if it's not the quantity that's annoying, let's say the desire to fuck – sorry, to make love – when you've spent your working hours with a certain number of renters inside you.

'He's been going crazy for three days,' smiles Dorothée. 'I'm getting loads of dirty texts, you can't imagine. Obviously I don't have the time to respond, with all the clients. I'm getting photos of his cock, fine, I like it, but between you and me, it reminds me of work. And the fact I'm a bit distant is driving him nuts.'

She hangs her long neck back to make herself a ponytail – and I understand this man. In a few moments she'll have put her normal girl's clothes back on, and I will still see Dorothée naked and shimmering with oil, magnificent even in her cycle helmet.

'On Monday, when I got home from my holidays, I hadn't fucked for ten days. Ten days, can you imagine? In the years that I've been here, that's never happened to me. Even after forty-eight hours I wonder what's going on.'

Dorothée has seen that I was listening to them, and she smiles at me too – so I nod.

'Now, my problem is knowing if I'll want to fuck between now and the end of the week.'

She zips up her jacket, looking like she's thinking. With her several years in the brothel, she knows the reply, she's said it herself: after forty-eight hours of drinking beers by the lake, she'll wonder what's happening. She'll have strange aches in her thighs and in her back that will remind her that it's been two days since… That may not inspire her with any particular desire, these positions she's learned and carries out daily for men she doesn't give a fuck about. Let's be honest, probably *no* desire; probably at the most, a sigh of happiness at the idea of not having to, if it's not with the man she loves. And the idea of having booked a room, she who spends most of her time in rooms booked by others, will give her the impression of having chosen to fuck, whether she wants to or not. When he's there, there will obviously be something professional in her reflex to bend her back, to tense her thighs, to half close her eyes and purr. Automatic actions that will look like keenness, whereas she'll already be thinking of the tenderness afterwards, of the feeling of a job done, of the possibility of not talking, of not looking at the clock, of going to smoke on the balcony. And she'll have the feeling of not wanting to, of being able to do it like she'd do something else, out of habit, out of resignation, right until the moment when he takes her, and that's when she'll realise that this cock, which is no different to thousands of others, has in fact nothing in common with theirs. Because this cock has a way of filling her, of resonating within her, that would make her fall in love if she wasn't already. And her cries will ring out like a piece of much-loved music you're actually listening to instead of hearing as background noise. Like a piece of Pink Floyd on a decent sound system, something real, powerful, that almost makes you want to cry. She will wonder if he feels it, if he perceives the sincerity; but how could he? These are the noises of his wife, in them there's something primitive and immediate, it's his wife who he hasn't seen in a long time. And the noises she's making, the way she abandons herself, all of that is as good and familiar as returning home after months of moving around. It doesn't really matter how many times you fuck others, and it doesn't really matter why, when you do it with the one who counts, it's like coming back into port. And maybe Dorothée will perplexedly say to herself, thighs open and eyes wild, that all these guys and all these acrobatic positions were only of value through the repetition they constituted – maybe she'll feel she thought of her husband through it all, when the accumulation of them put her in a bad mood and it felt like she couldn't see another one without having to scratch him in the face, perhaps she imagined herself taken by him, or perhaps by closing her eyes she saw him at the other end of the room, watching her – perhaps if he knows nothing about The House, it's not cheating because she was thinking about him, all the time?

(Sometimes You Gotta Be) Gentle, Heavy Trash

'THE PROBLEM WITH THIS JOB IS THAT after a while, your body no longer knows when you're pretending and when you really feel something.'

Hildie sighs heavily as she fans herself on the garden steps.

'You try so hard to build up this indifference, it becomes so automatic, that it takes a certain amount of time for your body to learn to feel again. That's the real problem with being a whore. The rest is nothing – what other people think, the money, the tiredness, putting up with the blokes… The problem is the playacting one has to do, which becomes the truth.'

At this point I have my hands on her long supple back, which is covered with beauty spots, smearing it with sunscreen. Hildie is twenty-seven, or that's what she says when a client asks her age, even if the website makes her five years younger. It's the embarrassment of pretending to be younger than her sister; she feels she would have to speak differently, more simply, like she did at college – and that's not her any more. She despises blokes who choose their hour-long companion on the basis of their age, and doesn't want anything to do with them. To do this job well, to manage this activity as reasonably as she does, one needs be more than twenty-five, one has all the advantages and none of the inconveniences. If she'd started at eighteen or nineteen, i.e. if the longest part of her sexual life had taken place in a brothel, then things would be more complicated today. This difficulty she describes in differentiating real fucking from the sex you create from nothing, that would have been completely impossible to do, and Hildie would have been ruined for the rest of her life. She needs to have fucked, and fucked well, to work so much and to whisper to her body, on those evenings she finds a man she likes, that this time it's for real. The good side of this professional distortion is that when submitting to a boy who is clumsy with her, or who doesn't satisfy her, it's easy for her to not take umbrage: she puts this disappointing embrace in the same basket as those in The House, doesn't experience it as a failure of communication, failed chemistry. Her body is a companion that she listens to attentively, and for which she feels a kind of gentle pity on busy days, when she goes home wondering if what she's been doing for eight hours is sex or merely physical activity. She measures the sacrifice she's making of her flesh; sometimes, when she's drinking coffee on the terrace, surrounded by women as young as she is, and as pretty, Hildie dreams that if she touched one of their thighs, if she leaned over to kiss her neck, the frisson that would run through the girl would be real, would be felt from the roots of her hair to the tips of her toes – whereas Hildie would experience it as a familiar friction, occurring daily, like being scratched by a thorn while walking in the forest. To really lose herself, she would need the same slow pace, the same patience as a virgin is shown, a man to caress the places she's chosen to stop caring for, her legs, her arms, her ribs, and all this even though she has in her head the same fantasies of savagery as many others. One day, after a session in the Studio, a client opened her eyes. He asked her if she'd tried tantra yet; Hildie laughed, *Of course not*, you really think I'd want to spend two and half hours being massaged on the promise of coming like never before… How stupid that seemed to her! The client must have perceived the sarcasm in her smile; without getting annoyed he explained to her that tantra wasn't for old people who can't get hard or wet any more and who have all the time in the world to chase after an orgasm – on the contrary, this slowness and this perpetual deferral were perfect for young women like her who fucked a lot (too much?) while giving scant place for foreplay, by necessity.

'For example, I'm sure you personally need very strong sensations in order to come?'

'Yes, pretty strong,' replied Hildie, thinking of the noise and the power of the motor of her vibrator, which were so great she hardly had time to think dirty thoughts before she came.

'Obviously, that's normal. Well, tantra allows you to reconnect with every part of your body, every centimetre square of your body. For example – may I?'

He'd leaned over her, waiting for her assent before lightly tracing the curve of her ankle with the tips of his finger, up to the back of her knee.

'You'd be surprised to learn that the lightest of touches like this can excite you. It's needs to be worked at, of course. It requires surrender, and god knows it's not easy when you do the job you do. But it could put you back in touch with your gentle side. You need gentleness, Hildie, just like everyone does.'

Hildie hadn't paid any attention. She feared, deep down, discovering that there was another form of sensuality she was obliged to disdain, one that would have opened her up much more. But sometimes, on the terrace, after observing how happy the other women are with the sun on their flesh, Hildie closes her eyes and with her free hand caresses her ankle with her fingertips, up to the back of her knee, very slowly. As she does, she thinks of a young man whom she'd desire. And while I'm finishing applying cream to her shoulders, I feel all along my calf a tickle like that of a blade of grass and I nearly swat away with the back of my hand Hildie's own hand, Hildie who, behind her sunglasses, is smiling, her beautiful face turned towards me, 'You see how it feels?'

And I will think back to this caress for a long time, especially after our duos in The House – threesomes that left men breathless. Half-hours cleverly orchestrated by Hildie and I, without the need to even consult each other, deploying gems of obscenity, unbelievable positions, the guy clenched between our four thighs, unseeing and unhearing, while Hildie silently articulated, while she rode him, instructions to me. Feigning full abandon, without ever taking her eyes off the man's hands or the condom, watching his pleasure mount and imagining the dream combination that would make him come. Hildie and I were not far off shaking hands afterwards. Not for one single moment had we been distracted from our mission by a moment of dizziness, staying in control of ourselves even during bursts of elation, even with each slap on our respective thighs. And yet, when I dived between her legs to tongue her, with an appetite I really didn't have to fake much, I thought of that ordinary caress of my leg and I wondered what could have come out of that for us, if I could have made her come and if she would have known what to do with me, which places to touch, which language to invent to breathe a frisson of life back into our flesh.

'But these are rich people's problems,' she sighs as she puts her hat back on, covered with cream from her lower back to her impressive shoulders. 'You have the time to feel sorry for yourself for not feeling much. I always think of the girls who work in brothels charging twenty euros a go. This is a bourgeois brothel. It's only here that you can hear girls complaining they didn't come.'

I'm So Green, Can

What the phrase 'bourgeois brothel' carries within it is the fact that girls like Victoria don't hear the bell ring without fearing the arrival of a man they know. Berlin has three and a half million inhabitants, but behind the door there's always a face she's seen god knows where, at work, at the supermarket, that of a neighbour, or the parent of a student – it's enough to make you believe Victoria emits pheromones attracting all the men who would like to fuck her but who, for a variety of reasons, can't. Which is perhaps the fault of her photos – you only need a few seconds to make her out beneath those badly Photoshopped features. In four years, she's changed names three times, but barely a week goes by without hearing her murmur from the sofa as she pulls her clothes on again at top speed, 'It's a friend of my bloke…!'

Which obliges Inge to come up with excuses as fanciful as they are implacable: *Victoria doesn't feel well and has gone home, Victoria is still busy, there's a mistake on the bookings list* – even, in extreme cases, *She doesn't work here any more, who booked you in with her…?* And sometimes, just before the heavy front door closes again, the corridor booms with the thunderous complaint of a client who's leaving empty-handed again and who hurls, like a bottle into the sea: 'I know you're here…! Silke, I know you're here.' And we can't work out whether Victoria is really called Silke or whether it's a pseudonym adopted years ago and forgotten by everyone except him. Are they there to trap her, as she thinks? Even dressed in everyday clothes,

Victoria doesn't leave much doubt as to the nature of her profession – something involving men, it can only be that. In time, she could have got rid of any risk of blackmail by being perfectly upfront about her job; the way she talks, her good mood don't give the impression she feels any embarrassment about it. I ended up thinking that these men who rage when they find themselves spurned, these youngsters who look about to cry when they are offered another girl, these sneaky men who book her under false names (in vain, because she always looks through the keyhole), far from wanting to corner her, are under the spell of some kind of magic that she dispenses in the bedroom, some unstoppable coup that they wouldn't exchange for anything in the world – like that guy that I took to the door one night, who overturned a bedside table, all butterfingers all of a sudden, who Victoria never wanted to see again. The next time, jigging around with impatience, with all the loved-up excitement of a virgin for whom a new world has opened up, he had out of pique chosen Hildie, who looks a little like Victoria – from a distance, on a foggy day. And Hildie told me he'd slumped around, from the bedroom to the shower, from the shower back to Hildie, and it had been hard work getting him erect and making him come, him keeping his eyes closed. As he was leaving, he took from his pocket a gift-wrapped box of sugared almonds with a label on which he'd written 'Victoria', in pink, with hearts over the two 'i's. He'd apologised; and, stuffing a twenty-euro note in Hildie's hand, he had made her promise to kiss the great Victoria for her, to promise that the sweets would get to her, with Laszlo's compliments.

'With some, you wonder what they're thinking about when they're fucking. At least with him it was clear,' groaned Hildie. She was a bit annoyed, as is understandable in a kid of twenty when someone prefers forty-two-year-old Victoria. But deep down, Hildie must be mulling over the same thing as all of us, as we nibble the sugared almonds Victoria's disdained: why *her*? Good god, what does Victoria/Silke/Yasmine have that brings them all running? I'd have Hildie ten times over before as much as glancing at this tall, huge, rough-cut Valkyrie, with a wide, almost square backside, outrageously blonde; she gives off the kind of moody languor that people associate with whores, she has a limp handshake, murmurs whatever name she uses now. She makes no effort whatsoever to pretend to be delighted to meet anyone – sometimes she forgets to take off her slippers and rushes in, trailed by a whiff of the food she's just gobbled down without thinking of the person about to hang from her lips. Her clothes, her fragrance – they smell of whores from miles away – but not any more, or any better, than many girls here.

Ever since I've been seeing these bouquets, these sugared almonds, since I heard these beautiful guys groan as they leave with their cock between their legs, or saw them close their eyes to beautiful Hildie to picture Victoria's mare's rump, I've been eaten away by curiosity. Maybe her size, her disinterestedness, whip up instincts that the sweet talk of the pretty girls leave dormant. Perhaps her air of not wanting to be chosen, her darting glance of a schoolchild not wanting to be asked a question, give men weary by the transactional goodwill of the other whores a desire to bend her under them either willingly or by force. Maybe this risky double-or-quits technique is a boldness you learn after ten years in a brothel?

When she walks past us – with, by the way, as many smiles for us as she has scornful looks for her clients – in our minds' eyes we lift up her super-short skirt: or when she's naked, which is often, we, at a bit of a loss, seek the answer to this mystery in the folds of her flesh. It's obviously something that men feel and that leaves us indifferent, our nerves blocked by jealousy. Esmée sent one of her clients on a mission – but the man in question, totally in love with her, gave her a disappointing report, assuring her that Victoria was *too wide* for him. Too *wide*? Could that be the secret?

I heard Victoria crying out behind a closed door. My client was in the shower, I went to get my fresh towels, and I stayed there, captivated, one ear glued to the dividing wall, by the sounds making themselves heard above the soothing music. My client found me there, arms dangling, and he just smiled: 'That's the tall one.' And when I asked him what she did that was so special, so intoxicating, Hector changed the subject with a wave of the hand, saying he didn't want give away others' specialities. As if, my god, Victoria was one of his colleagues and not mine. Proving in the end that even the men are more discreet, more respectful than I am – and from then on, with her long almost white hair and her silk dressing gown covered in stars, Victoria appears to me as a witch astride a white swan at dusk on an evening when the devil is visiting the world of mortals, an apparition you could blink and miss, and that Marc Bolan would have mewed about in a song.

If There is Something, Roxy Music

THIBAULT TAKES OFF HIS CLOTHES, CALMLY.

'Sorry there's only the Mauve room, but the house is full.'

'Oh, don't worry. I really like this room.'

'It depresses me.'

Thibault is used to the brothel, more so than me. He's used to hearing clients talk, used to the clicking of the girls' heels in the neighbouring room. And this vulgar room where we end up as if by bad luck, lit only by mauve neon, has never intimidated him. No more than he's been intimidated by the odours of deodorant or come, or the prosaic roll of kitchen towel on the night table. Thibault likes being amidst girls, their laughter, he likes them to tap him on the shoulder as they walk past each other in the corridor and the cheekiness of his regular girls as they pretend to tell him off for his infidelities. He likes everything right down to the preparations in their finest details, the towels laid in a cross on the bedcover, the condoms taken out of our little bags, the brazenness of those who get undressed while they're talking to him and roughly dry the parts they've just washed in the bidet.

'And how have you been?'

'Fine.'

'I thought you were never coming back.'

'I've had some health issues.'

'Wilma told me. You were in hospital, I hear?'

'Did Wilma tell you that?'

'Yes, because she cares, you know. We were talking about the fact you were coming less often. She was worried about you.'

'That's kind. I had heart surgery. I had to stay in bed for two weeks.'

'Are you better now? Have you recovered?'

'Yes, but the doctor warned me that I have to stop partying, drugs, girls. At least for a while.'

Fully naked he sits opposite me, cross-legged. I'd already noticed the sadness in his eyes.

'I won't deny that I'm a bit down. I was so used to going out, to taking speed, to not sleeping… I always had something to look forward to, like coming here. But since I've been out of work I have less money, so I come less. I'm bored, is what.'

'Do other things. Read a bit.'

'I've just finished a doorstopper by Franzen. It wasn't bad. But I miss all this.'

'Be patient. Read Philip Roth, you'll like it.'

'I suppose I pushed the envelope too far. Ten years ago, I'd never have imagined such a thing would happen to me. I fucked non-stop, I got drunk too much… I suppose I'm paying for it today. Money aside, I was coming here four, five times a week, and I never had any trouble getting it up. Now I feel that if I didn't leave three days between two visits, it would be difficult. I would piss people off. I'm not thirty any more,' smiles Thibault, who has just turned forty-one. 'Suddenly my life seems empty. I buried my father six months ago, I don't know if Wilma told you that…'

'No, I'm sorry to hear that.'

'It's a weird thing to bury your dad. Maybe even more so for a man. I don't have a brother or a sister, I looked at the coffin being lowered and I thought – this is weird, huh? – that I was next on the list. In my head I'm still fifteen, I'm still the son. And now my father is dead, and I have no wife or children… If I could still party, that would at least distract me.'

'Why don't you find a nice little chick?'

'And when would I see all of you?'

'You'd do like the others do, you'd see us anyway. It would feel like a transgression.'

'I really will have to grow up one day.'

'No one's ever said that.'

Thibault bursts out laughing, clutches me to him. In his chest I feel his heartbeats, and I have nothing to reply to them. Maybe they are slower than usual?

'No, marriage, I'm not sure it's for me. I'm married to this place, that's enough for me. I have several wives a week, and we never row.'

'Don't worry, it'll all come back. We all have shitty times.'

'And you? How are you? How's the book going?'

'Getting there, slowly. My head's not really in it at the moment.'

'Am I in it?'

'You should be!'

'You know if you want stories, we can go for a drink and I'll tell you about my long experience as a client!'

'I have your card. When I start writing again, I'll call you.'

His card is indeed in the inside pocket of my bag. I sometimes think about calling him, convinced I might find, in his laidback attitude, something to fix my writer's block – but I know deep down that we both have the same problem, the same book on our hands, the same fear of writing it badly, and of tarnishing all these stories inside of us that, in their wild state, feel like parables.

With anyone else, I'd wait until *afterwards* to start such a conversation. But Thibault doesn't need any kind of atmosphere to remember why he's here, the spectacle of naked flesh is more than enough for him. And already hard, snagging one of my lips between his, he has the serious look of someone who has no idea what we were just talking about, or even if we were talking at all (if he'd been a woman, Thibault would have made the perfect whore).

'And anyway, tell me, do you get laid a lot here? Tell me.' In this question that he asks Wilma, Esmée, these women who have worked here for years and are *only* in a good mood if they get laid a lot, abides his sole fantasy, the illusion of men who imagine that nobody but them pay for it. It's the only moment when it would be tempting to reply to him, 'What do you think, old chap?' Anyway, I contemplate it but then remember his sad eyes, and I chuckle into his mouth: 'Four times today.'

Which is untrue, as I've just arrived – but that's certainly not what Thibault wants to hear.

Beware My Love, Wings

FINALLY LOTTE, HAVING SAID GOODBYE TO NO one in particular,
goes down the stairs, pushes open the garden gate, and is
sucked into the hectic motion of the shopping street. She has a
big latte in her hand and in her head the peaceful plan to read in
the park a few hundred metres away. The smell of the next-door
Turkish restaurant, which brings to mind work when she arrives in
the morning, evokes freedom when she leaves; and just like that,
with a click of the fingers, she forgets her day's clients, she's just a
girl with a full wallet, exhausted in the same way as a sports teacher
or a masseuse. Anyway it's a nice kind of fatigue that has nothing
in common with the suffering that somebody who's never set foot
inside a brothel might imagine. It's a weariness that means you're
going to sleep well, the day is yet young, it's the kind of weather for
soaking your legs in a lake. Lotte has worked hard, the city seems
to open its arms to her as she steps back into it, tomorrow she'll go
and sunbathe at the Wannsee – she's earned this outing, after two
days in this dark house where everyone's flesh takes on the hue of
milk with grenadine syrup.

Lotte sits in the grass, at street level; it's a pleasure to watch
colleagues who've just left work go by, and those who are just
arriving for evening duty. Esmée, who's tackling the steep slope
towards The House by bike, fierce concentration on her face; Thaïs
swinging her big sports bag containing two pairs of heels that she
uses every day and as many outfits as the different moods she'll

have. Seeing people continue to work, amass money, construct themselves some creature comforts; shooting a discreet smile at the girls working the evening shift, which they may or may not return, is one of the delights of the *Feierabend*. A delight that nothing could spoil. Except maybe one thing, and you'd need to be a whore to understand; for an hour, or at least the time it takes to smoke the first cigarette, it would be ideal not to hear a man's voice. Especially not the voice of a man speaking to her. But there is always one ready to chance it, with an air of cocky confidence; and while Lotte gets a book out of her bag, in a hurry to get back to the passage she's been dragged away from several times, she sees a shadow extend over hers, block out the sun for a moment, and a feeble syllable drowns out the tweeting of the birds, the laughter of the children from the neighbouring school: 'Hey!'

Lotte hesitates for a second, shaking with rage, having recognised the voice, the weight of the shadow, even the consistency of the silence, before she's as much as raised her eyes. There's Heiko, hands in pockets, a sad smile on his lips, appeared from nowhere, and Lotte summons up all the friendliness she can muster, the politeness she'd left in her locker in The House, to smile, 'Oh! What are you doing here?'

She knows perfectly well why he's there. Heiko must have heard she was leaving and discreetly followed her. He must have waited for her to finish her shift and walked behind her, inhaling her perfume and looking at this rear that he's only ever seen half naked, strapped into suspenders; he must have waited for her to position herself on the grass and deliberated how to approach her, fearing he would frighten her, and then fully counting on the possibility she'd believe it was a lucky coincidence – as if she could forget that he lives several kilometres from there and that there's nothing to do in this neighbourhood once you've left The House. Anyway, that's why he has the honesty, as he crouches beside her, to admit without dropping his smile, 'You told me that one day we'd go for a coffee, and I was thinking why not today?'

I can imagine the hatred that invades her at that moment; hatred of herself, because she does remember having expressed this possibility, when Heiko was threatening to stay in her room forever. Hatred of him – because who, if not a client, could hope for such a thing, to have coffee with her? Why not today, Heiko? *Seriously, why not today?*

She's forgotten that within every client slumbers a man who aspires to become more than a guy who has paid. She's often thought that she should stop seeing Heiko – almost every time he's visited, since the one when he hinted at being in love with her (do they even exist, hints, in such a restricted context as a brothel?). But as soon as she arrived in the introduction room and saw his face light up with happiness, his bag filled with gifts on the end of his arm, she lost her nerve: something childlike and tender within her rendered her weak in the face of his joy at seeing her again. Yet this could have been the moment to tell him no, because this same something, a moment later, was suffocating with rage: the capricious little girl who was always looking for compliments was exasperated by his lovestruck gaze, by how hard he tried to hold back so that she came (a hope as vain as getting together with her outside The House). And exasperation turned to disgust; the spontaneous, desperate erection of this pretty boy barely thirty years of age invoked unease in her, the feeling of prostituting herself that months of dealings with old men, ugly men, fat men had never awakened in her. She could make out the shape of his hard cock before he even undressed and was immediately seized by the desire to hit Heiko. Furiously, she counted the minutes he spent in the shower, finding that time went by both too slowly and too quickly, vaguely hoping that he'd fall flat on his face coming out of the bathroom. Which never happened, of course; Heiko would never have allowed such a thing, he would have come even with a broken leg. Which had actually nearly happened the day before; he'd sprained his wrist falling off his bike and had blustered in covered in melted snow, and Lotte had had to sit on him and do the work in his place: she'd put Pixies on in the background so as not to hear him swinging between complaints and ecstasy (although any noise he emitted had been unbearable for a long time), and she had had to grin and bear it in order to get through this chore without letting the bad vibes come in, turning her back to him, taking care not to touch his forearm, which he kept raised like a standard. It was always hard work; Heiko loved snogging and she'd given her permission for this before she started hated him, and now couldn't deprive him of it without revealing the dwindling of her affection. He ran his tongue around her pussy for a long time, not in the least annoyed to feel the lube she'd applied so as not to present herself to him completely dry. And to cut short the ordeal, Lotte created an orgasm intensified by her impatience, an orgasm like a snort that had the advantage of making him come – but the inconvenience of bringing Heiko back to her, over and over. The short-lived smell of come that arose when Heiko took off the full condom, this smell that she generally put down to a job well done, awakened in her a feeling of intense revolt. Sometimes she was taken over by a nausea that she hid by bending over the radio to change the music (Lotte took to never putting on her playlist so that no song ever reminded her exclusively of Heiko); and when she finally turned round and saw him lying there, his eyes closed, his cock returned to an inoffensive size, she was seized by a strange guilt. She could no longer understand how she had been able to hate him so much, and how he could imagine the opposite to the point of coming – she was overtaken by heart-wrenching pity for the fathomless stupidity of men. Stupid when they had an erection – everybody knew that, including them – but no less idiotic when they'd come, in fact even more idiotic. Docile as lambs. Radiant, duped by the illusion of having made the girl come and ready to take part in the same lie. While he was vulnerable like this, Lotte could have grabbed the opportunity to let him know that she didn't want to see him again. The shaky explanation burned her lips, until Heiko got out his presents – normally a box of chocolates. It was too late. These chocolates he spent a fortune on in a French shop in Mitte and that Lotte found too bitter gave her a fresh excuse for putting off the impossible explanation until next time. She didn't want to know what would happen, whether Heiko would leave the chocolates or take them away again (which deep down didn't matter to her either way, but she preferred to spare herself the spectacle of this generosity or this rudeness), whether he would start to cry, whether he would get angry – and above all, it seemed inevitable that he would with impunity take fifteen minutes of her time to argue, to defend himself, fifteen minutes that she couldn't reproach him for, because in Heiko's head, the time spent with her was not made up of minutes each worth a certain number of euros, but of pieces of eternity; and the idea that another man was waiting for Lotte – as obvious as it was – wasn't something she could burden him with. No, if she spoke now, she'd have to shoehorn him out of her room, and she wouldn't even have time to smoke a cigarette to get rid of the memory of torn-up Heiko before the next client. She would have to lug, from one room to the next, the exasperation that he had evoked in her and lay it over the exasperation the others would evoke – because this kind of scene would follow you around all day. So Lotte took a chocolate, thanked Heiko, and at the moment of sending him away promised to meet at a café outside, just to avoid him lingering on the doorstep, bending three, four times in the half-open doorway, demanding a last kiss, then another, then a truly last one, already visibly counting the days until he would see Lotte again, taking a little bit of her lips for every day without her. Sometimes this promise had the desired effect: Heiko nodded energetically, convinced that no client until now had had heard such an offer by a whore at the end of her patience. And even if Lotte had never called him, had never even entertained the prospect, he left happy, at top speed, fleeing with this promise of a meeting as if it needed outside air to survive.

Lotte vaguely hoped that, filled with this idea, he would wait for her call and never come back to the brothel; but he came, not seeming to hold a grievance for anything. Lotte could count on his presence as she could the ineluctability of death, every Tuesday in the early afternoon. He was generally the first to call up for her on Sunday evening, when the girls' schedule was published on the website.

Heiko was becoming more and more sombre, the Hausdamen were beginning to call him *Der Trauriger*, the Sad One. Lotte could no longer go into the introduction room without him springing up from his seat, always smiling but with a melancholy in his eyes that was even more wearing, if such a thing were possible, than his previous enthusiasm. He was wasting away. One week, deep in some inner drama, he decided to not come back — not without having spoken at length to Lotte about his despair: he was unhappy, he didn't know where any of it was leading him, he was earning less money, he wanted to keep good memories of it… And two weeks later, having clearly scared himself, he had come back. He must have understood he was depriving no one but himself, and he gave a strong performance, bordering on the hysterical, of a man determined to be happy with his meagre ration. Wearied by having asked too much of Lotte, he promised to behave as a reasonable man, happy with the little he received from her (Heiko had no inkling that this small amount would have seemed huge to other clients less in love with her).

This wisdom hadn't lasted long. The proof: a reasonable man would never have waited for Lotte as she left work. In fact, an unreasonable man wouldn't have done that. An imbecile would have understood that you can't get anything from a woman by putting a knife to her throat. After behaving like an annoying lover, Heiko had put on his stalker's outfit. It was already painful enough to fear his visit every Tuesday, and if the world outside wasn't safe terrain any more, what would Lotte have left?

So she says, maybe it's time. Now he's there with a coffee in his hand, she with hers, now they're as close as they'll ever be to taking a coffee together, perhaps it's time to send him packing. It's difficult to assess whether Heiko senses it or not, because he's talking as if the slightest pause in his monologue might make Lotte flee. He talks about his work, about his next trip… The fact he's chatty is a trait she's grateful for at work, because time passes more quickly and because, hypnotised by the flood of words, she forgets, a little, that she detests him – because he's *paid* her for that. Outside, in this perfect warm day, with her book waiting for her, folded over on the same thrilling page, Lotte sees no more reason to accept Heiko's conversation than that of any other random man. And revolt growls horribly in Lotte's insides – Lotte who's no longer called that since the second she closed the door of The House. Heiko is talking about an article he read in a psychology rag; he's clearly trying to send her a message, because it so happens that this article, written by a psychologist whose clientele is made up mainly of whores, explains to men that the relationships they think they enter into in a brothel are artificially upheld by the workers to keep their clients coming back. As he talks about this paper, Heiko keeps giving Lotte the side eye, and leaving a few fearful silences in the hope that she will outright deny that, that she will swear to him that their relationship is real. If this isn't a hint, then what is?

Lotte would like to explain to this well-meaning psychologist that she's understood nothing about brothels; that she's understood nothing about what a brothel like The House demands of its women, and nothing about establishments whose regulars work by the quarter hour, racking up more than fifteen clients in a day. Even with all the empathy in the world, this psychologist can't understand how the girls' affection and irritation build up, and the survival mechanisms that hold them back from expressing one or the other. The girls who work in one of these money-making outfits where men stand in line have no need to be in a good mood; if a client doesn't like the conversation, there are ten more waiting and it's the same every day, two hundred girls and three times as many men, it's a never-ending chain – so what can it matter, if they come back or not?

To Heiki, she should say, 'I'm friendly because you are! I trust you because I have the vague impression of knowing you, caused by the simple fact of sleeping together regularly. I'm like that with you because I'm a bad whore, clearly. I'm a bad whore because when you left me, you didn't learn the matter-of-factness that all my colleagues' clients have – one that precludes any idea of being able to become friends with me. I'm a bad whore because you see the way I yield to you as being of the same value as that of any girl you're not paying; my acquiescence evokes the same hope in you – I do my job badly. I'm a whore who causes you pain, and a whore shouldn't do that.'

Evening falls gently over Heiko and Lotte, who look like a couple. A couple without much to say to each other, or such a solid couple that silence does the work of words. Soon Lotte will pack up her things, determined to go and read in a spot where there's no risk someone will recognise her. Heiko will watch her carefully dusting off her trousers, and he'll say, *I'm staying here a while*. He'll have his hands on the outline Lotte's backside has left in the grass. Without even realising. In the Métro taking her home, Lotte will send a message to Inge, very quickly so she doesn't change her mind, 'No more bookings with Heiko, thanks.' Thinking it's a real waste to get to this point, but suddenly freed of a huge weight – and the following Tuesday, at the time she should have seen Heiki, Lotte will be top of the bill for the herds of Italians that come for the annual Grüne Woche.

Who Loves the Sun, The Velvet Underground

'WHAT A DAY, KIDS!'

Gita lets herself fall into a sofa, wrapped in the rust-coloured kimono she slips into between two clients, like a boxer. She's just spent an hour in the Studio – while I was taking my morning shower I counted the sharp lashes of her switch – and now, magnificent, beaded with sweat, eyes shining, she's making a studenty ponytail out of her blonde mane. She takes off her pumps, moves her reddened toes.

'I hit him so hard, I don't know if he'll ever get over it,' she coos in her voice like that of a dove, like that of a rude kid who doesn't give a shit, because men would fight to the death for a session with her. They sprout like mushrooms; as soon as you open a door, one appears, flowers in hand, an anxious smile on his lips, hardly giving her the chance to breathe. Anyway, seeing her roll a cigarette in front of her full cup of coffee, I want to tell her not to get too comfortable. From my lookout, behind the curtain, I see the Doctor. When Inge warns him Gita will be a bit late, he gestures that he's not in a hurry. And shyly, Inge returns, places a hand on Gita's naked shoulder while Gita laughs as she recounts how she annihilated her previous client:

'The good Doctor has arrived.'

Gita stops, and Inge tries to make it up to her:

'Such elegance, that man. Always dressed up to the nines. If only they all looked like that, huh?'

So beautiful Gita, rolling her big angry eyes, slides back into her professional good mood and disappears into the room where the Doctor awaits her. There's no sound, no joyful outpouring. The salon must be filled with this passing, loving silence that he brings, along with his overly complex perfume. He looks at her. Absorbing Gita with his eyes and his nostrils, with every pore of his body. Unconscious of the countdown that's already been set in motion in her own head. Unconscious of the thoughts she's dialling through while he's taking his shower, putting his clothes back on so as not to impose on her the same indecorum as other clients who shoot out of the bathroom naked and with a hard-on – and how could he suspect that Gita is unable to support this thoughtfulness of his as much as everything else, as much as anything to do with him? Gita has no desire to undress him or to pretend to find him erect; in any case, he doesn't often even have a hard-on, so immense, so terrifying, is his hunger for her; if this hunger involved his stomach, he wouldn't be able to eat.

There was a time when Gita was strangely moved by his gentleness and by how slowly he penetrated her – another symptom of this hunger, one that made him take possession of her carefully, a tiny piece at a time. She liked his grave silence, was excited by his way of holding himself at arm's length. She had even come two or three times. And now she is angry at herself, convinced that he felt it and that, like so many men, he mistook this spasm for the beginning of a romance – even a doctor, if he's in love, can't imagine a woman's orgasm as not having a semblance of tenderness.

Now he's naked in front of her, breathless. She's there on the bed, laid out. Regal. He hardly dares breathe. Floored by the moves she makes, which never change from one appointment to the next. It's his adoration that infuses their tête-à-têtes with a semblance of novelty. He notices she's wearing a colour that suits her less, a light green for her pale complexion – but this error of judgement, far from making her ugly, actually makes her more human. He imagines her at home in her pyjamas, choosing her outfit for the next day and running the green satin through her fingers, in a rush to go to bed, thinking she hasn't worn this outfit yet and that that's a shame given how much it cost her. Anyway, some of his own money is in the chunky sum she spent. It's another thing that makes his heart, which Gita strains daily, race. He can see when she's slept badly. When she's been out late. When she's smoked too much the day before. When she's worried. When she's on her period. He feels deep inside her the sponge she uses to soak up the blood. He sees also when she comes – how could it be otherwise? It has nothing to do with him being a doctor, it's because he's in love. And when she fakes it, he doesn't see it as deception but as the delicacy of a mistress who, for excellent reasons of her own, doesn't want to come. He feels tenderness for the professionalism she shows on days when she's in a bad mood. As if she was playing at being a whore; as if all of that was just acting she was doing of her own free will. It whips up his blood to see her eyes calm and faraway, belying the fluid movements of her splendid rump. It makes him want to pull her hair, if he could find it in himself to be bold enough. Because the doctor is a very well-brought-up German. Straight out of a rigorously Protestant family – going to a brothel, whether he has or hasn't freed himself from his upbringing, means that sooner or later he's definitely going to end up in Hell, on Earth or elsewhere. So treating a girl in a way he's never treated his wife is a temptation he always brushes away. This man has something of Count Muffat about him, enough to annoy the trace of Nana in Gita. He's not stupid enough to hope to make her come every time, thank god, but enough to always watch her face while he's pumping away on top of her – when so many others are content to look at her breasts, her arse, her pussy, this trinity designed by love, with the simplicity and beauty of a scenic landscape. He's on the lookout for any kind of mirror, the smallest glass surface in which Gita's face could be reflected when she wearies of being on her back, arms wrapped around his own shoulders. And that often happens; in a fit of rage, Gita wonders what use it is cheating on his wife if it's to fuck in the missionary position. And for someone else that would certainly be true, but love, love… Out of exasperation, Gita has forgotten this thirst that people in love have, one quenched by insignificant details. At the same time, his humble demands tire her; the way he whispers *Look at me* has the same effect on her of a perversion that is impossible to satisfy. For a man you love, or at least desire, the act of opening your eyes would have a feeling of fiery wantonness to it. But with the Doctor, she's afraid he'll guess her dislike or her indifference. Faking wildness, hiding behind her eyelids as if her modesty was being assailed, all of that embarrasses her, and after turning onto her stomach she's intent on never seeing him again. On leaving a note on the board, forbidding anyone from taking a booking from him.

That's been going on for ten years.

After what he thinks of as love and she thinks of as the biggest chore of all, her relief at having finished is so great that she softens in her resolution, thinks back to the moments when he helped her with some administrative procedures; to the day when, sick as a dog, she called him and he came, at 7 o'clock in the morning, with his case stuffed with antibiotics, without asking for anything in return, not even a fuck as payment for the excuse he'd had to find to leave his wife and his children so early.

Gita makes the bed and thinks of that morning when she dragged herself, throat all raw, to open her door to him; and he, in his work clothes, bags under his eyes but those eyes also aglow with a fire sparked by her phone call, walking into the hallway, his medical bag in one hand, a hot chocolate in the other. He panics seeing her barefoot, instructs her to go back to bed while he washes his hands. And Gita, slipping between the sheets, thinks that because she won't be paying for a consultation, she'll have to show him some kind of gratitude even with a 40-degree fever… But he comes and sits on the edge of the bed, opens his bag, asks her the questions a doctor asks a patient, inspects her throat by the light of her bedside lamp, with impeccable neutrality, indifferent to her bad breath, to her coated tongue, to the pus oozing at the back of her throat (while Gita feels the embarrassment of a workman who's let his tools get filthy). Unsurprisingly he diagnoses her with strep throat, gives Gita two sachets, piles her bedside table with a half-dozen vials. She's barely swallowed the first medicines before she starts feeling better; watching him pack his things, she feels a surge of tenderness towards the Doctor. At this exact moment, she's struck by the hugeness of the tragedy they're both experiencing, albeit at different levels. Perhaps because she is ill and prey to sentimentalism, and because the thought of waking up feeling less horrible is so lovely… Suddenly Gita sees this man, who's no different from others, as being definitely better-looking than most of them; this man who's currently absorbing the details of this room in which they sit in silence – Gita's lair with its walls covered with posters, photos, Gita's mess, her clothes everywhere, her bookshelf, her shoe collection. She's vaguely aware of taking on a consistency, in his mind, that she's never had, despite the hours he's spent with his nose buried in the folds of her flesh; and she suspects that he prefers her now, in her pyjamas and almost incapable of speaking, rather than made-up, hair done and strapped into suspender belts, because he's in love with her, and because there, in the midst of her dirty knickers and empty Coke bottles, he's close to a truth he firmly believes he wants to enter into. Gita is temporarily neither a whore nor a patient, but a young woman with whom he could, in the right context, fall in love, whose company he could enjoy for a few months, a girl for whom he'd hesitate to pay for an expensive divorce and who he'd get over as one almost always gets over them. Because they're at her place and not at the brothel, she could fall in love as well, they'd wear each other out down to the weft with their secret meetings, with restaurants and louche hotels, they'd invent for themselves the semblance of a life constantly at the extreme limit of frustration until they really were well and truly frustrated and she, just twenty-six and free as a bird, falls in love with someone else and they separate in a thousand different ways. She sees all that pass over his face; and the possibility flits through her mind that he's something other than a client, that he has a different smell to the soap in the brothel and that she likes this smell. She regrets the disdain he evokes in her in normal times, in spite of him and in spite of her, this irrepressible disdain inspired by men in love with girls they have paid, precisely so they don't love them.

She lies back on the pillows, expending the last of her energy to reveal her breasts – which are small and swollen by fever; if her mouth is out of action, he can still take her on her side, quickly; she's so hot inside that he won't be able to last long. Ready yet again to give herself while hating all men via him, for fucking a half-dead girl as long as her arse is still firm and warm… But the Doctor doesn't seem to see her breasts, or if he does it's with the clinical coldness of his profession. He smiles, pulls the covers back over her, and this smile makes her feel obscene and pathetic – did she really believe he was so rotten?

For a moment he watches her drink the chocolate he's brought. The main thing is not to have anything too hot, that would only make things worse. She needs to sleep. She needs to rest. She needs ten days off work.

'Thanks,' sighs Gita, eyes full of all the gratitude she was counting on showing him lying on her side.

Before leaving her room, he seems to hesitate, then says, with a gravity that throws a shadow over his handsome, angular face:

'You know, I'll forget your address straight away. You don't need to worry.'

Gita smiles, replies that she never worried, but she suddenly does feel both relieved and worried – because she hadn't realised, not consciously at least, that from now on he does know her address. The thinking part of her brain suddenly rolls out all the unpleasant recourses she'd have to turn to if he decided to harass her, like moving house or calling the cops. She's tempted to believe him – but can you trust a man in love?

The fact is you can – yes. Count on the promise that he'll never ring her doorbell. As to forgetting the address of a woman you love, to order, I don't think that's possible. Especially when this woman you were in the habit of seeing twice a week disappears from one day to the next. That's what Gita did; she came one Tuesday, did her shift, said 'Goodbye', and no one ever saw her again. The Hausdamen who called her to come and get her things never got anything more than the automated voice of a standard answering machine, and after a while, another metallic voice informed them that number didn't exist any longer. Her locker stayed the same, padlocked, with the label with violet letters spelling out this name of hers she'd found in a book, which was nothing at all like her own, but at the sound of which she turned her head when she was smoking on the balcony, lost in herself, when you called her to come for a client. One day, her photos on the website disappeared – but I'm sure one man kept these images as screengrabs, images you'd at first glance describe as kitsch, Gita lying back to front on all fours in the most indecently floral room in The House, but that were actually fascinating because her eyes, not retouched, bestow an almost painful gravity on this debauchery of roses and daisies, of pastel organdie. Never, in spite of the lack of space, has anyone dared force the padlock on the locker to use it to store a new girl's things; and a part of Gita stayed there, in a very high cupboard, beautiful Gita herself seemingly evaporated from the face of the Earth.

When the Doctor came back, two days after Gita's disappearance – which Marlene had told him about on the phone – Lotte, Birgit and I hid behind the curtain and watched him come into the small salon.

'Poor man,' sighed Birgit as she came back to her reading.

Lotte went to talk to the Doctor. He resembled a shipwrecked person clinging to a plank to get a few extra breaths. He wanted news about Gita, and when Lotte told him nobody had any, an eternity unfurled in deathly silence. The Doctor held his head between his hands, and Lotte, starting to lose patience, moving her hips from side to side to give herself something to do, not daring to interrupt the thoughts of this potential client, noticed that all his fingernails, which were usually of an almost feminine neatness, were bitten to the quick; that there was, within this more than 40-year-old man, a nervous adolescent whose worst habits had been awakened by Gita's absence. Lotte was afraid he'd explode and threaten to trash the place if they didn't tell him the truth – that she didn't want to see him any more. But the Doctor wasn't that kind of man; and, overcome with pity, Lotte felt her own hand move away from her body, come and place itself on his shoulder; he raised his haggard eyes, the eyes of a madman, towards her:

'Who is there who looks like her?'

Bluebird is Dead, Electric Light Orchestra

'You know, I waited for her in front of her place. I swore I never would, but after a week, I thought I was going mad. The nurses were looking at me as if I was a different man, and that's something you notice right away when you spend your days surrounded by people the only part of whom you can see is the eyes. I could have killed patients I was thinking so much about her. In fact I almost did: I almost left a bandage in some guy's stomach. That seems impossible, almost like any of you lot forgetting condoms, but you can't imagine how easy it is. It becomes the same colour as the tissue, and before you know it you have septicaemia or a dead body. I was closing the wound thinking about Gita, and Gita's apartment, when the nurse placed a hand on my arm – and that never happens, not in the middle of an operation.

'So when I came out, instead of going home, I went into Mitte, I parked in front of her place. I waited and then I saw her. There was a guy with her. A guy of her own age. Someone who wasn't paying – that was clear from the way he was looking at her. She'd never been naked in front of him – that was clear too. I hated this guy immediately, of course, but I was mainly happy that she was okay, I'd been really worried. It's completely stupid, deep down I must have suspected that she'd just had enough. You have to be really stupid in the way only men can be to imagine that a girl who vanishes must be in a bad way – it's the opposite. She was radiant. I thought I'd seen her happy here, but it was like admiring a sunset wearing sunglasses, there was no comparison. She had a beer in her hand, which the guy took a mouthful of, and, by the way she laughed, by the way she devoured him with her eyes, I knew they were going to sleep together. That she wanted to. It's mad, suddenly I saw everything, right down to the excitement on her face. It was inky-dark, but I felt it. Nobody but me would have been able to see anything but just another pretty girl about to take a boy home with her. She sat on a windowsill on the ground floor, her arms around this guy's neck. I wondered if it was for him that she'd given up this job, but I don't think so. He was a chance encounter, one who probably didn't have the slightest idea about her past. That's when I understood that I'd only been a client for her, because she moved differently, she shone differently. With me she'd only responded to stimuli, she hadn't taken any of these initiatives, hands in his hair, wrapping her legs around his thighs, tipping her face back. It's crazy how apathetic reality can make you. I was there, in my car, my head full of all the times I'd felt close to her, when I'd thought I was getting more than she gave the others. The time when I came to hers, this moment of peace in her bedroom, in silence, she lying beneath the sheets and me sitting on the bed looking at her poor throat, all white. I didn't ask for anything else that time, I was happy with being close to her. That day, I dreamed she might fall in love with me.

'And suddenly, seeing her hanging around this guy's neck, I wondered if the cars all around me were really empty, whether I wasn't going to glimpse other clients frozen in horror, old clients full of the same exploding illusions.

'The idea that she could disappear without even thinking of warning me should have put me on the right track. If I'd been less stupid, I would have smelt the others on her. I took it as her smell, I loved it as I did everything else.

'I'd only been a client; and when, wrapped around her young guy, she looked in my direction and saw me, I understood I'd become an enemy. Those eyes…! I saw only her eyes, the rest was buried in the other guy's shoulder, it was just before they kissed. She didn't blink, didn't move, even in surprise… Just those eyes, fixed on me, huge, terrified, still. Terrified. Terrified.

'You know, the worst thing, when you have a wife, children and a mistress, is not to be in love with someone with whom you'll never be able to spend more than two hours at a time. It's not that this love is one-sided or doomed in advance. The worst is to have to go home carrying a collapsed world on your shoulders and to make sure that's not visible. To find the strength, god knows where, to smile and be normal, while during every second of this farce, the collapsed world is still crumbling, unceasingly. The worst thing is that that's possible. And doable. And that you do it. Days, weeks, whole months, with this gaping hole in your heart.'

Mambo Sun, T. Rex

HILDIE TAKES ANOTHER BUS TO GET HOME to Kreuzberg. I'd
like to go with her and have a coffee, but I want to sleep
and my eyes are heavy from crying. She goes off hunched over
with depression and the bag she's emptied her locker into. In
the bus, old ladies look at her with something between pity and
tenderness, thinking it's some insurmountable heartbreak that
within two days will have been sticky-plastered over by some
other louse. Kids stare at her, stiff candles of snot suspended
from their noses. Maybe it's a death, a personal disaster – Hildie
is sobbing so hard, with such abandon. But nobody speaks to her,
nobody comes up to her, which is perfect because Hildie would be
incapable of making anything up. She would pour it all out, and
who could understand? *The place where hundreds of men crawled all over
me for three years has just closed down.* These tears can only be tears of
joy, *can't they…?*

At home, Hildie goes to bed fully dressed, has a dreamless nap
from which she emerges four hours later. Starving – having thought
she'd never be hungry again. The deep sleep that has torn her day in
two has made the morning faraway, as if it belongs to another time.
And the sadness, in fact, also has something distant and imprecise
about it, a grief without suffering, as if, instead of her, it was a dear
friend who had lost someone.

While she's devouring some left-over pasta from the day before,
she get this text: 'An hour?'

The sender of the text is a man she's never seen and who she started talking to a week ago, when she realised she'd need a distraction from her grief. The photos of this stranger intrigued her. Hildie slips into a loose black jumpsuit, without any knickers underneath. And with her heart thudding in her chest beneath her small breasts hardened by the poplin rubbing against them, she walks towards the park where they've agreed to meet. It's a lovely June evening; the heat of the day seems to rise from the ground. Hildie had two clients that same morning; you might think the very thought of seeing a man would bore her; but Hildie is amazed to find that she's on fire, and that despite spending three years trotting from room to room to fuck perfect strangers, this stranger, because he's not paying her and because she's chosen him, excites her in a new way. More than excitement, it's fear she feels, painfully squeezing her stomach; fear of spotting the man, in the darkness. Fear of not pleasing him. Fear of no longer knowing how to do it, from having acquired at the brothel the habit of getting right down to business – lowering her jumpsuit and getting taken standing up against a tree, a thought that now has her mouth watering like mad. And how could you explain that to a stranger? Especially since this one is not like that. They may well have talked about it, Hildie has the strong feeling he's not going to jump on her or try to kiss her outright. At the idea of this delay, this wait, her stomach twists again – but Hildie won't consider turning back. She who's walked stark naked, without the slightest hint of embarrassment, around The House's several hundred square metres, suddenly feverishly wonders what she looks like dressed, what her arse looks like in this suit, if people can see in the darkness that her breasts are perked up and that she's walking with the languid softness of a woman running towards the possibility of pleasure – weirdly, she hopes so.

When she still had all her composure, and when she still wasn't sure she was going to honour their meeting, torn up as she was by the final closure of The House and by having sobbed her eyes out with the other girls, she'd told him out of bravado to meet her in a deserted corner of the park; an actual invitation to rape. She walks, and the conversations of the groups crowded around portable barbecues get further and further away, the calm jubilation of a summer's evening in Berlin fades as if in a dream; the silence that settles is an obscene intrusion into the tangle of her thoughts. Even if, in fact, she's not thinking of anything. It's been five hundred metres since she's thought of anything, her eyes watchful, her body trembling the moment she hears a man's steps behind her. Trembling at the thought of being seen without seeing and caught in a moment when her facial features show her anguish.

At the moment she descends, super-carefully, a flight of stone steps devoured by moss, a vast shadow detaches itself from the darkness, that of a large dog that looks at her and comes over to sniff her legs. Hildie daren't move, she can hardly breathe, convinced that despite her long shower the dog has detected the smell of her three clients, some vestige of them caught in her hair. A brief moment of fright at the thought that its nose will bury itself, as it often does, between her thighs, which she protects with a deceptively casual movement of her hand. If there's anything the dog can smell, without the shadow of a doubt, it's a female on heat. But this one is well trained, like all Berlin dogs, and goes away with a peaceful yap.

Silence, again. Only the distant plash of an artificial waterfall. Hildie has a feeling of foreboding she can't define.

'I walked right round the lake while I was waiting for you,' a soft voice behind her says in English.

It's a voice with a heavy Liverpool accent; in the darkness she sees a row of pretty teeth shining; the orange light of a streetlamp, filtering through the branches of the chestnut trees, illuminates eyes ringed by very dark lashes. From the shirt buttoned right to the top protrude hairs that go all the way up his neck.

In greeting, another guy would have kissed her. An American would have held her to him, killing all erotic tension at the same time. But he does nothing, he looks at her with a smile, and the hairs on the back of Hildie's neck stand on end. As they walk side by side, Hildie thinks that if they touched each other by mistake, one of them would get an electric shock and they'd no longer be able to pretend they haven't talked about his fingers in her pussy, that he hasn't sent a picture of his hard-on in pyjama bottoms, that they haven't agreed to meet in the dark to touch each other without being seen. He's not wearing any fragrance; if she got close to him it's his skin she'd smell, an odour she'll never have smelt on anyone but him.

After the lake a path devoured by tall grasses snakes towards total darkness. It's an entry-point into a sort of small forest without any domesticated plants, and the trees form a tunnel with a dense roof. Hildie's never been here, in normal circumstances she wouldn't risk it, but it's she who decides to carry on in this direction. Despite their carefree tone, Hildie knows that he knows that she knows what a girl is consenting to who lets herself be led away, on a summer's night, beneath a moonless sky. And the truth is, she's dying of longing to be taken here, in the bushes, by this young guy bantering away as he walks beside her. This guy who's probably telling himself it can't be this simple, who's expecting squealing protests as soon as he lays a hand on her. Who will end up going for it with the feeling he's throwing himself into the void. When they sit down in the grass, Hildie's legs are trembling a little. The fear she feels running through her veins is itself a pleasure that could keep her there, indefinitely. There they are, sitting a few centimetres from each other, unmoving, talking as if they were on a café terrace. She feels him watching her as she mindlessly pulls some tall grass out of the ground. Cosseted by his voice, she wonders if he has a hard-on from her being so close to him, if he is imagining like she is their furious coupling in this mix of wild thistles and wheat, her legs wrapped around his back. Seeing herself all new and fresh in his dark eyes is like a new kind of drunkenness. She's forgotten that frisson you get looking at a man who's looking at you not knowing if he will have you. Who hopes so. Who is getting ready to make his move, squatting in the shadows. A man who doesn't consider that there was, just a little earlier, another more efficient way of going about things.

Things are scurrying around in the moss, not far away. A bit confused by human presence, tiny organisms are emitting screeches, soft purrs. This wood has a dampness redolent of earth and soil, the ungraspable scents of flowers hidden by thorns and nettles, fumes so sensual Hildie's dizzied by them. Her courage deserts her; she lets herself fall to the ground, murmuring that it's a really lovely evening. It's then that he leans over her.

'Okay, I'm going to kiss you now,' he warns before she feels his mouth suspended above hers. *When you listen to Mozart*, said Sacha Guitry, *the silence that follows is also Mozart.*

He doesn't kiss her right out: he invests it with all the care, all the unbearable slowness of first kisses left lingering in the air. First he lightly touches her lips with his, then he pulls back. Silently, Hildie digs her nails into the soft ground, a mixture of sand and pine needles. He feeds her his lips slowly, patiently, pausing to take in small breaths. Hildie can't breathe, claws the thigh she feels against her own. He's biting her lower lip; Hildie stifles a hoarse moan that finally escapes her throat when he plunges his tongue into her mouth — and immediately she's cross with herself, ashamed of the atrocious excitement she suddenly feels. She must come across as a girl who hasn't been fucked for years — and in a way that's how it is, in fact; she realises that the clients from The House have literally passed over her without changing anything in her appetite or her capacity to experience pleasure, even when she came home aching from being held so much, her groin burning, dreaming of a TV series and a döner kebab. After having treated her pussy as a tool, she's been beset by the desire to be seduced and also to seduce, to be part of this bacchanal between normal people. It was like a reawakening of Hildie within herself, she became Martha again, the 25-year-old Martha with a devilish libido and eyes that went all gooey as soon as she went anywhere near a boy she liked the look of. And for entire days, the fantasy of this stranger stayed with her as she lay in the arms of clients, who she spurred with her heels for her own entertainment while thinking of the boy she'd never see again.

Hildie purrs, mouth full of this tongue, while looking for comparisons; it's as if she'd walked through a rain shower under an umbrella large enough to keep her dry to the tips of her toes. It's as if she'd been a painter-decorator and was suddenly giving herself over to her vocation of oil painting on monumental canvases.

I *feel* all that, marvels Hildie as he lowers her jumpsuit to her waist. It's as if I've been in a cage, she thinks now, conscious that her metaphors are becoming more and more extravagant as he undresses her. I *feel* the cold, I *feel* his hands.

She also feels, as she sits on him, the extreme stiffness of this hard-on. It has nothing in common with the calm hardness of cocks that know they'll end up all warm inside a girl, because that's what they're there for. It's an erection that's been readying itself since they left behind the world for this far corner of the forest that doesn't even appear on maps of Berlin, and it lays across his stomach, compressed painfully by his belt. Hildie rubs herself against it angrily, eyes rolled back, face turned up towards the sky riddled with stars. She feels like she's climbing a tree, a living tree breathing beneath her and accompanying her movements with its warm, responsive branches. Now she's left her matrix of indifference, information is coming at her from all directions, right in her face, without her brain – normally in a state of constant watchfulness – being able to process a single one of them; she's fully there, stupid, dazed by excitement, astride the thigh he's bent up for her, feeling only the damp skin between his thighs and the throbbing beat of her heart in her clitoris. Whatever's left in her head that is cold and calculating whispers to her that underneath her is a hard cock, a cock that will no doubt have to be sucked – but saying it, Hildie within Martha no longer has the indifferent tone of a professional. Memories from before The House assail her; she knows he's going to breathe harder when she lets him out of his trousers, that he will close his eyes, in a swoon, when she rubs her cheek against him, and will open them again suddenly when he feels her teeth grazing the length of his cock – the dread of being bitten, the almost unreal thirst to be swallowed. And when she sticks out the end of her tongue to trace slowly, very slowly, the beating vein to the end of his cock, he'll let out this exasperated whistle at the idea he might come too quickly; raising her eyes towards him, Hildie will see him suspended over what her lips have in store for him. When she opens her mouth wide to take all of him in, then wraps him as if in a warm cover, he'll let out a gasp and his back will lurch, his fingers will plunge into her loose hair in order to roll them up in his fist, not daring to pull, not yet. She'll hear him sigh *Oh fuck* while she slides her lips up and down, suddenly swallowing him right up to his bollocks, astounded at being able to take him in so far, and to realise that the feeling of suffocation, the gag reflex, far from oppressing her, is like the spasm of a pussy getting ready to come – the rush of saliva and tears, the warmth spread across her whole face. And there below, between her thighs, the intolerable feeling of lack that makes her flesh beat like a drum.

'I didn't bring a condom,' Hildie gasps against his torso, thinking of the stack she turned her nose up at as she left home, for reasons that seemed legitimate to her then – she didn't imagine they could get to this point in the Görli, she didn't imagine the Görli would even have a place remote enough for them to be able to exchange anything more than discreet caresses. He's been less subtle, or more farsighted; he takes a condom out of his pocket and she hurries to tear it open, clumsily, as if the secret of life itself might spill out of it. Ridiculously short-breathed. She slips it on him with her mouth, as she was taught to do by one of her friends who was taking her car to go and get sucked off by a transvestite, in a tawdry part of Potsdamer Strasse, at a moment when fucking and despair were one and the same.

Hildie's let go of his cock, which, exposed to the chill of the woods, hasn't lost an iota of its stiffness. Now she sniffs him from every angle, as if he were a rare delicacy. The long thighs, the flat stomach, the wide torso where the ribs surface, the armpits she exposes in an imperious gesture so she can bury her nose in them, the damp hair that covers him. And straddling him, supported on her heels, she impales herself very slowly, all her muscles contracted around his cock. The star-prickled sky casts a shadow in her rolled-back eyes. In her throat, storms are coming into being, a cathartic need to cry out, that this is real, that this means something. For the first time in three years, two months, seven days and a handful of hours, Hildie looks at the boy beneath her, attentively. He's caught in a puddle of light and she feels engulfed by darkness, in total impunity; but the moon has slipped away between the branches of the large lindens providing a roof over them, and as she's watching his beautiful, tortured face, the prominent jaws of a man who is suffering and won't cry out, he sees this searing gaze of a drunk witch, her heavy eyelids almost entirely covering her dilated pupils. It's a world in black and white, but he guesses that in daylight, between her half-open lips, her teeth would look like a ribbon of pearls, and all this creamy flesh undulating above him would have the rosy pinkness of very young girls.

At the first impact against the walls of her lower belly, Hildie knows she's going to come. It's incredible, unthinkable, but at the base of her spine she makes out that unmistakable heaviness. Before she can warn him, before she can prepare herself for this spectacular lift-off, Hildie is thunderstruck by an orgasm so powerful that she's paralysed, mouth open in a mute cry. The improbability of the thing, its nigh-on immediacy bring tears of amazement to her eyes. Raising her face to the sky, fingernails driven into the forearms of the man who's looking at her, unmoving beneath her, Hildie slowly empties her lungs in a ragged yelp – birds right by them take sudden flight, out of the instinctive fear of dogs and then of gunshots.

Collapsing back on him, dishevelled, Hildie realises that his thighs, his stomach are soaking wet; the cock he slid inside her, and is continuing to move with his hands gripping her hips, makes a lapping sound – and Hildie suddenly understands. She understands that she really has come, it's just happened to her here, on this man, in this dark woodland probably littered with fag ends, and she feels a strange embarrassment in the idea that it could be so easy, that this ease at coming with the first man who doesn't pay her has something so stupidly Pavlovian about it... And as he arches his back to get deeper inside, Hildie feels that it's going to start again, a waterfall comes out of her and she can hardly stammer a few indistinct words before the world suddenly goes dark. He makes her sway against him, they're wrapped around one another, swaying to the same clockwork rhythm, beneath the same warm shower. Hildie can no longer stop herself from coming, three times, four times; she's not even aware he's laid her out in a clump of ferns and is fucking her with great furious thrusts.

'We have to see each other again,' he moans in her ear; he grabs her thighs with both hands as he comes too, and his moan comes to her through the cotton wool filling her ears, like the only manifestation of a world that's been temporarily annihilated, only continuing to exist around her genitals, their inextricably conjoined genitals.

When they wake up, the silence is total. The moon's come out from behind the clouds and is draping Hildie and Ian in a blueish halo. The ground is not littered with fag ends, not even a beer can to remind them how near they are to the Görli, but the ground beneath them is soaked. Ian smiles; he's beautiful, his teeth are beautiful, he's not as young as he seems in the dark and it's even better. Hildie realises she could fall in love with him, that she probably already has: she has trouble distinguishing between love and extreme lustfulness, which is still, after this avalanche of orgasms, gripping her by the throat – her pussy is sending her brain signals that resemble tenderness, burning waves of gratitude. The same drunkenness as with men she loves is slowing and deepening her breathing – Hildie looks for his lips, which he tends towards her with the face of a very sleepy child. On his fingers, which she's sucking ardently, is a smell of cigarettes and the lightly woody musk of her pussy. If he was in a hurry to button himself back up and rush away on the pretext of having a morning meeting, Hildie wouldn't have this strange fear, this feeling of an imminent crash. It would be much simpler if Ian was an asshole brimming with self-satisfaction at having had her, and she could leave for home largely convinced she'd made herself come all by herself. But while they're coming back towards the park, without daring to take each other by the hand, catching each other's eye at regular intervals, Ian asks:

'How did that happen?'

'What just took place?'

'Yes.'

'I don't know. To be honest, it's never happened to me.'

'Give over!'

'You don't have to believe me, but I swear it's true.'

Indeed, how could he believe that a girl like Hildie, who sends the kind of messages she does and takes such initiatives, has come like that for the first time? At the same time, she thinks, both judge and jury, why would a woman make that up? The naked truth is magnificent: she came because she liked him, because she chose him, because a part of her life has just flown away, and because she hadn't fucked for a thousand years.

They get to the middle of the park, where the orange street-lamps make it seem like daylight.

'Wait,' says Ian, spinning her around to face him. 'Wait, let me look at you.'

He smiles at her again, and Hildie, who for three years has protected the power of her blue eyes as if they were her only valuable possession, instinctively looks away. Ian grabs hold of her chin, forces her with the violent gentleness of people from the normal world – who really do have some strange customs. She would have loved not to see, in this light, in his gaze, that he finds her beautiful and that he is beautiful.

'I have to go,' she murmurs as she heads away from him, and they are both surprised to find themselves retracing their steps back to each other, as if they already missed each other.

Their swaying kiss, endless, takes their breath away. Hildie feels that Ian is hard against her again. She frees herself painfully from his grasp, almost runs towards the alley leading to the street, to her apartment, to her fiancé who thinks she's at a girls' dinner. Out of the darkness surges a weed dealer who greets her in a low voice; he and his friends saw how Ian was holding the nape of Hildie's neck, with such sexual fervour, and they're laughing. 'Nice evening, Madam?'

Hildie knows she stinks of sex. That the smell of sex is all over her, caught in her thick hair, in the damp folds of her, impossible to locate but everywhere, like a ring of smoke.

'What are you playing at?' she whispers to herself as she trots into her street. 'What the hell are you doing?'

And in the anguish that assails her, in her delicious weariness of a loved-up woman, there's a morbid joy in thinking that her entire life could explode within five minutes, because of the ungraspable smell of this man whose surname she doesn't even know.

June 2014

Right in the west, just behind the Schwarzes Café where my sisters cheerfully hold court, is Schlüterstrasse and its lovely squat buildings; and you have to really love Haussmann, like Parisians do, to prefer those of our capital. Le Manège occupies the whole first floor of number forty-seven of this noble street. More or less two hundred square metres you can't see from the outside. Only a well-practised eye would notice from the outside that the curtains are always drawn — and that the only window is letting out a mauve, slightly gaudy light, a true brothel light.

You have to give one thing to Le Manège, aside its pretentious French name, and that's the talent of its interior designer. When you've read too much De Maupassant as a kid, too many descriptions of brothels that, on Sunday evenings, bring together entire villages under one dubious roof, you're very likely to be impressed by the superficial opulence employed here. They fully had me, at least, with the smell alone: a head-turning mix of white flowers and musk. You have to picture a vast apartment cleverly divided into a myriad of rooms all leading as if by magic to one or the other bar — and even the corridors exhale this intoxicating fragrance and this bourgeois humidity, right into the shadowy corners where the clients and the girls stand discussing costs and options in very low voices. I was as impressed as a hillbilly, right out. The girls were beautiful; no, not beautiful, *splendid*, all perched up on dizzying heels. I was there, sitting ingratiatingly on a sofa in the little salon, the one where the girls were waiting for the clients, with this stupid smile that I have all my life believed would bring me friends and that has clearly had the opposite effect. I didn't feel intimidated by the girls or the décor, at least not in any visible way, because I was jabbering away with the brothel madam, smoking fag after fag; but that evening, and for the two weeks I worked at Le Manège, I basely let myself be flattered by a whole host of details that concealed the classic dysfunctions of brothels. The daily life of a whore is not improved or softened by a pretty wallpaper or a cleverly placed lamp; but sometimes the cage is so cute you could almost forget the rest. You fall asleep, like elderly cats, fleeing lazily into dark corners when their master is in a bad mood.

And it was the master I was to meet this first evening; Milo, an Albanian who, someone told me hesitantly, after I'd stupidly asked if he was nice, *could* be. And in the end, I didn't see him straightaway; I had time, before that, to ask the question five times of five different girls. I remember Micha, the youngest, the most slender, looking left and right before replying, without frankly any assurance or enthusiasm.

'Yes, he's okay.'

'Is this a good place?'

'Yes, yes. It's okay.'

In Le Manège I used up all the questions I came with as an innocent newbie, and I received replies that would feel truly scandalous to me today. Like the disdainful frown from the housekeeper when I asked her if certain clients had particular fantasies: 'I make sure everything goes okay, that they finish on time and that the client pays. But I don't want to know what's going on in the bedrooms.'

She wafted her arms around her to signify that any possible confessions would inconvenience her as much as a bad smell. Aside from the housework and the supervising, this young woman took care of the following tasks: welcoming the clients, showing them around, gathering the harem back together and organising the introductions. Noting the clients' choices or guessing, from someone's clumsy descriptions, which of the six or twenty girls had caught his eye. Notifying the lucky chosen one and scrupulously recording her name in the register, the duration, which room. Taking payment, whether in cash or by card. Seeing out the doubly relieved client, making sure he's happy, but before that, and most importantly, with the diligence and punctuality of a governess, going to knock on the door of the bedroom, five minutes before the allotted time is up.

A brothel can't function without strict rules. You don't need to have worked in one to understand that it's more complicated to manage about twenty girls, with their hormones and their beautiful bodies as their way of making a living, than fifty waitresses. On top of the general commandments common to all, each brothel grants and limits freedoms at whim, each hones its own internal methods of working. Both the girls and the clients are quick to sniff out whether men or women are in charge. You can feel whether it's a place where the girls are ruled by an iron rod or whether they're seen as independent workers whose sensitivities are to be taken into account.

Girls at Le Manège never really arrive in their civilian clothes; thousands of details give them away at the top of their lungs. You'd think they were always in-between two shopping jaunts on Avenue Montaigne, these little Ukrainians weighed with shopping bags, holding, at the end of rhinestone leashes, improbable Maltese bichons called Treasure or Darling.

'You can make a lot of money here, if you're responsible,' the Hausdame tells me on the first night. 'But most girls spend it all. Sometimes they tell me they're struggling to pay their rent! I don't understand how that's possible.'

The only thing that's obligatory for working at Le Manège are heels. It's by their height and their instep that you can recognise a whore. Otherwise, the girls are left free to their own sartorial whims — as long as they play fair and don't expose more flesh than their colleagues. No fine lingerie, but ultra-short dresses, shorts, a whole festival of legs on display, lined by stocking seams. But would you concur that the girls at Le Manège are, as it says on the website and the business card, the most beautiful in Berlin? Believe me when I say that when I arrived I thought they were all beautiful. The type of women whose swaying hips inspire dirty thoughts and unplanned spending. Bearing all those cheap trimmings you wouldn't wear in the murkiest Paris club, the trowel-thick make-up barely concealing poor, sensitive complexions, synthetic materials shaping arses so much that you can't even see the folds of flesh, outrageously long extensions riveted to skulls to compensate for hair too fine or too lifeless… Something fiery and full of life, doused in this illusion of beauty that is so tenuous, that goes up in smoke when you look at it too close up, leaving only the smell of naked meat.

It won't come as a surprise to anybody that this career may be the one in which your virginity is taken away the most quickly. I'm talking about the innocence that inheres in thinking it's easy to sit around for eleven hours waiting for a client on the promise of receiving a monthly salary of around five thousand euros. And if, like me, you have a book waiting to be written, and more than half of these hours totally free, that seems a totally fair exchange. But god knows that during these two weeks of work at Le Manège, it's not writing I'm busy with. A certain modesty – snobbery, perhaps – keeps me from getting a notebook out and writing. Fear, too… The vague fear of someone seeing me making notes and of getting caught out in the middle of my investigation. That, but more than that, one undeniable fact: when you're surrounded by girls playing on their mobiles or making calls, it's hard not to get sucked into this cycle of laziness, all warm and cosy on Le Manège's sofas. How many packets of grilled nuts? How many *Apfelschorle* snarfed to pass the time? The whore's job is all about patience.

When he phoned me the next day and I brought up Le Manège for the first time, Stéphane must have stifled a certain feeling of guilt.

Five months earlier, as we were crossing Skalitzerstrasse having a massive conversation about prostitution, I talked about an article on whores in Paris: in certain neighbourhoods, and with the right management, girls were turning eight to ten tricks a day.

'That's okay!' I exclaimed. 'I'm sure I can manage that many, give or take.'

'You have no idea what you're talking about,' sighed Stéphane in reply. 'Ten guys, that's a huge amount.'

'I'll find out, if I go and work in a brothel.'

'Stop being stupid,' he replied in that cutting tone that sometimes gives him such a fatherly air. 'You laugh, but you wouldn't last two days in a brothel.'

I'm as ignorant as he is of how big a role bravado is playing in propelling me into this project. I no longer feel I have the naive audacity I had at twenty. So many things have happened since then. But for Stéphane, I am and always will be that young and unpredictable animal sent half mad by her soaring hormones and brand-new breasts. And I imagine the reproaches he must have directed at himself after hanging up, knowing his young mistress was in a brothel without a chaperone several thousand kilometres away.

Legal in Germany, prostitution is subject to a strict rule – the same one freelancers must adhere to – *Selbständig*. It's not a profession where you can do anything you want, whether you're at the top or the foot of the ladder. The girls, like the brothel itself, have to scrupulously declare their income – and even with all the honesty in the world (as rare in this milieu as others), the Finanzamt makes frequent raids, turning over brothels and bringing them to a standstill while searching for hidden cash and non-declared bedrooms. It's complicated for a girl, even pretty, even educated, to work without being registered at the Bürgeramt and without having a taxpayer number. Simple-minded types like me, who never imagine having to deal with an accountant or queue at the Finanzamt for the simple and good reason that they're working in a job no one wants to do, are very soon forced to think again. Unless they work in the street and in the pay of some mafia, nobody can count on banking cash that the state will never see.

The Hausdame on my first shift is a woman of about sixty-five, speaking an East German that is difficult to understand, and surly as hell – answering to the name of Jana.

I'm only slightly surprised to find myself face to face with this shrill specimen who runs the show with an iron fist, with her moods as changeable as an ageing cocker spaniel's and an admirable propensity to smoke silently in the darkness of the deserted small salon. It's 7 o'clock; for now there's only her and me. Two other girls live in the brothel, in the dorm offered to workers who need it, but they stay in their room until eight, only coming out for something to drink or to respond when the sound of the doorbell tells them a client might have arrived.

I named myself Justine, just like that, without thinking too much about it: a choice that would have delighted Valentine if we were still talking, because it was her pseudonym when aged eighteen we played at being escorts. Justine – because it was easy, and because of De Sade. Even though I explained the reference to her, Jana looked at me without blinking: 'No one knows that.' But this initial J, which Germans can't pronounce properly, has an exoticism that delights her, a sort of impenetrable charm evoking the Pigalle district – which she's never seen – or Ali Baba's cave: money, in other words. I'm certainly not the first to have waved the French flag; but in this gaggle made up of Sophie, Michelle, Sylvie and Gabrielle, I'm the first to have dared take on a consonant as cunning as this cursed J. Anyway, in Le Manège, my nationality served me very well; having never met me, the owner took me on on the simple basis that French women have secrets in the bedroom that other women clumsily attempt to copy.

A quick clarification about the rates charged at Le Manège. Having designated itself an 'upmarket' brothel, Le Manège charges the highest rates of any brothel in Charlottenburg – of which there are many. This rate includes one act of penetration, one orgasm (an hour gives a client the right to come a maximum of twice – if he dares); and at Le Manège clients can also get, if they have enough money, one of the infamous kisses on the lips (twenty euros) that according to legend are taboo with whores, a blow job without a condom (another twenty euros), and all sorts of fantasies not outlined by the management and that each girl is free to accept or not. The extras are a supplement that the brothel doesn't touch a cent of, even if, for reasons that escape me, the girls have to declare it to the Hausdame.

An additional benefit is the bar, provided the customer drinks champagne and drinks it with the girl. Equally, the rooms on offer don't all cost the same. The first rates listed only apply to the three simplest rooms (even if they're luxurious in their way – or that's not the right word, but the right word eludes me); the four other rooms, thanks to their size, the showiness of their furniture or their hi-tech equipment (I'm thinking about the broken jacuzzi in Room Five or the dripping shower in the Junior Suite, which could hold three horses or a whole herd of clients and girls), come at a supplement of a hundred and fifty euros, of which the girls receive a percentage. If fate blows in a client who wants to down a bottle in a room with a jacuzzi and to pay for a whore who'll kiss him on the mouth or whatever, will suck him off without a condom and take it up the arse – that client can calculate for himself the price of a good evening. But there's still no question of leaving before your obligatory eleven hours of shift, however much you earn. In truth, it's the clients who decide the end of the night shift. And clients who drink, or who drink and take coke, have the potential to keep a brothel open until noon.

That's why at the beginning I tried to start as early as possible – before realising that in the daytime the place was as dead as those round-the-clock casinos that Berlin teems with. In the daytime, the clients know that only two or three girls are there, and often not those they'd want. The profusion of evening is much more attractive.

*

On the first day I'm joined at 8 o'clock in the evening by Gabrielle, a tall Bulgarian who is always buried in her phone and who, after wondering if I was there to work or run the bar, gratifies me with a vague *Hello* – end of our communication. Shortly afterwards, Michelle and Nicola arrive: two Ukrainian sisters you'd say were barely eighteen but who are actually twenty-seven and twenty-eight. This evening, Michelle is returning from a client's hotel room, arms laden with sweets and chocolates. She and her sister have between them a few regulars – not many – who constantly encourage them to eat. Because contrary to what you might think, being slim is not that important in a brothel; or rather, if they give the illusion of being slim, when they're hidden away under a dress and perched up on heels that make them look like foals, once they're naked and prone, these skinny beans invoke slight pity as well as the fear you'll break them in two. Vulnerable as they are in this fragile state that makes them seem barely old enough for sex, they give clients more of a desire to feed them than to subject them to the demonic rides inspired by the truly flesh-and-blood whores with strong backs.

Between Gabrielle and the two sisters, we represent quite a broad palette, none of us really competing with the others. And contrary to my expectations, the two little ones reply to all my questions about the brothel's workings. I'm making a strong coffee for them when the first bell of the evening, the starting gun for my career, sounds.

A man with a physique so ordinary you wonder if it's even legal, in his early forties, slightly bald on top – after having promised myself I'd remember everything, here I am not even remembering the name of my first client. Rick? David? What the hell was the name of this holidaying Canadian who'd never before set foot in a brothel? We were each as clumsy as the other in huge Room 3, with its outsize four-poster and its marble fireplace. Because once the client is hooked, the hardest bit starts – for me at least.

You can fritter away five minutes on polite chit chat, and then what? If the guy's never before been with a whore, he's also paying for not making the first move. It's partly thanks to this random Canadian that I perfected my means of attack – talking nonsense while climbing casually onto the bed, and, without breaking my monologue, throwing my dress right across the room. But even when I'm stark naked, the game isn't yet won; the newbie's never been further away from taking possession of a nudity that quite literally confounds him with anxiety. It's not hard to imagine his Cornelian dilemmas: does he really want to fuck? Wasn't the idea of being able to enough? How to get a hard-on, here, and why? No doubt they feel a bit stupid for spending one hundred and twenty euros on a bad fuck, and a quick one, with a girl whose job it is to drop her knickers ten times a day.

And indeed, once the guy has undressed (at top speed, with a few embarrassed sniggers), I find myself in front of a timorous erection onto which it's very difficult to slip the regulatory condom. If sleeping with a guy in whom one feels as much interest as a broken strip light can be deemed unpleasant, the idea that this same guy then slows things down because of some dysfunction is the height of unpleasantness. Whereas this guy could turn the situation to his advantage by starting out with a solid, enthusiastic erection. Because – it's as simple as that – once you're lying down against some man or other, it's very easy to forget his face and only see this common denominator that puts them all in the same huge shopping basket. Even if no two cocks look the same, that part of the body is uniformly likeable and amenable enough. And unleashes fewer reactions of terror than certain faces. A wedding ring gleaming around a ring finger is also reassuring – it puts things in context. As banal, as lacking in sensuality as a man may be, the idea that somewhere in this world a woman contents herself with him, even enjoys him without any money changing hands, gives you hope that not all is lost.

There we are facing each other on the outsize bed, drowning in an embarrassed silence, against a background of the girls' clucking in the salon. In my head, the as-yet unused cogs of my brain as a loose woman are turning at top speed; don't go too fast; don't hurry things along, even if it's a tempting idea, because no one wants to spend their time sitting staring someone in the face. And above all, no one wants to get to the point of having to consummate the second act included in the rate, not out of laziness but because the second will always be harder work, slowed down by the anguish of coming too slowly or not at all, and constantly threatened by complete failure brought about by the problem of having to race against the clock to climax.

But you don't even have to get to this point for it to become hard work. In this example alone: the Canadian tries so hard to hold back and does it so well that in the end he can't come. Between the first contrite embrace and Jana's imperious rapping at the door, there's a moment when he feels in charge of his erection to the point where he can stop and ask me if he can fuck me up the arse. Uncertainly I tell him the price, convinced he'll give up on this fantasy. But whether it's because sodomy is rare even in couples, or because money stops being a problem when you have a rampant hard-on reaching up to your navel, he doesn't panic at having to get out another hundred euros to take me up the behind. On the contrary, my giving him a price – and hence permission – makes it a bit more real. But by the time I've got myself into the right position, his nascent erection has collapsed. Without much hope, I try everything in my power, somewhat impatiently. We're at the point of writing each other off when Jana knocks.

It's hard to tell a man he won't come, for all the trying. I have the professional guilt that beginners do. But the Canadian doesn't hold it against me. I imagine he leaves a bit depressed for his hotel room somewhere between Friedrichstrasse and the Gendarmemarkt, the golden triangle of businessmen, and lets me off the hook by finishing by hand what I began with the best will in the world. By concluding that he'd gain nothing from this investment or this whole disappointing interlude. Back in Toronto or god knows what part of English-speaking Canada he comes from, he will be able to tell his friends that he went to a brothel and treated himself to the rights over a pleasant young Frenchwoman who didn't rule out any of her three openings.

I imagine that the ending would have been slightly remastered.

That's how I began my career and this book at Le Manège, cosy and warm in the extravagant luxury of this vast apartment, without ever freeing myself of a feeling that a trap was slow closing in on me. I very quickly got scared and started losing sleep to the angst caused by having had eyes bigger than my stomach. The fact that almost all the owners and girls came from the former Eastern bloc didn't help in giving a feeling of legality; I was inhabited by almost constant visions of an Albanian brothel I'd be sent to after having my passport stolen. The danger could come from almost anywhere: from the owners, the girls, the clients, from the impassive handyman Maximilian. I lived in terror of the writer or journalist in me being seen right through – and like in certain nightmares, I told myself nothing would happen to me as long as I didn't show I was terrified.

Yet it didn't take me long to display a reaction bordering on horror. After the Canadian, the evening was looking dead as a dodo. No client in sight, not even the same two or three who came every day. All the girls – a dozen of them – were spread around the big introduction room. Voluble little groups of Bulgarians, of Romanians fending off boredom on their mobiles, their discussions impenetrable – to me at least, alone on the sofa, chain-smoking.

Around 2 o'clock in the morning, exhaling one last sigh, I told Michelle and Nicola I was leaving soon. It was surprising how time seemed to slide over them without ever making them weary, without giving rise to anything more than a migration to the other end of the salon.

In the corridor I bumped into the Hausdame, who was filling the shelves with towels.

'I thinking I'll head off,' I chanced timidly.

She let out a short laugh.

'Ah no, that's not how it works,' she replied, and at once my fears resurfaced, stronger than ever, of a military brothel in Albania, my stolen passport and the explanations I wouldn't have time to give to my heartsick family, frightened half to death. Only Arthur and Stéphane knew about this —and only the bare minimum — and the latter would have to turn his embassy in London upside down to get me out of there — and in what state? My heart started to beat like a drum, and I bleated, 'Ah okay,' when she continued:

'A shift lasts eleven hours. Normally, you have to stay until four in the morning.'

'But there are no clients, and there are too many girls.'

'Still. That's how it works.'

'Fine. No worries.'

But I must have looked so helpless that she caught up with me in the corridor.

'Listen, if you want, I'll ask the owner.'

I didn't stop her, but a shadow over her face, in her voice, clearly showed the embarrassment this favour caused her.

I don't know why I was allowed to leave early. I never saw Milo grant the slightest favour to anyone, far from it. I lost count of the times when one of the four Hausdamen came back from the little salon where Milo, his business partner and an assortment of other henchmen drank and talked until the early hours, fat cigars in their mouths; she gestured with a finger for one of the girls — often the same ones, often *the* same one — because Milo wanted to speak to her. I don't know what was going on in the heads of the girls in question, but they had the attitude of prisoners being unfairly sent to face a firing squad. Sometimes Milo came out in person to chat in one corner with a girl. He talked to all of them in the same language. I never understood a single word, but you didn't need to be a polyglot to grasp the contents of the sermon. Milo's attention was directed mainly at Gabrielle and Micha. Micha: a little gem who was often alone, from Romania, who looked sixteen and who, at nineteen, was indeed the youngest in Le Manège. The look of a beaten puppy, mistrustful but kindhearted, with smiles full of dimples. The other girls, some also Romanian, never sat with her. I don't think the management held her in very great esteem either, because even during introductions Micha retained her furious air of a teenager dragged away from a Facebook conversation (which she must have been), and in the evenings, when men arrived with the notion of being seduced over a glass of wine, she had a stupefying talent for disappearing into dark corners and reappearing once the client had settled on another girl. In short, she showed very little appetite for business. Milo told her off almost every night without her renouncing her stubborn look, ever, and it was the same when Sandor, the vivacious partner, attempted to talk to her much more gently.

Perhaps they let me leave because I'd had the only client of the evening. Or because I was French and because Le Manège had to manage the hype about this improbable windfall. Perhaps so as not to alienate my goodwill as a beginner, or at least what remained of it.

Going home, I already had, etched into my brain, a catalogue of fears that were all to some degree well-founded. I had all the cards in hand to justify never going back. Yet I went back the next day, and the day after that, and almost every day for two weeks. Because in one evening I'd understood everything that had inspired such sad books about prostitution. And also out of pride, because it was out of the question that I produce a naive or miserabilist book, or even worse, a book that only touched on one facet of this work; I'd convinced myself there would be something beautiful or funny to write, even if I had to scrape away at it from every angle. I hoped that my voice would humanise the reality of prostitution – because books have this power – even if I was the only one fighting for this lie.

Had I never known Le Manège, I would never have been able to appreciate the humanity of The House, which infused this book with a new light. And had I been stubborn, had I'd stayed at Le

Manège alongside Milo and his sad-eyed harem, I would have written a terrible book, saying the same old things. And maybe written it in Albania.

Manège alongside Milo and his sad-eyed harem, I would have written a terrible book, saying the same old things. And maybe written it in Albania.

'THERE ARE LOTS OF PLACES LIKE THAT in Charlottenburg,' Jana tells me – Jana who never uses the word brothel. 'But this is the best one. Everywhere else, the girls are crying out for help.'

So there are obviously worse places than Le Manège, to the point where working for Milo feels like a mercy by comparison. At T…, for instance, the management recently introduced a flat rate, which basically means in one hour the client has the right to come as many times as humanly possible – or at least to try to. Compared to that regime, Jana's little iron fist must seem like a blessing. At T…, equally, girls have been sacked for refusing to give blowjobs without a condom. Each brothel has its own hell. At Le Manège, for me it's the waiting – endless, abrasive. Boredom affects us much more than we think. Bring together ten girls who feel a cordial indifference towards one another, trap them together without any kind of fixed salary and with their only common denominator the feeling of wasting their beautiful youth in a scandalous fashion; by the time the first client shows up, unaware of the financial manna and hope he represents, you've created a riot of hysterical females. That's how bitterness and jealousy take seed; the exceptional scarcity of clients. That irritates the owner, who irritates the Hausdame, who spreads an impalpable, simmering tension around the sulking girls. On certain days, if not all the time, it's best to not go near Jana, and each of her blazing, grumbling comings and goings, arms laden with full and empty bottles, makes the girls lower their heads as if a spell has been cast on them. If she doesn't have much to do, Jana holes up near the bar with her radio or takes over the bed in Room Six, which looks out onto the salon, to keep an eye on us; there, she gets out her tablet and distracts herself from her bad mood by watching some German talk show, surrounded by two mobiles and a landline – you never know, someone may call?

When frustration starts to torment her again, she leaves her refuge and joins us on the sofas to smoke her fifty-ninth Pall Mall and tell us about the unspeakable hassles she'll have to endure to get back to Steglitz: bus M49, which is often early, and which she'll have to wait twenty minutes for if she misses hers, and please god don't let it be raining like yesterday, because she couldn't sleep all night long, and yet this morning here she was, changing sheets, a chore she could easily have got out of seeing that there were no clients, not a single one, what a load of shit, what a hellhole!

As in any job, it's motivation that palls, quickly. You start out with the idea of smashing all the records and you end up feeling an immense laziness, to the point that the first soul who strays in becomes a nuisance, disturbing the unhealthy tranquility. What clients see when they arrive in the large salon doesn't change from one evening to the next: bunches of girls all turning weary faces in their direction, like a fragmented colony of meerkats. An army of iPhones make their noses glow fluorescent-blue. The house music would be bearable if someone was dancing – but nobody is, and the ambiance recalls that of a provincial disco with ideas above its station, struggling to motivate its staff. A few girls get a vague glimpse of the clients and leg it, silently – knowing they'll be lectured later by Milo, who's dragging despairingly on his cigar in the small salon yet seems to have his eyes everywhere. It's because it's a tortuous process to win a client in a brothel like Le Manège; you have to present yourself in a sufficiently eye-catching way to be offered a drink and replace the fifteen other candidates one way or another. But nothing guarantees this girl that she'll end up taking the client into a bedroom. It's not always easy to tell the difference between the men who come to fuck and those who come for a flirty drink – and from whom a girl won't extract more than twenty euros. This isn't a risk that Le Manège's occupants are inclined to take. Getting trapped with a waffler is depriving yourself of the chance to end up with a less easily pleased client. And then if, by luck, you do end up working one way or another, the waiting starts all over again once the client has left, but worse this time, because you have to deal with post-coital fatigue, the lure of a restorative nap.

You might think that this free time would encourage intellectual activities or conversations between the girls. But you can't put Wifi in a place like Le Manège and hope for an atmosphere of frank camaraderie. And it never entered my head to open a book when we were vegetating in one or other of the salons. The only time I was bold enough to do that, I'd brought along a huge Paul Nizon anthology, given to me at Christmas by my German grandmother; and I realised then that literature can, sometimes, be more irritating than idleness. That day, I swung between the desire to speak to the girls and the fear of not knowing how to go about it; and it seemed obvious to me that cutting myself off from this micro-society with something as pretentious as a book wouldn't help me create bonds with them. I never discovered the right tone to elicit confidences from them. One evening, when I asked the two sisters whether some clients tried to make them do things together, I don't think they really understood me – Michelle replied that it all depended on the money; and in her eyes there was no trace of the repulsion that the idea of going down on your sister, or even snogging her, inspires in most mortals. Either I was too perverse for the simplistic and commercial eroticism of this place, or quite the opposite: vice was so deeply rooted in these girls that the taboo of incest ceased to be one when there was a price on it – but I doubt it. Up to a certain point, it's possible to ask anything of Le Manège's occupants without eliciting from them anything more than a frown. It has to be said that in a brothel where you can get hold of cocaine with a click of the fingers, the girls are used to all extravagances. Nothing can really unravel them; they learned, a long time ago, not to expect any help from the owners or the Hausdamen, whether physical or psychological. Inside their heads are padlocked cabinets where they pile up memories of clients who were too drunk or too off their heads to touch them or talk to them nicely, memories of being held too brutally or of degrading fantasies – darker corners than any of the alcoves of Le Manège in which the smells of rancid sweat, dirty cocks, tongues paralysed by poor champagne, dissolve, only to flood back out in the middle of nightmares and moments of solitude that no happy thought can penetrate.

I'd have liked to be able to penetrate, if only superficially, these solitary, grumpy spirits, these boudoir secrets that sit so heavy when there's no one hearing them. But it didn't take me long to drive away all interest in me, which was already tiny, on the part of the girls, while winning a certain respect from Milo and Sandor.

On the fourth day I was working there, Le Manège had an influx of clients as unexpected as it was unhoped for. The first has the choice between Gabrielle and me. He can't resist the languorous call of France. Later, I zone out at the bar over a glass of sparkling water, smoking the first fag out of my second packet, when two men come into the salon, taking nervous little steps. The first is a tall bald man in glasses – on the brothel's aesthetic scale, what the girls consider an okay guy, inoffensive looking and with a seemingly decent personality, a bit of a Henry Miller (or Bruce Willis). But not enough to give me the shot of adrenaline necessary to move my arse and go and introduce myself.

When my eyes meet those of his friend, on the other hand, something happens, like a very light humming, and suddenly there's nothing of the whore about me. We look at each other with a feeling that time has stopped, and he looks so like this man who, years ago, I loved so hard, that I forget to smile, petrified, and he comes up to me like little boys come up to little girls, with wide eyes full of an amazed timidity. I look down at my sparkling water to hide the fact I'm blushing, and that must demolish his boldness because when I raise my eyes again, he's at the other end of the bar with his bald friend, ordering gin and tonics. I light another fag and stay where I am, smoothing the seams of my dress; the moment I risk a sideways glance at him, I see his huge long-lashed eyes trained on me. And I swear we look for each other furtively, as if we were in a bar, as if it had never been about money and I was there by chance – until Selma, a young dark-haired Bulgarian, tall as a vine, comes and perches one thigh on my stool. She leans into my ear and, with the murmur of an insightful friend, says:

'Go and talk to him! Go and talk to him, he's looking at you!'

'Really? But the others have already introduced themselves.'

'He doesn't give a shit about the others. He's been looking at you since he arrived.'

In any case it's out of the question not to – unless I want to get a lively earful from Milo, which certain girls love to warn me about. From them or from Ronja the barmaid with her obtuse, bulldog-like face, who's been observing my inertia since this started.

My legs wobble when I get up – the feeling of being observed; no matter how many years go by, I still don't know how to feel different when I'm naked in front of men who from close up or far away remind me of Mister, and this in spite of the disappointments that incandescent lout caused me.

The client sees me approach, something he was about to say to his friend frozen on his lips. 'Delighted to meet you, my name's Justine and I'm from Paris.' His hand is soft and very warm. I ask if they're here for the first time, with growing consciousness of my hair, of the low neckline of my skater dress, of the seam of my tights; none of that seems to have the same dramatic effect on the bald man that is keeping his friend riveted to his stool – and for good reason; it truly feels as if he has dragged the other one into a brothel. They're both from Boston, university friends, and have been living in Berlin for seven years. One is single, that's obvious, but the other, the Mister, undoubtedly has a female partner and that's what all his shyness is about. Too awkward to buy me a drink, and probably unaware of the financial rewards I'd get out of that, he's waiting for the right moment – but is there ever a right moment, for a man in a brothel for the first time, when it comes to reminding a woman she's a whore? I imagine not, even if both sides are there for that. When he takes advantage of a moment of silence to ask me how much I cost, I see from the way he twists his mouth that he has the feeling he's taking advantage of me, and that he's sorry about it. And I too am suddenly embarrassed I work there. In front of men I like, I want only to be an empress.

But the brothel doesn't ruin anything. Quite the opposite. The brothel makes empresses of all the whores. I ask him to follow me and he traces my steps at a respectful distance. My pumps are too big and I'm a bit ashamed that he can see my feet slip out with every step I take. We wait in a shadowy corner for the Hausdame to designate a room for us.

'What's your name?'

We're speaking English, and talking a lot, because I want us to forget the moment when I take money from him; men's money has always embarrassed me.

His name is Mark. He is thirty-eight and has a wife, and has just become father to a little boy. He works in music, without being a musician in any way – admin or publicity, something of that ilk.

When we go into the bedroom, he asks me why I work here. I'm so *fabulous*. I'm a *dream*. He can't believe – like all Germans and many Americans – that prostitution and brothels are illegal in France: it's a difficult reality for me to accept too, especially if I think of our loaded lexicon of swear words: *putain*, *pute*, *bordel*. I say that I'm a writer and that I'm writing about brothels, omitting to explain that I also have rent to pay at the end of the week, and that a week is exactly how long it takes the people at my publishers to reply to my requests for an advance. I explain that it's a secret he mustn't make any noise about, especially here – a pointless warning, because the men who come to the brothel overflow with secrets that you can guess even without them opening their mouth. Mark is one of those who needs to open it, or perhaps he feels he's swapping his secret for mine. Since the child was born, the couple have been in a crisis that the exhilaration of parenthood can't dampen. Yes, he adores his wife, but his wife is a good little girl who can easily do without sex, or who at least doesn't see any urgency to start fucking again, six months after the birth. They argue all the time – this bad patch that people in love go through when they've put everything into having a child. And it's obvious that quite contrary to feeling at ease in a brothel or that he's here for legitimate reasons, Mark has a sense of guilty shame about it.

What are the solutions when you love your wife but need sensuality, need to come? The most sensible is not to take a mistress, who by the very nature of things you'll fall in love with, thanks to the rush of hormones and fresh air she represents. That's how you get yourself in the shit. As it's only about cock and pussy, the most efficient way is undoubtedly to pay a woman to be temporarily nothing but a body. It must be complicated, for gentle, romantic people like Mark, to reduce oneself to something as despicable as a pair of aching balls. And even that doesn't stop you falling in love.

Mark's resemblance to the first love of my life ends with his looks. I've barely straddled him when he comes without a word, without a sound, his teeth sunk into my shoulder; I only realise because he gets soft. Mark says nothing, paralysed by this fiasco that really isn't one, but rather an automatic orgasm, a terrible excess caused by six months of abstinence. We could have had an embarrassing moment of unnecessary apologies, but thank god, the condom had the good taste to slip off. It protrudes from me very cleanly, still full of spunk, not a single drop of which has escaped, thus having done its job perfectly. But many believe, like Mark, that this little piece of latex is an unbreachable armour not only against disease (pregnancy being chief among their worries) but more importantly against the evidence of adultery. Contact with the juices of a woman who isn't their wife, especially when she belongs to everyone, is like a nightmare from which you don't wake up — with a well-earned divine punishment. It doesn't take Mark long to go pale: the feeling of cold air on his cock is enough. I've hardly begun to take the condom out of me when I feel the feverish trembling of the married man who sees his empire exploding like a bubble and can already taste the bitterness of triple therapy in his mouth.

'Sorry,' Mark stutters a dozen times. 'Sorry, I'm really…'

He never finished his sentence, but I completed it in my head with a rage I was careful to conceal: really what, really ashamed? Really dumb? Really messed-up?

We parted on good terms; Mark wanted to see me outside the brothel, have a drink, and I gave him my number. I think I gave him my real name and the title of my book because I'm a coward and because I really wanted to be more than a whore — because despite all my good intentions I suppose I thought I was above all that. I wasn't expecting him to call me, and he didn't for a long time, and even though he was my umpteenth client (you quickly fall into the habit of mixing them all up), I didn't forget how the world melted around us when I kissed him.

'Please, take care of yourself,' he said to me as he went off down the corridor, only holding onto me now by one finger.

'Don't worry. This is a good place,' I lied, while still believing it a little. (And, quietly:) 'Will you come back?'

'Of course I'll come back. It's so *incredible*.'

But Mark, for the ten further days that I spent at Le Manège, didn't come back — and I can't blame him. Despite my pious lies, which were designed to reassure myself as much as him, even a novice like Mark must have latched onto the fact that I was the only one whose smile was sincere enough to hide the vast and sad shadow of the place, its reality.

The period of grace ran out after he left. I was named best employee of the evening, even the week, after my two virtually consecutive clients; and when I went into the small salon to put my two regulation towels in the wash, I heard Sandor having a big chat with Milo, telling him in English that *she,* the French girl, was a good worker. And indeed, if men don't understand much about this work, they understand enough to recognise a goose who lays golden eggs. If I had to shrug off the moodiness of the girls and the Hausdamen several times, none of these guys ever raised their voice at me; quite the opposite, their gazes displayed their surprise at having a girl who was neither reticent nor insolent nor a slacker.

Milo studiously ignored any displays of friendliness. Maximilian, who we called the Ghost, conserved his energy for his job of handyman, able to sort out anything at any hour of the day. The longest-standing girls had, over the years, earned the privilege of addressing him by gentle little nicknames and getting a few sentences out of him – sometimes a smile, which always seemed a bit pained.

Sandor was made of another cloth, of a colourful joviality that had a tendency to turn to a dark anger much more frightening than Milo's constant moroseness: it was the seductive kindness, the propensity for compliments and witty comments that made Sandor an especially useful intermediary between the chief and his harem, as much for tellings off as for encouragement; this same kindness that caused me to mistrust him like a plague. Yet Sandor had set his sights on me; he spoke good French, a bit rusty but full of charming mistakes, and I offered him the chance to practise. As soon as he'd been able to leave his country, he'd travelled, lived almost everywhere and spent years on Boulevard Suchet in Paris, which he evoked with nostalgia, using adjectives full of admiration. He never talked to me about work, and when I was waiting for clients, he came and lit his cigarette beside me after having kissed my hand, and spoke to me of Edith Piaf and Jacques Brel. His wife had left him two years before; he consoled himself in the arms of an ever-changing array of Bulgarians and Ukrainians – quite a nice solution when you're nearly fifty and yourself come from these countries where the women are so beautiful and so cold, when you speak their language. Every night he offered to run me home, an offer I always avoided, my heart racing at the thought that he'd guess my fear, irrational or not, of falling into a fatal trap.

Once Mark had left and the room was tidied up, I went to idle around in an armchair. No one had arrived in the meantime and the girls hadn't moved either. Michelle and Nicola were engrossed by Candy Crush, Selma was in the bar with Ronja, the Ukrainians and the Bulgarians were split into two groups in the annex of the large salon.

At the end of my shift, three guys burst into the corridor. It was almost light, I'd just told Madeleine I was leaving. But half an hour goes by quickly, doesn't it? For fun. For the satisfaction of trumping all the other girls.

It didn't take much; despite being in the middle of putting my clothes back on, I was cunning and looked deep into the eyes of the tallest of the three men in the way I imagine makes me irresistible. And that must be the case, because that's how I won the worst client of my career. I remember everything, especially the look on his face when he pointed a finger at me and said:

'I want to go with you. How much?'

A bit stunned, I announced my prices, thinking that even if he's rude, at least he seems familiar with brothels and may have the good taste to get a hard-on better than the Canadian and to keep it for longer than Mark. He doesn't want a drink, he doesn't want to waste time – he wants to fuck, now, right away.

I would have understood my mistake if I'd looked at Ronja before looking at him, the Greek man: because if Ronja seemed to be constantly and for no particular reason pissed off, she also exchanged knowing looks with the girls to advise them not to attract the attention of certain clients she knew. And she knew these three guys, just as Milo did. But in the end they were clients, and some girl had to attach herself to them. For Le Manège there are no good or bad clients, as long as they pay: *No one wants to know what goes on in the bedroom.*

However, and it can't be by chance, Renate puts us in Room Three, which looks out onto the small salon – onto the men.

The Greek must have a name, but I can't remember it. I started out with the idea of doing my job efficiently and shooting off home, but this rogue, who doesn't speak a word of English, has another plan in mind. After taking his clothes off, he lies on the bed, hands crossed behind his head, making himself at home. And while I, resolute, approach him with a condom in my hand, he gives a gesture and a Germanic groan to convey to me that the object in question won't be of any use. I stand speechless, one thigh on the edge of the bed.

'Cocaine?' he suggests.

What's he talking about, this nutter? We girls can't even have a drink while waiting, and this bedroom is strictly no-smoking, so it's certainly not for snorting coke in either; what on Earth are you thinking…?

'I want some cocaine,' he announces in the tone of a mobster out on the town – and this way of demanding it makes me want to slap him around the head.

I have difficulty repressing that expression of disdain that teens have when they're thinking *'Poor old thing…'* and reply dryly that we don't have any.

'Go and ask your boss.'

Shrugging my shoulders, I leave the bedroom in my knickers, convinced the Greek will soon be kicked out by Albanian feet for his cheek.

'What's happening?'

Milo puts down his cigar, looking concerned all of a sudden.

'Well…'

I approach their little circle and Renate puts down her gin and tonic.

'He told me he wants cocaine.'

I open my eyes wide to clearly display my professional integrity. Milo scratches his chin, thoughtfully. Then a smile lights up his face; he speaks to his factotum, who as per usual is hunched in a dark corner of the salon. He utters a mangled German phrase, at the end of which Maximilian stands up and leaves Le Manège, fag in hand.

The Greek, still lying down, gives me two ragged hundred-euro notes.

'One for you, one for me.'

I'll think of this gram as a tip, once he's off my back. Which is clearly not going to be soon. He pulls out of his jeans the end of a sachet purchased elsewhere and, by my standards, quite enough for the amount of time we have left.

'Make us two lines.'

I understand his basic German dulled by alcohol. And while I'm visibly thinking, he says with his face in my neck:

'Put it all.'

He accompanies this order with a slap on the bum that's more repugnant than any ejaculation in the face – and this gesture alone spells the end of my semblance of good humour. I force myself to adopt a horrible smile behind which beats the impetuous desire to impale him by one means or another, with my bare hands. And I create a kind of straw with one of the hundred-euro notes before making lines, badly, with one of Le Manège's business cards.

The golden rule, when faced with a client who wants to snort coke, is to not take any yourself. Just as when managing a pissed bloke, the solution is definitely not to get pissed too. But when you're getting started, you tell yourself that if faced with an arsehole like this, a line will give you the strength and patience you need to maintain your dignity. The problem: if you act well and don't let your eyes give away that you're feeling like you're being burned alive at the end of a sharp stick, the client may choose to extend the session.

Here I am loaded like a mule. The lines I made were so crazy that the ledge of the hearth looks like a baker's work surface. According to my measures, there are at least four lines awaiting us in this mess, but the Greek cleans everything with the back of his hand and licks the spoils from his palm. He lies back heavily in the middle of the bed, holds an arm out to me. And that's how hell takes over in this Charlottenburg bedroom, except for the few seconds when Renate passes me two grams of unchopped coke through the half-open double door.

It rapidly becomes clear that I'm not to expect to be leapt on in a virile fashion by this guy who's asking nothing more of me than to stay seated beside him, trying to decode his German rumblings tinged with English and a Greek accent. At the start, hoping for a miracle and more and more tempted to make him shut his trap by giving him a hard-on, I fiddle vaguely with his limp dick, which the coke has shrunk. Contrary to what you might think, it's very annoying to spend time with a client who doesn't want to or can't fuck. With a French man – don't quote me – there's a whole host of topics of conversation, and you can get away with it. But try a guy who's so fucked that he doesn't even know which language he's speaking… Cocaine is a bad drug for fucking or sensuality. There will always be people, men and women, who will swear the opposite – that coke gives you a hard-on or increases the libido. The truth is that even if it's possible to get a usable erection and an embarrassing tendency to share your secrets – including sexual ones – it's almost impossible to come after more than one line, and the appetite for socialising withers away as soon as you're getting down to it and letting go. Making love, or receiving pleasure, evokes no more than crass indifference. When the effect wears off, desire doesn't return, far from it – and you don't want to talk any more, just to take some more or to go home. In this precise case, the only 'advantage' of coke resides in the fact that you repeat the same phrases ad infinitum, just said in slightly different ways. The most occult jargon almost starts to make sense.

So I managed to grasp that his conversation turned around one simple topic: his wife. And a half-dozen variations on this theme, without my being able to determine whether his anecdotes were real or fantasy: his wife's best friend who plays with his cock under the restaurant table before they end up having a threesome in a hotel room, his wife falling under the spell of a young waiter on holiday and them ending up having a threesome in a hotel room. In Greece, on a yacht, his wife knowingly caressing herself in front of a young sailor and, what a surprise, them ending up having a threesome in the cabin of the boat. From these adventures, there's probably a moral message to be gleaned: his wife (or the fantasy he has of her) is a bitch. And far from taking umbrage, he encourages her to satisfy her every desire. Here's a subject I can talk about until Renate calls and saves my life! But it's hard to feel involved in a conversation where the laws of reason no longer hold sway. Coherence feels like an exhausting luxury at this point. I very quickly settle into my cruising speed and my vocabulary is limited to *ohs* and *ahs*. He regularly gets up, gets off the bed and stumbles over to the chair where his clothes are. And I tremble with the mad hope that he's suddenly got tired of talking nonsense with a girl who understands nothing and who, by stubbornly working on him, makes him face this impotence once more; but no, he's fine. He's just looking for a banknote in this pocket so I can roll him a cylinder.

'Make us another one?'

While I choke back my desire to jump at his throat, he watches over my shoulder to check that I'm actually making *two* lines.

(Later, a young Spanish girl with expertise in the subject will teach me that there are a thousand and one ways to not take coke while managing the sensitivities of a stoned client; in particular, the very simple trick of letting your hair hang loose down the right side of the line to flick it away. In any situation, it's never good for a whore to lose control, even within a brothel as closely surveyed as Le Manège. It's important that the girls are willing to take coke, but it's also important that they know their limits and stick to them, because none of the management will be there to listen to them sobbing after they've let themselves be fucked without a condom in the harmful euphoria of the moment, or be slapped because they said no.)

I'd have liked to hear the wise words pronounced in the alcoves of the brothel *before* crossing paths with this indefatigable Greek, because by the time Renate knocks on the door, I'm well on the way to catching up with my client in the stoned stakes. Relieved, I mentally formulate some farewells that are much more cordial than I feel. But quicker than a cockroach, the Greek stands up to extend the session, banknotes in hand. The tone he uses tells me I don't really have a choice.

We're on the brink of a fight when Renate sends me to explain to him that he'll be charged for an additional half-hour, not the better-value price for one hour, which is what this infamous tightwad had got into his head. It's clear there's no question of him loosening his grip; I have to go back to the salon completely naked to announce to Milo that the client wants to talk to him – and that's rarely a good sign. During their conversation behind closed doors, I realise that the air here, even though stinking of cigars, is a thousand times more breathable than that of my room, soaked as it is with sickly sweat. I can't hear a sound, and I expect at any moment the din of punches thrown, followed by a howl interspersed by babbling. Sandor tries to fill the silence by making conversation with me.

'Ah, France…!'

Milo ends up coming back out, pursued by the heavy odour of hot, rancid sweat. And immediately sends Renate into the room armed with the credit card machine. She comes out in turn with an expression of extreme disgust and only starts breathing again when the double doors are closed. Yet the way she points her finger to send me back to work carries a hint of pity. Milo and Sandor pretend to look elsewhere.

When I finally throw in the towel, I can't stand the sight of anybody or Le Manège itself. I've snorted almost a whole gram of coke and I'm word perfect on every detail of the Greek's fairytales for adults – over which the coke slides like a caress. Obviously, although I'm the typical customer for this substance, although my social skills increase tenfold under its influence, at no moment did my thousand lines give me any desire to speak; no, I crash-landed in a prison cell for a long and painful comedown with no respite. The closest I come to serenity are these very brief periods of lucidity when I reason with myself, *Come on, calm down you idiot, get a handle on this arsehole, soon you'll be out on Savigny Platz and you'll go for a drink at Schwarzes with Madeleine and between now and then no one wants to hurt you, everything is fine, you're high, that's all. Very high. Extremely high.*

Apart from these internal monologues, which don't help me at all, the simple fact of existing is problematic. All my feelings have turned to hate and, preceding the creating of the lines, the slap on the buttocks administered by the Greek brings a smile so tense to my lips that my teeth could shatter. I continue talking to myself but I'd like not to be able to; I disgust myself.

Renate knocks and, unusually, sticks her head through the half-open door to assure herself everything is okay. The Greek leaps right up, credit card between his shaking fingers. *Good god*, I think, *this monster wants even more.* Wouldn't that be a super-evolved form of torture to break time up like this, to not directly take two hours (because really, really, what better does he have to do before tomorrow evening, this Greek?!), with the perverse aim of seeing my hope unfurl, bloom and suddenly die? Perhaps he's delighting in my fear, which is evident behind my mask of workplace politeness and exquisitely fragile good humour. This *monster*.

The moment Renate asks me somewhat pityingly if I really want to stay, I flee:

'No, I really have to go, my sisters are waiting for me.'

The Greek hardly seems to notice I'm leaving, my clothes under my arm: he's already asking them to send him another girl.

Only three are left in the brothel, two of them already busy. While I'm getting dressed in the little salon, I see Diana, a forty-five-year-old (thirty-one on the website) Turkish woman with enormous breasts, doing her hair to take my place. Diana, who looks grumpy but is naturally joyful and gentle, is ready to be engulfed by this stinking hellhole – having no idea what's waiting for her there, this creature with his limp dick and his five stories, his obscene bum slapping. Diana has a son of fourteen who's sleeping in their apartment someplace and hopes to see his mother when he wakes up – and you can see she wasn't expecting a last client. And certainly not this client…

As she leans in to me to ask what he's like, Milo and Sandor are within earshot and I hear myself say the lie that is the rule in Le Manège, 'He's okay.' Even though I'm tempted to tell her the exact opposite through some miming action, I end up saying to myself, *What's the point?* It's too late. She's the only one who's free.

Diana doesn't give anything away as she enters the room, but I can feel her nausea at the moment she understands that it's not *me* who's stinking up the small salon – it's this guy, the one who joyfully swallowed me and spat me back out broken and wanting to get out as quickly as possible, without even taking a shower despite the good it would do me. And here he is, ready to take her.

I'm a lot more worried about her now I'm writing peacefully in the Midi. That morning, Diana's fate must have hardly grazed my conscience: each to their own shit, I've finished and I'm getting out, my friends, I don't exist any more, there's no point even saying my name.

Renate almost gives me a heart attack when she asks, as if she's really counting on me, if I don't want to join in in another room with another girl; and just like in a nightmare, the girl is there, wrapped in a towel, one of the five blonde Turks who never say a word to me – also looking pleadingly. I repress the urge to shout:

'No, really, sorry… My sisters… they're waiting for me.'

This entire scene takes place in full view of Milo and Sandor, but surprisingly, nobody fires me. Quite the opposite; Sandor springs up from his sofa and offers to take me back to mine in Wedding – god, I was *stupid* enough to say I lived in Wedding, so much for undercover journalism… That's all I needed, to fall into their nets at the moment when I'm probably about to tell them where to get off.

I stutter a barely audible excuse, spoken in an underground form of German, and make a getaway, away from Le Manège, away from the Schlüterstrasse, the furthest I can from this mauve window behind which Diana is beginning to understand what she's fallen into.

The most annoying thing about the comedown for me is how useless music suddenly is. I imagine that in any bad trip, whether it's weed, LSD or MDMA, *good* music can help make certain factors more bearable. But coke won't be fooled by such ruses. Coke is pragmatic, it needs tranquillisers or a few joints – without which it continues, tirelessly. It's also surprising that such a short euphoria can give rise to such deep distress, so relentless. Neither The Beatles nor Nina Simone nor The White Stripes (in fact, especially not them) – not even something gentle and neutral like Mozart or certain Velvet Underground lullabies.

The very idea of my racing thoughts being disturbed feels all wrong. The brain goes much too fast: when, aged twenty-one and in the same state, I listen to *Atom Heart Mother*, I'd already listened to the whole song in my head before it started. So this evening, I'm not even risking it.

It's quite a long walk between Schlüterstrasse and Zoo Station but it gives me time to think. First of all, didn't I *also* mention that I lived on Anrumer Strasse? For fuck's sake! What goes on in your head? What if one day I go home and find Sandor smoking his cigar in the lift of number thirty-four, with that scary smile of a well-brought-up pimp, and two or three right-hand men leaning against the letterbox? Okay, I was smart enough not to give my real name to anybody. Fine, but what if I don't go back? How much time will they need to find the piece of paper where they've no doubt already written my address and my passport number, ah yes, my passport that like a madwoman I leave in the 'changing room', a small room people windmill in and out of, leaving clothes piled on the sofa, where the only padlocked lockers belong to the Hausdamen? Wedding is rammed with menacing Turks who could jump me when I go out in the middle of the night to buy a packet of cigarette papers at the Späti on Müllerstrasse. And what if I'm not at home, if I'm writing somewhere or if I've gone out to stretch my legs, if Anaîs and Madeleine are in and they open the door without picking up the intercom because they don't speak German? It doesn't feel really possible, but most people who have come home to find their family tied up must have thought the same thing. Fat Sandor will be there with his fucking cigar, looking like he's sorry for intruding, and, before cutting off one of my fingers, will ask me exactly what my crying mother will ask me – 'Did I think it was all a game?' That I could go to and leave Le Manège like that and that nobody would take umbrage? Would I prefer to come obediently to a pretty little house in Albania, where the local soldiers and farmers will be delighted to get to know me, or do I prefer to help my sisters pick up their teeth this evening and their breasts in the morning? It's quite an easy choice, right? The great outdoors, the countryside, warm human contact, learning a dozen new languages and dialects…

Halfway to Zoo, the world seems unusually dark to me, and the only thing I can cling to to get the Greek, Milo, Sandor and the grumpy Hausdamen out of my head is the book. I'm going to write about it all, that's why I'm doing it, and the only reason I allow myself to get hurt in this way is because *it's not my life*. My life is to write, but for a few months more I can pretend to be a whore – and if blokes like the Greek believe it, it's because I'm a good actress.

Which gets me thinking about the other girls. Like Diana. What can they think about? When they, like me, are going back up Schlüterstrasse high and stinking of the sweat of a thoughtless arsehole who looked like he was talking to the Mad Hatter *and* the March hare – what do they think about? What dark thoughts suddenly settle over them like a heavy cape, when they're not writing a book and Le Manège is their life? How do you get to the point of saying to yourself Le Manège is your life? Do all other hopes, all other dreams disappear? Perhaps that's better. Perhaps you can cope better with the comedowns and the filthy bastards when it's only another day of *work*. Perhaps you say to yourself *what a fucking shitty day* and despite that you put on your iPod, and perhaps the music manages to create a parallel universe in which you think of nice things and from which you draw the strength to start again. I hope so.

I really hope so.

At home, I fill myself a very bubbly bath. I spend ages in it, wondering if the police can maybe help me in some way. In the state of paranoia I'm in, the mere fact of thinking about the police could very well have sounded an alarm in Milo's mind. It seems obvious to me with a gram in my bloodstream that they won't have any desire to let the French girl leave, the one who has genuine long hair and who scoops up the three clients of an otherwise empty brothel. They won't let me leave.

They won't let me leave!

Once I'm in bed, the sound of my sleeping sisters' breathing should calm me down, but it doesn't. The idea of them calling my parents in tears to tell them I haven't been home for three days and am not answering my mobile, the idea of my mother bursting into tears straightaway and asking where I was, and Madeleine snottily bawling that I was at a brothel, a *brothel* – and all that while I'm in the boot of a Berlin sedan – makes me shake like a leaf in my bed. I should have never set foot in Le Manège – what's got into me? All alone in Berlin with my sisters – what can have got into my head?

At dawn I'm on the terrace swaddled in two coats and it can't be said I'm feeling any better. Despite repeating to myself that none of these catastrophic scenarios is plausible given that prostitution is legal in Germany, the very idea of writing a book about brothels from the inside seems out of the question. But I don't know how to chicken out now, after all my swaggering talk to my sisters, and to myself, and to Stéphane. I don't know how to give up on this new book that is taking shape in my head at breakneck speed, the notes for which already occupy an insane space in my head. All of this for a fucking idiot who didn't even touch me? I have memories of much worse evenings in Paris when I didn't earn a penny.

At 9 o'clock in the morning I'm still not asleep, but on the upside, everyone else is waking up.

'Are you up?' I text Stéphane.

And I read: *Stéphane is typing.* I can almost imagine him on his sofa in London, coming out of the shower, still damp, and smoking a cigarette as he taps away on his keypad. Outside his windows a grey, very light drizzle is spritzing the city.

'Yes. Are you home from work?'

'Do you want a call?'

'It's a bit complicated. I'll call you when I get to work.'

His wife must be around. I sigh:

'Fine.'

Then, almost immediately:

'Shame, I'd have loved to hear a friendly voice. Never mind. Laters.'

While I'm still feeling annoyed with myself for this passive-aggressive message, Stéphane, unpredictable, calls me. At the end of the line, I hear his breathless voice, the calm ruckus of London streets. I'm almost sobbing.

'I didn't want to sound miserable, if Nathalie is around, I…'

'No, not at all. It's just that I'm on my bike…!'

Stéphane, who waited 'til he was fifty-six and in England to cycle.

'Is everything okay? Did work go well?'

I would need to decide to admit to him there's something to be afraid of, that I discovered my limits not get getting violently fucked but while talking with a Greek coke-head. If he hears that, from one thousand five hundred kilometres away, Stéphane will be worried sick and order me not to go back to Le Manège, to never set foot or anything else in a brothel again. And if I lose Stéphane, if he starts to share even secretly my morbid fantasies, I'll get really scared: he works in an embassy, he knows more than me about the pretty European girls who disappear from one day to the next and who, one finds out with closer inspection, were monetising their services among locals. A quiver in my voice would be enough to put an end to what's left of my rebellion: I mustn't scare the only person who can see the brothel as just any old job. Or who finds all my anecdotes so funny.

'It was fine, just long…'

I light a cigarette. Stéphane getting out of breath as he pedals around someplace in London suddenly makes the world feel lighter. And I tell my little stories, sprinkled with enough rather charming and funny anecdotes for me to remain, in his wild imagination, the literary little whore who rules an entire brothel that she's tamed by her moods. This is what brings my courage and my motivation back to life, as if by magic. I have to write, so that Stéphane knows everything I haven't told him out of fear of worrying him. And this Greek, this accursed Greek, will seem tiny once I've committed him to the page.

When I go to bed, I'm already feeling better at the thought that in London Stéphane is starting his day as an adviser at the embassy. I thank myself for having not mentioned the things that would reveal that Le Manège engages in serious cocaine dealing. You never know: if I disappear by one means or another, I'm certain *he* will know immediately where to look.

THE FIRST FEW DAYS I PULLED OUT all the stops and put on some very bright lipstick: something I never do because I think it makes my mouth look awkward, impaired – but there had never been a better time. But there's one place where you certainly don't paint your face like that, and that's a brothel.

It's obvious when you think about it, because all the retouching in the world can't prevent a shipwreck; and I felt a wave of sadness one evening when I saw Irina leave a room in a towel to send in the Hausdame with a credit card machine, the entire lower half of her proud little face smudged red. I didn't like Irina, who in any case never even seemed to have noticed me, and I found her bland look incredibly pretentious. But this redness spread all over the chin, like a mark of infamy, even on her teeth, which she'd tried to keep hidden when calling Jana, made her look like a doll left out in the gutter at the mercy of the wind and the rain – the failure of all artifice, without which all that remained was this pale little dork, unsmiling and, ultimately, not even pretty.

That quelled any desire to paint my mouth, or any of me. When you see the damage to two layers of waterproof mascara from a simple blowjob… Even more shocking is looking in a mirror after straddling a client without kissing. As if the make-up *feels* that you're fucking, and that's all it needs to disintegrate.

When the girls are gathered in the salons waiting for the regulars,

Le Manège can pride itself on a shit-hot, beautifully maintained team. Yet the place is still deserted, for reasons nobody can discern. (The client in me gives a little nudge nudge: *Are you surprised? The day I set foot or my cock – heaven forfend – in a dump like that...*) And it's true that I have difficulty working out which of the girls would be the least bad, if I had bollocks and a hundred and twenty euros to spunk. Although I'm not a bloke, the desperately empty grand salon is there to confirm that men feel the same as I do.

Where a business without customers would downsize its workforce, a brothel – which pays a fixed salary only to its Hausdamen – opts to recruit even more girls. Where a normal brothel would send in fighter planes, Milo recruits Paulette; a response that leaves us slack-jawed. Paulette appears at the end of a particularly deathly week. While most of the group are dolling themselves up as they wait for the salon to open, this German tall as a statue – I mean, huge! – introduces herself shyly. 'My name is Paulette'. No one seems to believe it. Paulette must be thirty-five years old, she comes from Potsdam but feels like she's come from much further away, from the depths of Schleswig-Holstein, from the depths of a countryside forgotten by the internet and telephones. Should this be seen as ballsy bias on the part of Milo who, weary of having about fifteen beautiful girls wandering the empty brothel like zombies, said to himself that a creature like Paulette would attract a new clientele, or at worst increase the splendour of the usual harem ten times over?

Paulette is enormous: with her every step I feel the heels of her pumps groan in agony, and her flesh jiggles with every movement. She pulls her bleached hair up high, and beneath this puny chignon her neck's been eaten away at by a butterfly tattoo the black ink of which is already turning green. Her fishnet stockings barely come up to the middle of her thighs and compress them into a thick roll of flesh, all granular. Only a well-practised eye could work out what size Paulette, who's obsessed with bodycon clothes, is. It would be hard to find underwear that wouldn't leave marks on those imposing buttocks. To crown it all, Paulette has a face as friendly as a prison guard's, an infrequent, pinched smile – and if her eyes carry not the slightest trace of an erotic predisposition, they have a gleam of determination that many girls would do well to take inspiration from.

Yes, Paulette has talents that many don't: she's nice. On top of that, she seems to genuinely wait for a reply when she asks how you are. Paulette isn't here to splash out on Vuitton bags or a jacket for her chihuahua; whatever the reasons that brought her here, you sense her instinct for survival. And that spur makes for much better business than a sudden desire for luxury. In spite of everything, I can't help wondering what was going on in Milo's thick skull. He's not Henry Miller. I'd be surprised if he got a hard-on for the obscene poetry of amorphous flesh. Or that he can grasp the euphoria of not being able to distinguish, in the darkness, between a breast or a buttock or a roll of flab. If you step back from it a bit, Paulette is the only girl here who might remind you of the brothels De Maupassant described, where people were preoccupied with flesh and eroticism, not frills. I definitely think there must be something sinister in the act of fucking her. An eclectically minded pervert would no doubt find some kind of new thrill in it – if that's what Milo was thinking. But I'd be surprised. The only things Milo thinks about are visual cues that reek of fucking: high heels, trowel-heavy make-up, fake boobs, hair with extensions down to thigh level, gold hoop earrings and floral or sweet eau de toilette that stagnates in the padded hallways. Everything that smells of females from kilometres away – in fact, maybe Milo said to himself that a mountain like Paulette, dolled up in good shoes and quite tight fabrics, would scream to clients that we have women here, lots of women, so many woman that we even allow ourselves the whimsy of having a Paulette.

For now, nobody can see this profusion from the street; also, I imagine that word of mouth is more effective that Milo's marketing brainwaves – and instead of fifteen, there are now sixteen of us sitting doing nothing in the big salon. The tour buses can come, we're ready for them.

THERE ARE SEVERAL OF THEM, LIKE PAULETTE, whose presence raises lots of questions.

Most of the girls live in-house or rent an apartment nearby in Berlin, but in both of the two scenarios, you sense the hand of Milo. For how do you rent an apartment by yourself when you don't speak ten words of German or have a payslip? What do you do when you can't deal with an accountant? It's always possible to invent a job for yourself on the forms if you're asked to explain what you mean by self-employed (no one really wants to rent a place to a whore, a human being with wavering levels of professional motivation and changes in address as capricious as they are unforeseeable), but you have to find something credible. That's why in Berlin you'll meet a lot of make-up artists who are incapable of communicating with their German clients.

Most of these girls have been brought in by Milo or by his contacts. While they were languishing in Eastern European countries dialling through shitty jobs paying peanuts, including nocturnal shifts in strip clubs, a tall, smiley man like Sandor came to talk to them of the West. Berlin, the big, beautiful city bursting with opportunities, full of men ready to pay handsomely for the chance to spend a few moments in proximity to this Slavic beauty revered all around the world. *Think, my pretty*: the same work as here, just about, but in a very special place where you'll be treated like a princess, kept warm and safe from men who barter for ages before reluctantly deciding to pay you two or three times less than what you're worth. Because there they employ people to defend and serve you, no one will be able to get their claws into you or take advantage of the fact you're alone to refuse to pay for something extra. You'll set your own criteria there – and believe me, not one German will baulk at getting more money out to hold something other than his Gretchen in his arms. I'm telling you, you'll hold the city between your thighs; I'm talking about the same work as here, sure, but for a flood of cash, so much cash you won't know what to buy any more – and when you come back to your country, you'll be a golden girl and anything will be possible. All you need to do is work, work hard, and trust me. What does it matter, leaving your family for a while, if you can send them money and before long go back and see them enjoying the means not to worry any more, ever? All you need is to be bold. To be less stupid than the naive girls from around here who prefer to run themselves down in crap restaurants than offer men the *real* merchandise that truly interests them, the only one they'll get their wallets out for and not keep tally. Do you know how much it's worth, a woman's so-called virtue? Of course you can still cling to your integrity that's already been damaged by semi-prostitution, hand jobs in toilets and dubious exchanges in parking lots, you can stay and save yourself for your lover, but your lover is a poor redneck who'll never give you the life you deserve, who fucks you badly, without paying, and whose only achievement will be marrying you, one day, maybe; and that will be the end, you'll become a fat hippy with a stomach ravaged by stretch marks, surrounded by snotty kids who will suck out your marrow before you're even thirty. At that moment, your feet won't fit in your pretty pumps any more, my lovely, it'll be too late and you'll never again escape from this hole. That's what you can do.

Yes, it's this kind of bullshit that must have seduced most of the girls in Le Manège, even if they seem disenchanted now. Which means they don't have the choice, they're trapped… I believe the Hausdame when she tells me that the girls never had a penny of advance. What can you do, how do you spend your time when you don't have any family nearby, no friends or relatives beyond your work colleagues? You buy things. Money doesn't seem real if it's not spent, it seems, at the tills of Kürfürstendamm's luxury boutiques. You'll think of escaping later on. And then at Le Manège, there's something to eat, something to drink, and there's coke; the girls' bad mood comes from the fact that their nostrils are rammed with it, and when they run short, they only have to send Maximilian to get some more. If you've worked. If you're working. And as most of the time you don't work, the long evenings at Le Manège can only be a terrible comedown, more mournful than violent, from which no random client could free you. Which is to say that the girls, with what they earn, are only feeding a way of life of deadening luxury in which rent and food must seem very secondary.

Paulette, Loretta, Sylvie, these are a whole other kettle of fish… The clan of long-standing girls and Germans who make up the lively, human hub of this silent seraglio all racked by desires. It's them you hear laughing and talking in the small salon, because after 10 o'clock at night, the small salon, and the company of the owners and the Hausdamen, is the privilege of the long-standing ones. When a client arrives, these girls don't have to go and introduce themselves or even leave their armchairs. They're allowed to order alcoholic drinks, and when they do come into the grand salon, it's rarely without a vodka on ice and suave nicknames for Maximilian or Ronja, with whom they're thick as thieves.

Loretta says she's thirty-five, but really she's forty-six and looks forty-eight; she's a bit beat up but she comes every night and obviously finds what she's looking for, because she never misses a call. She's a nurse in the daytime and has a twenty-one-year-old daughter. Diana has a child of fourteen. Sylvie. Paulette. They come here for a better life, whatever that might mean, to have a bit of breathing room once all the bills are paid. But where are their clients?

The only thing that could explain the presence of mothers, who have better things to do than await the whims of a local clown disdained by fifteen Bulgarian teenagers clamped to their mobiles, is the escort service Milo offers. The prices are higher, but the proposition is undoubtedly better than the in-house one.

One day Selma talks to me about escorts and I ask her if it doesn't make more financial sense to do your own advertising. In Paris, it's the only option anyway, and for girls who manage their affairs well, business is booming. But in Germany of course, given the confusing lawfulness of the profession, it's very tiring to throw yourself into the business alone. The girl has to go somewhere or be ready to let perfect strangers into her place without being sure if they have a knife in their pocket or god knows what else – without even mentioning the neighbours, who, in Germany, like to know what those around them are up to. The girl must never deviate from a few strict principles: never the same hotel twice in the same week, so as not to be recognised by the porters (the Finanzamt loves to get wind of appointments not included on annual tax declarations). Always get paid in advance, regardless of how nice a client may seem or the trust they inspire. Keep an eye on your watch and be able to stand up to guys who nitpick about the length of a session. Don't back down about condoms, unless the guy is ready to pay extra for it – and whatever the extras that are offered, get paid *before*, always. It doesn't matter if the guy decides he wants anal right in the middle of doggy style and the time it takes him to open his wallet is enough to make him lose his hard-on. The moods of a client are never those of a whore, ever; the only thing that counts is time.

But before getting as far as these considerations, getting set up requires certain background work of you. Buying a second mobile so you're not constantly hassled on your private line. Spending long hours on the phone repeating over and over the same flattering descriptions, the same exorbitant fees, replying patiently to the same stupid questions and recognising guys who call with their dick in their hand to get off for free on the pretext of a hypothetical meeting. Replying to all the emails, scrupulously sorting those who may be happy with a cut and paste from those who merit a personal reply (although you often make mistakes about this). And even before that, finding the right place to advertise in the brutal confusion of German websites, one who charges reasonably and can best showcase you. Finding a photographer who can knock out photos that are both suggestive and a bit classy; no one can hope to make it on their own with photobooth-quality images taken on the hop at home in their own bedrooms. Being fully self-employed is a vocation that takes over every moment, and the girl has to show proper talents as a secretary, accountant, organiser and publicist. As if it wasn't enough to be busy being beautiful and smiling, waxed, manicured, with great hair and make-up.

Isn't it better to let Milo do the dirty work? Even two boring evenings a week, as long as those may seem, don't equate to a tenth of the free time a self-employed girl loses to managing her business. If you don't know more self-employed girls, it's because prostitution is a job that for several excellent reasons encourages laziness. No girl loses sight of the fact she's selling something that most women preciously conserve and never even think of monetising; and this generosity brings, in addition to a handsome salary, several advantages such as having free time and not having to make any effort to hook customers. All the forms of prostitution that exist in Berlin aim to reduce, as much as possible, soliciting, which is exhausting for girls. Even those who walk Oranienburgstrasse all year long, in snow, winter or hail, in their eternal thigh-high boots in patent leatherette, are indolent about soliciting at the very least. *When* they solicit. They tend more to pose in full sight on the edge of the pavement – and you can walk past a thousand times the same evening, with rarely an exception, and see them still in the same place, fiddling with their mobile or talking to one another. And when you brush past them, they watch you lazily, as if to say *You know why I'm here, idiot, and I know what you want.*

At the very most you'll hear a murmur, a ridiculously low figure announced in a rolling German full of the accent of the East. And they'll lead you to the edge of the courtyards of Auguststrasse, through a *porte cochère* that is always half open – or in your car if you have the good taste to own one. You can expect nothing from them beyond a furtive, strictly surface embrace; imagine the waste of time if on each occasion you had to take off your trousers, your thigh-high boots, risk putting your bumbag behind you (although, can you keep a bumbag round your waist while fucking?), take off your pullover, your puffer jacket, your underwear… No, thanks, really. Having carried out my clumsy little investigation, I learned that the array of services offered in this honourable street is restricted to hand or blowjobs. There's no billing by duration, god spare us, but by ejaculation, quick and frustrated after a few jerky motions of the wrist or the neck – no conversation, no penetration, and, in return for considerable coinage, you get the chance to touch their nipples while the mute miss brings you off in the complicit shadow of the glove compartment.

I was told that in Potsdamerstrasse, another hotspot of prostitution on a public road, girls *can* fuck. You just have to put a price on it to seal the deal, and pay a supplement no less costly for the price of a room – one of the two rooms of a filthy hovel lit by striplight, underneath which the client discovers that what was promised him is less fresh, seductive and agreeable than beneath the light of a lamppost. The price of the room is generally not quoted until you're walking through the doorway, when the throbbing client is ready to empty his wallet. And here too, I wouldn't have to count on my week at Le Manège to have the talents needed to bring the customer to orgasm – leaving an intense sense of self-loathing as an aftertaste.

Those whores are confined in a dormitory, fifteen, twenty of them all piled up, regardless of the murderous frictions or critical issues between them. Although Le Manège, when compared with the pavement, passes for a family firm full of progressive ideas aimed at improving the wellbeing of its staff, just one visit there, even as a client, is enough to make you sense that the girls fear the management, and that quite a lot of them would have nothing against working in a restaurant – if only their lifestyle wasn't what it is.

If I spoke German better, I'd tell Paulette that it isn't here she'll find what she's looking for. The clientele of Le Manège is made up mainly of businessmen with lots of cash and guys who've come with friends: men of that ilk want to dream and to make their mates dream – their mates who will also end up taking a very slender girl with very long hair and pneumatic breasts. Blokes who tend to have a space for Paulette in their fantasies come alone and early, during a break.

I understood that one day when Gabrielle, Michelle, Nicola and I were all left hung out to dry by Paulette. The client shakes our hand without even seeming to see us. There's only Paulette, impelled by four evenings of going home empty-handed, introducing herself in her quiet manner, in a German of which none of us can avail ourselves. Paulette speaks the same rasping dialect as this fifty-five-year-old taxi driver and, more than that, she knows how to talk to him. She intuited better than we did the weariness of the guy who's *finally* sitting in front of a cool beer after ten hours of driving around Berlin. Taxi drivers are self-employed like whores, but their own job includes lots of soliciting, and also much less money. Yet the tiredness is around the same, it's about carting around people of greater or less degrees of niceness and decency, who you have to smile at when they slag you off or stick chewing gum to the head rest, and who you have to tolerate when they've been drinking to the point of not even remembering their address. You'd have to ask a taxi driver if transporting around a guy who's jabbering away on a phone isn't comparable to a consensual fondle, just for money. In any case, there's a tacit and strong link between these two professions that often work side by side on the street; and if we, the younger girls, the little princesses used to the warmth of the brothels, are not open to this, an old streetwalker like Paulette sees an excellent prey in this tired man.

I watch them, fascinated, oscillate between oceans of silence and unhurried conversation, both of them sitting in the same heavy, broken position of a worker at the end of his rope, sipping their beer in unison. It's easy for her to cheer him up, and she doesn't babble foolishly, because it's neither her style nor that of her client, she sensed that right away (perhaps because Paulette is *also* a taxi driver…) And having made him buy her some beers and some champagne, Paulette takes the client by the hand like a child who she's persuaded to be obedient. She tells Renate about her luck, and Renate a little dubiously (he's the *only* client up to now and it's *Paulette* who snags him) opens the door to Room Two. A few minutes later, Paulette comes back out with the money for an hour and a half in her hand, plus sixty for herself, which she announces in a low voice to Renate; but I heard. Ye gods, what does Paulette have in her armoury to get an extra sixty out of a *taxi driver*? Twenty to kiss him, twenty for a blow job without a condom, okay, and the rest…? What clever little extra could Paulette have added? Would she have the cheek to make him pay for going down on her? Or did she decide to bill him twenty euros for sticking a finger up his arse? Which would be very small-minded, and at the same time brilliant.

Seeing her grab two towels in the bathroom and shift her enormous nipples back into place, I seek in her face or her attitude the feverish fear of a novice, in vain: Paulette has a ferocious determination, and she responds to my smile of encouragement with a smile that makes her features less severe — and makes her almost beautiful.

When I end up going home having done fuck all with my day, Paulette has snaffled three of the four clients who showed up, and the girls who were at first amused by her are beginning to take it personally. Obviously, I'm wondering what Paulette is doing. As much as I wonder about all the others. I would love to know what happens in the bedrooms. That makes at least one of us in Le Manège. But to my question full of allusions and hints, *How was he?*, I get the same thing every time: a lingering look that says that doesn't concern me, that asks why I might want to know that. Am I nasty? Do I tell Milo everything? If the girls aren't too grouchy, I may eventually negotiate a terse response full of defiance: *Fine, he was okay.* And since the Greek guy, I know that one can put absolutely anything into these five words.

What I don't know, in fact, is where this unease comes from: them or the management? The Hausdamen, for instance, who combine greed and vague guilt. They act as if they have little in common with the girls they supervise; if they don't want to know anything, it's because they imagine that their stubborn deafness spares them from being splattered by the very vice they wade in just as the others do. I let myself be mistreated by Jana for a long time before the young Spanish girl, who advised me on how best to use coke in a professional environment, reminded me of the cutting truth: it's *they* who work for us, not the opposite. They're happy to do the housework and to get the money off the clients; nothing gives them permission to go after us like guard dogs.

This reality seems irrefutable when said aloud and forcefully; but it doesn't stop Jana from forcing her authority down on our little world in a manner not dissimilar to certain major institutions of incarceration. Like any bully, she has her favourites and her scapegoats, who fluctuate according to her moods. Sometimes, in thinking you're pleasing her, you only annoy her more – the only constants are not to get under her feet, and above all never to make her speak English. It's better to ask her to repeat something two, three, four times in German – which will in any case end up putting her in a trance-like state, but it will take longer, leaving you time to run away.

THE NEXT DAY, I'M ALONE WITH JANA for six hours. Six hours. It reduces me to the point of doing some horrid maths, to working out my income for the week, which painfully amounts to one hundred and five euros for thirty hours of fathomless nothingness. The day before, when giving me my share, less the thirty-five euros a day Le Manège takes in exchange for my *Steuernummer*, Jana, even more at her wit's end than I was, said to me:

'It's money all the same, Justine. You have to sort it out.'

And the fact is that I have my own idea on the matter, but this idea is only floating around my head for the moment, among a thousand other half-assed plans. In two weeks I would have had tenfold the amount of time I needed to go to the Finanzamt and get myself a number. If I haven't done it, it's not out of laziness – I'm tempted to think – but because I'm in no particular hurry to be registered at Le Manège for good. The sum siphoned off me every day is for me the price of a freedom that in my opinion fluctuates. I'd earn more with this *Steuernummer*, for sure; but wouldn't I earn more, on every level, in a place that actually has clients? Sunk into my sofa, I weigh up fors and againsts; not a day has gone by here without me wondering if it was possible to leave, to resign. In the eyes of the law this question seems grotesque, but Milo's eyes seem to lightly mock the law. I think about reading articles on the subject, but I don't want a slightly biased reporter to scare me even more.

Did I give them my address?

Let's say that nobody is following me – which would be really lovely. Can I in all decency show up in another brothel? It must be a very small world, one where everybody talks to one another all the time. How much time will it take for the news to circulate that a French girl has appeared in a rival brothel? However little that has to do with Milo, how could this news not interest him? I had more clients in two weeks than certain girls in a month. Will he simply allow me to enrich another brothel and spread it around that Le Manège is totally dysfunctional? I wonder.

These thoughts lead me to review the entire viability of this project, my book, the bet I made with myself – and this cowardice, this luke-warmth that isn't like me and that makes me fear and hate Le Manège. But I'm not going to abandon a project I'm passionate about because the first brothel I tried is managed by a bunch of idiots for whom sensuality and eroticism have almost as much meaning as thermodynamics do for me.

It's not really clients who are the problem, if you discount people like the Greek or the young traders who snooze stoned on girls' shoulders, usually with something ridiculous on their heads. You can always manage the assholes. But what's detestable here is that the only people who make money are treated rudely by those who are only really cashiers, bullies and door openers. This is not the way women should be treated who use, for the public good, a part of their body that girls like Jana only use for peeing. Why in exchange for this sacrifice should I be met by the enraged expressions of the Hausdamen and their exasperated spraying of Febreze as soon as I leave a room? They should crawl to serve us, the old goats. Who's paying them, after all?

It's the girls who keep me here, their stories. I cling to the desire to decipher them, especially Michelle and Nicola, the two sisters. Where else could I meet two sisters in a brothel? The chance seems unique to me. Have you ever heard of anything so unhealthy? And they don't even make a USP of it. I'm the only one to make a blasphemous added bonus out of it, and perhaps I'm the only one who talks about it at all.

And the old ones interest me too, all of them interest me. If there's the slightest chance of me one day getting confidences out of them, is not staying where I am, without making waves, without complaining and without bootlicking, the price I have to pay? Yes, but in two days of assiduous attendance, my pious desire to conform has only dug between them and me the same kind of trench that separates shopkeepers on the same street, the inevitable rivalry between businesses. I thought if I worked as much as them, as well as earning the goodwill of the management, I'd inspire the girls to like me, or at least feel some solidarity that would incite them to spill the beans. Total naivety: everything seems to slip under or pass through them – pleasure, displeasure, all the emotions most mortals associate with sex and which for them dissolve into cash. At the beginning, if I attracted some interest, it was because I was the shorn lamb, dependent on friendly nuggets of advice. That lasted one evening before I got up on the starting blocks, and now I'm enemy number one, relegated like a pariah without any company at all, the tricolour curse come to nick their clients, hanging on to Sandor's shirt tails like a prodigal daughter. The only way to turn their opinion in my favour would be to get really bollocked by Milo – but this option frightens me a bit, and most of all I'm not sure they wouldn't distance themselves from me even more, for legitimate reasons this time.

What's the point? How can I write human, funny or tender things about this job in a brothel that has stripped sex of all its emotion and reduced it to purely mechanical friction? This place is part of the truth, but it's far from being the most interesting. If *I'm* capable of starting out in this with a neutral or even positive attitude, there must be many others like me.

Perhaps I'm too alive for this place. Perhaps I don't see why sex, which is the great darkness and joyful light of human life, should be dull just because it's paid for. What will become of my enthusiasm if I stay here? What will become of me in general? I can't go to work with a knot in my stomach and go home every night praying that Stéphane's already awake in London. I can't work in a place where all the stories I collect are impossible to tell my sisters. This is also the problem of Le Manège; I don't want Anaïs, Madeleine and Marguerite to know how I'm treated, but the secrets I'm keeping are also choking me. In this moment, I'm in great fear of adopting, in spite of myself, Le Manège's verbal tic, that of always replying that *it's okay* (in writing it, I realise the defeatism of this phrase). Anaïs and Madeleine and Marguerite, by osmosis, have an infallible instinct to sniff out when I'm not happy: I can play-act for a few days, but I unfailingly move towards a moment when it will be visible. And the simple fact that their older sister works in a brothel is a problem sufficiently complex not to involve some sadness.

I'm still the only one in Le Manège, with Jana and Gabrielle, who haven't set foot out of the room. It's the start of the evening. I've made about thirty euros – which would almost make the Schwarzes Cafe, where Anaïs and Madeleine work, pass for a Geneva bank. What's holding me back? And anyway, is Le Manège really the kind of the place you resign from according to any rules? I don't owe them anything. They, on the other hand, still owe me the one hundred and fifty euros from the Greek, which they can't pay even if they want to because I haven't given them my bank account details. Without talking about the thirty-five euros a day they're supposed to give me. The total is an astronomical sum I'd be very happy to spend, but perhaps that's the price of my sudden defection: they wouldn't have the guts to piss me off with more than 300 euros belonging to me in their pocket. If I go, there's no coming back.

I don't care.

'Jana?'

She raises her head lazily towards me, one eyebrow raised.

'I'm going down to get something to eat, okay?'

'Go ahead.'

She's dived back down into her TV show without the slightest suspicion – nor the slightest sign of interest. It can be as easy as that.

I slip into the empty changing room. One last hesitation, a vague disappointment in myself makes me linger in front of the big mirror for one more moment. *You're not really okay here, are you? – No, not really*, I reply to myself. I put my civilian clothing back on. I take care to slip my shoes and my dress into my handbag, so Jana doesn't worry seeing me leave with two bags. An unnecessary precaution. When I cross the small salon and place my hand, for the last time, on the door handle, Jana doesn't take her eyes away from the screen. It's undoubtedly a detail she'll regret when she has to tell Milo I've upped and left.

'See you soon!' I fling at her as I rush out, and as I close the heavy door I hear her murmur the same thing back – this old fool certain she'll see me again munching on a sandwich.

Outside it's still daylight, still fine, the air has never seemed so breathable to me, and as if the whole world was favouring my escape, the bus towards Zoo arrives straightaway. I watch number forty-seven with its mauve curtains disappear far behind me.

The people in the bus seem perfectly normal. It's not a neighbourhood that means a lot to anybody, Schlüterstrasse, just a street linking Olivaer Platz with Zoo. No one looks at me weirdly, nobody can tell that I am free.

Free. This is another of my griefs against Le Manège. I've never left a job before thinking I am free. Peaceful, yes, but never *free*.

The Hell of It, Paul Williams

'THE FRENCH EXCITE ME. I LOVE THEM to talk during sex. I don't understand anything, but it excites me. The guy could be reading out his shopping list, I wouldn't know the difference. Like Jamie Lee Curtis in that film.'

There are lots of things I'd like to say to Bobbie, who's come out of a session in the Studio with one of my compatriots. French men in brothels are, for me, like an epidemic of gastroenteritis. I suppose there can be something touching in the amazement they try to hide at the idea that no cop lies in ambush behind a surveillance camera to jump on them as they come out of the bathroom. Is that a miracle for them, or just an anomaly of the law that they take advantage of at the same time as they're taking advantage of some poor girl? You'd have to ask them, but French men in brothels as everywhere else rarely have the gift of speaking other languages.

This is what spares my colleagues many of the impulsive vulgarities that only I understand – because faced with a woman from back home, French men get all chatty, often too chatty. And I can't put their clumsiness down to the language barrier, whereas an asshole from across the Rhine will at least have the benefit of the doubt before I class him as such. It's an advantage; and only grasping sixty per cent of the conversation keeps my mood stable – I'm very tolerant, for as long as we're talking. It's a soundtrack we produce together, tacitly, to give some consistency to this choreographed romance. A necessary evil that can actually turn out very nicely, as pharmacists who rarely sell a box of aspirin to an old person without getting trapped in a conversation would no doubt say.

But *French men*...! I don't blame them – you can't spend your life soaked in a culture that sends whores into the flames of eternal damnation (and before that, society's reproval) and know that brothels have, like everywhere else, rules of behaviour. I could illustrate this with a whole array of examples. You, the middle-aged estate agent, who, when I ask you your job, replies, 'Like you, I profit from other people's money!' (An estate agent is indeed a parasitic trade like no other.) Or you, the old fogey living in Berlin for thirty years, who, when asked this same question motivated by the most basic of courtesies, squeaks with a disdainful smile: 'Is this an interrogation?' (It turned out you were an accountant: thanks for having spared me this conversational cul-de-sac.)

Rather than compiling a whole list of the unfortunates whom curiosity or the inability to speak another language have herded into my nets, I'd do better focusing on that fat bastard whom unkind fate brought to me, and whose very presence confirmed the fundamental need to reopen brothels in France.

Where are you these days, you big fat loser, you whose incompetence still echoes inside me even louder than the aptitude of any of the good-looking guys? Your arrival coincided with that of spring – what an irony. I was waiting for my next appointment when Inge came looking for me to translate something urgently – there was a French guy in the men's salon – and guess what? He spoke neither English nor German!

I generally like being the spokesperson for this lovely brothel, explaining the prices, the way things work, helping them decide which girl will catch their eye – I'm an even nicer spokesperson because of always having a good excuse not to go with them. I adore escaping the French. That day, I had the time; but I decided to claim I didn't as soon as I saw you, painfully sunken into the leather armchair. You held out your damp little hand, and I introduced myself.

'Finally someone who speaks French!' you exclaimed, filled with the impudence of a tourist who thinks he's at home everywhere.

I'd barely started talking about prices when you shook your head, impatient.

'I saw that you offer lessons.'

'What do you mean, lessons?'

'Dunno. I saw it on the site. *Liebeschule,*' you announced clumsily.

'Ah, yes. And what do you want to know?'

'Bah, I don't know, how it works. Because you, for instance…'

'No, I'm sorry, I already have appointments.'

You protested loudly, arms in the air as if I'd accused you of rape.

'Yikes, I only asked…!'

Perhaps you were afraid that a Serbian security guard, watching us via the intermediary of a recording device hidden in my knickers, would rush out and break your fingers as soon as my voice rose. Infected by your panic, I replied to you in the same tone.

'There's no problem, I'm just telling you how it is…!'

'Ah, no worries, no worries!'

'Fine, all good then.'

'It's just that, as I don't know any English…'

'Yes, I can quite imagine. I'm sorry.'

And as your arms were shaking at the thought of having been out of place, I continued:

'There must be a lady you like?'

'A blonde, I think: Dorothée?'

'I'll go and get her.'

'But you, there's really no way?'

'Really, no, I'm sorry.'

What a relief as I shut the door on you! Normally I'm not that concerned what my clients look like, I feel that's the right way to be in this job — but faced with you, I was ready to renege on all my principles, to invent new ones. And as I rushed along the corridor to fetch Dorothée and put an end to this situation, I felt my chest freed from an indescribable weight — yours. I avoided looking at the face Dorothée was pulling – her unique and grave *Ach!* felt full of reproach. I understood her pain perfectly. Ugly and stupid clients, fine; true hell is when *on top of that* they come to be taught, and you have to be there, really there, and can't shut your eyes and imagine anybody but them. Anyway let's not think about it any more, I said to myself as I slipped off to my next appointment with the certainty that, whatever amorphous monster awaited in the introduction room, it would be a merciful fate.

The next day I was trotting along gaily to my first client – the one who sets the tone for the whole day. I was far – let's say, twice the distance between Paris and Sydney, *that* far – from imagining what lurked behind Stefan or Hans or Michael or whatever German name the booking had been taken in. You. It was you, the fat Frenchman with clammy hands, already relegated to the depths of my memory, and who I thought had gone back home; damn it.

'It's me again!' you sang, which did nothing to make you any more agreeable.

I thought I'd been nice enough the day before. But you dived right back in, as if your meeting with Dorothée had been nothing but an interruption in our conversation, from which nothing had stayed in your head:

'So, as I was saying, what I'm interested in are lessons.'

I thought this was my chance.

'I'm so sorry, but the problem is I'm a very bad teacher.'

Your nervous little arms had returned to their usual position:

'Ah, I'm only asking.'

'And I'm explaining.'

'Because I was told to go and see you, I was told *you must see Justine…*'

'That's very kind, but…'

Probably a very understandable ploy on the part of Dorothée. At my wit's end, I repressed a sigh.

'What do you want to learn?'

'Actually I've come to learn cunnilingus,' you whispered.

'*Cunnilingus.*'

'Yes, I think I have the fingers right, but well, I'd like to know more about it.'

My god, exclaimed Emma inside Justine, *How old are you?* I never asked men this, which shows how little of a fuck I gave about it, but you were well over thirty-five, which means there are here on this Earth men who at that age feel at enough of a loss with the female sex to come asking for advice in a brothel, and in such a way.

Why me? But as you were there, as I'd got too involved to easily extricate myself from this quagmire, as you were staring at me with that stubborn bovine gaze that doesn't hinder the language of the body, I decided it was better to get it over and done with.

'How long do you want to stay?'

'Well, at least an hour, right?'

'An hour is long enough, isn't it?'

'Or an hour and a half!'

'An hour is fine. Let's go for an hour.'

An hour of pure joy, I thought as I went back along the corridor to choose a room, the Red one, the darkest. It really would be difficult to find someone less attractive on first sight. I'd never come across such an unappealing physique, coupled with such a stubborn attitude – one that screamed out that it was in your very nature to make everything as complicated as possible. Fat, hair thinning on top, the remainder of the black strands swept over your skull in a pitiful attempt to not look too awful, squeezed into overly tight clothes, strangled by a belt that made very little difference – what a lovely team we made!

Of course, you didn't want to take a shower. You'd washed at the hotel, that was enough. I had to do my little routine while you watched – fold back the covers, fetch lube, condoms, hand sanitiser, all while making conversation with you. Thank god, you had enough questions for two men – and good ones, I note, giving me no option of dodging them with a chuckle:

'Did you do this job in Paris?'

'Er no, not really.'

'You'd earn shitloads more in Paris.'

'It's very dangerous in Paris.'

'Nah…' You tried to downplay it; you who certainly knew nothing more about the subject than a few websites with classified ads.

'It's very dangerous,' I repeated with a frown, defying you to come back at me with your sigh like that of a seal.

'But you'd be much better paid.'

'Yes, I know.'

I realised now that eighty-eight euros for an hour with you was far from enough.

'I don't do it for the money anyway.'

'Get away!' you hooted with the look of someone who won't be taken for a ride.

'I'm doing it for the experience,' I elaborated tetchily – because while experience was indeed my main reason, the promise of climbing on top of a guy like you was not exactly keeping me awake at night.

When faced by you, I really do have to admit that it's nothing more than money, and my stupid politeness. Charity, actually: for less than a hundred euros, there could be no other name for it.

You raised your eyebrows in disbelief while you were removing your clothes. I forced myself to keep a neutral expression, a half-smile that was the ultimate in courtesies. And as I was watching you take off your underpants and modestly fold them on top of the rest of your rags, suddenly very serious, a shudder of anguish chilled me from top to toe; how was I going to go about turning the situation around? Standing there sanctimoniously, you certainly didn't look like someone who'd help me by throwing themselves on me in a frenzy. It was written in huge letters on your French forehead; I couldn't hope from you the relaxed ways of Germans, who simply come and lie naked by me and caress my hips. We'd said everything; neither you nor I would find the least topic of conversation; nothing

I knew of you gave me anything with which to start all over again. You were an immigration lawyer; a piece of information I'd received with fake enthusiasm, before I realised it didn't inspire me in any way. I had no idea of what it might be, but it didn't interest me enough to ask you. At the word lawyer I did consider the possibility that you might not be a total idiot, before realising that it's perfectly possible to be both an idiot and a lawyer; you only have to be able to understand reams of arid legal meta-language and apply it – nothing in all that prevented you from being tiresome, in fact quite the contrary.

The place where you lived, in the Beauce, sent my brain to sleep: not even an RER line to complain about together. And you weren't fed by a historic or cultural passion for Berlin, which is why your presence lacked mystery; you'd been going to whores for two days. You'd come alone and as a sex tourist, without even a fellow sex tourist to swap stories with over a drink.

As for you, beyond the evidence that we had nothing in common, I didn't interest you because I was a whore. It didn't occur to you that I was a person, with stupid things to say just like everyone else – even more than anyone else. Furtively I took off my knickers.

'So, in short, you want to learn cunnilingus.'

No trace of any kind of enthusiasm on your face.

'You've already tried it, yes?'

'Yes, but not really; half, I guess.'

'Half? Meaning?'

'Bah, it was a long time ago.'

'Ah.'

'I think I've mastered the fingers. As for the rest, I'm not sure.'

'Fingers is a good start,' I pretended to reassure you, as if you were one of the rare specimens to have grasped the principle of putting fingers in a pussy.

But deep down, everything I heard bothered and panicked me. There would be no way of forgetting your presence, you didn't know how to do anything; to teach you I would have to feel things and tell you about them. I would have to explain the inexplicable to you, I would have to drag out of myself scientific words to name what shouldn't need to be named, and above all I would have to feign pleasure so that you made an effort. I tried to calm my heart palpitations:

'You've watched a porn film, haven't you? You have a rough idea of where the clitoris is, at least… I mean, the small lips, the big lips, all that, I imagine you're familiar with it?'

'Yes, yes, sure.'

'Fine. Well there's nothing very complicated about it.'

And I opened my legs carefully.

'Begin with your fingers, and then do what you already know how to do.'

'What, like this?'

Your stare…! Perhaps you were hoping for a slow dance?

'Yes, like that. Practice is the most important part of this kind of thing.'

You looked like you were leaning over a workbench. It's true I must have been quite a sight, with my arms crossed behind my head.

'So I start with my fingers, right?'

'Do what feels right to you, do whatever it inspires you to do!' I replied, impatient.

My god, so it really was possible, for a man, to find himself ten centimetres from a pair of gaping thighs and still believe there was a strict route to follow, a sort of warm-up with a procedure that didn't change according to day or mood or company or desire?

I'd like to have dreamt the rest or for it to be someone else's story. I was caught up in a matrix of despair when I saw you put your index finger in your mouth before putting it inside me, as if you were taking the temperature of a corpse. Brow knitted, you started a sort of in-out movement – it was the inexorable, perpetual rhythm of a drop of water falling onto the forehead of a torture victim until they go mad.

I leaned back gently against the pillow, panicked at the idea of you sensing me moving and asking my opinion. That was my current dilemma, which attitude to take. I could have faked it, but that wasn't helping you, was it, and I was afraid my bad acting would be blindingly obvious to an immigration lawyer. I could also take it all back to zero, raise the general level by telling you it wasn't okay, that that wouldn't work. Which ran the risk of annoying you. It was just that the abyss of your ignorance, your lack of sensuality, your lack of appetite, scared me. Even those afflicted with the darkest ignorance wouldn't think of doing what you were doing. Which crater, which planet inhabited by gastropods could you hail from for a pussy to inspire you to mark these manoeuvres like something out of a nineteenth-century marriage manual? I observed your silence with growing worry, aware that nothing, not even my inertia, would make you deviate from your course. No sound, no expression of pleasure would send the slightest real frisson through your flesh – there was no attraction or chemistry or creativity here – but only time; in your thick skull, you were turning an hourglass over and over at each laborious step that was supposed to lead to sex. And I had no idea where we were up to with the hourglass, or, even more importantly, what was going to follow; why you hadn't entrusted me, like everyone else, with the intelligible task of making you come. This time it was me who was supposed to come, just like that, by means of a stubby finger that made me miss my gynaecologist – if only because he talked to me at the same time. The thought of having to twist around at the end of this finger, lost in a laughable swoon, was a challenge comparable to the major oral exam at Sciences Po university. I was even afraid of coughing and you feeling it inside me; I was afraid of you becoming afraid, realising that *it* is alive. And because I saw no other solution to my misery, I propped myself up on my elbows:

'Right, you've got the basic idea with fingers.'

What else could I say to you? The comings and goings of an object of a vaguely phallic shape in the vaginal cavity is indeed the cornerstone of one aspect of foreplay.

'Shall I stop?' you asked me.

'Not *necessarily*, but you came to learn to go down on women, didn't you?'

'Yes.'

'Well, then I think there comes a moment when you have to throw yourself into it.'

'Shall I do it, then?'

'Go ahead.'

Bloody hell! Seeing you in between my legs, I had the impression there was a plate of raw offal down there and that I'd interrupted you in the middle of prodding food about with the tip of your fork. We reached the sensual apotheosis when you poked out the fearful tip of your tongue. I watched you through half-closed eyes; you hadn't reckoned on the hair, that probably didn't seem very clean to you. Seeing the frown of concentration on your forehead as you forced yourself to make contact without touching the hair, I realised you must be upset not to have everything spread out before you, to have to guess or forage your way in. I sensed you were thinking, too: aren't all whores completely hairless? So whores are protean projections of male fantasies? Maybe I wasn't taking care of myself: I would have bet my day's income that it hadn't even occurred to you to look at my description on the internet, which would have spared you this type of disappointment. Because the result was that I felt nothing. But you'd found the clitoris, and someone would have had to run over you to get you to back down. I transformed a sigh of despair into a vague squeak and was immediately intimidated by the noise it made in the midst of all the silence.

He stayed for three quarters of an hour! When you think of everything that can occur in three quarters of an hour! Rachmaninov's Concert for Piano No.3, for instance: it fits in its entirety, with even a bit of time to spare. Three quarters of an hour can contain at least three orgasms. It can go by very quickly, without you even realising. On the other hand, it's no less than three times fifteen minutes; we don't think about that enough.

Thinking about it now, right afterwards, made me want to cry with the unfairness of it, and I felt like I was giving you the nails to seal my coffin. I lifted my chin.

'The thing is, there's not just the clitoris.'

You stared at me uncomprehendingly.

'It is important, but there's a whole world surrounding it.'

No spark of understanding lit up your face.

'The small lips.'

Still nothing.

'The big lips… There are things to be done there.'

As it was obvious that you didn't have the slightest idea what to do with this extra, doubtlessly ornamental flesh, I added:

'You don't have to stick to the clitoris, that's what I mean. You can lick everything. A bit lower down, for instance,' I suggested with a lift of my eyebrows that I thought would save me having to say the word *vagina*.

You gave me a panicked look:

'But further down… There's something else!'

'Yes, and?'

I was slowly starting to see red. I summoned up my last shreds of patience.

'It's not colouring in, what you're doing down there. Nobody cares if you go outside the lines a bit.'

Livid, I watched you lower your snout and bravely carry on with your task, without taking any notice of my advice. There was no question of going *further down*, out of fear of coming across *something else* — but when you found yourself quite obviously faced with a fickle woman for whom the clitoris wasn't enough, you with great effort put another finger in your mouth and used that. Pleasure should now have been crashing down from all sides and utterly consuming me. But the sucking noise you made irritated me like the squeak of a knife on a plate — that was a kind of torture no book on brothels has ever described, the complete uselessness of men sometimes. This sucking noise and the music from the loudspeakers, like an affront.

When I saw there were forty-two minutes left, all the dams in me burst. I sat cross-legged, pulling this nonsense of incomprehensible flesh away from your mouth.

'Be honest, you were bored.'

You gave me an almost shocked look.

'No, why?!'

'I don't know. That's how it felt.'

'No.'

'Fine.'

'Why, were you?'

'It's not exactly boredom, let's just say I have the feeling that…'

Oh, shit.

'Firstly, if you have to suck your finger, it's because something's not working. Normally, it's already wet. You're doing things the wrong way round. You need to lick first and put your finger in afterwards.'

'Oh.'

'Yeah.'

There was an awkward silence.

'Why do you want to learn to do that?'

'Uh, because I have a girlfriend.'

Something that was staring you in the face!

'It's an honourable reason but it's not enough. Beyond that, it has to be because you like it. If you're not feeling it, it's pointless.'

You lowered your eyes.

'You don't seem to particularly like it. That's what I mean. Does it excite you, or not?'

'Oh, if I do it, it's mostly to give pleasure!'

'Indeed. That's the problem. You need to understand something about women, and that's the big key: if it doesn't turn you on, it doesn't turn us on either. Quite often, we can't come because we're wondering if you're bored. You have to communicate a bit. How does it make you feel?'

'Er, I don't really know.'

'Yes, but then if you really want to go down on a girl and for her to like it, even if you don't like it, you have to do yourself some violence! If not, you might as well slather yourself in lube and get right down to it. I have the impression it disgusts you, that it's not a nice situation for you. I really don't care, but I don't think it's money well spent.'

'Okay.'

'I quite understand that you don't feel like doing it to a girl who works in a brothel.'

'Okay.'

'But you can't learn anything without practising.'

'Yeah, that's for sure.'

'For the love of god, a pussy can't handle someone with no appetite for it. You have to feel you're being carried away, or pretend to be, but do it well. Because with this, I'm sorry to say, we're both falling asleep.'

'Oh right. But the clitoris…'

'Yes, the *clitoris*. It's good to know about it, well done. But we don't feel anything when you do it with the end of your tongue, because you don't want to get dirty. It's as if… Look! It's just like if I took you hold of between two fingers and waved you around, gently' – I explained while miming the gesture.

'Yes.'

'You might say to me I'd end up making you come, after an hour. But we won't have *exploded*, either. It will have been a lazy wank.'

Something told me this concept wasn't unfamiliar to you.

'Maybe for men it's less painful. But a girl, my dear man, needs to feel your desire. Feeling your desire comes through very small things, like for example the fact that your hand is doing nothing: place it on me. Or on you! Wherever you want, as long as I have the impression you like what you're doing.'

'Okay.'

'Am I explaining it okay, or is it all Chinese?'

'No, I understand.'

'And when you go down on someone, ye gods…! You have to put your chin, your whole face, into it, you have to behave like an animal; there's a sleeping animal inside you!'

'For sure.'

'So lick, bite, suck, smell, let yourself go! There's no bad way to do it.'

You had a look of such total lack of understanding, it pained me a bit.

'I'm telling you that to help you, you know. And you mustn't do things that you don't feel like, just to give pleasure.'

You groaned.

'You just need to remember the idea of enthusiasm, okay? That's what's exciting.'

It's at this precise moment that the solution came to me, blindingly obvious.

'Look at me for instance. I can assure you that if I did the same thing now, out of the blue, you wouldn't in any way feel that I don't want to do it. Do you want me to show you?'

'Yes, okay.'

You clearly understood nothing, since you came in total stillness, without a word, without a sigh, without even that frisson that goes through dogs mating in the street – too civilised to abandon yourself and groan, not enough to make an art form of love. Stuck, my poor man, between being an animal and a civil servant.

'You see,' I continued as I put my knickers back on, 'this is your whole problem. You don't need to look anywhere else.'

'What?'

'Just that.'

'But I didn't do anything.'

'Exactly. You didn't do anything, it's as if you were dead. You came, and the only way I knew anything about it was the condom getting hot.'

'I don't think I'm a very expressive person.'

'Sure, fine… But make an effort, dude. And that's from a professional.'

I watched you get dressed in silence, gripped by pity at the sight of your sad underpants, your old-fashioned vest, your way of putting on your socks before everything else – giving me a tableau of misery that even Houellebecq with his science of the sordid would have avoided painting. I could see you doing the exact same thing every morning in your little Beauce bungalow, without a woman's gaze to tuck your shirt into your trousers for – so alone and resigned that the rare presence of a girl didn't make you think to face me when putting your legs in your trousers to hide the horrible fat of your thighs. I understood why Dorothée had sent you to me, thinking a compatriot would understand you better than she did. But there was no need of language to understand you, it was universal: the only thing a Frenchwoman would understand more quickly than a German, or a Russian, or a Romanian woman, was that by depriving you of brothels in your own country, you'd been deprived of a sex life. Prostitution would simply have had to be legal and institutionalised, never stopped being so, for you to give your first kisses and all the rest to a professional at the age of seventeen, like your friends. You'd have still been impressionable enough to retain a few of the basics of desire. You'd have paid a girl you'd have fallen in love with as one does at seventeen, and this love would have made you want to understand; or at least an older woman, a bit gruff, would have lectured you, *Listen my sweet, if you carry on like that, you risk not doing it for free one day, I speak from experience.*

Was it immoral to think it was sad your sexual experience wasn't doled out by whores – rather than via the sex obtained by means of a misunderstanding with pissed girls at the end of a student party? What can we desire for nasty, disagreeable men, awkward and resigned to women's disdain, if not the kindness and smile of those who work in brothels? Your unpleasant side was the result of long years of shyness, of refusals, of snubs, of an adolescence spent invisible to girls – one more man swelling the ranks of those who've never fucked without making superhuman efforts, who fight for a meagre smile, and who at around thirty-five simply give up trying. The clumsy, good-natured kid was smothered to death in the body of a dusty lawyer.

While you were finishing getting dressed and, feeling a little more cheerful, halfheartedly joining in with my conversation, wearing your attentive auditor's hat you asked me how much I'd earned an hour in Paris:

'Five hundred euros,' I replied soberly, and your eyes grew wide before you expelled an incredulous chuckle.

'Ohhhh, wow!'

'What?'

'It's a rip-off.'

Uh, so there's no hope then for you French rednecks? We take pity on you for your solitude, your incompetence, but you also find a way to be assholes — as if it's funny to be so. I smiled at you. In my eyes there was more disdain than it was possible for you to digest; for a moment I wanted to explain to you how priceless the eccentricities of well-brought-up girls who like to be scared are for certain men. I wanted to explain to you to what point these men lose all common sense when they're horny and have the chance to offload this turgescence onto the pearly-white belly of a female student who wouldn't so much as shake their hand in the street.

I wanted to explain to you that even at less than a hundred euros a pop, it was you who'd ripped yourself off. Through your own fault. All you would have needed was to be smiley and nice for me to be those things too. Lout. You couldn't distinguish a gaze damp with desire from an internal combustion engine.

You shook my hand as you left.

Come On, The Rolling Stones

Septamber 2014. I've been at The House for two months, working with a professional conscientiousness that leaves no room for a social or love life. Overstimulated by the great heat I stored up spending a month in the Midi, I'm in a state of fragility that's never brought much good with it. I've worked like a dog, but clients can do nothing for me. During my holidays, I looked for a holiday romance to suit the languid heat, some heartthrob who'd improve my siestas. In vain. I traced this sentimental fantasy back to a desire to fuck well, with the head I mean, to really want to fuck and to have this desire crystallised in just one man. It's more complicated than I thought. I ask myself warily if the brothel isn't curing me of something: excitement having come to be more significant than pleasure to me.

And I'm back in Berlin, delighted with my tan, how blonde I've gone, and feverishly seeking someone to show them to, tasting the promise of this like a culinary treat. Fate, which has no taste, brings me a text from Mark. Here's a guy who must have spent summer lamenting the emptiness of life and who vaguely perks up when he sees my name on his contacts list. The promise of starting out again, for a young dad who's not feeling himself, is part of infidelity. And I'm not the kind of woman to refuse to be a symbol.

Bang on half past three in the afternoon, Mark and his bike ring my doorbell. Visibly emotional, terribly timid, he enters my apartment, most of which has been tidied up for the occasion. As I start walking towards the living room, Mark at my heels, I realise I have absolutely no idea what he's come here for. I'm quietly getting over a monumental bender, and sitting across from him at the table, I wonder when he'll go home and I'll be alone again.

I don't have to wonder for long. After ten minutes of listless chat, Mark lets slip, with a meaningful glance towards my bedroom.

'Would you like us to get a bit closer?'

I didn't for a second consider this possibility: sleeping with Mark. Or if I thought about it, it was to feel a barely believable indifference rise up through me; not the least desire for sex, even with myself. I stare obstinately at my nails, as I do when I feel incapable of masking the disdain in my eyes. And I grumble through my hair:

'What do you mean, get close? Like, on the sofa?'

'For example, or whatever you like,' bleats Mark, half choked by his boldness.

Thank god, I was lucky enough to have a sofa that would kill any excitement. A real IKEA sofa for skint students, in very hard wood barely softened by flimsy cushions. A couple never sat on it without looking like they were at a marriage counsellor's. We look so out of place that I ask Mark:

'What are you really doing here?'

'You mean in Berlin?'

'No, I mean here. At my place.'

Mark squirms, ill at ease. The reason for his being here was obvious before I asked the question. And unless he's honest, unless he behaves as an adult and considers me as such, everything that comes out of his mouth from this point on will be nothing but long, drawn-out cowardliness. Revulsed, I listen to him make us both look ridiculous, certain there's no longer a way of chucking him out politely.

'No, I wanted us to talk, to get to know each, talk about books, music, make love, talk about our lives…'

Tricky to work out if he thought *make love* would have gone with his other improbable suggestions, but just the possibility tips me over into a murderous mood. As I've never learnt to be nasty, I let him drown in his terrible replies and say in an acerbic tone:

'Let's talk about books then, as that's what you're here for.'

A heavy silence, which Mark breaks with an embarrassed stammer.

'Can I kiss you?'

In his huge eyes flutters the assumption that he'll be able to convince me – what's wrong with Justine today, for goodness' sake? How could it be so easy, so natural at the brothel, and so difficult here? I don't reply. His lips, briefly making contact with mine, leave me as cold as if I'd been elbowed by a passenger on the Métro. I hope he can feel it. More than that, I hope he can feel my annoyance.

'You realise you're right at the point of getting yourself in the shit?'

'What do you mean?'

This type of question normally rocks married guys to their foundations, and Mark should be the first to show signs of anguish when I evoke the fatal destiny that waits around the corner for adulterous family men. But he has his set idea, which makes him impermeable to the voice of reason (the fact it's embodied by me undoubtedly makes reason very improbable).

'You have a wife, a child and no desire to have an affair. As long as you saw me at the brothel, it was fine, you were keeping all that inside a sort of security fence. It's here, now, that you're losing control.'

'Yes, I know…'

I hardly listen to Mark's pathetic babbling; he resembles Mister to some degree but doesn't have the breathtaking nerve to persuade me that what's evolving between us is a forbidden romance. There's nothing much worth keeping from this babble beyond the naked truth, which is demonstrated by his trembling fingers: Mark, poor guy, wants to fuck. That's what he's here for. It's bad of course, but he will only fully become conscious of this after having been relieved of the seminal burden robbing him of all his common sense.

'I also don't want an affair while I'm writing my book and while I'm working at The House. I've already tried and it doesn't work. It's a luxury I can't allow myself and honestly, I don't feel like it. I'm too busy. Neither you nor I have any interest in having an affair.'

Mark bleats that he knows, he knows. He's turned the problem around and around in his head a thousand times and of course it's a bad idea, but well:

'I feel so attracted to you,' he sighs as he places a hand on my thigh, this thigh so cold and rigid that beside it even the indifferent arm of the sofa seems sensual. 'I can't fight it, it's stronger than me.'

Of course it's tempting to fuck a whore without forking out a penny. I can't disagree. I leap up, light a cigarette without giving out the slightest sound. Mark wrings his fingers and sighs:

'I don't know, I can't get you out of my head.'

He stands up, in agony:

'I *jerked off* thinking about you.'

It's strange how hearing that does *nothing* for me. It brings *nothing* to mind.

'To be totally honest, with my work I have ten times more sex than I need. Most of the time it's shitty sex, but anyway. So I don't see what I have to gain from this situation.'

Mark doesn't really see it either, how could he? It must be hard enough as it is for him to admit what he's here for, since his desire to talk has evaporated. And he stares at me in silence, so expectantly that my nerves give way bit by bit.

'Since you came to mine, you could at least have the decency...'

'The decency?'

'To tell me it's just pussy you want. Nothing else.'

Because I'm not that stupid, jerk, even if I deserve slapping for my naivety – deserve, in truth, to let myself be fucked. Was I really that stupid to imagine we'd just talk?

Mark gets all tangled up in a messy soliloquy in which the only trace of honesty is his eventual admission that it's 'the physical side' he misses; in other words, that very warm little spot between the thighs of a girl where he can place his anguish and his grievances against his wife, so pure, the mother of his child – a warm, damp haven in which to forget himself and from which to draw the strength to be nice and gentle and loving, and steeped in guilt when he goes home in the evening.

'Yes, it's exactly as I thought. Pussy.'

Despite the fact I have the eagerness of a dead goat, Mark stays where he is, taking my hands in his and stammering inanities in which are buried some shreds of genuine entreaty. This would be the moment to kick him out of the door. But the only thing that comes out of my mouth makes no sense:

'So, that's what you want. Pussy and that's all. Without a thought, without anything. *Brainless sex.*'

And as Mark emits one of those pathetic sniggers that cowardly guys do when they're unable to say yes, I walk without a backwards glance towards my room, where the door stands wide open onto this bed where I don't think I've ever been held in a way that's meant anything.

'Come on, then.'

Nothing can keep Mark on his end of the sofa, not even my glacial voice, which is more professional than ever. I hear him run over like a dog, the clicking of his heels amplified by the high ceilings. And as he entwines himself around my back, I suddenly realise, and with a horrible joy, that I have no condoms. And I'd bet everything he doesn't either.

'Do you have the necessary?'

Just as I thought, Mark stiffens against me.

'Huh… No.'

I turn around.

'I'd love you to explain to me how you aim to cheat on your wife without a condom.'

Another snigger: yes, how stupid of him. From my side, the lack of contraceptives speaks for itself: I'm not with someone, and obviously I've got used to this idea.

'So. What are we going to do?'

'Bah, … but I…'

Bah, bah, bah, you idiot, oh yes.

'We're fucked, then.'

'Perhaps I could just…'

'Just what?'

'Just touch each other?'

'You mean, I can jerk you off?'

'For example. I don't know.'

I raise one eyebrow. Mark opens his mouth, closes it, opens it ten times. Poor Mark. A few minutes ago I was talking about his baby, and he made this painful, transparent speech to convince me that fatherhood was the best thing that had happened to him. That I couldn't understand, but that it changed everything. Nothing and nobody had brought him, however hard they tried, as much as this baby who was happy to simply exist in his crib. You became a dad and suddenly nothing else mattered, this little packet of flesh, so dependent, made everything else obsolete, both responsibilities and the freedoms you thought you could never live without. But you *can't*, in fact, Mark: it may actually be the exact opposite of this miracle of fatherhood to find yourself in the apartment of a girl begging for a fist around your cock. We know all about this miracle of fatherhood, which would elicit a forced laugh from any man if it didn't include the prospect of a hand job. One day not so long ago, Mark was a young Bostonian filling his beak with illicit substances, banging away at girls he *could* fall in love with. And then he had a baby and suddenly hand jobs became scarce. There's nothing like a child to reconnect a man of forty with the up-for-it adolescent slumbering within him. I'd have loved a young father to say to me, after having banged me like a convict on parole, that his relationship was a car crash since the birth of his child, and that you shouldn't believe the stupid things people say to save face: it's splendid to be a dad, but it's also unspeakably shit, and even if he loves his child more than anything else in the world, he no longer makes love with his wife and nothing can replace that love. Wouldn't that feel better afterwards? Wouldn't both of us feel better? In any case, what girl with any sense at all could swallow Mark's speechifying about fatherhood with this painful pole deforming his trousers?

Endlessly weary, and determined to push to the limit this waking nightmare, I chuck Mark onto my bed without encountering any resistance. He pulls his jeans down to his ankles. And in the silence of a tomb, I gratify him with a robotic blow job, devoid of any emotion but frighteningly efficient – because barely two minutes have passed when Mark exclaims that he's going to come. I can hardly believe it to start with, given the enthusiasm I'm putting into it. But it's the truth. How long is it since this poor boy has fucked? It's a question that throws a particularly miserable light on the scene: it really was an emergency; at the first sneeze he let everything out into his trousers.

I rub his thigh softly, at the edge of his slightly twisted jeans. Mark gets up; as he tucks his shirt into his trousers, he devours me with his big deer eyes.

'It was fantastic. Really.'

I howl with laughter. I never gave such a sad blowjob in all my life – in fact no, *sad* isn't the word, as I already gave sad blowjobs that had nothing in common with this diligent, furious friction. I have given some shabby blowjobs – and it's not that either. No, the word I'm looking for is more serious, it implies a heavy, bitter disillusionment. However, looking at Mark, you'd think I was the bringer of light. The same as all the guys who come to The House do – but at The House, it's my job. That's it: it was a whore's blowjob, what I just did. A blowjob that wouldn't seem out of place in some dark alley in the Bois de Boulogne, quick, efficient, leaving one's knees covered with mud and gravel – except that it's happening at my place!

I show Mark to the bathroom, undoubtedly so he can wash his cock as I taught him, with water but not soap, the idiot. If his wife doesn't fuck any more, how would she notice that his cock smells of sperm? It's a question I've been dying to ask all the married men the brothel throws in my path.

I lean against my bookshelf, fag in mouth; I imagine Mark is taking in details about me in my bathroom in spite of himself, my soaps, the make-up, the colour of the towels, these ridiculous posters torn down in the street by Madeleine, all these little things clumsily whispering stories to him about the true Justine, about the false Emma, who's a real girl with a real life, and I think he already feels ill at ease without all that.

I've been reduced to reviewing my book collection when he comes back and hops about behind me, and that's how we have a clumsy, aimless conversation. He doesn't know how to take his leave, and I announce in an expressionless voice that I have an errand to do. That's twice today that I'm saving our lives. I haven't looked him in the eye in ages and Mark asks:

'Is everything okay? Are you okay?'

Does he think I'm going to burst into tears? That I'm going to start to bawl and drag myself along the ground and, taking Mark hostage, tell him how I'm just a poor girl who lets married men persuade her to give them their first blowjob since the arrival of their firstborn? If I wanted to annoy him, the way to do it is already right there in front of my eyes.

'Everything's fine.'

There's no way I could recreate the conversation that followed, because Mark issues something so huge it effaces everything else.

'Listen, I don't know if I'm supposed to ask you this…'

I immediately know that whatever it is, it stinks.

'Should I give you something?'

Somewhat revulsed, I feel a certain joy seeing him dig himself a hole.

'Give me what? Money?'

'Uh yes, I don't know...'

I look away. Mark immediately gets himself knotted up in pitiful apologies. And I can't really blame him, in fact. I was so glacial, so robotic, that he sees no other way out but paying me. It was a whore's blowjob – so I must be one.

It can't occur to him, but a whore would *never* do that. A whore doesn't have the time to waste on stupidities like this. It's sad girls who behave like this. This phrase of Mark's sticks in my head for two or three days, this handful of clumsy words to try to dig himself out of it using money. It hits the nail on the head; after six months in a brothel, after having pulled through situations that would have made many girls cry, this is the moment when I feel like a whore. Mostly, this is the moment when this state of affairs bothers me. You'd almost think I had limits: fascinating. And I got there all by myself! Mark has nothing to do with it all, I've led myself to it, and it's our shared lack of dignity that's given rise to this consummate scene of contemporary, utterly pathetic quid pro quo.

As I show him to the door, Mark chances:

'Could we consider it as a sort of... warm-up? For a next time?'

That this idea could even flit through his head is a great source of consternation, but I'll have lots of time to devote to thinking about it in the remainder of the afternoon, slumped on my sofa chain-smoking – alone.

'Safe trip home,' I smile at him as I close the heavy door of the building, and Mark waves at me until I disappear. He goes as far as writhing around under the blinds of my room to ask me yet again if everything is okay and, as he can sense that I'm pondering slamming the shutter on his fingers, he cycles off stammering goodbye again.

As he heads peacefully towards Mitte where his pretty little family lives, I suppose the physical relief gives way to a gaping void, a feeling of self-disgust and of guilt that no shower, even with lots of soap, could wash away. And to reassure himself when he's in his wife's bed, Mark will imagine that basically there's nothing to confess. It's as if he'd been to Friedrichshain for nothing more or less than a wank – and no one has forbidden that, huh? The thought that his sex life has been reduced to that, to this kind of sordid embrace with a dishevelled kid who he'll always wonder about giving money to, will keep him awake and trembling – that would be only fair. At any rate, proof that fatherhood really does have a price.

Is She Weird, The Pixies

I DON'T REALLY KNOW WHAT TO DO with the trivialities of daily life in a brothel. I don't know which story to integrate them into if not mine. There must be a moment in the life of every writer when they would like to be able to draw. These images would have more weight if applied to the blank sheet of paper using precise, airy little strokes of felt tip or paintbrush. There are moments so light in a human life, moments of grace so fleeting that words would only weigh them down. Sometimes I'd like to be Reiser, Manara, that would be the ideal.

My head is full to bursting with these gems; and I can only tell them this way, juxtaposing them randomly in the hope that this page can convey their beauty. All in vain.

It's an October afternoon, I'm early and, as I like to do as soon as I get a job, I go for a coffee at the Italian on the corner. At least that's my plan, which I adapt slightly when I see Birgit at a table on the terrace, in my favourite place.

She's on the phone; I slip away like a fox to the bakery next door, where I'm served a coffee full of froth on a rickety table. There I scribble a few silly things in my margins, perturbed by the none-too-distant presence of a colleague in civilian clothing, drinking her *Feierabend* coffee. I hear, between two gusts of autumn wind, her Berlin accent so mystical and so familiar. She looks in my direction; in a cowardly move I grab my mobile, pretend to take a call in French that keeps me going to the end of my fag. Birgit must have recognised me, and I absolutely don't want her to think I'm a snob. I inwardly evoke the excellent argument that the girls from the brothel have no desire to be recognised; two pretty girls together two steps from The House, that's a bit much. But let's be honest, it's mainly that I don't feel like talking – and I know that Birgit knows that. She's worked here for ten years.

That doesn't help me stop feeling ashamed. And as I walk back past her, I address her a discreet hello, buried in my scarf. *Oh, hey Justine*, smiles Birgit – who saw me from the start, I'm sure of that now, and doesn't seem to hold it against me.

We exchange banalities, *How was the shift, when did you finish?* It's Wednesday, she has her kid at home; she's waiting for some food she's ordered for both of them.

The House would be a bit sad without Birgit, without her laughter and her expert advice as someone who knew the place when it still had only four rooms. Not much surprises this woman, which is a quality the new girls find reassuring. It's Birgit who, inevitably, walks past us in the line to introduce ourselves, bends her five feet nine inches at a right angle to look through the keyhole at whoever's sitting in the salon; and often she backs away, saying 'I'm not going in there,' and sits back down, all regal, on the big sofa in our salon. *Why?* asks the trembling troupe, certain of being able to rely on Birgit to sort the perverts from the good guys, the simple from the complicated.

'He's not my type,' Birgit replies simply, already immersed again in her copy of German *Marie Claire*. *He's not my type*, that's something you'd never imagine from the mouth of a whore, especially when she has to feed a big girl of fourteen – but Birgit has her principles. Money has nothing to do with that. She never rushes to introductions, and in any case she has her regulars, guys like Berthold who spend whole mornings with her in the Gold room, her favourite. And that's plenty for her, because it's obvious that Birgit isn't venal, it's a bit of extra comfort that she comes here for five days a week, from

10 o'clock to 5 o'clock, in rain, in hail and if the knights of the Last Judgement are on their way. And if she doesn't get any work, Birgit doesn't rage, unlike the other girls; she has lots of other things to do, her paperwork, her toenails, a blow dry, those and chatting with colleagues – but not normally me, because my German, while getting better all the time, leaves me impervious to the subtleties of their conversations. I don't understand, but I listen. And the words I grasp, coupled with those that I guess, tell me that Birgit is a mother to this whole little population. You can tell her everything, Birgit won't say anything. She's fully present at work, and when she leaves, her life here gives way to the other one she navigates with a different first name. Everything in her head is perfectly compartmentalised, except perhaps right at the end of a shift, when released into the fresh air, we all separate out our thoughts: then it's always a bit fluid, a bit warm – it's all still alive in us.

And it's at this precise moment that I surprised her, looking sad. It's obvious behind her smile, obvious like the grief of mothers who've dried their eyes just before their children get home from school. And if I feel the need to pretend not to have noticed anything, it's so as not to open Pandora's box, because that would call everything into question. And what could I say to whatever is bothering her? There are so many silences within her, a woman's and a mother's silences that are alien to me and that I can't deal with, I'm too cowardly for that. There are, within her, ten years she's spent learning the sang-froid and black humour not to be hurt by anything, ten years of making excuses for her regular absences, ten years of resignation that she hates calling that. Ten years of saying to herself that there are worse things, deep down, than prostitution, such as dying of hunger or dying of hunger with your child, or of being close to being kicked out by your landlord at the beginning of each month and losing sleep about it, and of begging from friends, relatives. Like bearing a life that allows you the basic minimum not to die of boredom; like feeling your dreams of youth wither away, one by one, for lowly and unsparing reasons to do with money. You can keep all that quiet, but there's always a moment when this wave of despair crashes down on any prostitute, even on me hiding behind a book, an experience, I who at twenty-five still have fantastic days before me, as much at the brothel as elsewhere.

And it weighs on me sometimes. To the point that I selfishly don't want to imagine the torments that eat away at a forty-six-year-old prostitute or the heaviness of this unanswerable question: what happens in two years, in five years? What will I do? Who decides, if not time? There's always an age when willpower and resignation don't count for anything any more: no one wants to fuck you any more. There's a moment when even prostitution becomes an inaccessible luxury.

C'est la vie, as Birgit would say in my language.

'I have to go to work,' I stutter, stepping away.

'Go on, beautiful, off you go,' Birgit replies with a shooing motion and that smile, so sad, so tired, my god, her voice all singsong as if she was seeing me off to school – whereas we both know I'm about to get screwed by men I've never laid eyes on. Birgit has something about her that says, *Needs must, such is our job, and who said it's a job without scruples?* C'est la vie!

Birgit with her black coat, her blonde ponytail, the leaden sky and this wind that smoked all my cigarettes for me, this depressive end of a day. I've forgotten everything before and after – and neither do I know what to say about this scene. However, there's an important message in it. Somehow I feel that if I don't talk about these women, no one will. No one will go and see the women hidden away behind the whores. And we have to listen to them. Within this empty shell of a whore, these few square centimetres of skin rented by whoever so desires, who no one ever asks to have a meaning, is a truth that shouts louder than in any other woman who isn't for sale. There's a truth in a whore, in her function, in this vain attempt to transform a human being into a commodity, one containing the most essential parameters of our humanity.

And may Louis Calaferte excuse me for having understood him so badly when I read him at the age of fifteen: it's neither a whim nor a fantasy to write about whores, it's a necessity. It's the beginning of everything. We should write about whores before we can talk about women, or about love, life or survival.

LA MAISON

And may Louis Calaferte excuse me for having understood him so badly when I read him at the age of fifteen: it's neither a whim nor a fantasy to write about whores, it's a necessity. It's the beginning of everything. We should write about whores before we can talk about women, or about love, life or survival.

'YOU KNOW THERE'S A NEW FRENCH GIRL in the house?'

Egon buckles his belt, shooting me a shining gaze from beneath his lovely brows. We've already gone beyond the time allowed, I must have made him feel something in spite of myself; and, you have to hand it to him, if he wanted to pique my curiosity and steal my precious minutes, he's succeeded.

'What do you mean?'

'I saw it on the internet. She arrived a few days ago, I think. Do you know her?'

'I don't know *all* French girls, you know.'

Yet I'm interested, so I sit down on the edge of the bed. 'Have you already seen her?'

'No. You know very well I'm faithful.'

'That's very nice, my friend. But for how long can you resist French temptation?'

Egon must have perceived the irony and the jealousy, the unlikely jealousy, contained in my raised eyebrows, because he bursts out laughing:

'Are you scared of losing your empire?'

This word *empire* puts me in an excellent mood, so I pose like an odalisque on the cushions, my arms thrust into my hair.

'Do you think I need to worry?'

'Not at all.'

'Victory without risk is triumph without glory.'

I give Egon a pitiful translation in German, then in English, of this noble quotation, which says more than I'd like about my confused anxiety: because this is the first time I've talked about war in the brothel.

It's all the girls can talk about, the new French girl. They wonder, as much as I did, if the arrival of this competition sounds the death knell for my unchallenged reign. And even if I force myself to stay calm with, let's say, the beautiful conviction of a sovereign, my first concern as I descend to the salon is to look at the little note stapled to the list of girls, describing the new girl as tall, voluptuous, long brown hair, dark eyes, large breasts (42D). Of course, Pauline is overbooked.

Two days later, when settling down to work, I pick up a scent I'm not familiar with. I follow it feverishly into the bathroom and she's there, Pauline, as different to me as it's possible to be, tall, statuesque, with a Parisian air that needs no words. I go up to her, feeling like one dog sniffing another:

'Pauline?'

'Justine?'

How does that happen? Two French voices make themselves heard and a whole domain appears, our own private boudoir materialises in the midst of the other girls. A friendship based on the fact of being French; I don't think this argument holds much sway in normal life. But in a Berlin brothel, it's a quite feasible kind of glue. To the point that I never seriously asked myself if, beyond that, Pauline and I had anything in common. Perhaps not. It's the irresistible power of attraction of your own language when you think you've got used to the fact of never fully understanding the people talking around you. It's not without charm, mind, this flow of words that gets a bit clearer day by day, without you really noticing. But when a compatriot murmurs and you understand, suddenly — it startles the brain awake!

Of this day when I met Pauline, I remember nothing but that — this excitement. I didn't leave a room without looking for her in the common rooms or the kitchen – even just crossing her path, like a gust of wind, fragmented my re-reading of *Germinal*. I followed her into the bathroom, delighted, bubbling with the need to know, with no other excuse than the pleasure of speaking French. By a happy coincidence, I was, in *Germinal*, at the part about the poor horse Trompette, who is taken down into the mine: at the bottom, the other horse, Bataille, the doyen, smells him, and it makes him go mad; his nostrils tremble with it. He inhales from his fellow, who's come from up there, the fields, the wind and the sun; the elusive memory gives him an immediate tenderness for this new recruit who's shuddering with fear. The latter has scarcely put this feet on the ground when Bataille caresses him with his muzzle, as if to transfer his veteran's courage to him. There's no point saying that the parallel, while pretty, stops there, for the reason that in Zola there's no tender paragraph without a tragic backlash: destined for the same terrible fate, the two horses will, I imagine, finish up drowned like rats. It's to my dramatic temperament that I owe my comparison of Pauline and me to two nags martyred in an imaginary mine. The metaphor doesn't go much further than the sensation of seeing the arrival of a being similar to oneself, speaking the same language, awakening the irrepressible desire to comfort them, even if it's in vain, to translate everything for them again, so they feel at home. Pauline smelt of newness; and I could never see a new girl without remembering myself at Le Manège. That's also why I was irresistibly attracted to Pauline. She had gone for the simplest option, had opened the first door her Google search had presented to her, hadn't bothered looking for something classier, more pretentious, more expensive. She didn't know what she'd escaped, she strolled into this, lucky, unaware of the paradise on Earth she'd unearthed by chance. She was fine here, there were no surprises, it was as the website promised; and I imagine that through her I was dealing with my nightmares, a return of the anguish I felt in Le Manège, when I didn't understand anything, when nobody spoke to me and it was no doubt better that way.

Not everyone had the luck, like Pauline, to take their first steps as a whore in such a homely environment. It's through the prism of the newbies that those who've worked at The House for a long time and myself measure how lucky we are. It's like a sudden revelation, to see them ask a thousand questions before daring to help themselves to a coffee, while we're stuffing ourselves with cookies, laughing open-mouthed, dresses hitched up to our bellies. I remember one girl roaming the narrow corridors like a grieving soul, mobile in hand, waist cinched by a fuschia-pink bumbag: an item that shows you've come from somewhere else, in this case a brothel like Le Manège where nobody would leave their things unattended. When I spoke to her, she threw me a fleeting half-glance over her screen. *Did she like it here? It was alright. Not enough money, not enough extras. Not enough clients.* From her way of evading the conversation, I understood she hadn't started counting on her colleagues to pass the time. Unless her career started in one of those brothels where girls kick their heels at the bar in a bid for clients, and perhaps her legs got numb in this house with such little pointless movement.

I'd thought we'd end up reeducating her in spite of herself. In the middle of a shift, Nadine, who had a bit of time to kill before her next booking, had got dressed again to go and get some clementines from the fruit shop on the corner. She'd offered to bring something back for the new girl: the latter had opened her eyes wide and, putting down her mobile, whispered with a glance toward the Hausdame's office:

'Are we allowed out?'

A painful reminder of Le Manège, where this was frowned upon. Nadine suppressed a moment of horror.

'What?! Of course we can go out, darling. We're all free and independent here.'

But apparently this freedom didn't make up for not earning the extras you work hard for elsewhere, and that here are often a question of generosity towards one another. After a few days, no one had seen the new girl again, and a few days later, no one would have remembered her name.

*

You need more than a common nationality to become friends. Having the same job doesn't guarantee it, for sure. But talking, that's what makes mine and Pauline's friendship: speaking the same language, not having to reduce or polish our thought in order to translate it as closely as possible. Saying the right thing straight out, instinctively.

In any case, it keeps us so busy, we're in danger of forgetting to work. Our tricolour coalition comprehensively *anschlusse* the kitchen, driving out the Germanophones, who daren't even ask us to at least speak English (and what a sly pleasure, after months of effort, to be those immigrants who do nothing to integrate!). The others listen to our nonsense as if it were music, smiling at the obscenities we enunciate in such dulcet tones – and why not, when nobody twigs on! The girls repeat a few of our words with indulgent clumsiness, delighted to have spoken some French. And we – untameable, holding forth, howling with laughter, imagining we're shouting in the smoke-filled Procope – imbibe hectolitres of coffee and philosophise about clients past and future: we savour our analyses, rectify our respective conclusions, delight in the nuances that come so naturally to us in French. We have a whole universe to reconstruct, to bring up to scratch; it's a mammoth task that intoxicates us, to the point that each new client makes us sigh like wenches who are tired out from doing nothing. And when Inge half-opens the door to announce the arrival of some layabout without an appointment, I go to introduce myself while inwardly praying that neither of us two is chosen. I shake the client's hand sluggishly as I murmur my name – because we're busy, Sir, isn't that obvious? What thug is this disturbing our conference in comparative semantics about the word *bite* and its – *weak* – German equivalents? Who else is there than we two whorehouse Barthes to point out the poetry of the French language when it differentiates between *pine* and *queue*, *con* and *chatte*, while our Rhine neighbour flounders in the inevitable repetition of *Schwanz* and *Muschi*? Certainly not the aforementioned

Rhine neighbour who has chosen Pauline and is waiting, big fat thighs crushed into the armchair of the salon, all cheerful at the thought of riding a French girl. Cursed German. Will the war never end?

'You can search as much as you like, the only real choice, for them, is *Schwanz*.'

'There's *Pimmel*. But who would say *Pimmel* in bed? *Pimmel* is for a little boy you're telling off for fiddling with it in public.'

'Really, I'm telling you, beyond *Schwanz* there's no hope. They have a smidgeon more choice when it comes to *pussy*, but experience shows they're often too shy or too well brought up to use *Votse*, which is the exact equivalent of our *cunt*.'

'I love *Votse*. It sounds filthy.'

'*Schwanz* is the protean word *par excellence*. It changes its meaning according to context. Perhaps there's only one word because it's a symbol?'

'Who needs more than one word? What about the hypnotic grace of…?'

And the ding dong of the bathroom bell cuts short a huge conversation we'll have to continue some other time – but so many things will have happened between now and then that we'll no doubt have forgotten this portion of the linguistic iceberg we've exposed. Perhaps there'll be a client, vaguely francophone, who, having exclaimed *minou*, will get the conversation going again from a new angle: how full French is of charming faux pas, like *minou*, and how tricksy this language is in its undisputed elegance – except for the uncontested masters of erotic dialogue: the French, goddammit!

I try to forget I know her real name. Anyway, she's now more Pauline for me than Léa; Pauline, this deliberate choice, describes her better, says more about her than the Léa she is to the rest of the world. She's Pauline even on the short journeys we make together, from the Métro to the brothel, from the brothel to Yorckstrasse, where I get off and she carries on. Yet it's in those moments that I feel myself brushing against another world, when we meet at the bakery before our shift, each of us bringing to the air we move the smell of our lives from outside, or when we leave at midnight in our civilian clothes. Perhaps because she speaks my language, I don't have any difficulty at all in imagining her apartment or her activities outside work, what she eats, a little of what she thinks; I wouldn't be surprised to bump into her on her bike, in the park, or on a café terrace with friends – whereas after months of being close, I still marvel that the other girls and I inhabit the same world. What poetic chance seems to be at work every time one of them materialises in the street in front of me! Thaïs brushing past my table in Krossenerstrasse, without make-up, in a baggy pullover. And that morning, too early for anyone, Lotte, dishevelled, her long brown hair swirling around her hips, crossing the road and without seeing me crouching down close by to do up the laces of her trainers… Each time it's like a violation of the half-dream in which they all gambol around. Even if Lotte's obviously coming home from an evening of MDMA and Thaïs is just coming down to get her order from the Thai restaurant, I sense inside myself the bad faith of a poet who won't admit to any coincidence not having a meaning, no banal reality – no, it feels like they've been placed there on purpose, by some conscious force, their fugitive presence providing me with yet another verse for this poem I'm writing without knowing the ending.

When I see her in front of the bakery, Pauline gives me the warm, familiar feeling of recognising a friend in a big crowd. The fact that we don't see each other outside work, except for these coffees before or afterwards, which are always in the vague context of work, is symptomatic of the value we place on the world outside, and how ferociously we defend access to this other world: not out of mistrust or fear – but out of a reflex created by the pressure that whores endure. That Pauline and I feel good as prostitutes, that we share opinions on the subject – does that also mean we want to have the sense of ourselves as whores outside what we are together? In the street no one suspects us of being good-time girls, but we know.

Because we only know each other within that framework, and it's impossible, in such a job, not to talk about it. It's as if there was always something to say about it, an endless amount, and the more you talk about it, the more you want to talk about it. It's true that it's fascinating and funny like few jobs can pride themselves on being, and Pauline and I are young, and wily, enough to see it as no more than a game we win on every level. But within this job are bloodier realities that we are too sophisticated to ignore; and perhaps we fear, in the long run, not lying to ourselves well enough, not being able to confess to our passing moments of depression without each depressing the other.

In April I'd spent a week in bed with angina. I hadn't been able to eat, drink, or of course smoke, a right I'd believed inalienable until then — and because I easily fall into despair, this defeat of my organism broke my morale. I thought so much while I was in bed, between gulping back the mucus and between poultices of coarse daisy salt, the comforting feel of which made me sob — I'd reached the degree zero of self-esteem that pushes a person to suicide or to shut themselves away in front of TV they hardly watch, they're so stuffed full of sombre thoughts. How precarious my situation seemed at this time! My noble objectives, my idea of transcending the world of the brothel had melted, leaving place only for the naked truth, which neither I nor anyone around me could escape in the long term: I'd worked in a brothel. You can write as many books as you like, this was the only thing on my CV anyone would remember — so smart. When I returned to The House I needed Pauline's smiles and enthusiasm, that unshakeable drive of a hussy who's being paid to be sexy; and the way we'd spur each other on. *Of course we make men happy. Of course we're the queens of this house. Of course this job allows us to live better than most other mortals.*

It was a lovely day; most of the trees had turned green in my absence, and the warm air carried pollen, lazy wasps, a scent of late spring. I was already downplaying my little basket of complaints in a playful tone: we need to get a new job, if only part-time, if only to be able to reply to those who ask us what we do in life. Because it entertains us, at the moment, because we're young, but we can't be whores all our lives, even if we wanted to – and objectively we don't want to. You only have to look at those who've worked there for ten years, since they became of legal age, to work out that it's not a deadly turn of fate that makes you stay at a brothel: just being used to this lifestyle, to this warm comfort that allows you to put everything off until tomorrow, the ease of earning this money. I know this word, *ease*, is highly relative; it's the word the others use, those who don't know if it's easy or not to fuck six times a day, to suck so many cocks and to do it well, with a smile, without a clumsy nip of the teeth, without a sigh of impatience; but we know, you and I, that as long as we are pretty and strong, as long as it amuses and flatters us, this money doesn't demand a lot of effort from us – that's what I call *easy*, I have the right to use this word. As long as a significant part of us is fed by men's attentions, by their desire, as long as we feel we're being paid for being beautiful and intelligent, this money seems easy to us. As long as we like fucking, and god knows it can go on, and even when it annoys us, we know very well that you get used to everything, you only have to look at the number of idiots who force themselves to run and end up liking it. And that's precisely the problem, the fact that sex becomes a habit, the *dura mater* of the conflict. How fucking becomes a sport, exercise – and even if it's the most complete, the most entertaining of all sports, in the long run you don't know when you're having fun and when you're only in it to win.

This job calls on women's capacity to lose their bearings and to find them again unchanged in the same place. Basically, to be able to fuck without feelings and without soul when they're paid for it, but outside the brothel, to give sex back its magical powers, and to the words used in sex all their meaning, as if no transaction had ever come to disrupt the notion of something sacred. Total compartmentalisation. You can't be whole at the brothel and outside. Of course we know, you and I, how much the cock of the man one loves (or that of any nincompoop one's slept with for free) is different – how much it counts. If all the others merge into one single neutral phallus, these all have their own smell and taste and unique ways. We know how much the noise we make with them sounds true, the emotion of it. And for a certain amount of time, it's we who decide to feel something more than friction or not. But that doesn't come from the brain; that comes from a part of us that gets tired, in the long run, of opening and closing these valves from one hour to the next. Because it often so happens that we go home and have no desire to fuck. Of course. You know that; already, in the Métro, you realise how nice it is to sit down. How good it is to do nothing. The program is written up in your head; when you get home you see yourself scoffing a falafel in front of the latest *Game of Thrones*, sunk into the sofa, wearing thick socks and a dingy dressing gown. That would be the ideal. But you can't hold onto this idea too much because your boyfriend is also home. Some evenings, you have to admit it's annoying. Even just talking: because we *also* spend our days doing that, for god's sake, almost more than anything else, we literally get talked at non-stop. He may well be your boyfriend, this man who waits for you with a smile and who legitimately truly desires you and is also a man who wants to talk. He has *plenty* of things to say, and undoubtedly many interesting things: but in the end, wasn't silence what you yearned for the most in this combination of falafel–TV show–dressing gown? And when bedtime arrives, as he murmurs in your ear fantasies that have you as the main character, you unenthusiastically gauge your keenness to make love, right then and there, and to commit to being penetrated for the umpteenth time: *Waterloo! dismal plain!*, my lad. Choosing between that and knowing if Tyrion Lannister is going to get his head cut off is a no-brainer.

It's hard to admit that to your boyfriend, especially in those terms. From any other girl it's understandable, to not really feel like it, to be tired, have tummy ache – any of these excuses trotted out in a disingenuous, moribund tone. It's more difficult when you spend your days satisfying other guys for money. I like the idea of the plumber, let's go with the plumber: no one would reproach a plumber for wanting to talk about anything but their work in the evening, however passionate they are about it. Yet at home, there are also leaking tabs and washers to change, and which heartless monster of a plumber would reply to his wife that that can wait, for god's sake, that he's fiddled about with pipes all day long, will it never end, is the world nothing more than one huge dripping tap? Well no! His wife asks nicely, she can't do anything about it; and it's not a lot to ask, a last, quick turn of the wrench for the sake of conjugal harmony. It may even be the turn of the wrench that legitimises all the others.

Except that the plumber may want to fuck when he gets home. Some evenings, I think I'd rather unblock the drains.

It isn't that bad either, I didn't say that. But before doing this job, did it often happen that you said, *Come on, let's get it over with* as you were starting to fuck? Did you let it happen, and did you surprise yourself wanting to make him come as quickly as possible, as if that was the ultimate goal, the one where all pressure suddenly goes away? Not to mention the idea of you coming too – it's sort of the point, after all. There's no money on the table to define the simple aim; no, it's simply about wanting to. He may well be your boyfriend, but some evenings sex is an effort, and you need the same patience, the same consistency, the same self-mastery as you do for the clients. And his desire and his tender actions have the same feeling of being demands that need to be satisfied. Sometimes I can no longer bear their smell in my hair, the compulsory smile, the fact of having to think about them, and I need time to remember that the man opposite me is the one I've chosen – and why have I? Sometimes I would be very happy having no one other than me to keep me company after nightfall.

The problem remains the same whether you have a partner or not, except that when you're alone you can moan in peace. When you fuck all day long, what do you think about in bed to send yourself to sleep? Countless times I surprised myself by thinking about what keywords to use on my collection of porn sites – honestly, the actual definition of doing your own head in. All the variations of sex between human beings passed in front of my eyes without inspiring in me anything but the yawns of a worn-out old libertine. Long moments of thrilling suspense as I near the limits of my twisted imagination, because there must be in this palette of frantic copulation one detail that will pique my interest and *make me feel like me again*. But what a heap of lies! How can I like the woman, how can I not dislike the man, who takes all that on the chin and asks for more? And lastly, more than my orgasm that is rapidly beating a retreat, that's what I'm regretting, the capacity to be credulous when it suits me – and that would suit me well, right here and now, to not know as much as I do about the work demanded by these awful films. It would suit me to be able, like everyone else, to let go of my personal little stress and fall asleep like an animal, without the shadow of a thought.

Since when have I been having this kind of conversation? Since when have I been able to watch ten, twenty, thirty scenes of double penetration at the same time as saying to myself that I need that as much as I need gonorrhea – and anyway, who says I haven't got gonorrhea? If I'm thinking of sex in these terms, like a long-distance race you risk coming out of with your throat and the rest of you riddled with thrush, what's left that interests me except art (my book that I'm not writing), my tax declaration and my impending coming-out to my family? I mean, what's left when it comes to thoughts that don't bring me to the verge of a heart attack?

This is when I realise that it may actually be progress. Perhaps Arthur is right, the aim of this experience could be to liberate me from this slavery to sex, and I only have to read or knit in order to fall asleep, like normal people (like *old people*). My god, it could become a habit, one no less unhealthy than any other. This is undoubtedly my chance – as the two Foucault books ordered on the internet and now gathering dust whisper to me – to learn as much about philosophy as I do about the human genital apparatus. When I think about the incalculable number of films, of musicians, when I think of the scary number of writers waiting for the public to see their worth, there's the promise I could still be happy for a long time without taking my knickers off once. I who have nobly planned, in some vague future, to read all of Hugo, all of Proust, all of Joyce… Here's my long-dreamed-of moment to elevate my soul above this obsessive fiddling, these lowly preoccupations. And who cares if Hugo is never as scintillating as a damp crotch, when the sinner emerging from his very warm mud, full of disdain for his flesh, is steeped in the conviction of being better than he is: now I've sated this pathetic part of myself, let's get to it and nourish my immortal soul.

But detached from the rest of me, my soul seems dull, lacking in appetite; the possibility of being immortal in these circumstances makes me despair somewhat. Some evenings I miss my soul as it really is, bawdy, unwholesome and yet ruled by its own morality, preoccupied, while awake or while resting, by this science of pleasure and the ways of adding my own stone to this beautiful turgescent edifice – some evenings I miss the monster I am. It's me who lures me to the depths, where I keep myself exquisite company. Where's that voice gone that murmurs to me, after a few pages of Aragon, that an orgasm would be the most vibrant of homages to this beauty? It's not easy for me to lose myself, but when it happens, I have no idea where to find myself again.

The problem in this job isn't what others think, it's what happens within us. Although it's not out of the question that one isn't influenced by the other. The fact of being convinced of doing something good doesn't make the word *whore* any gentler, nor prostitute, which implies total passivity in a job where in fact you never stop moving. You can't do a lot to counter the weight of a thousand-year-old religion, even in Germany where we have as many rights as anyone else. Renting out that part of our body as well as such huge, vague intimacy has nothing in common with any other job. To be clear in your own mind, you have to imagine the contrite face of a bank worker to whom you've replied 'whore' to the question *What do you do in life?* You can be as strong and sure as you like, it's not nothing to always be different. You don't need others to feel it, but others don't hold back from making it known. And I'm not talking about my bank manager or my landlord, or my gynaecologist; I don't care about the knowing smiles of the girls in the hair salon downstairs when they see us walk past, or the loaded silences of the building's tenants when we cross them in the staircase with a client who could be our grandfather. The real problem is guys. Guys outside, and the moments when they become attractive. Because I did try, one evening when god knows how but I wanted to fuck; I went on Tinder, where it's practically impossible for a girl to leave empty-handed. Unless you're really *very* ugly, or very fussy — or a whore, obviously. I don't know why, I didn't want to lie. Or in fact, yes, I do know why — I must have been more curious than truly excited, I only wanted the possibility of it. And also, for Christ's sake, because you have to stay polite, even when it's only about fucking, and what better question to empty out someone's stash of banalities than *What do you do in life?* The guy asks me, and it wearies me to make up a job; I don't want to come across as snobby by saying writer. I prefer to come across as slutty rather than pretentious (this moral tug of war, huh?), so I reply that I'm currently writing my third book, about brothels — thus far I'm doing marvellously — and for that reason I work in one.

There you are. *And you?*

Well, believe it or not, I'm still waiting for a reply. And I don't blame this poor boy. For sure, there must be men on Tinder who are cynical enough to leap on this golden opportunity to sleep with a professional without spending a penny. But deep down is this what I'm looking for? Do I really want to spend my free time and my hormonal ardours on men who are never more than another client, who only stay out of brothels for financial or vaguely moral reasons? Because no one ever *just* wants to fuck. You want to respect the other or be respected by them, or you would like to get to know each other, insofar as it's true that you fuck better when you know each other; and in a corner of your head, you don't exclude the possibility of liking each other, you aspire to unearth, even on such a trivial platform, something more consistent than anonymous sex. You never stop hoping you'll fall in love, because, everyone agrees, it's tiring to look. If couples have met at the Späti, why not on Tinder?

Spending a night with a whore is just about conceivable – but what if you happened to get a taste for it?

In this boy's defence, I could have gone easier on him. Doesn't this embryonic conversation contain in its entirety the irrational fright men have faced with the complex, avid sexuality of women? Isn't there a dark continent that's even more frightening than the simple fact of selling your body and your time? Because isn't a whore who come evening roams about on Tinder quite simply a nymphomaniac? A whore and nymphomaniac, that's a lot to announce to one's loved ones. There's nothing can be done about it; in the eyes of the world a girl who prostitutes herself carries around a placard shouting in bold letters, *I'm a lost woman*. It's possible that via the whore it's men you're really judging and condemning, their baseness, their misery, it's possible; but women have been a perfect scapegoat for so long that we don't see it any more, and this fact is not about to change. And I want to fuck who I like, without having to lie or justify myself, I don't want to scare men I see in the street and who are really attractive. You can't reeducate them all *manu militari* – so, my poor Pauline, when are we finding a job?

All of these lovely considerations haven't stopped us entering the building, although I feel there are now two of us ruminating *my* doubts. But we can hear, above, in the stairwell, Rosie with her ethereal laugh seeing her client out. Simultaneously, in response to our ring on the doorbell, Sonja opens the door, cooing the stage names of the two stars we are. We've hardly entered when Bobbie, always a bit sour, announces to everyone at large: 'Justine, there's already been ten men calling for you!' And Pauline's schedule is already swamped. The morning girls are slowly getting dressed again, because is there anything nicer than ogling the ones who are starting when you've finished? Lotte, who already has her headphones over her ears, is encouraging us to eat the strawberries she's brought from her garden. Margaret is brushing her blonde wig, the bathroom bell rings, 'What, already?!' exclaims Marianne and she rushes to swallow the last of her yogurt, not without whispering abuse at her client who must still have hardly washed his hands. Pauline and I, in this continuous flow of words, are starting to unlace our shoes and the doorbell below sounds twice, the telephone is screeching out too, Sonja doesn't know what to reply to any more. Delilah takes the best place behind the curtain to see the clients coming in, and despite the din you hear her emit joyfully:

'The French are here, all the men are coming!'

Which makes Pauline and I laugh — except it's not a joke, not really. Let's admit it without false modesty, if there's a place on this Earth where we are adored, desired, renowned, flattered like adorable despots, sniffed around and understood, envied and accepted, it's here, at The House.

And there, you see, may be the nub of the problem.

Twist and Shout, The Mamas & the Papas

I MISS THE HOUSE. THE WAY THE morning sun fell on the old parquet, the girls stamping around in the doorway; maybe I'm exaggerating the beauty of the flesh, the symphony of laughter, the lightness at the end of the day, that ungraspable magic when I stopped on the threshold of the salon to look at them. Perhaps it's just the distance that's making me sentimental; but I'm remembering this fleeting intoxication, this jubilation at being surrounded like this by women either naked or in suspender belts, like a heaven I hadn't needed to die for. It took my breath away. Even when they annoyed me, when they talked too loudly or when they were stupid, moody, brutal, bossy, bitchy, when I could have strangled several of them and mouthed off others, I found them beautiful. Theatre laid on just for me, the only spectator, the only public capable of loving them all equally. No one looked at them with such delight, with such calm sensuality. To the point where I often ask myself if I didn't come to The House for them. Oh, now I'm writing it, it's obvious: *men*, men are everywhere, you meet them in the street, at parties, almost everywhere. But whores, these heroines of my erotic imagination, there was only one place to meet them – and to think that I could never have found that…

I've always believed I was writing about men. I can't re-read my books without realising that I've only ever written about women. About the fact of being one, and about the millions of forms that takes. And that will undoubtedly be the work of my life, killing myself trying to describe this phenomenon, accepting the feeling of having in many hundreds of pages advanced by half a centimetre. And trying to be satisfied with this half-centimetre as if it was a major discovery. Writing about whores, who are such a caricature of women, the schematic nudity of this state, being a woman and nothing but that, being paid for that, it's like examining my genitals under a microscope. And I feel for it the same fascination as a laboratory worker looking at cells essential to all forms of life multiplying between two glass slides.

It's here that I realise just how fine the line between journalism and literature really is. That I'm not at all made to be a journalist, deep down. As egocentric as that profession can be, it doesn't come knee high to the narcissism that puffs up a writer like me, one incapable of writing about anything other than myself. I try sometimes. When I was in The House, or to be precise whenever I left it, my head was full of their witty remarks, of their laughter, of these essential phrases they let slip without noticing; I felt them alive, so alive, I had the feeling I'd seized a part of their soul. And that's not innocuous; it may be because their voice is ultimately only my voice. Between the moment when they talk to me and the moment when I put it down on paper, their vivacity seems to have got lost in translation, being that of someone totally outside myself. I write about them with too much love, too much reverence, too much thought; I mislay their stupid laughter that has such truth in it, the insignificant details of days spent in their warmth. Some bias within me, something outside of being a writer, wants to describe them like statues, like icons. I'd like them all to be unique in these pages, all splendid – but we ended up fusing into a single Woman, and their conversations sound like mine. This approval annuls all objectivity, a kind of feminine solidarity so deeply rooted that I don't even feel it.

When I'm with men, my critical faculties have always been deliciously dulled. In their company I always felt the swooning docility of religious devotees. My piggybank overflows with such blazing memories, always strangely linked with a feeling of happiness and regret. That struck me, one evening, while I was listening to *I'm Sticking with You* by The Velvet Underground; despite having chopped up some vegetables in my kitchen, I was on my bicycle whizzing through Steglitz, a few years before, during that sumptuous summer; the chestnut trees in bloom had an intoxicating fragrance, I was riding at breakneck speed, my headphones on my ears, thinking of that man with such violence that I almost got flattened at each corner, and I arrived exhausted at the café, drunk on Berlin and burning with passion. I was so young then. Since then, I've loved others who have made me happy, so why was this song that I've always listened to evoking this man, and only him? Why, as soon as I thought of the word *love*, was it he who appeared? That had floored me; as unhappy, as lonely as I'd been with this lover, my twentieth year had otherwise been a golden age that I'd chased after ever since, tirelessly, despairing of feeling as alive again, as full of the world. He'd never loved me in turn, and all the men who'd bothered to had inspired in me a love less devastating; the notion of surrender, of passion, was only brought to life in me by one-sidedness. And I know that as I breathe my last breath, it's this man's face that will appear to me, like the most formative love story this world had in store for me.

Who knows, if our paths hadn't crossed, what would have become of me. Diplomat? Doctor? Psychologist? Professor emeritus in some university? Instead of this melancholy writer full of herself, working in a brothel, washing up on shores she never dreamed of. All these things I could have done, all those I wouldn't have known! And this man knows nothing of this; I imagine his existence is following its implacable march, whereas mine, lacking in the slightest sense of organisation, has the impulsivity of an environmental catastrophe that's impossible to stem. When I think of him an image comes to me of a river that's escaped its bed and would engulf, without the slightest conscience, entire parts of a continent, villages, houses, other rivers – and I don't who is who in this metaphor: the black, raging torrent, is it him or is it me?

Dead Leaves and the Dirty Ground,
The White Stripes

FOR SURE IT'S EASIER TO SEE WHORES as sex machines lacking all feeling, throwing all their clients into the same basket of disdain and hatred, and miraculously falling in love the moment they step out of the brothel – because that's how women are made, isn't it? Let's just say this is how they wanted women to be. It would be too complex to give whores a voice and to see them as they are really, no different from other women. You don't need to prostitute yourself, to be forced into it by misery or to be completely crazy, or sexually hysterical or emotionally lacking. It just takes simply having had enough of slaving away to buy the basic necessities. If someone has to pay for the lastingness of this trade, it's probably the whole of society, the obsession with consumption – not men or women. Men and women suffer together under the same yoke. And I think about those men who don't have two pennies to rub together and who lack the possibility of selling their body – what do you do then? Of course it's less tragic to fuck for money than to sit in the street with your hand out. I impatiently await the idiot who tries to persuade me otherwise. Of course it's less tragic to be at The House than at Lidl busting your guts for a risible salary; the only superiority of the cashier over the whore is being able to say without blushing how you spend your days. Or maybe not without blushing… Maybe the day women are offered suitably paid jobs they'll no longer consider taking off their knickers to pay their bills – and the world will be better then, no? Or morality will be?

'Each person has their own idea of what's the worst thing,' says Birgit as we drink our first coffee.

That's what I think I hear; the phrasing is perhaps slightly different. Perhaps the words have nothing to do with it. But what there is to be understood slides between the languages and I grasp it very well.

'For me, it was not having time to see my daughter. For two years I had two different jobs, one in the morning, one in the evening, six days a week. A nanny was getting her to do her homework and putting her to bed. At night, I came home from work to an apartment as silent as the grave. I exchanged a few words with the nanny who told me that everything had been fine. I found myself alone in the living room with the left-over portion of dinner, and I said to myself *Shit, all of that for* this? You see what I mean? You can't, you don't have kids, you're still young, but I can assure you that more than once I cried, oh, as if I would never stop. I said to myself. *And tomorrow it starts all over again, and the next day, and the day after, and the day after, and…* I was exhausted.'

Birgit takes a long drag on her Vogue Bleue. Paula, who also has two children, makes an approving movement with her head while silently powdering her cheeks.

'We're back in contact with the father. He now takes her three days a week. I come here in the morning, I have a few hours elsewhere, I sleep enough.'

Birgit solemnly puts down her cup of coffee.

'Each person has their own idea of what's the worst thing. But you don't know what the worst thing is before having children. You find the best excuses once you have babies to feed.'

Lightly touching Paula's shoulder:

'You want the flowers from Berthold? They're pretty, but they're not my colours at all, I've just repainted my bedroom.'

Love Me or Leave Me, Nina Simone

LORNA. I WONDER IF SHE CHOSE THIS name after reading *Druuna*, by Serpieri. The eight-year-old girl who with a red face devoured her uncle's porno comic strips while the rest of the family was in the garden always shudders with embarrassment at the idea of admitting she knew this book and the names of each of the characters. Lorna: engraved in my memory, these two syllables will forever evoke the scene when the big lumbering Druuna is brutally taken by a family of wacky humanoids, and the mother, who is running operations, has the name Lorna, which always makes me think of a disgusting sexual practice. How many fluids gushed onto these three pages of such poor taste! As soon as I close my eyes, the line drawing and the areas of muted colour come back to me with the vividness of childhood memories, and I now know how marked I was by Lorna's huge breasts and the way she caught hold of Druuna's arm to inject her with the product that transformed her into a bitch.

Lorna, my Lorna, is built the very opposite of her namesake. Blonde, elegant, fine-boned and always wearing an impeccable chignon that's hardly any looser when she comes out of the bedrooms, and which she turns into a ponytail after her service. She has a sumptuous mane that she's stopped leaving down after noticing that men can't stop grabbing her by it – and what a haven for germs so much hair provides when you spend your days lying on the groins of a dozen men.

Today Lorna's in a sulky mood: lying on a mattress, on the ground, I'm sunbathing as I listen to her grievances, eyes wide open behind my dark shades.

'Anyway I felt I shouldn't have come. There are moments like that when the vibes are shitty. But it's two weeks since I've worked and I've got a massive pile of bills to pay. I didn't have a client all morning – and I was starting to think I would've done just as well staying at home when Sonja came to tell me that a guy called Klaus had booked me. Obviously we knew each other, but she has a way of telling you that, as if I could remember hundreds of guys called Klaus that I've known here, or Hans, or Peter… And in short, this Klaus arrives, this old bearded guy, and suddenly I remember and I say to myself, *Oh no, shit, not him…*

'But I simply had to go as it was my only client of the day. I vaguely remembered that he was annoying but I was convinced I could get rid of him. Already, in the men's salon, he started to piss me off, to say it was lovely to see each other again, he'd wondered where I'd gone, blah blah blah… Suddenly I said to him I'd had a child. It came out without me even thinking about it. And he was off on one again, eyes wide at having gleaned this information: "I knew it as soon as I saw you!"

'I already felt huge, but then he goes on: "I had the feeling I had a different woman in front of me, a real woman. Not a child any more."

'Thanks, jerk.' Then it went from bad to worse. As he's a psychiatrist – well, that's what he says, maybe he's lying, but he's so crazy that I tend to believe him – he talks to himself, it must give him a break from his appointments. I was lying there, in the Tropical room, looking at this old man's body next to mine, my body that was ultimately not so bad, despite being a bit chubbier than before, and I was thinking of the first time he came to see me. Late evening, at the end of the shift when I'd really had enough – but when you start this job you have truly mind-blowing reserves of patience. It fascinated me that he was a psychiatrist. Or let's say, it fascinated me until he started talking in that pedantic tone that they all have in that profession. This obsession with wanting to guess who you are, why you do this job, where you come from. I was playing this crazy game, I was telling him lots of things just to see what Freudian dung he would drag out of his skull to heap on my childhood memories — and in truth I was blown away by his lack of boundaries. He was afraid neither of being difficult nor of me abruptly stopping him to say *It's not that at all, you're completely off the mark*. I didn't do it, primarily because, even in my beginner's enthusiasm, I had no desire to set him off again, secondly because it was a bit like with horoscopes, a lot of what he said sounded right. If you go into a brothel to talk to a whore about her father or about her relationship with men, about the way she perceives her femininity and femininity in general… Good god, there's an eighty per cent chance that that will hit the nail on the head. I don't need to be a psychiatrist or even to have read Freud. I was right there looking at us, it was late and I was knackered and also very quarrelsome, and without even realising it I started tinkering out loud with the concepts of abandonment, the Oedipus complex, love and hatred of the Father, and I suddenly started to cry my eyes out. It's hard to remember what about, but I must have touched on something so true that I found myself sobbing on this old man's torso — something that must have reminded him of his consulting room and he certainly liked that, fucking a patient. I was so embarrassed at spending the hour he'd paid for like this that after a moment I got hold of myself as best I could. I was completely emptied out. Then I wanted to do what I'm best at beyond feeling sorry for myself and for my *abandoning* father — I wanted to suck him off. Within the idea of sucking him off, fucking him and then throwing him out, and of tidying the room while listening to CAN in my headphones, was something uplifting that would get me back on track, and I hoped he would do me the courtesy of getting an erection and coming quickly; but he was already in his seventies, and obviously he didn't have an erection. My tactfulness at that moment is what misled him

– because today, in a similar situation, I would start with my hand and it would be sorted out quickly. But at the time I still saw all clients as men and I feared their gaze, I wanted to be the whore whose tenderness redeemed the coldness of all the others. The fact he wasn't hard annoyed me, for the strategies that that demanded of me in my nervous state, but the idea of wanking him off with the so obviously professional intention of making him hard enough to slip on a condom embarrassed me. Embarrassed by something in me that wasn't prostituting myself. And as for putting a condom on his limp dick… So there we have it, I sucked him off without a condom. There was one within arm's reach, but when he started to get hard I felt he was going to come very quickly and I was afraid that the time I needed to tear the packaging and unroll the condom would make the soufflé collapse. So I carried on. He came in my mouth, I didn't even think of running to spit it out in the sink, especially since with all the micro lesions there are in the mouth it's less dangerous to swallow than to walk across an apartment with your mouth full of spunk. Off you go, swallow, it's done. For me that's all it was, the practical side of things, and I didn't think about it again until today.

'He came back a week after, all hot and bothered, and it annoyed me to see him again. The first time he depressed me for the whole evening, and I had no intention of letting myself be dragged down again. I was in luck because he hadn't come to fuck me or even to sound me out with his stupid questions, he'd come to tell me he couldn't carry on seeing me. I still remember the relief and the effort I made to look like a rejected lover. He said he'd end up getting too involved; he was married, he had no desire and no time to fall in love and I was a young girl too full of life for an old man like him not to lose his head about sooner or later. And I was thinking, *So get out of here, you imbecile.*

'Two weeks later, I was behind the curtain spying on the client who'd just rang the bell when Klaus appeared. I started in exasperation, thinking he'd changed his mind – but he was there for Gita. He had his Gita period.

'Anyway, whatever, just now in the bedroom, I'm listening to him enjoying the sound of his own voice and already imagining myself getting a Post-it and writing on it in lovely script *No meetings with Klaus!*, when he starts to talk to me about Gita. How Gita stopped receiving him after a few appointments without even explaining why to him; it's the Hausdame who told him he was being given the heave-ho. And I remember perfectly Gita telling Sonja that she didn't want to hear his name again, that it was beyond her, she would willingly have explained to him but she risked getting nasty. Sonja spoke to Klaus, but he came back under another name to see if that might sort out any misunderstanding. After that, he must have gone to haunt another brothel. He tells me this story as if it was the ultimate affront, and then his theory that Gita and he had got too *involved*, and that's why she'd decided to deprive him of her company. Note that he doesn't for one second imagine that he might just have pissed her off.

'"You see, deep down it was better for me too," he says, "because it would have ended badly. Gita – well, her real name is Julia but I don't tell anyone that (*as if you were telling me something I don't know, you asshole*) – I could have given her a child."

'He comes out with it just like that; it took my breath away. And also he used the word fertilise, as if he thought it was his job to perpetuate the German race or god knows what, and he'd seen in her a more or less conscious, yet very strong desire, to be fertilised too, so obviously… I look up at him, forcing myself to be quiet; I don't know if I want to laugh in his face or give him a couple of slaps, when he starts to tell me he also stopped seeing me, if I remember rightly. And without having to use the Hausdame – no, he took the initiative all by himself. He must sense a question in my silence because he starts to rave – there's no other word – about how receptive I seemed to him. What he means by receptive, I realise, feeling as if I've turned to stone, is receptive to being impregnated. At this point it's my turn to give my own savage analysis; I want to see how far he's ready to go in his insanity without a single sign of encouragement on my part, and I ask him to elaborate on the topic of impregnation. This word in my mouth gives me the feeling I'm lying on the torso of Doctor Mengele. And he gives me this bizarre portrait of myself two years earlier, young, full of life, hormones dripping out of every pore – my first sign of assent according to him was the way I threw myself on his shoulder when talking about my father. Second sign, which literally rooted him to the spot – I swallowed his *seed. Donnerwetter*…! That's when I understood that you can catch things much worse than chlamydia by sucking off a man without a condom, things that unleash not discharge or itching but that flare up in your face years later when you're not thinking about them any more. So I swallowed some *seed*, without asking for anything in exchange and as part of a total gift of myself, bordering on the most brutal desire to become a mother. In my state of shock, I decide to play the idiot in order to make him face his own vacuity; I tell him I was certainly not in any danger of falling pregnant by that means. He assumes the most erudite air to explain to me that I do know that this mouth and *that one down there* are psychoanalytically the same thing, that with both it's about absorbing the man's seed. And I'm consumed by the need to laugh, to laugh so much I piss myself, until he decides to leave with a slam of the door – but what stops me is always this unhealthy fascination with what's happening in his head. I need to know if he really believes in what he's saying, and I think of the face Gita must have pulled hearing him say these kinds of things… Obviously I imagine how much fun it would be to hurl at him, *But big fella, the only reason I sucked you off without a condom was because you weren't hard and you were already pissing me off too much for me to waste my time playing games with your dick, I wanted to go home and smoke a joint the size of a nuclear warhead. And since you want to talk about psychology, I also studied some at university; it seems totally logical to me that a young lady would prefer to be fertilised by you rather than by a guy of the same age, with the physique and the aura of a good breeder, if indeed she's hoping to be fertilised in a brothel. Thank you, but I fuck four guys a day who'd make more alluring parents than some crusty old fool.*

'Why didn't I say anything? Because he never stops talking! He had already left for Planet Klaus, filled with woolly theories and semantic crevasses – saying that now I was a mother he felt less threatened, and I wanted to say to him, *Klaus, listen, I can feel myself becoming a mother again by the demiurgic power of your words, it's best if we stop seeing each other.*

'As if that wasn't enough, there he is, ruining my shift for good by saying that once they're mothers, whores lose a lot of their clients. Which first of all isn't true, and secondly fuck you, old man. Yes, because the power of very young girls over men can't be matched. And I knew that he was basically right; I wanted to knock him out with my bare fists – but I saw from the clock that by talking so much rubbish, he'd eaten up pretty much all of his hour, except the five minutes he needed for a shower. I had a flash of jubilation, and as I started to slip my knickers back on, I protested that yes, fine, men love very young girls but, to my mind, those who prefer them to others are severely lacking in confidence in themselves; it's disconcertingly easy to impress young girls with minimal effort, you don't even need to be good at anything. Men who get fixated on young women have small cocks or are impotent, or both, that's what I think. And real women show up the men who need pristine bodies, or breasts that point at the ceiling, as losers. Obviously, now he's cornered, Klaus, who has a reply for everything, throws himself into a flimsy soliloquy to explain that he isn't like that, of course, no, really – but on seeing me getting dressed again, he looks crestfallen, as if he'd forgotten where he was and for how long. At one time, I'd have interrupted him so I could do my job, something to do with having a clear conscience, but in fact it's *his* problem if he talks too much. He asked me if he could add another hour, and this is the point when it felt like hell was opening beneath my feet – and I looked at him, with his underpants as tired as he was, his Doctor Diafoirus beard, this poor old guy who imagined his seed was so ardently desired by girls who are just trying to work and to stay polite, and I replied *Sorry, I'm booked up 'til next week.*'

Lorna lights a cigarette from the butt of the last one, spits out the first puff in a furious sigh:

'You see, this guy is sixty-three years old, his wife is seriously ill and hasn't wanted anything to do with sex for ten years. You don't need to think about it for long to understand why he comes to a brothel. He must feel like his fire is going out. That upset me – for a moment. And then I said shit, my life isn't always easy either, I've got a baby to raise and a heap of problems that go well beyond money, and in fact I don't need a small-time psychiatrist to come and tell me that I'm getting on, that my clients are all going to flee into the arms of the young ones, that I'm looking for a father by proxy or a symbolic parent, I don't need someone to come and break my balls when a hundred, a thousand other men are happy to pay me to do my job.'

At that moment Gita flies past, summoned by some professional obligation, and Lorna grabs her en route:

'Gita! What if I say the name Klaus to you?'

She slows down just a little, puckers her pretty nose, as if assailed by the smell from a sewer.

'You see,' Lorna goes on, 'when a name as ordinary as Klaus brings a specific client straight to mind, it's a bad sign. In short, I wanted to tell him so many things, things that would have put him back in his place with a click of my fingers. I don't overdo it. In retrospect, the whole world is there at the ready with all the brilliant comebacks you could have used. Indeed, what kills me in this job is this possibility, as a woman, to annihilate in one fell swoop this masculine pride that puffs up at the least thing and is based on nothing, and to stop yourself from doing so. Some manage, not me. I don't want to spend an hour, or even thirty minutes, next to a man to whom I've just said no, his cock isn't as big as he thinks it is, that he may well be cute but he still has to *pay* girls, so enough of the attitude… All these guys who go home convinced they've made a girl come. Those who take the condom with them into the bathroom because they heard – you wonder who from – that some girls inject themselves with the come of men they plan on blackmailing. Can you imagine everything there is to say to *that*? All the replies that pile up, in the long run it's like a cyst I can feel beating inside me, right there, in my belly. And I will never be able to write a book about it, I have no talent and it would seem like revenge, but fuck, there should be a book about it. Reading that would make me laugh. Would make all whores laugh. And everyone else, because brothels, deep down, are nothing but a magnifying mirror where all the faults, all the vices of men that are tempered by daily life become deafening.'

In the beginning, I understood Lorna even less than I did the others because she was always launching herself into debates in the Berlin dialect with other Germans who didn't care about being understood either. And Lorna didn't decide to speak more clearly, in a twinge of conscience, when she saw me with my eye sockets twitching as if I were watching a tennis match between her and Birgit – but I got used to it. Through continually being faced with this strange accent that chews up most words and reinvents the rest, Lorna's voice and intonations became part of my familiar musical vocabulary – and, astonished, I realised I understood her. I understood her, and above all I knew her well enough to ask her to repeat fragments of sentences that escaped me, and one morning I surprised myself by replying *Allet Jut* to a client who asked me how I was in the way Lorna did when she arrived in the mornings. *Allet Jut, Schnecke.*

The German I speak, this loony lexicon made up of Berlin slang and badly declined scholarly words, the only thing I've picked up that I can boast about to my dumbfounded family – I find it quite funny that I've acquired it in the brothel, from contact with Germans who come from all four corners of the country, and especially with Lorna, with Birgit who, without wanting to, allowed themselves to be deciphered like one of those great books that you normally don't finish except at uni, after a term with a dry teacher. They are my Molly Bloom's monologue – and yes, once you're inside it, once you've overcome all the obstacles, it's the kind of gratification you rarely get, and it makes you happy to your very core.

Summertime, Janis Joplin

THIS MORNING, IN THE MIDDLE OF THE list of appointments, I saw a little note stapled to the schedule: 'Svetlana has finished.' She isn't on holiday, it's not a break – no, she's finished working here. I imagine that a normal employer would have written, 'She has resigned'; finish is a word unlike any others. Straightaway, without thinking, you fill in the rest of the meaning: 'She's finished with all the stupidities.' Or not even that, you don't need any kind of precision – just, she's finished. She's no longer of our ilk. She's no longer a whore. I'm reading things into it for sure: but in this choice of verb, I sense the tacit agreement between The House and Svetlana to not call her any more, not even as an occasional escort, nor to relaunch her every two months as happens with the girls who make themselves scarce for unknown reasons, but to whom they wish to convey that if the chips are ever down, they are always welcome. Her photos disappear from the site. Her locker no longer has a sticker on; inside it is the emptiness of abandoned rooms where a hairpin will forever linger…

A whore who disappears; that necessarily makes the others think. Birgit said one day – that must be the first joke in German that I got – that every time a man gets married, a whore is born. I look for an equivalent joke that would explain their disappearance, but I fail.

No one knows where they go – the world has, quite simply, taken them back. What becomes of them? Well, they become normal people, I imagine. But I wonder: now she's stopped, now her embraces are free, does she walk in the street, all peaceful, like all the women who've never prostituted themselves? By abandoning the brothel, do you lose from one day to the next this very highly tuned sense of being a woman? Do you lose that habit of wondering, every time a man looks at you, if it's an old client or a future one? On a café terrace, sitting alone near a table of ten guys who daren't flirt and are pretending to tap away on their mobiles – do you still vaguely fear that they're in the middle of comparing us with the photos on the site?

How do you isolate this piece of your life from the rest? Whore is not so much a career, in fact, as an agreement made with yourself one day: the decision to shift the idea of emotion that is attached to sex and not to care about it any more. Once you've worked at the brothel, you can't go backwards, you can't pretend that sex has never been a job. Everyone else can carry on not knowing that, it's not written on a girl's forehead – but *we* know.

Do you ever really stop? What becomes of that feeling in the stomach region when you hear someone say, for whatever reason, *whore*? You can't debate prostitution objectively – and you need to avoid these debates, anyway, unless you want to betray yourself through your uncontrollable vehemence.

Svetlana has finished. And at the brothel as elsewhere, life goes on; her absence will create a void for her friends, which others will rapidly come and fill; there's nothing of the wake about it, nobody seems to think of it that way – either that or perhaps it's also part of the job, not to get attached. To think that she was, for a time, a centrepiece of the evening shift, that you could recognise her voice from afar, that from her scent you know what room she's just occupied, the sound of her laughter, of her *cries* – and that on departing she can leave only a tiny trail that is swept away by the need to carry on working, carry on living: it's this same pattern according to which we like certain clients but spend six months realising they may never come back. And if they don't? There will be others. Being a whore is a job that can only function through forgetting: clients efface the memory of their predecessors, girls efface girls.

I think they all have – that we all have – a space inside us for the girls and the clients; but it's not regret that fills this deeply buried space. It would be out of place to regret that one of us has changed lives, has passed to the other side of the mirror. We all know why someone finishes.

Perhaps I shouldn't even mention Svetlana: she's left and she's fine, she undoubtedly wouldn't like me saving her from oblivion by remembering her, because she was pretty and funny, and because her adventures have made mine more interesting. But whores aren't called, in some cultures, public women for nothing, I'm afraid. If we are different people at different times of our life, then Svetlana, this precise part of herself (which is as theatrical as Justine is for me) will always be public. Svetlana always exists in that dimension of the universe where she is nineteen years of age, with thick blonde hair and the most beautiful breasts I've ever had the good fortune to see (may the women to whom I've whispered this compliment please forgive me).

What breasts! I forgot to be jealous of them; sometimes I muttered within myself, *Yes well anyway she* is *only nineteen*. Svetlana came back from the bedrooms superb, naked – as much as the others: but in the middle of this benevolent forest of nipples, my eyes recognised hers immediately. They were of that blessed species of breasts that are small but bulky, heavy and sometimes sticking two fingers up at all the laws of physics, insolently taut like a disdainful chin, wobbling very slightly when she walked and I imagine – oh, how I imagine! – bouncing exquisitely in the purple darkness of the rooms. Juddering like two flans, with these tips only slightly pinker than her white skin, and this affecting curve between the bottom of her breasts and the protuberance of her ribs that was lightly accentuated when she leaned over the ledger to record, in her strangely plain handwriting, what time her client left. Her client who'd spent every minute of his appointment in a state of mute adoration. They took care of her; sometimes you saw her coming out of the Studio with her buttocks and thighs red from having been smacked, but some divine grace seemed to save her breasts from the obligatory punishments. Seemingly waterproof, pale as milk, the nipples lazy, indifferent, those of a virgin to be worshipped through the gaze.

Yet a client made her cry one day when I wasn't there; she didn't come back the next day. It was Delilah who whispered it to me in the kitchen. Nobody had remembered what he looked like, something that is, however, of the greatest importance; but the Hausdame got mad and warned him that if he behaved in this way, no girl would want to go with him again. Behave in this way? No one knew, either, what he'd done to Svetlana to reduce her to tears and make her rush out of the room before time was technically up. The debate was still raging in the common room, each girl combing her personal history for a client who'd been flagged up, who could have got past the vigilance of the Hausdamen – there are too many! And then each girl is disgusted by things that others don't mind; how do you distinguish one madman from another? Svetlana may well have been young and new to the job; it's not so easy to make a whore cry, especially here: it suggests you've frightened her, hence to have made her forget for a moment that nothing can happen here without her wanting it to. It suggests you've been speedier than a whore's lightning-fast process of thought, to nip in the bud the idea of leaving the room to call for help.

This idea reminds me what a sword of Damocles hangs over our heads, and I talked about it with Pauline to lighten the load: if tomorrow a fanatic shows up with a razor blade in his pocket and decides to redesign a girl's face, nobody here can stop him. There are no bouncers, but that wouldn't change anything much: they wouldn't have time to reach the first floor before the girl's throat was cut. And even leaving aside the razor blade, interjected Rosamund, who was listening to us, one buttock perched on the kitchen work surface, if tomorrow one of those regular clients who we've grown to trust blew a fuse – say he has a burn-out and comes with a gun under his coat, determined to leave neither calmly nor alone… Rosamund enumerates the possibilities while cutting up some ginger, without looking up at us weighing each of her words, slight chills going through us. Let's imagine that the girl is lucky enough to find herself on the ground floor, near the common room, so in a position to alert someone: who says that the feverish entry of the Hausdame, the door handle being turned or any old noise from outside wouldn't push the desperate client to pull the trigger? Just like that, without warning.

'BANG!' says Rosamund flatly, pointing her finger toward the table where Pauline and I are smoking.

But even if he doesn't fire, not straightaway; even if he contents himself with grabbing the girl by the hair while shouting, eyes wild, that his life has no meaning and that if they call the police… If he backs away towards the half-open windows with the whore shaking with fear against him, the two of them clamped together like two mating beetles… Is there some kind of manual to teach staff what to do in the presence of a maniac? No, we're fucked: if a maniac decides to reduce our flock, the only thing left to do is hope that God will recognise his own.

This incident makes us more careful for a week, before time passes in its usual way and we forget (even if since this day, as soon as a client looks for his wallet in his inside pocket, the image comes back to me of Rosamund peeling her ginger, thumb and index finger holding firm, hideously calm – BANG!). We can't all forever squeeze into the ground floor and nobody plans to – and anyway, we all know that bad things only ever happen to other people.

For a few days I wondered what awaited Svetlana outside; I pictured her already lying in the arms of a youngster like herself for whom the past mattered little – at nineteen years of age, the past is only ever a tiny bubble filled with sensations, nothing more. I didn't think a rough client had made her run away, not given the psychological coalition we all represent to one another – no doubt because I'm twenty-five years of age and the day when a client makes me cry will be the day I'll curl into a ball and die.

The fact remains that I fell for it hook, line and sinker. He looked completely normal, at the start – I wasn't at all wary. He was handsome; but just like bad things only ever happen to other people, madmen rarely wear their vice on their sleeve. With age I should have learnt this, and understanding this releases me from my inertia. I did feel a certain tension in the air when we arrived in the White room. This man filled the space in a strange way, not quite normal. But I've seen so many things here; there's no more childlike, more innocent room than White, and it's always there that the most banal men feel themselves grow claws and fangs – as if immersion in this world that smells of little girls inspires them with the desire to pillage.

I was standing up, smoking a cigarette as I looked at him, and I wondered what had brought him there, *him*. A handsome boy like that. The heaviness of his eyelids put me in mind of a universe as hopelessly lost as Atlantis. He must have felt this spark of desire, and he must have been one of those who like whores who display a calm resignation – perhaps he was even one of those who get excited by the almost palpable disgust of first-timers.

'You look so young,' he sighed, nose pressed against mine. 'How old are you?'

And it was obvious I was going to reply truthfully, he clasped his hand over my mouth:

'Don't tell me. You don't seem more than eighteen. Shit, you could even be younger.'

'I could even be younger,' I cooed while slipping down the straps of my slip, in doing so delivering one of those shameless lies that only have any credibility in the bedroom, and which he will only have believed because he wanted to.

'No wait, stay dressed. It's very pretty, what you're wearing there.'

He had a superb nose, which he moved around my neck very

gently, and in a deep voice he emitted these words that brought Atlantis stealthily back towards the surface:

'I like young girls, you know.'

His hand grasped mine and placed it on his thigh.

'Can you feel what you're doing to me?'

I was straddling him and his breath had the smell of men from outside; I felt awaken within me a sickly desire for his hands on my normally numb body. I had in my lower back this atrocious and delicious itch, this desire to be taken, soon, not straightaway, not like that; this sensation of being alive, my god, so suddenly alive, without a clock in my head, without the least idea of where and how this would end – and the scene could have lasted forever if, while I was humbly caressing his cock with my cheek while holding back moans of desire, I hadn't heard this same voice, full of the violence of men who have a hard-on.

'Suck me like that, without a condom.'

And just *like that*, I was a whore again. I felt something like a bucket of ice cubes in my back; I tried to maintain the cold politeness of a geisha to explain there was no question of that – when suddenly a torrent of professional observations rained down on me, *I don't know him, he didn't take a shower, he seems weird.*

Wanting to be sucked off without a condom, there was nothing weird in that. It was his face that looked different. It was his way of insisting, again and again, to such a degree that nothing was left of my desire but the wish to scratch him, which worried me. An instinct, nothing to do with the one you learn in a brothel – just a woman's instinct – whispered to me that I couldn't trust him any longer.

I don't know exactly when I realised it was him. From a range of things, no doubt: his obsession with age and the contained brutality of his slaps, as if he was holding himself back from punching me. I was fascinated by what I saw sweep across his face, fascinated and terrified. I was telling myself that the moment when I couldn't bear it any more was coming very quickly, he looked just like a dog about to bite, to tear me to pieces – I was stupidly delighted not to be bored. From outside, it looked more like we were fighting than making love; I was thrown around, pulled by my hair, crushed beneath his weight, still in control but convinced I wouldn't be for long – like a wave devouring an entire dam, I could pull back again and again, but I'd end up going there too.

My mistake was to believe I could keep him in check by what seemed to excite him so much – my supposed youth. His way of repeating, somewhere between astonishment and anger, *You're so young, you seem so young, you look like a little girl.* I was laughing to myself, bewildered by this obsession with youth in men who see their own crumbling away; I found this caprice to be so bland – when suddenly a resounding slap yanked me out of my reverie. Struck down, I raised myself back up on my elbows, ready to protest, but a second slap threw me back against the pillow, trapped beneath the man looking at me, his face in mine, inhaling the fumes of my anger:

'You want to escape, is that it? Just try. Try, little whore, try.'

I didn't give him the pleasure of trying, I knew full well it was impossible. This guy that I could have shoved over when we were still dressed had, naked, pulled out from heaven knows where a titanic force. He licked my cheek, for a long time – I hated him at that moment, and I couldn't get rid of this hatred.

'You can't escape,' he continued, 'because you're so little. I could do anything I want to you.'

I laughed in his face, which he didn't make a big deal about. He was still inside me, his eyes fluttering behind their lids.

'You look sixteen. Tell me you're sixteen.'

As, stunned, I wasn't replying, he gave me another slap that would have made me jump up, teeth bared, if I'd been able to move. He must have felt it, because he took hold of my chin with a sudden sadness on his face, impossible to describe:

'You can get your revenge, you know. You can hit me too. I know I'm sick, I really do. Tell me you're sixteen,' he groaned in misery.

All I saw was a poor bloke about to hit his fifties, who could have passed for thirty-five had his lovely hair not been peppered with white, one without this pitiful need to assert his authority over a very young girl because women were stronger and more intelligent than him. My own role was not to redo this man's education – just to insert myself into his game, and for as long as he wasn't slapping me, there was nothing very difficult in all that. I bit my lip as I repeated, right next to his ear:

'I'm sixteen years old…'

I felt him trembling between my thighs, not vindictive any more but calmed right down by the intoxication of hearing himself repeat such an aberration, deeply calm like a man making love – and malice, as well as curiosity, took hold of me once more:

'… I'm fifteen…'

He let out a little cry, as if I'd touched a particularly sensitive part of his brain, and a little hesitantly I continued my languorous backwards count:

'… I'm fourteen…'

Seeing myself again at that age, all chubby and imbecilic, mouth spiky with braces – and seeing this guy, too, in the crowd of parents picking up their kids from school, all stiff in his trousers with the embarrassed air of someone who has just come on himself:

'… I'm thirteen…'

I went down to *eleven* before shocking even myself – because it was obvious I could have pushed it down to six before he lost his erection; and even then, I wasn't sure. The only certitude was that I'd just infused his desire with an extra dose of sadism. He stood up suddenly, grabbed me by the throat, and because his eyes suddenly scared me, I tried to roll out of the bed. But he grabbed me by the hair, laid me on the ground, unfazed by the way I was blindly kicking out my legs above me. I heard him spit into my hair that I was nothing but a whore, a dirty whore, and he would do what he wanted to me. And before I could formulate the idea of stretching my leg out to where it would have stopped him, a volley of slaps rained down on me, right in the face. I lowered my eyes to my torn silk slip and I saw, as if I'd actually been present, Svetlana leaving the room in tears: I saw the contrite face of the guy receiving the Hausdame's reproaches; this vision had such clarity, it could only be him. There was no doubt, and I felt on the brink of tears myself; tears of rage, a pure, murderous rage, shared between the fact of having been slapped and the idea that he drove a girl away from the safest brothel in Berlin, and the fact that he imagined himself sufficiently immune to come back to the scene of the crime less than a week later. And that such a thing can happen to me! I who was clearly older than nineteen and had much too much experience to be brought to the verge of tears by this type of situation. If I was in this state, I could hardly imagine the storm inside Svetlana's head. I pictured Svetlana keeping her cool as I'd thought it possible to, then little by little realising there was no safe word capable of stemming this kind of desire, no more than there'd been a mutual agreement about slapping or this sickening atmosphere of there being a murder about to take place. That this wasn't a theatrical client easy to put in his place but a sort of wild animal panicked by the power of his own claws. I thought that by saying the word *whore*, he must have convinced Svetlana, dragged her into his fantasy against her will – and that beneath the hail of blows she must have felt so alone, all of a sudden, so small faced with the realisation that the brothel, prostitution, were all that *as well*; and that such a thing would perhaps never have happened to her in the normal world. The word *whore*, generally, belongs entirely to us; you don't hear it from the mouth of clients, or rarely, at the height of passion, and for men it has something so blasphemous about it that they apologise profusely after coming. With him it was different. His way of saying it made me face my situation too, and it was a highly unenviable situation given that it allowed for these kinds of relations. Suddenly I had the impression I'd written pages and pages of lies – and this man arrived like the angel of death to reestablish the truth: write what you want, embellish things as much as it's possible for you to do so, but a whore remains a whore, and do you know what that is, a whore? Your job is to be quiet when a normal girl would demand respect. A normal girl would kick me out of there, but not you: you, you're going to shut it and let me fuck you, let me hit you, and when I've finished with you, you'll say thanks for coming and you'll groan like they all do because you have a few bruises and because that deserves a little bit extra – and why not, but only if I feel like it? What else can you do? You'll tell your whore friends not to go with me, but what do I care? There are so many other brothels in Berlin, where no one knows me yet, or I can persuade younger girls than you it's the life they've chosen, that that's what being a whore is.

I thought once more about Le Manège, I thought once more about everything that my proverbial professional conscientiousness had thus far pushed me to do with a smile, without ever preventing me from sleeping soundly at night, everything I'd tolerated by telling myself it would only make my book funnier or more interesting; I thought about everything I'd known outside the brothel, and that I would never have borne today – everything I'd accepted because I was young, and nice, and filled with the desire to please people. Memories came back to me of the power that all the men I'd loved, some only for a short time, had over me; that I'd loved so much I'd forgotten how much that power weighed on me. I thought of Jules, my new boyfriend, whether he saw me. I thought of the hours spent in The House to puff up my bank account before my trip to New Zealand, and of the miserly sum that that was given the patience I was now showing. I thought of Stéphane, and how to tell him that – tell him I'd let this man inflict this on me because he'd paid me, and that I hadn't been able to defend myself. This really was an anecdote that summed up in its entirety the situation of whores, and I really must be one since I was taking part in it, and that wasn't funny at all. I asked myself what the fact of not being able to tell something to my best friend was worth, in financial terms, or to have to keep silent about a bad experience to my boyfriend who was waiting for me thousands of kilometres from there. I thought that if I talked about it to Stéphane, he'd get scared for me, he'd smell my fear, and that had nothing intelligent or sexy or amusing about it – thought that you can't play at being a whore forever, you had to be really one for a time, with all that that involved in terms of abnegation and sacrifice; but good god, no! No way!

His last slap swept away my numbness; I wormed my way out of his arms, sliding onto the parquet because of my slip, and I shouted:

'No! No! For crying out loud!'

He immediately collapsed, an air of unbearable repentance melting his features. I got up, a bit shaky, thinking about the flowery room, my favourite slip ripped to shreds, the sugary background music in the loudspeakers.

'Who do you think you are, exactly?'

The shamed silence of a child who's bitten another.

'The spanking, fine, the smacks are just about okay, but hitting a girl like that? You really must be crazy!'

My anger went deeper still when I realised I really was about to cry – even if I was standing up again, showing him my indignation, I was still in his eyes nothing more than a whore who was suddenly aware of the fact she wasn't being paid enough to get beaten up. Not an offended woman, no – a whore fearful about her work tools. And deep down that was true, *too*.

He was there, on his knees, dishevelled, cock stiff against his stomach, devouring with his eyes the beaten-up little girl who was rising up against Dad's all-powerfulness. Delighting in the tears I was holding back. And he threw himself at my feet:

'I didn't want to hurt you, I didn't think I was hurting you...'

'And when I told you to stop? And when I was trying to run away?'

'You didn't tell me to stop.'

'First of all, don't touch me. If you touch me again, I'll punch you in the face, understood?'

I lit myself a cigarette; he staggered as he got up and went to sit at the other end of the sofa. It's mad how much he resembled the first man I loved, to whom I would never had dared say no, not in this tone, not like that.

'I'm sorry,' he sighed, sheepish. 'Is there anything I can do that will make you forgive me?'

'You can leave.'

'I'm going to go.'

'Excellent.'

He pulled up his fly, put his shoes back on, his long coat. Just before I closed the door on him:

'Can I come back and see you?'

I was already no longer in the same state of fury; I had wisely returned to my place, outside of my body, and my mechanism was back running at full throttle.

'I promise you I'll be nice.'

'Don't push me, because I'm going to get nasty.'

'You can be, you know. I know I deserve it.'

And he left; in the way he stared ahead there was such sadness, something so desperate, that I knew I would see him if he came back – because now I knew it was Him.

I said nothing to the girls when I went back downstairs. Thaïs, seeing my red cheeks and hearing my breathlessness, asked me with a chuckle if I'd come – which she certainly had, because she'd just left the arms of a regular who spent an hour with his face between her thighs. I could never have explained what I felt then; I didn't feel much at all, I was already busy writing. Images from the previous hours tramped through my head with an exasperating precision: I want to call the owner and get a good old *Hausverbot* pinned on this guy – no, to let him come back, to let him fantasise about the beating he would give me, and then to tell him no – *No, as far as I'm concerned, and no for the others too, old chap, never set foot back here again.* Before that, I would have spread the word to the girls, even stuck to the wall of our salon the most exhaustive possible description of him so that he could never again, however much money he offered, place his hands on anyone in The House. I would have clarified that it was him, Svetlana's client. I would have spread the news as far as the neighbouring brothels, where he would of course try his chance; if he hadn't already. If he hadn't already been to get shot of that unfulfilled orgasm between the traumatised thighs of a barely legal Polish girl.

Now I've calmed back down, this former client of Svetlana has given me my first real dilemma in the brothel. It's a new kind of torment, a curiously interesting one, having to decide if such a client is manageable or not, compared to the usual debates that occupy my mind, like deciding if I'm going to see Walter again because he always tries to stick a finger up my arse even when I say no, or Peter because the incessantness of his role-playing games shatter them all into a thousand pieces for me, impossible to stick back together. Both of those, and most others, don't pose any moral issue; there's nothing in them that would legitimately scare off a respectable woman – and whatever he says, Peter should talk to his wife about his fantasies, that would save him spending his salary in the brothel. Same for Walter, who comes for want of anything else to do and probably out of laziness; it's not for these men that brothels are useful, fundamentally. Or that's not how I see it. It's a place that was thought up at a time when there were only whores or respectable women, and within them you could ask for things that would break up a marriage or have you finish up on the end of a rope in a public place. Widowers distracted themselves from their loneliness, okay – but it was also and above all a place conceived to protect wives from the outlandish inventions of men whose cocks, it seems, took over from the rest of their internal organs once they were hard. You only have to read De Sade…! In among the thousands of anecdotes he recounts or invents, it doesn't matter which, are fantasies that would make my clients seem pious; in *120 Days*, one of the *lady historians* (well there's a pretty word) recounts her visit to the home of a prominent man while she was very young:

nobody had warned her about anything, she was handed over into a dark room where after waiting many hours, some servants rushed in dressed as ghosts armed with sticks; during this time the master of the house was wanking frenetically while listening to her hurling herself against the wall and crying out in fear – she was handsomely paid for that. I note that at the moment of telling this story, she is fifty years old and has only a few fingers and fewer teeth, some pulled out by a client who spent a huge sum to fulfil this whim. No doubt the narrator here is more De Sade's idleness than De Sade himself; it's hard to imagine how years in prison must shape a man's imagination. The fact remains that there is still a grain of truth in it; brothels have always had the vocation of being places of freedom, as outrageous as the latter can seem. And the resignation, the patience of whores have always allowed them to stifle their indignation while raising the price. It's still the case today, even when whores are almost considered to be normal people, having the inalienable right to say no.

It's not that he's demanding the impossible: wanting a girl who's very young or who seems to be, nothing about that would raise a whore's eyebrows, unless she's old or in a bad mood. Pushing your luck as far as asking a twenty-five-year-old girl to whisper that she's eleven – that's borderline morally unacceptable; but for that to be decided, a debate needs to occur that doesn't have a place in the practical mind of a whore in the midst of a shift. Adding a few slaps to the fantasy – just about acceptable. Of course, we pretty girls in The House are oversensitive; he wouldn't have much chance finding a volunteer. But I imagine there must be a place where, for a chunky sum, it's possible to abuse a girl, to treat her like a slut, to make her play at being a little girl and as a bonus to get sucked off without a condom. It must even be possible to slap her, and hard, if you've agreed on it beforehand.

But the delicate matter of agreeing *beforehand* – because a whore is still a woman who is still a human being who has rights that no payment can slice away – isn't that a twentieth-century perversion of the concept of brothels, part of this movement towards respect for everything that moves, breathes and speaks?

What gets this man going is precisely the act of taking a girl by surprise – that's exactly where my dilemma lies: I understand it. His pleasure lies in seeming like a normal man who has come to leave his seminal offering in this collective donation box, and then to see fear appear little by little in the eyes of a woman, to observe this professional mask that, as it slips, reveals the whore's real face; the whore never being anything other than a girl with fears and disgusts similar to those of her peers. That he uses his fists to assuage this, as primal as that is, is nothing more than an attempt to humanise the sex machines that whores represent.

Except that it's not about money any more; no girl would accept not knowing where the client is going to go. It's a terrible thing, for a whore, to be left hanging in the moment. To not be able to imagine the end – whatever it is. Even if the client went as far as clearly formulating this request, *I want to punch you in the face*, and having obtained permission – that would be disconcerting, definitely, but you'd know the score. But this man has no control when he gets turned on, that's why he doesn't even think about warning you; he doesn't know himself what's going to happen. It's impossible to know how to unravel the tangled web of his sexual imagination; there are as many very, very young girls in it as whores, they're both very slutty and extremely chaste, they're totally submissive but capable of turning on him; he needs them to get revenge but they fear him, terribly, and rightly so because they end up beaten to a pulp… Perhaps he feels, as he fucks, how obscure and inaccessible his ideal is, how frustrating this formless desire is, when its only discernible incarnation is the smell and colour of blood. He has a thousand scenarios in his head, and what links them all is hitting, constraining, shouting, crushing – without anyone knowing if it's the frustration that creates this shortcut, if that's its apogee, or if on the other hand he hits in order to not do worse.

Nothing is impossible in a brothel; in theory it's a safety valve saving men from embarrassment, from the need to justify themselves and, above all, from prison. For several decades, porn has filled this role: there are on the internet at least a million films showing what this guy desires, namely girls being massacred by men. And you don't need to look for long; you don't need to look at all. The homepage of one of my favourite sites teems with unambiguous titles; there's no need for keywords, it's a lexical field that seems to have been generated by the computer itself – but if you want romantic films, fucking between people who love each other, then you need to resort to semantic ruses, and what ruses! Good luck to anyone who wants to find a film in which it's not about smashing, taking apart, exploding, defiling, treating like meat, covering with spunk, piss, shit, strangling, smothering, abusing, raping… And the opposite of home movies, which manage the feat of being both the most exciting and the most tender, are studio productions in which porn actresses, clearly weary of playing corrupted students, pretend totally illogically to be whores. So in our day we wank in front of the pantomime of a meta-whore playing a whore, i.e a professional feigning excitement; we wank to a girl who doesn't feel like it playing a girl who also doesn't feel like it, but who is being paid – so she doesn't have any say in the matter. And it's fascinating to see these expressions of fake desire and of resignation, these reflexive movements as they open their legs and moan *ooh ooh* as their eyeballs roll up and down, left to right, following their own thoughts, which are all to do with when these gesticulations will end. As if, after sucking all the substance out of stories in which a student or the mother of a respectable family gets herself a spanking and asks for another one, the masculine imagination had resigned itself to getting turned on by the docility of a whore to whom one can do anything in exchange for a substantial sum. As simple, as depressing as that. What that says about the world in which we live, I don't need to explain. Perhaps these films are a necessary evil, the chance to expel fantasies of violence and domination, and thanks to them both normal women and whores don't need to deal with as much brutality as before, when technology didn't have the means to embody fleeting images.

An apparently normal man, but one in whom simmer impulses no one can satisfy or eliminate, a woman killer at loose who tries to get as close as possible to the limits of legality by counting on the shame a whore would feel in speaking to the police. To get where? To what extremity will this need to hit women carry him if you let it happen; what will be the next stage? If even the brothel can't appease this tension, if it's not actually a tension that can be appeased but a killing instinct inherited from animals; is that to say that he's stuck, alone, with his product defect? Stuck between his psychiatrist and himself, between morality and this sly voice in himself, whispering in his ear as soon as he sees a kid girl, *Do you think she'd cry if you gave her a slap? What kind of noise could she make? Would she bawl or would she try to stifle that in the pillow while praying that you hurry up?*

And I think of my sister. I pass the high school close to the Métro, I see all these young girls shimmering with life, with their pretty white teeth and these little chests harbouring all the hope and all the tenderness of the world, without an ounce of mistrust of the human race. Seductive, seductresses, and crassly ignorant of this beauty. Full of winsome looks aimed at no one in particular, towards the whole world, but that such a man, roaming the area, would pick up on and take personally – and how do you resist the temptation to lead on an old man with his tongue hanging out when you're seventeen and have such a need to feel pretty? I think of my sister, I think of these girls, and above all I think of me, at the same age. And how easy it would have been to remove myself from the company of my friends to get sweet-talked in a café and invited later, at a dark hour, into some hotel room. Oh, how I would have been transformed! Keeping my secret through bravado, I would have thrown myself headlong into it. And at the moment when, turned on, he raised his hand, I would have persuaded myself that that was something adults did and would have bravely let myself be beaten up, too brave to protest, to admit I was frightened. Such docile quarry, this flock of little women who laugh too loudly, whose joy is too conspicuous; barely two-hundred metres separate the high school from the brothel, and what assurance do I have that when I leave the Métro he didn't ask himself the question? If there wasn't the brothel in which to get all hot and bothered legally, who's to say he wouldn't go and rub himself up against younger girls more easy to manipulate? I'd be ready to wager that the only argument that could keep him far away from this school or from another is the idea of a jail with his name on waiting somewhere in Berlin. And all I can do is pray that this idea stays hidden away in his head, or that one day he's heavy-handed enough with a whore to get himself locked up – and that this whore isn't me.

Ballrooms of Mars, T. Rex

There are no bars on the windows. No locks on the doors. Only doorhandles to turn, and straight afterwards, the courtyard, the street, the world. Girls who want to leave can do so, The House isn't going to stop them. And often they come back. Unexpected defections, girls resigning in the middle of a shift could have led the owner to take severe measures – it's commonplace in the trade. Many establishments demand of the girls the same reliability as a hair salon or a restaurant – but not this one.

At the start, when I felt ill or when the sun was shining, I bombarded The House with fantastic excuses: my period, angina, my family descending on me, the Métro not working… As soon as I'd sent the message, I was flooded with guilt; I imagined Inge or Sonja letting out a long sigh and crossing out my appointments one by one, having to announce to my clients that yet again I wouldn't make it. Until the day when one of them replied by text: 'My dear Justine, when you don't come, there's no point explaining why. You just need to say you won't be able to come.'

I'd registered her irritation at getting landed with a convoluted message in the middle of the chaos, with the bells of all the rooms ringing, some for people coming out, some for people going in, with one of my clients no doubt kicking his heels in the salon. I'd felt as if I was at college, when having forgotten my textbook for the umpteenth time, I saw the teacher shrug his shoulders instead of getting annoyed, as if to say he was washing his hands of it – which was much worse than a reprimand. I later understood, no doubt at sunset, the time I should have been coming out and skipping home, full of men's joy and girls' laughter, that in spite of the annoyance, this message carried more goodwill than my dishonesty deserved. I'd read, *It's fine, liar, slacker, stay at home loafing about*, when I should have read, *We know that there are days when it's just too much, men riding you, endless conversations, idiotic demands. You probably feel fine, you don't hurt anywhere, but if you had to come you'd end up in a bad mood and the clients would feel that — but we don't care about the men; what counts is that we want you here freely. So don't waste too much time justifying yourself: it's enough to let us know.*

Which of course, on the terrace of the restaurant where we were stuffing ourselves, my sisters and I, while polishing off bottles of Chianti, in the lovely heat of a summer's evening, made me feel even more guilty. This place was definitely too good for me. Flattered my basest instincts, which were to not go to work when I was feeling lazy. This place didn't think, like I did, that we were doing any old job. And thought that to do this job, her ladyship had to be in a positive mood, even if it meant trying the patience of certain men. If she cancelled too often, they'd no doubt end up looking elsewhere; but experience taught me they never go looking elsewhere. They wait. Several weeks if needs be — but they come back. The more a girl eludes them, the more they need her. Not counting those who, infuriated at being sent off yet again, ask the Hausdame if I exist or if Justine is a fabrication to attract customers.

Certain Hausdamen held back tart remarks; a magnanimity the owner had taught them. And on the last night of The House, when Désirée is there, surrounded like a guru by all these women who cherished her without once seeing her in twenty years, when we are alone I ask her (I feel love pulsing in my eyes as I look at her, and I feel she sees that):

'How did you manage to make this place work while being so nice? Where did you learn this goodwill towards women? No other brothel permits what we're allowed here.'

'Really?' Désirée exclaims, as if she didn't know the other establishments, as if she hadn't opened her doors to all the girls deemed too unreliable elsewhere.

'No brothel I know of lets the women come and go, change their days and then change their minds, cancel at the last moment, sometimes without even letting them know, while knowing they can resurface without a reproach from anyone, or at least very few. There's nowhere that happens. Rosamund, who's now at the T..., got fired because she had a week off work even though she let them know... Lotte was let go because she was ill. And there are also those places where the girls can't say no to a client, or are frowned upon because they consider that four guys a day is enough, because they don't want to suck someone off without a condom even for more money... They're asked to wear heels, to put on make-up, the Hausdamen decide when their shift ends... So I have to know. Did you work in places where the owners were as nice as you, is it that?'

'As nice as me... Is it really about niceness? It's about intelligence. Not that I'm particularly intelligent. But I know what it is, this job. I know it's no use running after girls, policing them, reproaching them for their bad mood or their unreliability. One day, a girl who has ten appointments decides to stay at home; well fine, that's a lot of money – but no doubt, of these ten clients, five fall back on other girls, and girls will show up on the spur of the moment, and the day the girl reappears, she'll have other clients, even more of them. In fact, we don't lose money. The money is distributed differently. And the profits made from a girl who doesn't want to work, the state she'll be in when she goes home... I don't think it's worth it. You don't get anything from a woman by forcing her hand. And then, you know...'

Désirée sweeps her eyes around the room, this room that's all sorted out ready to disappear. And I look at her hands that have become virtually useless, these hands that built everything here, decorated everything, set it up in such a way that girls she didn't even know, who she may never see, felt prized, precious, and I feel like crying.

'… I think you need a lot of love to do this job. Mine. You have to have been one of them yourself, of course. Before goodwill, before business sense, before good taste – it's love you need. No one can work well without love.'

I think of Romain Gary when he wrote that after you've been loved by a mother, for your entire life you have the impression of eating cold food. I think of the girls now scattered about the mediocre brothels of the city, ones that are undoubtedly better decorated, more expensive, but where the high ceilings and the staff exude such an icy breath that it doesn't even occur to the girls to huddle close together to recreate that tenderness they took for granted – orphans. Oh, I know, I know how that sounds. I don't care. There are more than fifty of us who know it to be true. This was the only place that you could call a house. But not of ill repute, because it never was. Everywhere else, it's all about money changing hands, without the slightest hint of poetry.

What a waste!

I went to drag myself around an establishment the girls had told me about; it was our last few weeks together. The atmosphere had already changed; the prospect of not having any work made many of them blind and deaf to the grief that was poleaxing me, and in a frenzy they were going through the list of brothels in Berlin. That one didn't look bad. I went without any conviction, I came back dead inside; it stank of Le Manège, the girls were as streamlined as hunting dogs, and that's exactly what the men were looking for. Naively I wanted to introduce myself without shoes, in black tights, but the Hausdame categorically refused – and I saw myself, just like two years earlier, in a dump furnished with posh fabrics, sliding on uncomfortable pumps to go and shake the claw of a guy who wanted to fiddle with fake breasts and to be blinded by false nails. The voice of revolt growled in me, in perfect German – *Bunch of misery guts, demanding we wear heels – you wear them, the heels, if you think that all femininity comes down to that, if you think that men want girls who are very obviously doing a job.*

I ended up having a client, a regular from The House. The ostentatious dimensions of the place literally crushed us, used as we were to our warm little hutch, to my music, to our smell. We were all sheepish, all self-conscious; I no longer knew what was what or what I should do. When he left and I came back with my arms laden with sheets to put in the laundry (the rough white sheets of cheap, unrestful hotels), the Hausdame took me to one side:

'I noticed the bedroom wasn't very tidy. Look over there, the cushion: you have to put it back straight. I know it was a bit different where you were before.'

Different? You don't have the slightest idea, sister.

I pictured The House once more and the note pinned to the corkboard, next to the bathroom, where the new girls would all read it: 'Dear ladies, here you are free to choose what you wear, as long as it doesn't reveal too many of your charms. Choose what suits you best: you can present yourself in high heels, in ballerina pumps or in sandals, or even barefoot, like a little elf.' Sic! An elf!

I'm talking about a world where whores could choose to be princesses, elves, fairies, sirens, little girls, femme fatales. I'm talking about a house that took on the dimensions of a palace, the tenderness of a haven.

The rest of the world, for the girls, is now an abattoir.

Memory of a Free Festival, David Bowie

I DON'T REMEMBER GIVING ANYTHING ONE LAST glance. From the start, I looked at everything with the gravity, the slowness of a farewell. I always left The House convinced that, behind my back, it was disappearing like a dream. So much so that the last evening, after the party organised the day before moving out, I ran to the Métro, refusing to believe it would be the last time, not backing down, because farewells revolt me.

It was hard to believe: all the bedrooms were open, the soft air of May entered via the balconies where the smokers were all crammed together, and the salon had been reserved for Désirée, whose fragile lungs couldn't tolerate clouds of smoke.

Music, very loud, rose from a small hi-fi system rigged up in the garden. More than fifty girls had come, all the ones I knew and then the others, the mythical ones whose names could still be seen on the lockers and the lists but who had stopped a long time ago. There were my colleagues in civilian clothes and also well-dressed women who had become respectable, dressed for their new jobs and there out of loyalty, because even holding the status of upright citizens, they still carried in their heart immense gratitude for having lived so well here, despite having had enough at the end, despite the desire to be normal, despite their wish for people to forget that they'd been paid to suck cocks. And these besuited women, as soon as they'd come through the heavy security door, relaxed back into their sashaying gait; in the purple light of the salon their sensible outfits looked like a secretary costume thought up for businessmen who daren't jump on their own. Annette, who was a PA in a law firm, looked at the garden with her huge eyes, no doubt replaying these five years of her life like a fantasy, some realistic dream she'd never tell anybody.

Now the telephone has stopped ringing, the girls talk very loudly about things they're not afraid of the neighbours hearing. I look out for Pauline, who won't come, and I see Hildie, who follows me out onto the balcony of the Yellow room to smoke a joint.

'This is where I had my first client,' she says without looking at the room, which is still full, curtains drawn.

She looks at this balcony, which we've never been out on before, and opposite, on the other side of the street, the apartments where a guy with binoculars used to hide behind the curtains to glimpse some naked flesh.

'It's funny, yesterday a guy asked me what effect that had had on me, my first client. I'd have liked to say something fascinating, like a huge shock, a sudden splitting of my personality – or whatever guys imagine. It didn't have much of an effect at all. Either I actually was in shock and I didn't give myself the option of being hurt or disgusted, or I'm made differently to other women – I don't know. I found it easy. I was surprised not to feel dirty. Something told me I should have done. With my first trick, I bought some tights and some socks. This money felt no different from the money you earn from working.'

Hildie seems to ponder for a moment, and she smiles:

'It felt better.'

I spent two years thinking I should have felt dirty, guilty, humiliated. I spent two years wondering where that surge of joy when I exited the Métro came from, on days when the weather was so lovely that the windows of buildings in the distance, encircling The House, dazzled me as they reflected the sun. I spent two years marvelling at myself for having this regal bearing when I caught my likeness in shop windows, for feeling so light in my body, for seeing the world as so peaceful and so filled with promise.

It was perhaps having so much money on me. Perhaps living for two years without any financial considerations weighing on my mind. The only shadow over my happiness was this absence of guilt, this pride even, and the idea that I wasn't normal, was destined never to fit into society. I constantly had on my shoulders the disdain and the embarrassed commiseration that the world feels for whores. It was not my anguish, it was that of other people.

My first client… If you mean by first client the first guy I slept with without desire, to please him, well then you have to go further back than The House or Le Manège. I don't remember. That's perhaps why, like Hildie, I didn't feel any shock or disgust when I was a offered a setting and a salary in exchange for my surrender. My first client at The House, I remember very well, was just next to the Yellow room, where Hildie was on her knees in front of a construction worker. It was in the louche half-darkness of the Mauve room, a man who was smoothing his moustache as he flicked through *Der Spiegel*. He wanted a hackneyed student and professor scenario, and it took us a good few moments to understand each other, because I hardly spoke German at that point. He didn't hold it against me, and, in a very teacherly way, he spoke carefully to make me understand the jargon of submission. Yes, he was ugly, that I will concede, to the crowd hungry for details – with a small, slightly threadbare moustache, unassuming but very nice, wearing a wedding ring he didn't bother to take off. The idea of seeing him naked or of being taken by him didn't disgust me; it was this ridiculous scenario (to have to come back out of the room, knock on the door, and pretend to be a student who'd given in her homework late and needed to be punished) that seemed embarrassing to me.

But I did it. And that didn't stop me, afterwards, from swallowing an egg sandwich and forty pages of Nicholson Baker; it didn't stop me from sleeping like a log the following night. Is that the problem? I should have lost my appetite, had horrible nightmares. I should have looked at myself in the mirror and said: *That's what you are, a whore.*

Never, in two years, did I have this kind of thought. It would have been a very different deal if I'd stayed at Le Manège, I'm very conscious of that. This is not an apology for prostitution. If it's an apology, it's for The House, for the women who worked there, for kindness. Not enough books are written about the care that people take of their fellow beings.

If I only rarely despised or hated *them* — at the end of a shift, or when I was in a bad mood, right in the middle of my period or just feeling fragile — it's because I feel it too, this masculine obsession with women's bodies, with women's desire, even faked. This endless being led around by their cocks is exactly the same as me being led around all my life by my pussy, in the hope of understanding it. These guys are no more pathetic than me. It's myself I was looking for in their eyes, whereas they were only satisfying a physical itch.

'And now it's all over. And that's the hardest part. Today, everything is different. There's no action. I have to wait around like everyone else. Can't even get decent food. Right after I got here I ordered some spaghetti with marinara sauce and I got egg noodles and ketchup. I'm an average nobody. I get to live the rest of my life like a schnook,' as Henry Hill said in *GoodFellas*.

Our humour. That's what I loved too. That my dirty jokes, which normally offended everyone, were so successful with the girls. In the kitchen, torn between giggling and throwing up, Betty, Delilah and Hildie listen to me describe the English client who comes at me in the morning with his ideas about strap-ons — and as it is, outside the brothel it would have taken me a long time to get my head around saying the word *strap-on*, but here it comes out as easily as a coordinating conjunction; I don't see any of them frowning or shuddering; all of them have had this big belt in black nylon and this translucent phallus, like an extra colleague, around their waist. Then, encouraged by their receptivity, I hurl the rest of my story in their faces: how I take this guy clumsily, without daring to look in the mirror, a bit vexed that being with me inspires in him this type of fantasy and not the very simple one of fucking me. Is that what he's been mulling over since the first time we saw each other? Really? Me and my silk suspender belt, and that's what he wants? That's what I'm thinking about, surprised to still be astonished by how questionable men are, when I realise, stunned, that we're literally covered in shit – and now that I'm writing this for chaste ears, obviously, it sounds bad; I need to forget for a moment that two years have passed and that the rest of the world is slowly forgetting who Justine was and who Emma is.

'I pull out to gain a bit of momentum, and that's when I see that there's shit everywhere, there's some on the strap-on, he has some on his buttocks, I have some on my fingers...'

Betty yelps, her mouth full of ham and cheese, Hildie chokes on her cigarette and Delilah, her beautiful canines sparkling between the carmine of her lips, repeats on a loop *Oh my god oh my god oh my god*... Exactly the effect I was counting on.

'I have a moment of fright when I realise he's not noticed anything, he doesn't see or smell anything; yes, even better, he's starting to try to turn over onto his back, because he wants to carry on – and I stammer *I'm going to wash my hands, don't you think you should go to the bathroom?* The guy replies *No, it's okay, I'll wait for you.* So I run to the toilet; I'm so choked up I don't even feel like vomiting, and yet I'm so enveloped by the warm smell of shit that I wonder how it's possible he can't smell it, there's some on the bedcover, on the cushions; the real question is how I didn't realise before, I was so lost in my thoughts that it went miles over my head... Anyway, I clean myself up, I clean the strap-on, and I go back into the bedroom convinced that in the meantime he'll have got the measure of the disaster. I'm even expecting him to have left – but no, he's there. Happily, he stays no longer than five minutes; I ask him again if he wants to take a shower, he repeats that he doesn't, and I watch him starting to put his trousers on – is this guy for real? Is he going to put his pants back on and go back to work with his arse covered in shit? But at the moment of pulling his boxers back up, he stops, he realises, all while trying to look impassive, and that's when he says to me that actually maybe he will *nip* to the bathroom. When he comes out, he really doesn't know what to say, he wants to get the hell out, and he'll probably never come back. And surprise surprise, the guy didn't leave me even the tiniest tip.'

'If he'd left you a tip,' remarks Betty, 'it would have meant he knew.'

'But how could he not know?'

'As long as nobody talks about it, it's as if it had never happened. No doubt he told himself that if he left you a tip, you'd think he'd known it was going to happen.'

'Who's to say he didn't know? I'm coming to the conclusion he did know. It wasn't a tiny little bit like: I took my precautions but there's always a risk. It was *a lot*. A lot like: I wanted a shit when I arrived. Like: I knew what was going to happen and maybe it was what I wanted but I wouldn't have dared ask. I mean, these kinds of things don't happen here, or do they?'

'That can happen,' says Delilah, 'but in the Studio, because there are plastic sheets, and the guy has to pay at least twice as much.'

'Yes, and the Hausdame generally sends them to B… for those kinds of things,' says Betty. 'They have what they need, and above all, the girls are used to it. But Justine, why didn't you yell at him?'

'I was embarrassed for him!'

'I understand,' says Hildie. 'I wouldn't have said anything either.'

'If he'd wanted that, he would have given you more money so that you carry on.'

'Unless what really excites him is taking me by surprise.'

'Maybe he woke up with the desire to get fucked up the arse,' says Hildie, 'and he washed himself out at home, but he used too much water or he left too soon, and there was water still inside. I know all about it, that happened to me once.'

'It's quite possible. And he didn't leave you any money either because he was sad and disappointed at the idea of saying to you, *Listen, I'm sorry about what just happened; look, here's a hundred euros, it won't happen again.*'

'My tip is the satisfaction of knowing he's going to be thinking about it with horror all day and trying to get it out of his head.'

My tip, in reality, was this conversation.

Perhaps there's a kind of brothel humour and this was the audience I was always destined for. Recently I was talking about my taxes with a girlfriend, and I brought up this eighteen-thousand-euro threshold that you must not cross in order not to be eaten alive by the Finanzamt.

'Eighteen thousand euros *a month*?'

'A year!' I clarify, a bit flattered she thinks I've been able to earn such a good living; and I round it off, already giggling at my wit: 'Eighteen thousand *a month*, can you imagine? My fanny would go up in smoke!'

Deathly silence. I can almost hear Delilah and Hildie roar with laughter. Perhaps from now on I'll always need, in a corner of my brain, a half-dozen giggling whores as soon as a horrible joke comes to mind – which is often.

It's the same friend who read a first draft of this book and said to me that, deep down, she found it very sad. I was completely depressed when she said that; I needed this feedback as much as I needed a rope and a stool. And I re-read myself carefully, trying to understand the text in the spirit of someone who'd only seen whores with the eyes of an innocent, the way I did when I started. It was no use, I still laughed in the same places; I felt I was transcending exactly those things she must have found sad – and for a long time, months afterwards, I was still prevented from writing by the idea that, perhaps, the only person it made laugh was me. Or that if it had a certain kind of humour, it was very black, like the essential, cathartic bad taste of the medical examiner who places a funny face on a corpse's bashed-in mug. Despite my clumsy attempts to make people laugh, the rest of the world would probably carry on seeing only horror in its pure state, a trade between pariahs and other pariahs – and I dreamt of asking this friend, because it was the only thing that really counted: *Do you mean by that that I give the impression of wanting people to like me?*

As if that wasn't obvious.

After having draped myself in writerly high-and-mightiness by deciding that I was funny and that the whole world could go fuck themselves in front of Kev Adams shows, I stopped writing because of my family. I prefer to say it before someone asks me the question: yes, I thought about it. Yes, I thought about it all the time. No, I didn't kill my parents, okay? May god be my witness, I tried, but clearly they're immortal. Oh the cold sweats I've have, that I still have, when this idea comes floating into my mind after I've smoked a bit...! In the daytime, sober, I have a sense of mission that allows me to swat away my scruples with a bellicose backwards sweep of the hand – but in the evening, the sissy that I am behind my swaggering exterior starts to collapse. I have the feeling that if I send this manuscript to someone in the industry, my arm, my shoulder and finally the whole of me will find themselves crushed by unspeakably huge gears. From moment A when I click on 'send' to moment B when my father says, drily, that it was really a good investment to pay for me to go to a Catholic school for ten years, I see nothing but a rapid descent punctuated by vain attempts to cover my arse by calling it a novel, adding to the infamy the outrage of never having the courage of my convictions. There's no way of hiding – that's a thought that twists my innards until the second I fall asleep. When I wake up, again, this cowardice, these strategies dreamt up to diminish the initial shock revolt me: why should I hide? I was proud. I was happy in The House. I'd adored hanging out with these girls, I loved these men, loved the colour of my flesh in the pink light and the play of shadows on my face, the feeling of inventing over and over a new Emma, new Justines, I loved the feeling that nothing was impossible. And if I was capable of diving into what many consider to be a hell, it's because there must be within me some instinct for life that my parents passed onto me. I am them; and this constant jubilation, this eternal laughter, it's my father and my mother, my grandparents, my sisters, they are all there in this capacity to be me and to laugh about it, and to find poetry and tenderness everywhere. My strength was nourished by seeing them live and hold one another when something was wrong. And if I so loved being in the midst of women who laughed when they could have cried, who didn't give a damn about anything, who caressed one another's hair to soothe their sorrows and tapped one another on the behind in mutual encouragement, it's because the little girl in me remembered those moments when despair was kept far, far away, at astronomical distances, because of all these people whose smell I knew so well.

Wir müssen hier raus, Ton Steine Scherben

THERE WILL OF NECESSITY COME A TIME when people run out of arguments against happy whores. We're already there, and behind the now obsolete arguments, there's just a paradoxical jealousy burdened by other names. It's no longer a career one dies of at the age of thirty, eaten away by syphilis or any other illness you can now cure with a month of antibiotics; the days when a whore constantly played Russian roulette is over. Whores no longer have in the pit of their stomach that oozing wound, reopened each day, and whose screams they have to stifle. Where their activity is legal, whores don't have to drag themselves through the rain to carry out dubious exchanges in dark alleyways. In brothels that take care of them, they no longer have to keep a constant eye on their bag inflating their inside pockets with the day's takings; they don't need to be cold or be afraid of the men who provide their bread and butter. They can use their earnings to rent an apartment, to have a credit card. They have more or less as many administrative advantages and annoyances as any other taxpayer. And the fact is, they don't have time to spend it all on the various drugs that, traditionally, in some people's eyes, will these days kill them as quickly as venereal diseases did at the beginning of the twentieth century.

Whores have time… Oh good god, and then some! The happiness of not having to wake up at dawn, and when the sun is shining, of going and sitting on a terrace, behind dark shades, to give themselves over to the only activities that make this pitiful existence liveable: reading, writing, smiling at boys, devouring girls with your eyes. Holy cow, I knew I couldn't be totally wrong, in Paris, spending the large part of my days hopping from café to café, my manuscripts in my hands. Calling Pauline, who's not working today either, and having a quiet breakfast while other people run to the office. Generously tipping the pretty waitress and trotting off in a leisurely manner, in the fragrant warmth of Berlin, toward the botanical gardens all dense with flowers.

There are moments when I wonder what better anyone could offer me. And I do feel that the hatred, the whole world's mistrust of kept girls, is mainly about the jealousy inspired by their freedom. And their reticence to admit that all this free time, this drunkenly unbridled frolicking, makes it worth being caressed or pummelled by strangers. It's not me you need to ask, my opinion is set in stone. Oh, I hear what people can counter this argument with; that I'm lazy. That I've chosen ease. That there is, in this odious compromise, an abominable renunciation of hard work and perseverance. To be socially acceptable, I'd have to spend most of my time slaving away in a shop; and the salary I would be paid, and then begrudgingly, would allow me to read, to write, and to fill my nights with sometimes satisfying, sometimes mediocre encounters. That I ingeniously combine work and seduction is clearly some unforgivable offence to industrious functioning of society. But when I see what this same society does deem acceptable, I'm even happier holding up a cold beer and toasting the health of all the world's whores.

The difficulties I'm experiencing in finishing this book are only slightly to do with how little I wanted to leave The House. From the moment I was there, I literally saw the book write itself before my eyes, with the right nuances, and as much tenderness and humour as I dream up in the darkest depths of the night when I can't sleep. Then the girls seem to me to be straight out of books full of colour, like a flock of rare birds getting too close to my hands for a connection not to exist between us. But as soon as I have a day to myself, as soon as I have nothing better to do than write, it's like a curse comes crashing down and I can't squeeze out another line. Because I've realised that from the moment I finish this book, I won't need The House any more. I won't need the girls any more. And I go right back to breathe in a mouthful of their oxygen, chilled to the bone by the decision to manage by myself, in a moment of intoxicating inspiration.

I'm now walking around in my sack dress, belly swollen, my belt pushed up under my breasts so no one can ignore my five months' pregnancy, a Romain Gary book in my hand; my best friends, all the loves of my life with the exception of Jules, are in my books in their entirety and I'm tasting their company like never before, as I stake out my space on sunny terraces in a state of inner bliss in which my perception of my body has fully dissolved. I've held a peaceful wake for my sexual self; it seems only to live now through this belly in which I sometimes feel something move.

I imagine a time when I'll be as slim again as all these girls around me. Sensuality, my constant obsession, appears to me like a distant past or a strange future, almost imaginary. No doubt that's due more to the age I've reached than to pregnancy – I have a poignant nostalgia for those mad romps through Paris when every occasion when a man looked at me was a breath of fresh air to me. The way they turned their heads; as I then turned mine. Dizzied by possibility. Panicked by what I imagined them imagining. This consciousness of my flesh, this infinite comfort of being and of moving, this love of myself. These looks that I took away with me to the confines of my suburb, on fire from having floated past their noses like an exquisite smell. These inner machinations about men in the street I'd never see again, about those I rubbed shoulders with daily; this relentless effort for a smile I deemed more meaningful than usual. The enormous bollocks I felt myself growing. This pathological need to know I'd hooked them – the worst and the most delicious of all my servitudes.

It's surprising that I can now not give a fuck about it to such an extent. Or let's say rather that I gave up this distraction while I was pregnant.

Closed in on myself, Romain Gary by my side, arm in arm. I'm laughing out loud. *Your ticket isn't valid beyond this point*; aren't these human contingencies miserable? This mania for a hard cock, when goddammit, love is more than enough for a communion of souls. Coming – yes, fine. It's limited, so restricted. Hours of contortions and panting for the simple pleasure of coming at the same time, by another's hand – when you'd do it yourself with such brio. All this racket for a spasm; any sensible man would give it up.

Now that sex seems pointless to me, I'm in the perfect state to be surprised by an affair on an unprecedented scale. I'm the obvious candidate, and I can even almost imagine what he would look like, the man for whom I'd consider the possibility of leaving my child and husband. The real impossible love. To finally know what I'm talking about. I imagine myself, sitting on the edge of a window, sighing for a man lying behind me on a bed soaked with our juices. *I really don't know what to do any more*; and behind this window, it's still the rooftops of Paris I can see. I can feel in my calm chest the short breath of a woman who's going home covered with the smell of another. My fingers know by heart the steps to take to delete a Facebook conversation. It would take me a minute to break everything to become that woman again. And thinking that this guy already exists, somewhere in the world, probably a few hundred metres from me. Perhaps even having brushed past me, having seen nothing or only a pregnant woman. The miraculous irony of the thing…!

At the table next to me are two couples somewhere in their forties. The women are talking with one of the men, and the other, who is rolling a cigarette, isn't bad at all. I must for a moment have had the face of a woman thinking about her next lover. He looks at me; he's not supposed to, but he does it anyway. It's not as if his girlfriend was going to stop talking, and it's a conversation he's heard a thousand times. No one's going to ask him his opinion because he doesn't care. They've given up on him; they're happily leaving him to roll his cigarette. They are four people who met on holiday; he and his wife live in Berlin, the other couple come from Munich (yes, that's the type), they got to know one another in Spain; but not the Spain all the Germans go to, a side of an island where there are no tourists; they'd rented a villa and hung out at the same tapas bar, and that's where they met. The two women were friends at high school, what a coincidence! And although they lost contact for fifteen years, they basically grew up in the same world, they are very similar. One is blonde and the other brunette, but they are the same type of beautiful forty-five-year-old woman, tanned, made-up, with overpriced but casual-looking clothes, a few non-blingy pieces of jewellery, obviously looking after themselves and drinking Aperol spritzes. They look like the wives of doctors, or lawyers, or financiers. Look, they may have had a foursome. In any case, you can see they all still fuck, individually. They're couples who still get on well, on the whole; anyway, who cheat on each other quite discreetly, careful to not disgruntle each other. But the one rolling his cigarette, that one, he looks as if he's been cold all winter; perhaps he didn't even think about it, but now the lovely weather's coming back and girls are walking half-naked in the streets, the idea of a foolhardy romance is coming over him like slow inebriation. May also be the beer (a wheat beer, a true middle-class beer). He's that type of man: the type who fucks his wife well but who's panicked by the theoretical idea of sex with another woman, a stranger.

In fact, it's not the man's glances that are the most troubling; it's the indifference that lies in-between them. It's this looking away when our eyes meet. It's this idea that it's not being done on purpose. It is, in the middle of the tangle of conversations, the silence when he looks at me and when I look at him. This way we have of being a bit forsaken by the rest of the world for the blink of an eye. It's not his look, it's the certainty of being looked at; this calm conviction that murmurs, *Read your book, in peace; I will still be here when you look up again. I will study you at my leisure for the whole time you're pretending I don't exist.*

Venus in Furs, The Velvet Underground

DELILAH'S FICTIONAL CANE HISSES THROUGH THE AIR. It's pouring with rain today and I'm watching her with delight, in this ambiance of a pre-apocalyptic cocoon, unspool her piece of grand theatre.

'What the hell are you thinking? You think you're going to feel my little pussy? Huh, is that what you'd like; you'd like me to let you bury your disgusting cock in my little pussy? Lower your eyes when I talk to you!'

And I, overcome, complying.

'What makes you think you can set eyes on me? A sick man like you, who comes to pay young women to be treated like shit. You disgust me!'

Her voice changes imperceptibly, to indicate the stage directions to me.

'You can hit them lightly with the whip, on their cocks for instance. Never with your hand, or at least not until the end. What also works well is laying them on the ground and walking over them, one foot on either side. With heels; you always need to keep your heels on. The advantage is that they can't stop themselves from looking at you, and that gives you a good reason to hit them.'

Sticking out her pubis, which is outlined insolently by her little pink-coral knickers, the two lips all plump – and always this extra-large cane, which I feel crash down on my neck.

'Did I give you permission to look at my pussy? You know what state that puts me in, when you disobey? Apologise, you disgusting creature. Sorry, who? Sorry *Madame*; did nobody teach you good manners? You're going to count every lash along with me to teach you to stay in your place. And your place is on the ground, with your eyes lowered. I swear to you that if you make a mistake while counting, I'll start again from the beginning, until your arse is so bruised you can't go home to your wife, am I making myself clear? *There, you make them get up and you tie them up with their arms over their heads.* Did I give you permission to get turned on? You fucking maniac! I'm warning you that if you get another hard-on after your punishment, it won't go well. Pervert! Nothing annoys me more than this fat cock nobody's asked anything of. Do you think I'm going to sit on it, is that what you imagined? I'm going to stop you having a hard-on.'

Delilah sits down with a huge smile:

'Everything's an excuse for punishment. The thing is to get a bit closer right until the end. After an hour of letting themselves be hit, if they can smell your arse or your pussy, that will make them come as well. You just have to remember that a dominatrix doesn't fuck, and above all doesn't give BJs. Never give anything other than your hand, and even then, look disgusted.'

'I could never be as good as you, in any case.'

'*Ach, quatsch.* I've just given you the basic outline, you can't go wrong. *Especially with this French accent you have.*'

Delilah does a nice imitation of my fanciful German, one I never know is mocking or tender — but however perfectly she apes the length of my vowels and the singing texture of my consonants, what I don't tell her is that half the words she puts in my mouth are completely unknown to me.

'Obviously,' she continues, 'it's easier when they have some fetish. Those who like feet, for example, those are good clients. You get your feet licked and caressed; in the end you give them the delight of your toes on their cock and that's it. A bit extra if they want to come on your shoes, and it's all done.'

'Like those who want to get fucked up the arse, I imagine.'

'Well that, you see, that's what relaxes me. That's how I most feel like myself.'

What I have no trouble imagining is Delilah methodically going at her clients, hardly noticing the straps around her waist, linked to the strap-on. She chooses the right words, the right rhythm, and above all she carries this air of not giving a fuck that all the lovers in my fantasies have. I hazard a smile:

'It's a bit of revenge, yes? For once it's your turn to fuck them?'

'For sure. It's very natural. Ever since I started fucking, I've known how good it is.'

She crushes her cigarette butt, thoughtful:

'And even if I didn't know anything about it! What they want when they come to get themselves fucked up the arse, deep down, isn't it to get well and truly pounded?'

'I imagine so. I don't know, actually. I've always heard people say that to dominate someone well, you need a lot of love and empathy.'

'You must be kidding!' snorts Delilah. 'Another thing men made up to make women crawl at their feet. When you're dominating a man, I assure you there's no need of love. It's a lot simpler than that. Do you think I like all my clients? I really like some of them, but it doesn't go beyond that, they're still guys I wouldn't say a word to outside the brothel. No, to dominate, what you need is to have no pity at all. Guys want you to remind them that they're pathetic, with their cock and their pathetic need to put it in women. Because they forget.'

Delilah stretches; the shiver of a yawn deforms her face for a moment, giving her a look of impatience as her mouth gapes, full of cruel teeth.

'But women don't forget. How could we forget? Especially us lot.'

Her client's just arrived. She puts her phone away in a pocket with a keyring in the shape of a teddy bear hanging from it.

'Honestly, I don't know how it works outside, but I think

everything's very simple in a brothel. You're either nice or nasty. And that depends on the girls, but it takes me less effort to be nasty than nice. Looking down on them and being rude to them is almost automatic. That's why I'm good, in the Studio.'

That's why she does her job so well. Disdain.

Disdain! I'm still thinking about that while Janus, who's just tied my hands behind my back, ferrets around looking for a whip in the umbrella stand. Just take a look at that, this guy nearly six feet six inches tall bent over an umbrella holder, pretending to himself he doesn't know what he's looking for. With Janus, it's always the same: the whip with three lashes, or the one with a flat paddle, which looks like a carpet beater. After six months of weekly appointments, I detect in this man no will to change, no temptation to try the myriad of instruments piled high in the drawers of my chest, not even another whip. Like the bamboo paddle with its petrifying efficiency — unlike the other ones, it's just right for reddening the delicate posteriors of middle-class men excited by *Fifty Shades of Grey*.

As hackneyed as his scenario is, Janus doesn't need any help or any progression. There was a period when, while he was conscientiously taking his bath, I put handcuffs in my size, ropes, condoms, his two favourite whips on the sideboard in advance. He came back butt-naked and I greeted him already undressed, with the smile of a model employee on my lips: *Look, I already got everything ready for you*. Zealously, I'd turned out the big light to leave the half-light of the small red lamps as he did himself; put on music, pulled the Berkley horse to the middle of the room, placed the towel on the bench where our session generally ends. That embarrassed me, once I was tied up, to feel him stop to find the accessories spread out around the Studio by the others. I had the impression that our disorder unfairly cost him precious seconds. In the face of this thoughtfulness, Janus had a contrite little smile of thanks and I finally understood that I deprived him of the pleasure of looking himself; that these lost moments were for him an exquisite, primordial gathering of momentum. This silence full of moments of hesitation – heavy as the silence before a storm, populated only by the sounds of drawers opening, slow footsteps – totally enriched the action to come. His epicurean jubilation at the idea of making me languish; this time-lag, this constant deferral that is the hallmark of great dominators – placed within reach of working men who go to the brothel.

Rattling my wrists about in the handcuffs for want of something to do, I realise that if I really wanted to free myself nothing would stop me, and certainly not Janus, who never ties a knot without assuring himself, in his gentle voice, that I'm not hurting and my blood is not cut off. This affability makes me all the more receptive to him: it's a fact, nothing nasty can happen to him with me. Which also makes him lose credibility. To tell the truth, nothing can happen at all. The only risk would be that I dribble a bit when he kisses, deeply, implacably, once his excitement has reached a critical point. He holds me by my hair in the nape of my neck; it's the only moment when Janus seems invincible, when his impassive features of a good guy playing at being a hangman tense a bit, in a way that to anyone else but me would seem frightening.

This is what makes his simple, childish satisfactions even more moving. Unfolding the ropes. Pulling down my knickers – which I don't take off any more since I understood what happiness he gets from undressing a girl, from stealing her modesty – even if this girl is a whore for whom modesty has become a pretence, pieced together from distant memories. Activating the crank to raise my hands above my head, that's a heavenly delight. Almost as much as grabbing me by the chin to force me to look into his eyes: a task I carry out with lots of shivers and terrified flinches. In his eyes there's an abyssal void, nothingness. And I have to recognise in Janus a certain talent, even if it's only in this psychopath's gaze; he could teach apprentice doms a thing or two. Janus speaks little; he's understood the erotic dimension of silence. And when he gives orders, it's quickly, in a low voice that truly shows the German language in its best light.

What he also does really well, the small detail he's finally mastered, is the transition between his early movements and what I'd call *the eye of the storm*. The condom is placed on the sideboard, in the shell tidy. Janus starts by untying my arms; I express my theatrical suffering by massaging my wrists, groaning weakly to depict the relief mixed with fear of a girl who would have been hung up for hours (I've counted, we're up to eighteen minutes). Right, *on your knees*. He turns around, gravely, to go and fetch the condom. A stroke of genius – he throws it at my feet, in a way he obviously hopes is disdainful. I don't know if he's proud of it, but it's his most credible move; he needed some time to hone his gesture. From one appointment to the next, he adjusts his way of moving towards me; he perfects this backwards jerk of the elbow to make himself look uncompromising. I truly would like to agree to this really small thing that gets him in such a state, pull out of my hat a reaction that would give extra depth to his fake disgust, but I never find anything but an abyssal silence, eyes lowered, shoulders hunched; I tear the wrapping feverishly, as if I'd given up on getting out of a well-deserved punishment. Once the condom's slipped on, there are no more surprises to hope for. Even this pretence of domination withers away; the condom – and hence, intrinsically, the prospect of coming – signals to Janus the permission to let himself go. As this stage, he's at the gates of the abyss. As he's organised, without glancing at the clock he knows there are five to ten minutes left. And with a click of the fingers, his mask will fall, like a dead skin.

It's laughable, but there's nothing contemptible in all that. It's pretty, the smile he has when he's holding himself back. Bobbie, one night when she was leaving a session with him, told me with a laugh, *When he comes, he becomes really beautiful*. Beautiful, indeed, with that murderous grace of very gentle men when they lose control, when the stifled death drive flits across their face. And this silence, thrilling, as he moves slowly inside me, contracting and relaxing his fingers. Straight afterwards, humbly folding the weighed-down condom into a paper towel: 'All good. That wasn't too hard?'

No, I don't dislike Janus. This type of man has no other aspirations than to sacrifice himself to his little fantasy of a girl who says no. Janus has nothing in common with those who we do dislike in the Studio – and that's easy to do, when you find yourself tied up any old how by a man with clumsy hands. More so than when you're on the right side of the whip, like Delilah.

Olaf, for example. Olaf, this specialist in wasting time. You have to wonder about the usefulness of demanding Satie as background music, of arriving dressed to the nines, of turning the Studio upside down looking for the most exotic instruments, when after twenty minutes the narrative framework slows down dramatically. You'd be justified in imagining that a man who books for 10 o'clock at night has had a whole day to think about what would give him pleasure – but no.

Generally speaking, my goodwill withers away very quickly when I'm waiting, tied up any old how, for an idea to come to him. Nobody needs to know anything about BDSM to guess that he doesn't know a thing about it. Ignorance, excitement and the will to do good make him clumsy. He may well have been a tailor by trade, but the knots he ties are too loose or too tight, make you want to laugh or to hit him.

Because he's a nice boy, and because I'm too nice myself, I let him put the rope around my neck – not without remaining afraid of losing my balance and ending up hanged like David Carradine: you can bet that with his method and the time the knots take him, I could die five times over without him knowing how to back-pedal.

The way he slaps also betrays his lack of technique; he hurts himself more than he does me. He quickly gets out of breath and dishevelled. I look at him, irritated, wading about in this setting of oppressive domination that he's imposed on himself. So conspicuously racking his brains that I myself feel embarrassed – and as it always comes at the end of a shift, when I've already expended all my patience on other clients, the embarrassment quickly turns to rage. Or to hatred, more accurately. *Olaf, sweetie, this is actually expensive, two hundred euros to seem like a beginner!* He's there, arms swinging, asking himself what the next stage is. Total malfunction:

'What should I do to you now?'

'What should you do to me?!' I spit behind my loose gag.

'What do you want?'

All tied up as I am, I stare at him astounded.

'But… I don't know!'

'Do you have some kind of idea?'

'But… no, frankly, not really! It's me who's the sub here.'

Olaf scratches his skull. Not only am I not helping him, but before long I'm going to start judging him, so he decides to walk me on a leash across the Studio, armed with a supple stick he can't make up his mind to use. Even with my wrists tied behind my back and my cheek against the warm lino, I'm not in the most uncomfortable of positions.

'You do want something,' he says sitting on the bench at the other end of the leash, looking like an old man stopping in the park to let his dog take a shit.

It's outspoken enough outside the Studio to ask a whore what she wants; like any other worker, a whore will reply, *To be on holiday.* In the Studio, being fed up takes on a whole other intensity. I'm not exactly burning with the desire to be hit or to be having to move my toes and fingers discreetly to get rid of the pins and needles. I'm doing it with good grace, because it's the game, but don't ask me to take any initiative. Whoever heard of a dom who asked a sub their opinion? Or a dom who runs out of ideas? The way this is going, Olaf's going to make himself some study cards so he can swot up the night before.

'Do you want me to untie you and let you tie me up?'

'Bah, no. I'm the slave here. And also I have no idea how to dominate.'

And also, what the hell, you don't randomly invert the roles like that when lacking inspiration; you don't demand of a girl that she makes up for the client's lack of creativity, especially in the Studio, where the rules are fixed in advance. There are some ambivalent girls, like Margaret, who'd be enchanted by the idea of taking her turn to hold the stick, and who'd be delighted to make the client atone for his gaucherie, just like that, on the spot – but Margaret is a brothel chameleon, blessed with a seriously admirable capacity for adaptation. There is no worse public servant than me in the Studio; when someone assigns me a role, I have no impulse to come out of it; my spontaneity nods off like an old cat in front of a fireplace. But Olaf is drowning and he's dragging me with him, while I sigh with relief:

'I don't know, why don't you try the bamboo cane?'

To win myself a bit of peace, I'm happy to count out loud for Olaf, who isn't bored any more. By the time he ejaculates against my thighs, relief has replaced irritation; I've even perked up. On the clock I see we only have fifteen minutes left, and I feel sorry for him:

'You know, we can do everything, but you have to let me know in advance. If you want to inverse the roles, I have to get myself ready; I can't go from sub to dom just like that.'

'No, but it was very good!'

Olaf politely wipes the sperm off the black lino. I notice he's got a bit on my stockings, but as he's my last client, I don't make a big deal about it. Unlike him, I don't have any on the outfit in which I'm going to have to cross Berlin to get home.

'Want a smoke?' he suggests as he collapses on the small sofa opposite the Berkley horse.

And when he's come, Olaf is no longer detestable. He's cultivated, he's interesting, he has beautiful features. As I open the windows I see him like I see the Studio, suddenly, for what it really is: a little room hung with black leatherette for our jack of all trades, its walls naively bristling with handcuffs and straitjackets intended to be menacing but that are polished too often with antibacterial spray to be feared; when the pulleys get tangled or jammed, you have to call a proper repairman, and while waiting for him to come, the Hausdame hangs a DEFEKT sign on the door. As for Satie's *Gymnopédies*, which I've turned down to a respectable volume, they barely hide the gurgling of the pipes in the next-door bathroom where you can clearly hear a client washing his mouth out. As I light my cigarette, the sound of the doorbell in the corridor comes to us from beneath the door, stifled. The Studio is hermetically closed as a matter of principle but ingenuously lets every sound filter through, just in case; the activity that takes place inside escapes nobody, neither the girls nor the Hausdamen, who've always instinctively recognised the cries of fake pain and the most suspicious silences. Janus and Olaf undoubtedly don't know this, but that's what you'd have to build on, to scare the girls. You'd have to play on this latent time, persuade them that in barely a few seconds and without the slightest sound being emitted, something terrible could happen.

The one who could hold his own against all others, the one whose very name sends the house into tumult, is Gerd. Generally he makes an appointment, but sometimes he just shows up, wanting to surprise and to be surprised — and then a fraternal war tacitly divides our ranks while we're introducing ourselves. All the girls who agree to go to the Studio, whatever the position they occupy there, jostle one another in the corridor while they re-do their hair with their fingertips. It's not about money, because Gerd doesn't leave bigger tips than the others, and it can't be said that he makes up for it with his physique. With his big briefcase and his long woollen coats weighing him down, Gerd resembles an elderly family doctor who brought us all into the world. Yet when the Hausdame opens the door to him and, with the ravished reprimands of a young débutante, relieves him of the roses he invariably brings, the whispers spread like a powder trail: *Gerd…! Gerd is here! No, without an appointment…!*

The rumour spreads as far as the salon; sudden emotion makes the stockings on a half-dozen feverish thighs squeak. The phone rings, but no one gives a fuck, and one unlucky girl complains: *I already have an appointment.*

Gerd's understood the theatre of it all for a long time; and though he can't see anyone from the corridor, except the shadows and Birgit's pumps going past below the curtain, he raises his hat to us, greets the corridor with a tilt of his chin. The roses are always beautiful, his clothes impeccable; he's wordlessly friendly, to the point where even the most nitpicking girls forget he's at least a thousand years old. But above all, Gerd knows what he's doing. Any of the happy elect would tell you that – except Delilah, who wouldn't allow herself to dominated for all the gold in the world and is, in fact, missing something huge.

Maybe she's afraid of the briefcase. We've all been afraid of it. I remember our first meeting. Gerd had purposely asked for the little mauve room at the end of the corridor, the furthest away. You could hear things in it despite all the comings and goings of the girls, but I was tied up there in such a way, my neck attached to my arms in turn attached to my ankles, that it would have been physically impossible for me to emit the slightest sound of alert. Little by little I felt myself grow anguished. Out of the corner of my eye, from the half-cupboard framed by curtains where Gerd had put me away, literally, I look at him looking at me with a hard-on. Impassive. Totally conscious of the little room for manoeuvre being like this left me to breathe, of the few seconds left to me before exhaustion set in, and therefore possibly of strangulation. It seemed to me that this was the end. Never has a tragic end felt so close. At least, I thought, I would be found in a warm place; at least there would be a tearful Hausdame to explain to my parents, *We do keep watch, we do take care, but we can't be everywhere.*

I stared at Gerd with the eyes of a panicked horse, my throat contracted by my desire to say, *Untie me, untie me, I'm going to die.* He was now walking around me, almost up against me, trawling the end of his cool fingers over my skin. I closed my eyes so as not to see my own end, as he murmured *Calm down* in my ears, and I thought that was the last sound I'd ever hear, that Gerd was a sort of angel of death trying to appease me as I gave my last breath; my legs gave way. I pictured all the lovely things you no doubt see just before dying – the house in Nogent, sunset over the beach at Sainte-Maxime, the smiles of men I'd loved. There's never enough time, basically, or there are too many beautiful things. But in a jiffy Gerd undid the knot that linked my neck to the hook on the ceiling, and I fell like a bundle into his arms – which suddenly no longer seemed so frail. My heart was beating so loudly, I'd been so frightened that I felt a wave of gratitude and devotion for this man invade me like a flood of tears. He made my breasts protrude painfully in a clever macramé of cords; I had my knees up as high as my ears and the feeling of being a piece of meat deprived of all will – but something servile and completely moronic within me foamed at the mouth at the thought of Gerd's next moves. I could have been dismayed, as I often had been, seeing him slip on a latex glove before putting his fingers inside me; how many fingers? I don't know. And even if I'd wanted to count, the pillowcase that Gerd had slipped over my head rendered me blind and deaf to everything; to my flab sticking out between the ropes, to what I looked like, to the shame I'd have felt if a stunned Hausdame had opened the door. All I remember is coming so hard that I bit my tongue 'til it bled – and afterwards, seeing me reappear all ruddy-faced in the common room, Esmée and Hildie burst out laughing: *Okay, Justine? A little Schnapps to recover?* Obviously I wasn't red with anger or exhaustion, and strangely for me, who always walked naked amidst them without the slightest hint of embarrassment, my reflex was to wrap myself in a blanket, as if my body was also loudly proclaiming how satiated I was. There was something intimate in the pinkness of my cheeks that went well behind nudity and gave me the desire for dreamy solitude, for a siesta as deep as death. Afterwards, like the others, I kept a look out for Gerd's appearances.

Gerd doesn't risk inspiring disdain through his conversation, either – he doesn't have any. A few sentences of preamble, of genuine courtesy, that's it – good man. He takes his shower, he makes girls come with fearsome efficiency, he goes home, relieved of his roses, two hundred euros and a stockpile of sperm that no girl has ever seen come out. The spectacle of a woman coming, who doesn't have the choice, who has given up fighting, is plenty for him and he's happy with his clever little hand, which you couldn't believe capable of such things. There's a nobility in this little old man who we praise to high heaven in the kitchen, Hildie, Thaïs and I, one beautiful morning, while he's torturing Bobbie (who doesn't deserve it, because she comes as soon as you touch her). And Delilah, who comes in to smoke a cigarette, listens to us before squeaking:

'You piss me off, all of you, with this guy who could be your grandfather. Seriously, have you seen his briefcase? You'd have to pay me just to touch it. Have you never wondered how many girls his toys have been inside? Repulsive. Maybe he goes to all the disgusting brothels in the city and when he gets here, you're in raptures about him diddling you with a vibrator that's not long come out of a *Hartgeldnutte* infested with chlamydia.'

'He cleans everything in front of you,' retorts Hildie. 'He has his bottle of disinfectant.'

'Yes, *his* bottle… Who says there's not just water in it?'

'You're so mistrusting…! He puts condoms on all the dildos and plastic gloves everywhere he can.'

'I don't trust him. He's crazy, that guy. And on top of that he doesn't leave the tiniest tip.'

'Yes, but he makes us *come*,' I blurt out, determined to fight to defend Gerd's honour.

Delilah shrugs.

'I don't need a fossil to show me where my clit is, darling.'

These comments almost put me in a bad mood, but I feel Delilah is vexed by our unanimousness; above all by the fact our conversations don't carry the slightest trace of mockery of Gerd. That goes against the workings of the world, that whores suddenly start feeling affection for a guy who ties them up. That opens a breach in her conception of this job – on one side boyfriends, on the other clients. Delilah's disdain extends to the very concept of men; what saves her boyfriends is the love she has for them – fed by the hatred of those who pay.

Jack on Fire, The Gun Club

How sweet the way home can be, sometimes! In summer, when the star-filled sky between the ugly buildings has the colour of violet fizz. Leaving The House, I have such blasts of happiness that I could greet everyone in the street – and in fact, I wave like I do every evening at the guys in the Turkish takeaway next door, who know exactly what these pretty customers wearing too much make-up and never taking onions in their döner do for a living. And what of it anyway?

How I love my little U-bahn compartment. Nothing more intoxicating than knowing you're a whore in the middle of a respectable crowd who suspect nothing – because though I put the proper effort into this job, I'm often, at this late hour and in this neighbourhood, the girl who looks most like a student. Just imagine! When I've spent a whole day in a negligee and high heels, hair hanging loose down my back and more mascara than I need, my treat to myself is to slip back into my slightly loose jeans, a shapeless pullover, my shredded Bensimons, and to pull my hair up into a messy ponytail; then I like to look at the other girls who are on their way out for the evening, who, it seems, go to insane lengths to resemble what they think we – the whores – look like.

Which are the ones who appear to have loose morals, ladies and gentlemen? Them, with their jeans so tight in the crotch they leave nothing to the imagination, or me, reading peacefully with the look of a babysitter about me? I'm cracking polite smiles for the old ladies who nestle up beside me because I'm a more reassuring neighbour than these clusters of dolled-up young girls downing cans of Kindl before getting turned away from Berghain. This vague odour of men's sweat can only come from them, caught in their too-long hair; they have a loud laugh that drowns out my music; I see the little old ladies raise their eyebrows — *Young women don't know how to behave any more.* I have an air of complicity that says that youth has to run its course.

How can you read in these conditions? I feel like Superman in civilian clothes, just having narrowly saved the world to unanimous indifference — and I wonder if men feel it. It's not the make-up which is in danger of betraying me, because I washed my face before leaving — but my eyes that have kept the audacity of the brothel, a laid-backness that comes across as brazenness. I've just come down from my last client, and I know full well you can still smell that. That it's fading in me, very slowly, if in fact this kind of thing can fade in me. On the U7, except for some old men who are always looking at girls, there is hardly anyone travelling beyond a few sleepy old women and, on occasion, Bobbie or Thaïs who get off at Yorckstrasse with a wink in my direction. But it's actually on the U1 that the experience is most interesting; it's there that my intoxication at having done my job well is supplemented by the general jubilation taking over Kreuzberg. There's about one chance in three that in the tide of young Berliners conveyed here by the Underground I bump into one of my clients, or one of those I share with Pauline (the pair that we form brings in more young penniless artists than Western businessmen). If I recognise them all straight out, it takes them more time, by means of stolen glances, to establish the link between my hair — which I tie up in the same way before I bend over them to suck them off — and the book in French that I'm by now only skim-reading. Like Werner, for example, who rushes on at Hallesches Tor; I made him come on my face forty-eight hours ago, we have the same memory of it, but if he blushes about it, I just smile. I touch the rim of my stupid hat in greeting. Werner lifts his chin and we dive back into our respective books, Zola for me, a Le Corbusier overview for him.

Look at me, beautiful friend. Raise your eyes from your phone. Bear this naked gaze if you dare. How can a girl in a hat like me have so many things swarming in her eyes? I'm going to tell you, it's because I've spent the whole day getting laid. I've made men come from 4 o'clock to 11 o'clock and, to tell you the truth, I still could, if I wanted. And perhaps I do want to. I would know exactly how to go about making you beg the Almighty to not let me devour your soul.

Oh, I've never had such serenely obscene relations with men as those I've constructed in the Underground with perfect strangers. Leaving work exhausted, I thought I was voided of all sensuality, but there is always in my head, as in the final scene of *A Clockwork Orange*, Beethoven's Symphony No. 9 screaming out while the passengers of the Underground, naked, do unmentionable things to one another.

Words of Love, Buddy Holly

A PINK EARLY MORNING OVER THE HOUSE.

Sarah yawns as she fills her locker. Bobbie leans over to pick up her socks, crouches gracelessly, totally indifferent to the flesh she's exposing – which is as poignant as that of a woman getting out of bed, bored, at least for now, of seduction. Birgit is folding towels in the bathroom; she's listening to the radio via her headphones. Slippers on my feet, I drag myself to the kitchen to make coffee, but Paula, visibly furious, is already taking care of it. The bell that's just rung, wrenched us out of our complaining, is her first client, visibly keen to be punctual, and already ready and waiting for her in the Green room.

She lights a Winston aggressively, with adorable vulgarity, all frowns as she inhales the first drag. She takes me to task:

'That drives me crazy, that, when they arrive bang on time. You can't say anything to them, it's noted everywhere that we open at 10 o'clock. But I've *just* arrived! You have to wonder if he was right behind me on the stairs. Now I think about it, I'm sure I heard him!'

'It's unbearable,' I pitch in with the complacent indignation of someone whose first client isn't arriving until noon.

'It's already *astounding* to wake up wanting to fuck before going to work. Your wife, maybe, fine, she's next to you in bed; you only have to reach out your arm. But *going to the brothel* before work! I don't understand, I've tried, but it's beyond me. In the morning, I dunno, you want to have a peaceful coffee, to read the newspaper!

Come at midday and eat into your lunch break, yes. But arriving *bang* on opening time, just because you're allowed to…! What does he think, that I live in suspenders and high heels?'

In fact, I can't even remember how she was dressed when she arrived. Her bobbed hair is still a bit wild, she's wearing her pumps like slippers – Paula really could live in suspenders and high heels; she looks like she's just crawled out of bed.

'I'd hardly opened the door before Brigit jumped on me. *Your client's waiting for you.* I had to step on it to get dressed and put my make-up on; luckily I'd showered at home because I wouldn't have done it for him.'

She widens her made-up little eyes in barely contained annoyance.

'Yes, because I looked through the keyhole, to see his face! I had an intuition, I thought it might be him. I could kill him, that man. He's tender, he's needy, you can't get away from him, it takes forever to make him understand that he has to go. And what about my coffee?'

'*But drink your coffee!* Quarter past ten is quarter past ten. Like clockwork. Try to be where you need to be early.'

'The coffee won't be ready for ten minutes; I can't wait knowing he's there, with his little hands on his little thighs, staring at the door. That oppresses me. I'd rather get rid of him now. But I can tell you that that annoys me, this kind of behaviour. I also have a life in the mornings.'

And having crushed her first cigarette in the clean ashtray, Paula strains to put her pumps back on properly. Stays crouched down for a moment, the smoke slipping voluptuously out of her superb nostrils in a resigned exhalation.

'When it starts out like that, I can't tell you how long it takes to get me back into a good mood.'

Between the curtain and the door to the kitchen, I see her walking ahead of her client, in the direction of the bathroom – a tall boy who covers her with a look of adoration, and who can't see how she's screwing up her little nose, above that regulatory smile.

While he's doing his ablutions and she's filling out the attendance sheet, Paula sighs:

'He's smart, the animal; he brought me a coupon for KaDeWe. That's kind, huh? But now I'm in a doubly bad mood; because I am, and because I can't really be so.'

He'll leave ravished, as always – ravished in the true sense of the word. And hearing Paula burst out laughing on the balcony with Genova, both of them haloed with smoke and the aromas of coffee, you think to yourself that this client will in the end have passed through just like the others: they annoy us, they move us, for as long as they are there. Once they've left, it's a bit like they never existed.

Tainted Love, Gloria Jones

AT MOMENTS IT'S DIFFICULT TO SAY YOU'VE forgotten it's prostitution. You look between your legs at all that moving flesh, you listen to the laborious, outrageous, exhausted noises that people make without even thinking about it, and you realise how all that is, deep down, absurd.

I was going to write – I felt it at the tips of my fingers – that our exhaustion must be similar to that of a nanny forced to play tirelessly with other people's kids, to contain their frustration; in my head, god knows, the two activities demand the same sacred energy, the same abnegation. But I very much doubt that there exists on this planet a tiredness comparable to that of whores, even within the most physical professions. Without even talking about the mental energy that's mobilised to make conversation with eight different blokes, to be equally friendly and smiley with each – a titanic energy! No one knows how much the body is linked to the head after eight men, how tired the vagina is – and what it is to obligingly open this vagina and to contain your anger at each thrust, every time the cock bashes the end, like the umpteenth punch in the numb mouth of a man being beaten to death. Deep down, you don't feel anything any more. Or just bad things: what remains of sensitive nerves now transmit nothing to the brain beyond a feeling of intrusion, a discomfort that could become torture, which must have been one in the days when lube didn't exist. That too: the violence towards yourself, this resignation when you coat your vagina with lube so they can carry on going into and up against everything, to silence the reflex contractions – and when one is struggling to keep smiling, so that at least *that smile down there* stays dazzling. That violence, that's us, women, imposing it on ourselves, by repeating to ourselves that that hole has 'been there done that', that it's made for that, and if it's already the eighth time for you, for him it's the highlight of his day, he won't have another, think of him, *think of him*, because thinking of the money isn't comforting at all. This sense of the sacrifice that makes us turn the other cheek so that they, at least, are happy.

If I'm thinking about that today, it's because I got my schedule wrong, and instead of arriving at 2 o'clock in the afternoon, as I told the Hausdame, I arrived bang on 10 in the morning. By the time I'd realised my error, I'd already been booked up to the end of my shift and, with my recent multiple cancellations, I didn't dare change my timetable off the bat. An eleven-hour shift seems like torture to my sisters who work in a café – but when you work in a brothel, the torture is mixed with a feeling of inhumanity directed at you by the rest of the world, especially men, and including the Hausdamen who, thinking they were doing the right thing, overbooked me.

In the kitchen, Genova has just started her shift. She does her make-up calmly in the little mirror with two faces screwed above the table, and I sit opposite her and smoke, discreetly fascinated by the countless stages of her transformation. First the foundation, coppery, that you'd have thought could only jar on her fair skin. And yet, against all expectations, it works: she has an army of sponges and brushes that change these two squirts of tinted cream into a second, undetectable skin. I would never be able to do that. And what's more, she's talking at the same time, showing just how natural this procedure is to her, as much as rolling the perfect joint is for me (and that definitely won't sort out my skin).

'How are you, Justine?'

'Fine. You?'

'Fine, as ever.'

She's crayoned on her eyebrows any old how, she looks like a little girl disguised as a witch; there's some grey, some black, some brown, and, from these rough areas of colour she's going to come out a miracle of sophistication. That must be all down to that strange suppository-shaped sponge.

'I can't stand them any more,' I come out with, suddenly in the mood to share confidences.

'No shit!'

'It'd be fine if this guy didn't come. There's one of them in the bunch I'd rather pay to stay at home. He's nice, but I told him I didn't have time today and he somehow managed to scrape together two hours. That's a real drag on my day, you can't imagine.'

'Just tell him, tell him that you don't feel like seeing him.'

'Yes, but what do you do if you don't feel like seeing him one day, but later, perhaps, you don't mind or you like it?'

'But you can also very easily say to him: *I'm not in the mood today.*'

'Yes, but that gives the impression of being a bit…'

Genova stops mid-movement, waiting for the word I'm looking for, which turns out to be *capricious*. Intimidated by her eyebrows, raised by a thick line of kôhl and with a disdainful air to them, I sigh:

'I don't know…'

'Listen, *baby*, I'm going to tell you something: I, for example, do this job to live. I have bills to pay, my rent, my health insurance; I need this money, and generally I'm not choosy when it comes to my clients, it's kind of the whole idea. But if I mess up one day, if that puts me in a bad mood, then the next day I know I'm going to cancel, and that will be money that I lose and never get back.'

'Yes, I know you're right.'

'I'm sorry, we're not selling bread rolls here. It's about human relationships. And sometimes that's just how it is, you don't feel like it. It's not even up for debate. They can easily complain to the Hausdame or even write to the owner; nobody will be able to object to that.'

'I'll bear it in mind for next time. It's done now, I feel better already, but an eleven-hour shift is too much.'

'I know what you mean.'

Now it's the lipstick. A neutral colour that makes her beautiful full lips shine without her looking made-up.

'Certain days are like that. You know, when it gets to evening and it's just *too much*. It's the mirrors that drive me mad. The one in the Golden room, for instance. It's like another circle of hell in there. You can't take any more, and you have to look in the mirror at this guy grabbing you by the buttocks, by the waist, shaking you in all directions… I really like that normally, I like it when it's a bit bestial. But sometimes, I can feel anger rise in me, I want to shout at him *Take your fucking hands off me, you dirty fucker!* Do you understand?'

I don't reply, content with smiling at Genova, who I'd never have imagined getting to the end of her tether, invaded by this hatred of men that I feel dawning in me today. It's that, it's like a flare up in the middle of your goodwill; the reflection in the mirror is suddenly that of a ravaged doll, beautiful pink, firm skin beneath the body of an animal. The sound of a massacre – a noise as old as the world, the sound of a woman oppressed by a man, suffering beneath him, of impatience, of fatigue. And I look through my hair at these curtains, these mirrors, these lights and these flowers, the whole room shaking to the rhythm *he* has chosen, and I tell myself that this decor is just an attempt to make people forget what is really happening. It's not surprising that the truth resurfaces for short moments. The comfort, the pleasantness may well make an impression for a while, but the starting point is absolutely inhuman conditions; this job has never been really human. The legislation, which is on the side of whores, may soften working conditions, but these are painful efforts by society to try to tone down the basic premise: a whore is a sex object. The possibility for a whore to say no is pretty restricted. Yes, of course you can say no, especially here – but what kind of no is it, actually? No to what *in particular*?

*

And then there are those days when I don't understand the clients at all; when I've arrived late, and the first one is already waiting for me, and I start my shift without even putting on my make-up or smoking the fag that allows me to transform myself into Justine… And I have to think about everything right away, the towels, the music, the lube – while my head is still full of my literary thoughts, or of fantasies about the latest nitwit I'm shagging.

It doesn't have to do with anything, but I'm not there, god knows why: I'm not inside it, my moans sound fake, I'm disorganised… And because it seems like the guys guess it too, because I feel they are less hard, that they take longer to come, after being angry at myself, it's them I start to despise, just like servers who suddenly hate customers who confront them for their bad attitude or their carelessness. I'm angry with them, and the tiniest details of sex become intolerable to me: this one doesn't get as hard as he should; that one sweats like a donkey and I can't bear any contact with his dripping torso (*and fuck if I get one drop on my face I'll scratch him 'til he bleeds*); this one wants to kiss me and as I turn my head to the side he contents himself with licking my ear; that one, whom I've expressly forbidden any anal mumbo jumbo, won't take his finger away from my arsehole; this one has an odour that without being good or bad gets on my nerves, and who on top of that makes such a din while going down on me that I have to resort to sticking my fingers in my ears in a way I hope is discreet – but if it isn't, he can go fuck himself!

Is it because they're used to me being nice that my sudden coldness takes the wind out of their sails? Weary of alternating between a flimsy embrace and a useless blowjob, my gullet hypersensitive on bad days, I take off the condom like you do a sticking plaster and baste my hands with lube. Delicately to start with, I put them to work with misguided faith in the warm touch of my naked flesh and indescribably advanced kneading techniques. But as that continues, my talents evaporate and my expert caress turns into the furious juddering of someone milking a cow, until the unconvinced cock between my fingers withers away and my scorching defeat, my lack of professionalism, stands out in bright red letters: this is what happens when you cock up your job. You wanted to go faster, make the least effort possible, this is what you get. Where do you think you are, exactly? This is an artist's job, for fuck's sake. What did you think it was? Look at you, you have no desire to talk, no desire to fuck, you're only here because you hate yourself for spunking six hundred euros at Agent Provocateur; you bloody idiot, honestly! Six hundred euros for *one* set of underwear. As if nobody notices, when you really become a whore. And you believe that that kid has enough money for one hour with you? He's a social worker, for god's sake, and married, and with kids. It's a sacrifice he's making – and you're huffing about with rage? For one hour of your time – that's two hours less than you spent on Tinder yesterday while painting your toenails in your armchair. Where's your heart? And aside from your heart, where are your principles? These famous principles that set you apart from other whores?

So, I become nice again. I become just nice and tender *enough* for my hands to be worth more than theirs. And as he comes with moans of ecstasy, I'm hit by a gust of mixed gratitude and affection. He looks so happy. He thanks me with such an air of weary blissfulness. Doesn't that move you, oh stone-hearted one, that for one moment of loveliness he forgives you fifteen minutes of relentless milking. That it can be so simple, deep down?

And because I've botched my masterpiece, I'll resolve to be cuddly with them, just as they are – I'll caress their hair with a purr, soothed by the intoxication of the full condom, by my remorse, and by my strange solidarity with these men who've come here to feel more beautiful afterwards. A bit like going the barber's; without the least guarantee it'll work.

Strange Magic, Electric Light Orchestra

WHEN MY FRIEND ARTHUR BECAME A FATHER, at the beginning of September, I wasn't around to celebrate that – I was vegetating in the Midi, convinced I was pregnant too – and it was someone else he was quaffing champagne with on a Vincennes sofa. It was Anne-Lise, after ten years of love and low-level bitterness, finally resigned to not being *the one*. There had been, all through this decade, many declarations of bloody vengeance and tragedy on the doorstop of his apartment, and many had seemed to be the last. But by hanging out with him for so long, Anne-Lise had understood Arthur, and if she cried, if she shouted sometimes, she'd understood that nothing viable would come of being angry about this boy – and she was always there when he didn't want to be alone, just as he always opened his door when she was tired of being so. They talked to each other daily; Anne-Lise was that ex who Arthur's friends didn't know what to do with; they ended up resigning themselves to cohabiting with this shadow, with the vague certainty of approving in a cowardly way some deceit of which there would never be any proof. Deep down, Anne-Lise was like a best friend one tells everything to; and it's her he called the evening his daughter was born.

Whatever the confused pain, conscious or otherwise, she felt after Arthur called her trumpeting *She's arrived!*, Anne-Lise had invited him to her place, three days after the birth. There was champagne in the fridge and Anne-Lise, who didn't yet have any children, had melted with that enthusiasm that is to be expected of women in the face of young fathers. Arthur, drunk on his new status and carried away by her willingness to listen, had got a bit carried away in small talk about the episiotomy and cutting of the cord, about floating on air and his love for all humanity. Without thinking that there wasn't any place in all that for Anne-Lise.

He wasn't surprised when she took off her blouse, saying it was time to raise another toast. He opened his arms to her in serene jubilation, convinced that in doing so he was celebrating all womanhood, the marvellous fertility of their orifices, this blind and imbecilic joy that creates babies. She made love to him in a glorious fashion, full of expressive abandon, inventing for him some perilous contortions that left him panting, hands clinging to this young, supple body. He thought, and said to her, *I'll never forget that*.

Afterwards, falling on top of him as he struggled to regain his breath, rendered dumb by a diluvian ejaculation, she smiled and caressed his cheek, suddenly such a mistress of herself: *I like that*. It was a gift she'd given him, a performance to mark the occasion. Nothing, in their embrace, could have given rise to such a suspicion, or at least nothing concrete, nothing palpable. She had red patches on her chest and heavy eyelids beneath which malice glimmered – and Arthur wondered where this malice came from, from the fact of having come? Or from having made him come? It had given her pleasure to offer him this frenzied ride; and she had done it from the good of her heart, perhaps even love. With the consciousness of each movement, of each posture, of each feverish glance through her long brown hair. With the consciousness, maybe, of each contraction of her vagina when she had come, *maybe* – the world was suddenly overflowing with *maybes*. Not that that made a difference of any kind; pleasure was pleasure, even if Anne-Lise's had been motivated by anything other than simple desire. And he thought: *Is it really possible that they can be double, triple, quadruple like this; can they really be monstrous enough to have no control over their deception? Can it be that we have to truly resign ourselves to never knowing, have to grant them blind trust, or always doubt them, at the risk of never being happy?*

And he thought it was perhaps lucky, deep down, to have a cock to sort out the problem; to achieve a sense of repleteness, even a superficial one, which lessened the importance of the truth. That the cock always ended up winning when the spirit got tied up in endless dilemmas; and while Anne-Lise was falling asleep, hot and calm against him, he had a sudden fleeting and yet unforgettable awareness of women's misery, of their sensuality being so complex that they themselves often understood nothing about it – because they didn't have a stupid cock to indicate physical satisfaction to them. A man could lie about everything, but not about ejaculation – even if the pleasure had been mediocre. Ejaculation was a full stop – while a woman, able to take her satisfaction everywhere and nowhere, led an endless race towards Pleasure, weighted down by her thousand personalities. For a woman, there were a billion reasons for fucking without any really being physical. Among these reasons was the noble and egocentric one of effacing the memory of someone else, of paying a compliment, of continuing to exist, of celebrating the birth of the baby of a woman who Arthur had preferred to her. Perhaps physical pleasure was born of this altruism, from one moment to another; perhaps a woman who set out with the resolution to make someone come got caught in her own game and perhaps that's why Anne-Lise's pussy against his thigh was so wet.

But maybe she was just wet because that's what a pussy does, even a half-hearted one; perhaps she was excited by her own noises, by the effect she'd had on him. It was best not to know too much. My cynical testimonies about the brothel were encumbering his thoughts; Arthur thought about me fucking and thinking about something else. So women could, by their essence, be fully whole and completely compartmentalised, simultaneously present in multiple dimensions.

Was it really misery? And if so, was it the misery of women or actually that of men who despaired of differentiating between true and false? Wasn't that the only real misery, deep down? And this extra soul that women, who could be both here and there at the same time in multiple dimensions, didn't that belong more to the realm of magic?

Yes, that's what he thought as he fell asleep too – that must be magic.

Surrounded by Anne-Lise and by me, surrounded by all these women he'd made scream and possibly come, and the memories of whom were spinning around in him, dizzyingly, he'd thought that if that was called magic, then you had to carry on watching this performance like a child, without malice, without mistrust, without wanting to spot the trick – and especially not to give in to this adult perversion, the need to know why you become a magician, to fill what lack, to satisfy what deeply buried hungers, when it's enough to say to yourself that a magician likes to see their audience's eyes shine, that that's where their own pleasure is nested: in that of others.

Always See Your Face, Love

THAT SOMEONE COMES TO A BROTHEL ONCE is a thing I have no trouble getting my head around. That they come back is the proof that the place functions in a satisfying way, that the choice is vast enough to adapt to the eternally changing forms of male fantasies. That someone abandons the brothel, whether it's forever or for a little while, is a necessary evil, understandable to people like me who are always trying very hard to diminish the guilty pleasure of cigarettes or weed or rosé.

Since I started at The House, I tell myself that the vast palette of us offers any man the possibility to have seven different wives a week, if his budget allows it: the brothel – polygamy within reach of respectable citizens. But after more than nine months on the job, I note that my daily schedule, full to bursting, includes few newcomers; in most cases the names are familiar to me, and I rarely enter the introduction room without cooing, in an increasingly fluid German: 'Ah, it's you! How have you been, since I last saw you?'

And many of them I hug like I'd hug friends. *Friends*, the word undoubtedly falls short. Friends I'd do without, without too much difficulty. Friends I could totally do with not fucking. That they inexorably come back to me could be explained by the huge power of habit over men. Most of them consider the one hundred and sixty euros that an hour costs as a significant enough sum to not take the risk of being disappointed (or satisfied) elsewhere: a wise resolution that would meet the approval of the average wife from whom this investment is disguised by fictitious expenses. On the other hand, what would she say about the bonds fatally created by these steady relationships that in some cases go back more than six months?

Money should make everything insignificant, as it does with a Thai massage – but in the eight months we've been seeing each other, Lorenz has learnt my real name, Robert has read my book, Jochen has my phone number, and my kisses have lost some of their professional indifference and resemble those their wives submit to when they get home from work in the evening. What still differentiates me from a mistress, and few people but they and I will believe it, is this payment, which encloses us within a time-frame. They are paying to have a mistress; nothing has really changed since the nineteenth century. They pay to only have one, the same one; nothing will ever change in the need that men have, as much as women do, to put substance where there should only have been money.

Yes, but what about those who aren't married? Do brothels, when you find a girl to your taste, make you lazy? Let's take a look at Theodore: after six months of my seeing him, his mediocre physique doesn't make me raise my eyebrows – quite the contrary, a whole heap of other parameters have made him more than pleasant, *likeable*. Theodore must be – what? – thirty-five at most. He's a biologist, a solitary occupation, and his chat has nothing inspiring about it. Theodore loves nothing more than roaming the four corners of Germany all alone, bringing back cuttings of mysterious plants. With the exception of his friends whose names have become familiar to me, I don't know of any female in Theodore's entourage. So it's not out of order to consider myself the closest thing, in this solitary existence, to a girlfriend. Theodore is a brilliant boy, full of resourcefulness. Tender, funny, patient; and these long months together have taught me that he is also far from being bad or selfish in bed – him being one of these clients who make it a duty to make me come. Let's sum it up by saying that this man has everything to make a decent woman happy. And in fact, over time, I've started to wonder if the time that I spend with Theodore isn't a bit of a theft at the expense of a lady as solitary and tender as him, and who won't demand a penny to kiss him. I wonder if I'm not keeping him stuck in the mistaken idea that there's no love possible for him without prepayment.

With Theodore, and with certain others, it's harder and harder to define my place. Money, which should protect us from one another, is just the last mendacious barrier placed between us in the hope we can't love one another. And when the illusion vanishes, the truth appears more cruel, more stinging than ever; there is only ever a man and a woman who all the gold in the world won't stop penetrating each other, in all senses of the word (and the most literal is not the one you think, far from it). The chore of sex done and dusted, the moment arrives that I prefer, the moment when they talk and laugh and caress my thighs, comment on my music, tell me about their week. Things that have made them happy, sad. The little nothings that define them in this existence that I'm part of, without really being so.

It's December, Lorenz and I have just fucked and I'm at the point of grumbling about the Christmas parties looming large, bringing in their tinselly wake my entire family and the diabolical obligations associated with the birth of baby Jesus – presents, the meal, New Year's Eve… I try to rally Lorenz to my cause, but Lorenz can't stop smiling, arms crossed behind his head, eyes riveted to the small red lamp above us.

'I think it's going to be a good Christmas,' he says finally.

'Ah really? Why?'

'My girlfriend is pregnant,' replies Lorenz, eyes suddenly all pink.

He sounds like a woman announcing his pregnancy to her husband – and, as if I was this husband, I feel my chest swell with a rush of euphoria:

'No way!'

'Yes! Twins!'

Lorenz is literally glowing. And now we're on our cloud, Lorenz and I, talking about his girlfriend whose first pregnancy this is – he already has two grown-up sons, and the new ones are taking twenty years off his meter.

At the start I'm a bit flabbergasted, however, by the force of desire, or of joy, that sends a future father not between the thighs of his pregnant girlfriend but into the belly of someone else, a belly as empty and indifferent as it's possible to be. That this someone else is a whore makes no difference of any kind.

In Paris, a few dozen months earlier, I'm having a clandestine and god knows really very unenjoyable affair with a married man – a man, let me be clear, who doesn't feature in any of my previous books; in short, just one among many. This forty-six-year-old man has at this point been married since he was twenty, the age at which he had his first son. Meeting briefly – our favourite way – one evening, I ask him about the exact day of this birth, and he gives me this anecdote: that night, the young father comes out of the clinic in a trance, shaken up from having held in his arms a bawling little red package – his son. Was it possible? Him, a son? Nobody had ever invented such a feeling of happiness and agony, a more contagious ecstasy – even Ecstasy, of which he'd had his fair share, doesn't make you fall any more in love with everything, with Paris, with the world, with God even, who at this point, strangely, seems to exist. He buys some wine and straddles his moped, crosses the whole city with a blissful smile on his lips – headed where, do you think?

Towards the apartment of the girl he screws in addition to his partner, whose name he can only remember now because it's her, that evening, the evening he becomes a father. He climbs the stairs four at a time, bottles under his arms. He takes the girl with the calmness and the virility of an emperor. *While his wife, huge bags under her eyes and an inflatable ring under her buttocks, feels her pulse beat in the episiotomy cut*, I think, and he must think about that too because he guffaws, gently:

'It's weird, huh? I wondered if I was a bastard. It often happened that I behaved like a bastard, I'm not hiding from that. But it's hard to explain, what I felt that evening. I had so much love inside me, so much. It's as if I was going to explode. I had to share that with someone. Victoire was at the clinic, tired…'

'What about your friends?'

My tone is harder than I am, because something quite primal in me understands the paradox of this man, or at least wants to understand it. Something in that is indubitably human, poignant even.

'Yes, my friends… I saw them afterwards. That wasn't what I needed right away. I needed a woman. Do you understand?'

'A woman who wasn't yours. With whom you didn't have any children.'

'I suppose so.'

'You don't think it was fear? I mean, that you clung desperately to what was closest to freedom for you, at that moment?'

'Of course,' he responds gently. 'I was dying of fear. There was something terrifying about this love.'

Yes. Something like a trap closing, a very soft, comfortable trap in which one would willingly drowse off. The feeling that love itself is this trap. And you go and fuck others because this breath of air doesn't make you dizzy, doesn't shoot you kilometres above common mortals. Is this the price to pay for having by your side a good father, a father who is present, in love with his wife and his kids? To continue to ignore, or to understand, that obsessive love combined with the fear of screwing up can make a young father unfaithful?

What did he say to his mistress? What can you say to your mistress, to what extent can you admit you're afraid, that you've perhaps made a mistake? An erection that punctures this anguish is enough of an admission in itself.

I can clearly see that Lorenz is a bit embarrassed to find himself here, with me, rather than by the bedside of his wife whose complicated pregnancy is forcing her to stay recumbent for six months. There's no question of sex at this time, or only in a very gentle, very careful way. But even with all the consideration in the world, when you know that the slightest contortion is endangering the life of two foetuses, I imagine you suddenly have the tendency to find your cock too thick or too long, that you tremble at the thought of going all the way in.

(As I write these lines, thousands of kilometres from The House and my situation, I say to myself, god, give me an easy pregnancy. Give me a happy, sensual pregnancy, a pregnancy I can and must fight; it's such a terrifying thing for a woman to suddenly be a body entirely devoted to the survival of a child, to be invested by this serious role and to feel all those shadows swarming around you – women with empty bellies – to feel the silent fear that seizes the other by the throat, and the fact of knowing that being the Wife, the One, is exactly what condemns you to being deceived.)

To come back to my starting point, since I love nothing more than deviating from it – it seems that with a bit of pragmatism you could say that whores are uber-mistresses for bourgeois couples. And why not? One hundred and sixty euros a week is very little compared with the total costs of a not-too-shabby hotel room, champagne, a meal, gifts – all these stupid things that make the fact that a married man never leaves his wife less stinging and less sad. The investment seems better in all aspects. It took me some time to understand that in the eyes of many of these men, my status as a whore is the ultimate excuse that they'll give their partner, if one day, god knows how, they get caught out.

There are of course some who just come to take a shot. I have difficulty understanding these too. I'm thinking especially of the dynamic young businessman who sometimes goes as far as calling just ahead of his arrival so I'm ready, washed, refreshed. The first time, that rather annoyed me. He smiled at me, explained that if there was a way of staying less than half an hour he would – and that's often what actually happens. He jumps in the shower, and once he's in the bedroom he fucks as if the universe was about to collapse from one minute to another, eyes rolled back in his head. A brief groundswell, from which he immediately awakes; while I'm getting my breath back in bed, he's already putting his trousers back on, buckling his belt. On his lips, the smile of a guy for whom a great service has been provided. No shower afterwards; he's equally happy doing that at home, in peace. Sometimes I drag a few scraps of conversation out of him. He has a girlfriend, who he loves but of whom he's grown weary, as he has everything else. Coming to the brothel is a bad habit he'd really like to get rid of and that costs him quite a lot of money. But it's not because of money that he arrives and leaves at top speed, we know that. He's like a heroin addict from a noble background who's fallen in the mire through some bad luck, without him ever feeling linked in any way with his companions in misfortune; once a week he has to mix with the populace to get his dose – but he will only devote to it a hasty round-trip, at arm's length, hating the idea that pleasure is written all over his face, convinced that this time will be the last; but such things don't exist, the proof being that we always say *See you soon*. During our rendezvous, we've talked a bit about his girlfriend; what's not quite right, or what's wrong. Isn't it just down to boredom, which razes so many things you might have thought would be lovely forever? If there's an archetype of the whore, I can see that girlfriends and wives come out of similar moulds; and the epitaph on the tomb where they lie for several half-hours a month is this grave grumble: *One day I was a fantasy, and then I became the One, and I died of it.*

Before, they say, she loved sex. Before, we spent whole nights fucking. Before, I knew all her holes. Before, she sucked me off. Before. Before what? Not everybody is like this young Turk, already father to three little girls and married to a devout woman whose captivating mouth, capable of so many marvels when they were engaged, articulated this sentence the day after the wedding: *No more blowjobs.* Rare are the women who deliberately nail themselves into the coffin of conjugality and drag their husband with them.

The real problem is time. How can you fight time? Perhaps faced with this supreme, invisible, invincible enemy, men resort to the weapon of the brothel as a minor sin, more excusable than something on the side, but perhaps also shoddier.

The brothel is society's inexorable humility, man and woman reduced to their truest form — that of the flesh, which tastes and smells and quivers without the shadow of a thought, without the slightest rationalisation, a positive and a negative that penetrate each other stupidly because it's the ultimate aim, the finishing line of this mad race. And in this stupidity, in this flat graph of the brain activity of animals desiring other animals, no one is aware of the mainly cerebral war these two human beings are waging against time. Time. Because there is nothing else. Time, and at the end of it, death — the big sister of boredom, the one who's been taught honesty.

Here's something to make you ponder. Anyone who's been in a couple knows or can guess how double-edged letting go is. You allow yourself to slip into it with the best intentions, as if into a warm bath. You suddenly feel the need to look good fading away. This is the time when slowly, within the cradle of mutual love, the courtesies you created to soften your edges disappear. Little by little you stop forcing yourself to do anything; which is a good thing, I imagine.

Or is it? Who's never been part of a couple — one with a Twix in their snout and shapeless jogging pants on, the other in the same outfit busy trouncing Bayern on FIFA — without getting flashes of a vague danger hovering over on their libido as a couple? Certainly not me. Which doesn't necessarily mean that the quality of the sex is suffering — but that the sex is a game won in advance. What's missing is the possibility of failure.

And this possibility of failing must have a phenomenal power of attraction. I remember Margaret showing a client to the door, and hearing the man ask her in a whisper if she'd enjoyed the time they'd spent together. Standing in the kitchen in front of the half-open door, eating chocolates meant for clients, I tremble at the audacity and the naivety of the question; I imagine what it will cost Margaret to reply with a smile, *It was very nice, darling*. But instead of that, she lets an embarrassing silence hang in the air before sighing:

'Can I be totally honest?'

'But… of course,' replies the client, definitely regretting opening his mouth when he could have just accepted the goodbye kiss and left pumped up with illusions.

'If it had been a Tinder hook-up, for example, let's just say that I'm not sure I'd call you again.'

There's a strong chance that, even separated by the kitchen partition, her client and I are paralysed in the same stunned position. It makes me stop chewing.

'But, uh… What didn't work?'

'Darling, don't take it badly. I didn't ask you not to come back. If you like it, you can come back when you want to.'

'I wanted you so much; was I too fast?'

'That was part of it. But it doesn't matter. It doesn't stop you trying again. You can't come and see me for the first time and get everything just right.'

'But you seemed to be happy.'

'Yes, I seemed to. But because seeming is not enough, I'd rather tell you the truth.'

'What do I have to do? Tell me.'

'Ah no, I'm not telling you anything. You have to teach me. As with any other woman. Now darling, I have to say goodbye, I have a lot to do.'

The guy came back a few days later.

A woman or a whore, to a man who finds himself alone with one, are the same mysterious creatures with faces one would really love to put a smile on.

Bold As Love (instrumental), Jimi Hendrix

THERE'S NEVER A DAY, NEVER AN HOUR, goes by when I'm working on this book that I don't realise I've undoubtedly chosen the bad side of this story. Not the bad – let's say, not the good one. Not the most interesting. Which forces me to ask myself if deep down I wasn't born on the wrong side. My god, I should have been a man; in this exact situation, I should have been a man.

I would have been the king of clients. If only it was possible for one day (one very long day) to have my woman's brain in the body of a young man –not too young or too handsome. Especially not too handsome; that's not how you have the most effect on whores, how you get a little of that precious lack of inhibition out of them.

My heart would be thumping, and perhaps my boner too, in the steps leading to The House; a smell unfurls itself in them, like a red carpet, greasy and musky, a smell of freshly laundered underskirts around feverish haunches, the childish, maternal, nasty breath of well-maintained young women smoking in secret in the laundry room. I wouldn't know, as a client, where this smell comes from; no more than I knew, when I worked there, where it escaped from, through which microscopic gap in our reinforced door. And it's this mystery that would attract me like a fly, which would make me ring the bell with a trembling finger; and already the music from this bell, disturbing for a moment the laughter and the conversations, would produce this muffled racket like that of schoolchildren gagging one another to give the illusion of a quiet classroom.

As I'd enter, I'd sense them all, hiding behind the curtain to see what the new arrival looks like. The curtain would move a little; someone less discreet than the others would flash for a moment a long leg veiled in black, a few strands of hair.

I wouldn't book an appointment. I'd come at a time when I know the girls are kicking their heels.

'I'll call the ladies for you,' Inge would say in her joyous voice, full of a delicate emphasis on this word *ladies*, to refer to these women who very often aren't even called *girls*.

I'd sit myself right opposite the keyhole, so the girls can observe me before introducing themselves or not; and I'd pretend to ignore the blue, green, brown eyes of those fussy girls taking turns assessing the customer, just as I wouldn't listen to the murmurs of those having relations with others. Ah, the joy it would be to be placed there, belly twisted by cramps, in this ochre light, with the stupid, lascivious music.

And then the door would open, slowly: who would it be, first? Birgit, with her resolute voice and her long legs, the heels she slips on and off like slippers? Thaïs, with her smile full of mercenary vice and the plump, firm arse of a young filly, that unequivocal gaze of a girl who's not there to be cuddled? Manuela, her eyes kind, her breasts huge beneath a slightly ugly but always cheerful face, excusing even the most undignified requests? Odile, her bust of a Murillo virgin above very wide, perhaps too wide, hips, adorable from the front and scary when she leaves the room, with this monumental arse, the flab all shuddering? Margaret, her five foot nine of black and golden skin, her odour of jasmine? Genova! Genova, queen of whores, inventing affectionate nicknames for each client, with her predatory pout that leaves no room for doubt and dimples in her thighs that make you want to eat her? Eddie, her look of a respectable woman lost in a brothel, her fingers elegantly tense as if they were about to be kissed? All, send me them *all*. I would clasp their fingers in veneration. I would mentally undress them with the greatest respect, too delicately for them to feel it.

I'd choose one who's not too pretty, not too confident. One whose belly sticks out too much, or one who has a ladder in her stockings. One I'd disturbed in the middle of her break, bringing with her the smell of cigarette and some impatience. I'd take one who isn't too keen, who's indolent, who sighs when the Hausdame announces: *It's for you.*

Sonja was telling me one day that if The House belonged to her, she'd have the rooms decorated to men's tastes – leather armchairs, beautiful dark wood, steel. Odours of tonic, taupe colours, no flowers or shutters or pink linen – giving men the sensation of being at home. But it's exactly this impression of barging into a women's world that's the genius and success of The House; and if I was a client, I wouldn't want to change anything; I wouldn't move a single plastic peony, not a single prune-coloured organdie curtain, because this is where women live, because their eyes know each frou-frou, each piece of furniture, because they're inside every silly little flower on every bedspread. Because they're at home here, in this humble, unpretentious illusion, and it's like they're honouring clients by receiving them in their room. I'd bestow on each trinket a gaze moist with tenderness; I'd grant huge worth to these ornaments, these little efforts deployed by women to make pretty and poetic these rooms that are just for fucking in. I'd cherish the fake fountains, the false chimneys with buttons to light false flames, make false crackling sounds. Sofas you hardly sit on except to tie your shoelaces, yet where a discerning eye can spot, in the worn velvet, the phantom smiles of pussies that were set down there, in distant times, by mistake.

I'd have already taken a shower at home but I'd be good and take another one, even if only to open the tap, to leave her time to get ready. Sitting on the edge of the bath, as emotional as if it were the first time, I'd imagine her unfolding the towels on the bed, throwing condoms, normal-sized and large, all over it – because we never know what fate has in store for us. I'd make her wait a bit longer than necessary, so she wonders what the hell I'm doing and from there starts to think about me, precisely me. So that she wonders what type I am: the type who isn't going to manage to get a stiffy, or who'll take a thousand years to come, or who'll want to exercise his contractual right to ejaculate twice. Going back into the room, I'd see all these questions float behind her professional amiability.

I wouldn't get undressed. I'd say, *I don't want to fuck you, I don't even want you to touch me, not even look at me.* I don't want you to pretend to like me or you to say anything at all. I just want you to close your eyes and take off your knickers, just your knickers, if you're wearing any.

She wouldn't be. She'd be wearing just a body, of which she'd undo the central flap with the throaty laugh of a girl who's fine with all the lies, even the one saying you're not there to have her. She'd be lying on the bed, in the puddle of yellow light of a ray of sunshine caught in the voile curtains, beneath her buttocks a cushion lifting her up slightly. It's of little importance what her pussy would be like as she'd be only the first in my collection; but I'd be touched by her own particular way of showing it to me, of spreading her legs. She'd do it without procrastination, that's how I'd like her to be. She'd show it to me in the manner of a woman who's forgotten, slightly, how far god is in the details, how far it remains a gift in spite of the money.

It's of little importance what her pussy would be like, but I like to imagine it fleshy, full, enclosed in a dense bush. A woman's pussy, framed by plump thighs like the binding of a bible. A pussy she'd have had some embarrassment, some scruples, about showing off when she was around sixteen, before her job made her proud and indifferent. With long lips the colour of fresh meat, like a deep cut in the midst of all the bushy hair. When she'd spread her legs, her lips would have their own existence, each independent of the other. One would be folded back on itself, the other unfolded on the side, revealing a little of the red and pink depths; that she doesn't give a shit about this pretty chaos, this humility, would bring tears to my eyes. This mute crack in her centre, washed by the gazes of hundreds of men, would grab hold of me like a masterpiece reserved for my eyes only. I'd like it right down to the fake moistness, that blob of lube applied while I was taking my shower, in case I'd want to take her right away. I'd kiss her there, on this lie that other men would swallow whole. She'd tremble a little, without me being able to work out if it was a real frisson or the beginning of her usual performance. And in doubt, I'd say to her, *I don't want you to pretend.* I don't want you to come; obviously that would make me happy, but I don't want to ask the impossible of you. Come if you want, or don't. I've come to look at you. You're beautiful.

I'd look at her and wonder how many men have had her without moving her, and how many have moved her. What it would take to move her, what dose of indifference and selfishness, what size love to make her surrender herself to a man who's not paying. I'd skim, so very lightly, the delicate skin around her slumbering clitoris. I'd look at each fold, each blue vein, wondering which really led to her head. I'd blow softly on the hairs around the lips to see the whole cunt contract surreptitiously, like an oyster squirted with lemon juice. I'd kiss her in the middle of this mess of flesh and hair. This is how I'd spend the time allotted to me, ogling her along all her seams, watching incredulously the rhythmic changes in her breathing. I'd caress, slowly, each pearly stretch mark, every specificity of this body-altar on which so many men, every day, come to pour out their heart, to bring to this goddess of pity and indifference their frustrations, their joys, their whims. I wouldn't come; I'd press my erection, as proof of the high esteem I hold her in, against her overly large arse, while listening to another girl cry out in the other room, with the repeated slapping together of flesh as a metronome. I would go and masturbate obligingly in the bathroom, the open tap my only alibi, without disturbing either my girl or this other one who, having seen out her client, would be busy tidying the room, singing as she does so. They'd undoubtedly think I was impotent. The one who doesn't fuck. The one who just comes to piously kiss this cohort of dark, blonde, red, bald or hairy cunts, who fills his herbarium with a thousand clitorises with the sophisticated designs of cathedrals, with the smells of pussies and arseholes, and who nobody even suspects of relieving himself in the toilets with a feverish waggle of the wrist.

Being the way I know they are, they wouldn't give a shit about me. But they'd end up knowing my first name. They'd speak of me as an easy client, albeit a strange one; and the most difficult ones would end up swelling the ranks of those lining up to introduce themselves when they saw me arrive behind the curtain. I'd know them by heart, in the long run: what perfumes they wear, what kind of make-up, the lingerie they love. I'd recognise, from their distant and desirable breath of girls you don't kiss, what their last meal consisted of, the rash ones who eat a kebab, those who sip a coffee, those who've filed out to introduce themselves forgetting the cake crumbs in the join of their lips. I wouldn't talk a lot, I wouldn't be one of those clients who replace coitus with interminable chit chat – yet they'd be familiar to me. I'd read their moods in the folds of their pussy, in its changing colours; their nipples would tell me what part of their cycle they're in when I visit; I'd perceive the coppery tinge of blood behind the soap, the lube, and the bad eaux de toilette of the previous clients. I'd know, from the set of their eyebrows, if their tummies were hurting, and I'd place my warm hands in the place where their uterus was throbbing painfully. I'd be silent, in poignant humility. To such an extent that there would always be one, eventually, who'd see it as a challenge to take on this client whose cock might not even work. There'd definitely be an impertinent one irritated by my silence, a cheeky one with an insatiable ego, who'd undo my belt and force me to close my eyes, and would suck me off out of defiance, on hands and knees above me, her slit obligingly spread apart a few centimetres from my delighted face. There would end up being one who my tranquil gaze would have slowly conquered, reassured, and who would make up her mind to surrender herself a little. One whose obscene thoughts I'd try in vain to guess as her clitoris blossoms, who I'd prevent from coming at the last moment, and who, caught up in the game, would forget I'm paying her and moan again, revolted; and who after the orgasm would rub herself against me, a little embarrassed perhaps. One who'd suddenly want a hard cock right up inside and wouldn't say so. One I'd take, suddenly, without a word, sucked into her as if into a mouth, with the good taste to not last too long and give her too much time to think. One who'd end up finding me sexy, *as clients go.*

The delicious shyness of the beginners, the docility, the indifference of the older ones who know every fold of their flesh and deliver it fully, without a shiver of fear, without the least embarrassment, like beasts of burden whose look matters little. The unforeseen charms, the faults you hadn't reckoned on, those that make you sigh to yourself *What a shame* while imagining what it was like before. Breasts badly put back together, with large scars bearing witness to the time when surgery was clumsier – you wouldn't have chosen this girl had you known, and that's how these details displayed in the most laidback way seem like a gift. The pale, chapped skin from an ancient episiotomy that I would kiss gently – this creator of children who still finds the time, the goodness, the need to let out to the highest bidder this brave, hard-working cunt. I'd hunt down badly shaved legs beneath black stockings, the smell of their sweat in damp armpits; I'd cherish improbable and gross finds, a strand of hair stiff with sperm, the white spatters of an enthusiastic spurt inside knickers pulled up and down ten times, the chipped nail polish on the toes, on the hands, quite badly bitten nails – this approximate cleanliness of girls who between two clients give themselves a splash of water in the bidet, and who in the evening carry a bit of all of these men.

Out of the words they utter in their serious, laughing, frayed, exhausted, hoarse or caressing voices, I'd construct a story; I'd invent for them a childhood, a difficult age, a family and some projects, a whole life I'm not part of, or very little. And I'd roam the neighbourhood so constantly that I'd end up bumping into some of them dressed, in their civilian clothes, those coming out of work or trotting along to their shift, and greeting them with the almost invisible smile of a friend who wouldn't betray their secret for anything in the world. I'd spot them in jeans, with trainers on their feet, a loose jacket around their shoulders, laughing and chirping away on the phone, just like all the women who bring splashes of bright colour to the grey streets. I'd end up seeing them everywhere: the lady in front of me at the pharmacy, at the Späti, reading some detective novel next to me in the U-bahn, in every Amazonian on a bike rushing like the wind between a thousand others; I'd think I saw whores everywhere. This one, barely twenty-five years old, swinging her hips too freely, this other showing too much cleavage, ogled by men who feel betrayed by her beautiful indifference similar to that of a lady baker whose hair permanently smells of sugar. Or this one, who holds the gaze of men as she brushes against them in the street, out of defiance or habit, because it's a long time since she's been afraid of them.

I'd be the silent biographer of these dream priestesses, who understand everything without the slightest word, who never lie except to be nice to us. I'd read them poems in languages they did or didn't understand and that would make them smile; I'd read them books in which they are the heroines, from the era when there were only ever wives or whores. And I could say to them, since I'm a man, that I'm writing a book about them, a book in which they will all be beautiful, heroic, where garbage will become nobility and where there will be no garbage, unless it gives you an unbelievable hard-on. I would explain to them, in my broken German of a Frenchman in exile, the gracious obscenity of their postures, crouching as if to piss, how they hold their thighs so that nothing of their slit escapes the gaze; these ruses to make you come more quickly and that give you the urge to hold yourself back until the world turns to dust. I'd translate pages by Miller, by Calaferte, by García Marquez for them, despairing of not being able to hatch something more beautiful myself. I'd inevitably fall in love, like a man, dragged into it by the weight of my own lyricism. And through being with them, in them, I'd undoubtedly forget that there is on this earth, on every street, girls you don't pay, at least not in this way, not as honestly, who you pay by other means, by tactics I'd be too lazy for. Perhaps I'd be one of those who marries a whore for the pride of being, among a thousand cocks, the one that matters, the one whose fingers without doing anything different make her breath quicken, her cheeks turn pink, the only one for whom all her resistances collapse.

I'm writing these words on the terrace of a café in Boxhagener Strasse, one very sunny, slightly chilly afternoon; past me moves, fluidly, this brightly coloured crowd from the elegant and the crappy parts of East Berlin, bearded guys with good haircuts, chicks with pink, blue, green hair, parents holding the hands of scruffy brats, punks stinking of beer, old men and women covered in tattoos, men and women, whores and clients, all mixed together without you being able to say who is who, who does what to whom. Yesterday I started this passage after a week of black depression that I fought with panicked doses of Zola. My day was finished, I'd just taken a shower in the clients' bathroom. And in the mirror of the corridor I suddenly saw, looked at, myself; the embroidered towel around my hips, the towel that I hang on my hook, the one that says *Justine*. Inge had turned out the lights on the ground floor, cut the music, I heard her having a big conversation with herself, laying out what was done and what needed to be done, all this uphill work to which she gave herself over so indifferently, without ever allowing herself the slightest sign of irritation.

I was gripped by the awareness of being at home here, in this brothel, and that this home could be so lovely. And I asked myself, a little warily, when I'd changed, when these rooms, this smell, these girls, had stopped intimidating me and become this strange home. When had I taken my first shower in the men's bathroom, when did I first sing without realising while I was making a bed, the first time

I refused to introduce myself – when exactly had I made here, like in a familiar place, my first free choice and acted on my own will?

In the common room I'd tried to count, vaguely, the number of lockers on the walls and read the names on them: each one having its label and its decoration, each one adding its little voice to the choir: 'Kein Sex mit Nazis', 'Komm Zu Mir,' 'Für das Recht auf Faulheit', a naked Father Christmas, his legs crossed, near Thaïs' name. The postcards they sent one another from their holidays. And in this multitude there was my name too, Justine with a heart instead of the dot on the *i*, and when had I felt sufficiently happy, proud here to draw something as stupid and childish as a heart? When you open my locker – two drawings by my sisters, to mix a bit of my family in with this other one.

Butt-naked, the clients' soap drying on me, emitting this smell recognisable among thousands of others, I'd walked in silence in this empty shell of a closed brothel, this fairground at rest.

I interrogated myself about the word *family*. If it really applies to this thing that links us all to one another – if we can call family the fact of being women, just that. If family simply designates that moist, warm part of humanity that makes people get up and move about. I hold family to be a place, a moment, an environment, where you laugh and talk and confide in one another more than anywhere else – where you have the same problems, the same victories, the same defeats. Family is a place where the human race seems more beautiful, more noble and fragile, elevating a community above the mire. This is undoubtedly a specious argument, because independently of the context in which it arises, whether it's in the light or in the shadow of general disdain, the notion of family or fraternity blossoms as soon as you bring together people who share the same fate. Moments of love, of understanding and of communion have been seen in any old conglomerate of mafiosi, criminals, of wretches, in every fringe of society with dubious morality. And I think it's natural that about thirty women living naked side by side with one another, brought together by the simple fact of having been born women and being paid for that, can, if they don't see themselves as enemies, consider themselves sisters. The family doesn't burden itself with any idea of morality but its own; it prospers in the pursuit of the aim that is right for it, indifferent to what the outside world thinks of it.

I can't say anything about noble enterprises openly working for the good of society, to elevate it – where the quest for greatness brings together and bonds the families who yoke themselves to it. But between the obvious common good and undeniable bad things lies this bright shadow I'd like to talk about. I want to talk about this nest of women and girls, of mothers and wives, all comforting one another in the knowledge of also working a little, with their flesh and their infinite patience, for the good of the individuals who make up our society. By definition forgetting themselves, transcending their weaknesses and lending, for a few moments of joy, this body that, it was decided one day, in the name of a blind, deaf and dumb heaven, could only belong to a man or to the devil. I want to speak of these women who make and unmake, with their delicate fingers, the illusory notion of the sacred, these beings higher than women, who seem to exist only between the walls of a brothel. I want to talk about them because they exist; and because as they head off from the brothel, they leave in this empty boat the throbbing, maddening smell of a thousand different types of love, of different ways of tenderness, sought and found, each in their own fashion, a smell of fullness achieved every day and pursued every morning. There's no nobility to it, but there are poignant truths such as are found nowhere else, testaments to happiness and promises of joy – and someone has to talk about them.

About the Author

Emma Becker gained recognition with her debut novel *Monsieur* (2011), followed by *Alice* (2015). In 2013, she moved to Berlin, where she worked in a brothel for two years to research her semi-autobiographical novel *La Maison* (2019), which won the Prix France Culture-Télérama. After several years in Berlin, she relocated to the south of France in 2021, where she continues to write.

Bedford Square Publishers is an independent publisher of fiction and non-fiction, founded in 2022 in the historic streets of Bedford Square London and the sea mist shrouded green of Bedford Square Brighton.

Our goal is to discover irresistible stories and voices that illuminate our world.

We are passionate about connecting our authors to readers across the globe and our independence allows us to do this in original and nimble ways.

The team at Bedford Square Publishers has years of experience and we aim to use that knowledge and creative insight, alongside evolving technology, to reach the right readers for our books. From the ones who read a lot, to the ones who don't consider themselves readers, we aim to find those who will love our books and talk about them as much as we do.

We are hunting for vital new voices from all backgrounds – with books that take the reader to new places and transform perceptions of the world we live in.

Follow us on social media for the latest Bedford Square Publishers news.

bedfordsquarepublishers.co.uk